序 言

　　單字的累積，對於閱讀英文確實有很大的幫助。但是難免會碰上「每個字都懂，意思卻不懂」的情況，這是因為沒有徹底瞭解文法的緣故。尤其近幾年來的各類英文考試題型，幾乎是克漏字和閱讀測驗的大本營，這二者與文法間有著密不可分的關係，只要具備足夠的文法實力，答題時必能迅速準確；然而想要徹底瞭解文法，光靠背幾則公式是沒有用的，惟有**從題目中吸取經驗**，才是真正將文法融會貫通的不二法門。「**文法練習 1000題**」便是根據這個原則編寫的。

　　本書共分二十章，每章分兩部分：**文法重點和練習題**。文法重點部分是將重要的文法規則，列出條理，並力求敘述簡潔易懂；練習題部分則收錄國內外最新考題，按規則分類，是驗收實力、加強記憶的精華所在。

　　文法規則精簡，題目眾多是本書一大特色，目的在讓學生有充分練習的機會，避免一味地死記；只有從做題目著手，才能徹底瞭解文法，不怕任何變化題。

　　嚴謹的編校，是我們一貫的目標和原則，但仍恐有疏漏之處，希望讀者能給予我們批評和指正。

　　本書另備有教師手冊，附練習題解答，歡迎教師來函索取。

編者　謹識

CONTENTS

1. 不定詞（ *Infinitives* ）‧‧‧‧‧‧‧‧‧‧‧‧‧‧‧‧‧‧‧‧‧‧‧‧‧‧‧‧ 1

2. 動名詞（ *Gerunds* ）‧‧‧‧‧‧‧‧‧‧‧‧‧‧‧‧‧‧‧‧‧‧‧‧‧‧‧ 17

3. 分詞（ *Participles* ）‧‧‧‧‧‧‧‧‧‧‧‧‧‧‧‧‧‧‧‧‧‧‧‧‧‧ 33

4. 被動語態（ *Passive Voice* ）‧‧‧‧‧‧‧‧‧‧‧‧‧‧‧‧ 47

5. 語法（ *Mood* ）‧‧‧‧‧‧‧‧‧‧‧‧‧‧‧‧‧‧‧‧‧‧‧‧‧‧‧‧‧‧‧‧‧ 58

6. 基本動詞句型（ *Verb, Sentence Patterns* ）‧‧‧‧‧‧‧‧ 74

7. 時式（ *Tense* ）‧‧‧‧‧‧‧‧‧‧‧‧‧‧‧‧‧‧‧‧‧‧‧‧‧‧‧‧‧‧‧‧ 90

8. 助動詞（ *Auxiliary Verbs* ）‧‧‧‧‧‧‧‧‧‧‧‧‧‧‧‧‧ 105

9. 敘述法（ *Narration* ）‧‧‧‧‧‧‧‧‧‧‧‧‧‧‧‧‧‧‧‧‧‧‧ 118

10. 名詞（ *Noun* ）‧‧‧‧‧‧‧‧‧‧‧‧‧‧‧‧‧‧‧‧‧‧‧‧‧‧‧‧‧‧ 132

11. 代名詞（ *Pronoun* ）‧‧‧‧‧‧‧‧‧‧‧‧‧‧‧‧‧‧‧‧‧‧‧‧ 148

12. 關係代名詞（ *Relatives* ）‧‧‧‧‧‧‧‧‧‧‧‧‧‧‧‧‧ 164

13. 冠詞（ *Article* ）‧‧‧‧‧‧‧‧‧‧‧‧‧‧‧‧‧‧‧‧‧‧‧‧‧‧‧‧ 180

14. 形容詞（ *Adjective* ）‧‧‧‧‧‧‧‧‧‧‧‧‧‧‧‧‧‧‧‧‧‧ 194

15. 副詞（ *Adverb* ）‧‧‧‧‧‧‧‧‧‧‧‧‧‧‧‧‧‧‧‧‧‧‧‧‧‧‧‧ 210

16. 比較（ *Comparison* ）‧‧‧‧‧‧‧‧‧‧‧‧‧‧‧‧‧‧‧‧‧‧‧ 223

17. 一致（ *Agreement* ）‧‧‧‧‧‧‧‧‧‧‧‧‧‧‧‧‧‧‧‧‧‧‧‧ 237

18. 連接詞（ *Conjunction* ）‧‧‧‧‧‧‧‧‧‧‧‧‧‧‧‧‧‧‧ 250

19. 介系詞（ *Preposition* ）‧‧‧‧‧‧‧‧‧‧‧‧‧‧‧‧‧‧‧‧ 263

20. 特殊構句（ *Constructions of Other Kinds* ）‧‧‧‧‧‧‧ 277

1. 不定詞(Infinitives)

═══ Points of Grammar ═══

1. 不定詞的形式

時　式　　語　態		主　　動	被　　動
現　　在	基本形	to do	to be done
	進　行	to be doing	
過　　去	基本形	to have done	to have been done
	進　行	to have been doing	

2. 不定詞用法上應該注意的事項

(1) 感官動詞 see , notice , perceive , hear , feel , etc. 後用原形動詞。

　　I did not **hear** you **call**.

(2) 使役動詞 let , make , have , help 後省略 to。

　　They **made** me **go** there.

　　＊但 help 後可接有 to 或是省略 to 的不定詞。

　　I **helped** him (*to*) **do** the work.

(3) had better , can not but , do nothing but 後省略 to。

　　You **had better make** haste.

　　I **can not but feel** sorry for him.

3. 不定詞的功用

(1) 作名詞

　　To teach English is no easy work.〔作主詞〕

　　Everybody wishes **to enjoy life**.〔作動詞的受詞〕

　　The only way is **for you to do it yourself**.〔作主詞補語〕

　　He likes his wife **to dress well**.〔作受詞補語〕

(2) 作形容詞

　　Water **to drink** must be pure.

　　You are **to stay** here till six.

(3) 作副詞

　　① 修飾動詞

He stood up **to see better**. 〔表目的〕

He awoke **to find** (= and found) himself famous. 〔表結果〕

She wept **to see** her son seriously wounded. 〔表原因〕

She must be kind **to say** so. 〔表理由〕

I should be glad **for Mary to go**. 〔表條件〕

② 修飾形容詞

Only human beings are **able to laugh**.

③ 修飾副詞

Harry is not old **enough to go** to school yet.

4. **獨立不定詞**：不定詞有時與其他部分沒有文法關聯，而獨立存在。

To tell the truth, I don't like him.

He is, **so to speak**, a walking dictionary.

5. **完成式不定詞**

(1) seems, is said, is thought, is reported ＋完成式不定詞，表示發生在主要動詞前的動作。

$\left\{ \begin{array}{l} \text{He seems (or is said) \textbf{to have been} ill.} \\ \text{= It seems (or is said) that he was (or has been) ill.} \end{array} \right.$

$\left\{ \begin{array}{l} \text{He seemed (or was said) \textbf{to have been} ill.} \\ \text{= It seemed (or was said) that he had been ill.} \end{array} \right.$

(2) 表希望、計劃等動詞，如 wish, hope, intend, mean, expect etc. 其過去式加上完成式不定詞（～＋ to have ＋ p.p.），表過去沒有實現的願望、期待或計畫。

$\left\{ \begin{array}{l} \text{I \textbf{wished to have come}. = I \textbf{had wished to come}.} \\ \text{= I wished to come, but I could not.} \end{array} \right.$

$\left\{ \begin{array}{l} \text{The meeting \textbf{was to have been} held.} \\ \text{= The meeting was to be held, but it was not.} \end{array} \right.$

6. **疑問詞＋不定詞＝名詞片語**

I am at a loss **what to do**. (= what I should do)

Few people know **how to do** it. (= how they should do it)

7. **表明不定詞意義上的主詞時，用下列表示法：**

(1) for ＋受詞（意義上的主詞）＋不定詞。

It was good **for** him **to take** the medicine.

(2) It is ＋形容詞＋ of ＋受詞（意義上的主詞）＋不定詞。〔對 of 後的受詞稱讚或責備時，用此句型〕

It was good **of** him **to help** me.

8. 不定詞中的原形動詞，與前面的動詞重複時，不定詞只要用 to 代表便可。

I don't know him, and don't **want to**.（＝to know him）

His book will sell well; it's **bound to**.（＝to sell well）

9. 不定詞的修飾語及其位置。

I failed **to entirely avoid** it.〔entirely 修飾 avoid, 語氣較強〕

I failed **to avoid** it **entirely**.〔entirely 修飾 to avoid〕

10. to 的省略與保留：

(1) 表對比、強調或為維持平衡時，每一個不定詞的 to 都要保留。

To be or **not to be**; that is the question.

Anybody who wants **to buy stamps**, **to send a telegram**, or **to get a postal order**, must go to the post office.

(2) 使用感官動詞的句子，改為被動語態，後面仍用有 to 的不定詞。

I saw him **come**. →He was seen **to come**.

(3) 數個不定詞由連接詞連接，前者有 to 時，後者可有可無。

She ordered the old man **to leave** his village and **not** (*to*) **come back**.

(4) **come, go**, etc. ＋原形不定詞。

Jack, go fix your car!

Better **come join** us.

(5) try to → try and; come to → come and

Try to be punctual. ＝ **Try and be** punctual.

Come to see me! ＝ **Come and see** me!

EXERCISE 1

I. 請根據句意和文法選出一個最正確的答案。

1. She could not but _____ to hear such a sad story.
   (A) to weep
   (B) weep
   (C) weeping
   (D) to weeping

2. We saw him _____ out of the gate.
   (A) to go
   (B) go
   (C) to going
   (D) went

3. A magnifying glass will make it _____ larger.
   (A) to look
   (B) looking
   (C) look
   (D) looked

4. She does not know _____ to open it with.
   (A) how
   (B) what
   (C) who
   (D) whether

5. She was unhappy because her father would not _____ her go to the party.
   (A) let
   (B) permit
   (C) allow
   (D) get

6. She ordered the room _____ before breakfast.
   (A) sweep
   (B) to sweep
   (C) to be swept
   (D) sweeping

7. It was _____ that he climbed to the top of the tower.
   (A) true
   (B) easy
   (C) dangerous
   (D) difficult

8. It was _____ for him to finish the work in a day.
   (A) false
   (B) likely
   (C) hard
   (D) certain

9. It was considerate _____ him not to play the violin while the baby was sleeping.
   (A) for
   (B) of
   (C) to
   (D) with

10. I had no idea _____ to go or not.
    (A) when
    (B) whether
    (C) why
    (D) which

11. We have _____ him to be more careful in everything.
    (A) suggested
    (B) hoped
    (C) proposed
    (D) expected

12. I will have _____ writing the report by next week.
    (A) finished
    (B) hoped
    (C) expected
    (D) promised

13. He was _____ to leave the room, when the phone rang.
    (A) just
    (B) soon
    (C) about
    (D) immediately

14. _____ with, I have no time to have a date with you.
    (A) To begin
    (B) Beginning
    (C) Begin
    (D) To beginning

15. I am sorry _____ waiting out of the room for a long time.
    (A) to have kept you
    (B) having kept you
    (C) keeping you
    (D) have kept you

16. His wealth enables him _____ to England.
    (A) to have gone
    (B) to be going
    (C) to go
    (D) went

17. She makes it a rule _____ early in the morning.
    (A) get up
    (B) to get up
    (C) to be getting up
    (D) got up

18. Too much drinking will lead him _____ himself.
 (A) ruining
 (B) to ruin
 (C) to have ruined
 (D) to be ruined

19. This apron has no pocket _____.
 (A) to put things
 (B) to be things put
 (C) putting things in
 (D) to put things in

20. I wanted you to help me _____ my assignment after school.
 (A) finish
 (B) to be finished
 (C) to be finishing
 (D) finished

21. I would rather study than _____ to such a place.
 (A) to go
 (B) go
 (C) going
 (D) have gone

22. On my way home I stopped _____ some bread at the bakery.
 (A) buying
 (B) to buying
 (C) to have bought
 (D) to buy

23. The dog needs _____.
 (A) to train
 (B) train
 (C) to be trained
 (D) to have trained

24. She isn't rich enough _____ the piano, let alone buy it.
    (A) rent
    (B) renting
    (C) to rent
    (D) to be rented

25. The workers accepted the cut in salary without complaint
    because they were afraid _____ their jobs.
    (A) to lose
    (B) to be lost
    (C) to have lost
    (D) lose

26. It is sometimes difficult _____ you have just met.
    (A) to make pleasant conversation among people
    (B) making pleasant conversation to people
    (C) making pleasant conversation to for people
    (D) to make pleasant conversation with people

27. Almost everyone fails _____ the driver's test on the 1st
    try.
    (A) passing
    (B) to have passed
    (C) to pass
    (D) in passing

28. When inflation is rampant, many families find it difficult
    _____ the life style to which they are accustomed.
    (A) to maintaining
    (B) to maintain
    (C) in maintaining
    (D) maintain

29. She has no alternative but _____ him.
    (A) to see
    (B) seeing
    (C) going to see
    (D) see

30. I never know _____ when I go on a trip.
    (A) what clothes should be take
    (B) what clothes to take
    (C) what clothes will I take
    (D) I take what clothes

31. Pragmatists were hardly the first men _____ beliefs control behavior.
    (A) insist
    (B) insisted
    (C) who insists
    (D) to insist

32. He asked me if John had the capability _____ .
    (A) to do that
    (B) to doing
    (C) doing that
    (D) do that

33. Inland canals are used _____ farm and factory goods to nearby towns or seaports.
    (A) shipping
    (B) to shipping
    (C) to ship
    (D) in shipping

34. I am free _____ I did not quite know the sort of creature I had to deal with.
    (A) to confess   (C) confess
    (B) confessing   (D) in confessing

35. He wasn't _____ six miles every day.
    (A) strong enough to walk
    (B) enough strong for walking
    (C) enough strong to walk
    (D) strong enough for walking

36. _____ , my tennis went daily from bad to worse, and the worse it became, the more I loved it.
    (A) To honest be
    (B) If I be honest
    (C) To be quite honest
    (D) Being honest

37. After studying hard to become an accountant, he discovered that it was not what he wanted _____.
    (A) to do
    (B) that
    (C) doing
    (D) to

38. I muttered encouraging words to myself _____ up my courage.
    (A) to keep
    (B) being kept
    (C) keeping
    (D) to have kept

39. When a molar started to ache, I decided it was time _____ a dentist.
    (A) see
    (B) to see
    (C) to have seen
    (D) seeing

40. The tennis champion has been asked _____ an exhibition
    game at the tennis club next Sunday.
    (A) play
    (B) to play
    (C) to be played
    (D) to have played

Ⅱ. 請根據句意和文法，選出一個錯誤的答案。

41. (A) He seems to know something about it.
    = It seems that he knows something about it.
    (B) I happened to be present there.
    = It happened that I was present there.
    (C) She is likely to come here tomorrow.
    = It is likely that she shall come here tomorrow.
    (D) He ordered the room to be swept.
    = He ordered that the room should be swept.

42. (A) He is sure to pass the examination.
    = He is sure that he will pass the examination.
    (B) He is not a man to do anything by halves.
    = He is not such a man as would do anything by halves.
    (C) I have no friend to advise me.
    = I have no friend who will advise me.
    (D) Is this the way to do it?
    = Is this the way in which it should be done?

43. (A) His composition leaves nothing to be desired.
    = His composition leaves nothing that can be desired.
    (B) The next thing to be considered is the matter of food.
    = The next thing that should be considered is the matter of
    food.
    (C) It's time for you to start.
    = It's time that you could start.
    (D) Have you decided a place for your new house?
    = Have you decided where to build your new house?

44. (A) He lived to be eighty years old.

    = He lived till he was eighty years old.

  (B) Bill left Taiwan never to return.

    = Bill left Taiwan and never returned.

  (C) This river is dangerous to swim.

    = It is dangerous to swim in this river.

  (D) They are certain to arrest you.

    = It is certain that they will arrest you.

45. (A) The story was sad to listen to.

    = The story was sad when it was listened to.

  (B) He was surprised to hear the news.

    = He was surprised when he heard the news.

  (C) This bed is too short for me to sleep in.

    = This bed is so short that I can not sleep in it.

  (D) You are not old enough to drink.

    = You are too old to drink.

46. (A) He must be a fool to do such a thing.

    = He must be a fool that he should do such a thing.

  (B) To my surprise, I found her gone.

    = I was surprised to find her gone.

  (C) I expect to have finished this work by tomorrow evening.

    = I expect I shall have finished this work by tomorrow evening.

  (D) I can not help admiring her.

    = I can not but to admire her.

47. (A) I intended to have married her.

    = I intended to marry her, but I couldn't.

  (B) I hoped to have found something to eat.

    = I had hoped to find something to eat.

(C) It would have been wiser for you to leave it unsaid.

= It would have been wiser if you had left it unsaid.

(D) He was to have dined with us yesterday.

= He had been with us to dine yesterday.

48. (A) He worked hard to support his family.

= He worked hard so that he might support his family.

(B) I tried to persuade him only to offend him.

= I tried to persuade him, but offended him after all.

(C) It is impossible to please her.

= She is unable to please.

(D) It is comfortable to sleep in this bed.

= This bed is comfortable to sleep.

49. (A) The teacher made the children leave early.

= The children were made to leave early by the teacher.

(B) It is said that he was very generous.

= He is said to be very generous.

(C) You must tell them they should wait for me.

= You must tell them to wait for me.

(D) This is not the book that we should read this semester.

= This is not the book for us to read this semester.

50. (A) Father is to arrive in London next week.

= Father is due to arrive in London next week.

(B) You are to stay here till we return.

= You should stay here till we return.

(C) Nobody was to be seen in the house.

= Nobody should be seen in the house.

(D) Mozart was to die young.

= Mozart was destined to die young.

Ⅲ. 選出下列各句中錯誤的部分。

51. He <u>quickly</u> stepped on the brakes, and his car <u>came to</u> a
     (A)   (B)

  stop just <u>in time</u> <u>to be avoiding</u> an accident.
           (C)   (D)

52. <u>After</u> <u>a great deal</u> of initial confusion, the antiwar dem-
    (A)   (B)

  onstrators decided <u>protesting</u> inside the administration
                  (C)

  building <u>instead of</u> in the gymnasium.
          (D)

53. There are <u>a great many</u> stars in the sky <u>which</u> are <u>too</u>
          (A)   (B)

  <u>far away</u> from the earth <u>of</u> any instrument to detect.
    (C)   (D)

54. <u>To get</u> <u>some information</u> on <u>the economic problems</u>, <u>it</u>
   (A)   (B)   (C)   (D)

  should read this book.

55. I had hoped <u>to have learned</u> French before my trip <u>to</u>
          (A)

  Paris, but I <u>did not have</u> any <u>extra money</u> for a course.
  (B)   (C)   (D)

IV. 在下列各空格中，填入適當的字。

56. I expect that there will be no argument about this.
    = I expect _____ to be no argument about this.

57. I am only too sorry to hear of his failure.
    = I am _____ sorry to hear of his failure.

58. It is not likely that it will rain.
    = _____ is not likely to rain.

59. I am afraid to wake the baby.
    = I _____ not wake the baby.

60. I will try and teach him English.
    = I will try _____ teach him English.

61. I met him by chance at the station.
    = I _____ _____ meet him at the station.

62. He was so careless that he broke the vase.
    = He was so careless _____ _____ break the vase.

63. It was _____ heavy _____ me to lift.
    = It was so heavy that I could not lift it.

64. It is generally believed that he died in Russia.
    = He is generally believed _____ _____ died in Russia.

65. There is _____ denying that health is above wealth.
    = It is impossible _____ _____ that health is better than wealth.

66. You signed the document without reading it, which was very stupid.
    = It was very stupid ＿＿＿＿＿ you ＿＿＿＿＿ ＿＿＿＿＿ the document without reading it.

67. He made a note of my address ＿＿＿＿＿ he should forget it.
    = He made a note of my address so ＿＿＿＿＿ ＿＿＿＿＿ to forget it.

68. I believe that it was a mistake.
    = I believe it ＿＿＿＿＿ ＿＿＿＿＿ ＿＿＿＿＿ a mistake.

69. The window was very dirty and no one could see through it.
    = The window was ＿＿＿＿＿ ＿＿＿＿＿ to ＿＿＿＿＿ ＿＿＿＿＿.

70. I hoped to visit him, but I could not.
    = I hoped ＿＿＿＿＿ ＿＿＿＿＿ visited him.

2. 動名詞 (Gerunds)

Points of Grammar

1. 動名詞的形式

語　態　時　式	主　動　語　態	被　動　語　態
簡　　單　　式	doing	being done
完　　成　　式	having done	having been done

2. 動名詞的性質

(1) 名詞的性質。

Loud **talking** is certainly out of place in a library.

His only fault is **sleeping** late in the morning.

I remember **stopping** at the hotel.

He left the room without **being** seen by anybody.

His **sayings** and **doings** are liable to disagree.

Some people read only for **reading's** sake.

(2) 動詞的性質。

After **reading** the novel, I went to bed.

My dream is **becoming** a teacher.

She is proud of **having won** the contest.

He is ashamed of **being scolded** by his teacher.

3. 動名詞意義上的主詞

(1) 在下列情形下，動名詞不須再表明意義上的主詞。

Fishing in this lake is forbidden.〔眾所週知的事〕

I'm sorry for **giving** you so much trouble.〔動名詞意義上的主詞與主要動詞的主詞或受詞相同，或由上下文可推斷其意義上的主詞〕

(2) (代)名詞當主詞時，必須用所有格。當受詞時則可用所有格，也可用受格。

Mary's being diligent cannot be denied.

He objected to $\left\{\begin{array}{l}\textbf{John's} \\ \textbf{John}\end{array}\right.$ **joining** the party.

He explained about **his son being** absent.

Do you mind **me smoking** here?

4. 動名詞和不定詞都可做為動詞的受詞

(1) begin, like, love, continue, 等動詞後，可接動名詞或不定詞為其受詞。

He **began studying** (*or* **to study**) English.

(2) avoid, enjoy, stop, finish, mind, go on, put off, give up, etc. 之後只可接動名詞為受詞。

She **enjoyed chatting** with her students.

(3) wish, hope, decide, desire, seek, etc. 之後只可接不定詞做受詞。

He **decided to leave** his own country.

(4) 有些動詞可接動名詞或不定詞，但意義上有出入。(詳見文法寶典 p.435)

$\left\{\begin{array}{l}\text{I } \textbf{forgot going} \text{ there.} = \text{I forgot that I } \textbf{had gone} \text{ there.} \\ \text{I } \textbf{forgot to go} \text{ there.} = \text{I forgot that I } \textbf{must go} \text{ there.}\end{array}\right.$

$\left\{\begin{array}{l}\text{She } \textbf{tried cooking} \text{ meat in wine.} \text{（她曾試驗用酒煮肉。）—— 試驗。} \\ \textbf{Try to get} \text{ here early.} \text{（盡量早來此地。）——盡量，企圖。}\end{array}\right.$

5. 動名詞的時式

He is proud **of being rich**. (~ that he **is** rich.)——與主要動詞同時發生。

He was proud **of being rich**. (~ that he **was** rich.)

He is proud **of having been** rich. (~ that he **has been** or **was** rich.)——發生在主要動詞之前。

He was proud **of having been** rich. (~ that he **had been** rich.)

I am sure **of passing** the exam. (~ that I **will pass** the exam.)——發生在主要動詞之後。

6. 動名詞的慣用語

(1) **There is no +V-ing = It is impossible to-V = We can not + V** (~是不可能的)。

$\left\{\begin{array}{l}\textbf{There is no saying} \text{ what may happen.} \\ = \textbf{It is impossible to say} \text{ what may happen.} \\ = \textbf{We} \text{ (}or\text{ One) } \textbf{can not say} \text{ what may happen.}\end{array}\right.$

(2) **It is no use (good) + V-ing.**（～是沒有用的）。

> **It is no use (good) crying** over spilt milk.
>
> ＝**It is of no use to cry** over spilt milk.
>
> ＝**There is no use** (＝**good**) (*in*) **crying** over spilt milk.

(3) **can not help + V-ing**（不得不～）。

> I **can not help thinking** that he is still alive. ＝ I **can not but think** ～
>
> ＝ I **have no choice but to think** ～. ＝ I can not choose but think ～.

(4) **worth + V-ing**（值得～）。

This book is **worth reading.** ＝ **It is worth while to read** this book.

(5) **On + V-ing**（一～就）。

On hearing this (＝**As soon as I heard** this), I changed my plans.

(6) **of one's own + V-ing**（自己～的）。

> These are pictures **of my own painting.**
>
> ＝These are pictures which I **myself painted.**
>
> ＝These are pictures (which were) **painted by myself.**

(7) **It goes without saying + that -子句**

＝ **It is needless to say + that -子句**（～是不用說的）。

> **It goes without saying** that health is above wealth.
>
> ＝ **It is needless to say** that health is better than wealth.

(8) **go (come) near + V-ing**（幾乎要～）。

He **came near being run** over.

(9) **make a point of +V-ing**＝**make it a rule to-V**＝**be in the habit of +V-ing**（經常～）。

> He **makes a point of taking** a walk early in the morning.
>
> ＝He **makes it a rule to take** a walk early in the morning.
>
> ＝He **is in the habit of taking** a walk early in the morning.

(10) **be on the point (verge, brink) of + V-ing**

＝ **be about to-V**（快要～）。

He **was on the point of dying.** ＝He **was about to die.**

(11) **feel like + V-ing = feel inclined to-V.**（想～）。

I don't **feel like eating** now. = I don't **feel inclined to eat** now.

(12) **need, want, require, deserve, bear, stand + V-ing** 表被動的意思。

The shoes **need mending.** = The shoes **need to be mended.**

The story doesn't **bear repeating.**

This cloth will **bear washing.**

⊙ **The culprit deserves punishment.** = The culprit **deserves to be punished.**

（詳見文法寶典 p.431 ）

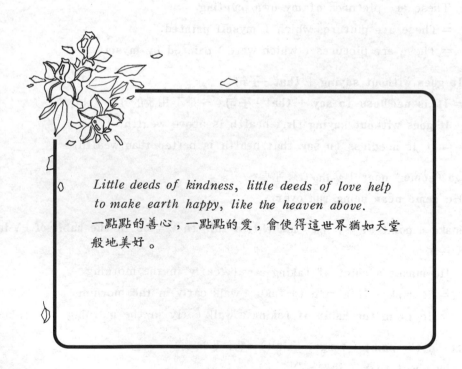

*Little deeds of kindness, little deeds of love help
to make earth happy, like the heaven above.*
一點點的善心，一點點的愛，會使得這世界猶如天堂
般地美好。

EXERCISE 2

I. 請根據句意和文法選出一個最正確的答案。

1. He_____ taking the key.
   (A) admitted
   (B) managed
   (C) hesitated
   (D) hoped

2. The government_____ to lay down a railroad there.
   (A) avoided
   (B) gave up
   (C) postpone
   (D) decided

3. The student_____to sit for the examination because he was ill.
   (A) expected
   (B) failed
   (C) meant
   (D) put off

4. Did he appreciate _____his mistakes?
   (A) you to point out
   (B) for you to point out
   (C) your pointing out
   (D) your being pointed out

5. Have you considered _____ for a scholarship?
   (A) to apply
   (B) to be applied
   (C) applying
   (D) being applied

6. I want to swim, but they do not allow_____in this lake.

  (A) swimming

  (B) to swim

  (C) swim

  (D) to swimming

7. We avoided _____over the unpaved road by taking the new highway.

  (A) to drive

  (B) to be driven

  (C) driving

  (D) being driven

8. That boy earns his living by_____papers.

  (A) selling

  (B) to sell

  (C) having sold

  (D) to have sold

9. I asked the man if he would mind_____off the radio.

  (A) turn

  (B) turning

  (C) to turn

  (D) having turn

10. When questioned, the students denied_____the practical joke.

  (A) to play

  (B) to have played

  (C) playing

  (D) having played

11. Why do they object to _____here?

  (A) smoke   (B) smoking

  (C) to smoke   (D) to have smoke

12. We aren't accustomed to _____ up so early.
    (A) get
    (B) have got
    (C) getting
    (D) having got

13. Watching a fine player is a good way of _____ one's own game.
    (A) to improve
    (B) being improved
    (C) improving
    (D) to be improved

14. I am certainly looking forward to _____ the champion _____.
    (A) watching, play
    (B) watch, playing
    (C) be watched, play
    (D) being watched, playing

15. There is one more book worth _____.
    (A) read
    (B) of reading
    (C) to reading
    (D) reading

16. I remember _____ the maid _____ out of the office yesterday.
    (A) to keep, to wait
    (B) keeping, to wait
    (C) keeping, waiting
    (D) keeping, wait

17. What do you say_____ on a hike?
    (A) to going
    (B) to go
    (C) about going
    (D) going

18. He could not help_____his lot.
    (A) satisfying with
    (B) satisfy at
    (C) being satisfied with
    (D) be satisfied at

19. Every morning he spends two hours_____papers and magazines.
    (A) for reading
    (B) on reading
    (C) reading
    (D) to read

20. He is not capable_____such difficult work in a day.
    (A) to finish
    (B) to have finished
    (C) for finishing
    (D) of finishing

21. We never listen to Beethoven without_____.
    (A) being deeply impressed
    (B) impressing deeply
    (C) having deeply impressed
    (D) to be deeply impressed

22. _____no persuading him to buy the car.
    (A) There was   (B) It was
    (C) Here was   (D) That was

23. He repented_____idle in his youth.
    (A) of being
    (B) of having been
    (C) to be
    (D) to have been

24. Don't forget_____to me. Let's keep in touch.
    (A) to write
    (B) writing
    (C) having written
    (D) to have written

25. Being easy to break, the article wants_____.
    (A) carefully to handle
    (B) careful handling
    (C) to handle with care
    (D) for careful handling

26. It is no use_____to deceive her.
    (A) try
    (B) tried
    (C) trying
    (D) being tried

27. Unless you both stop_____, I will call in the police.
    (A) fighting
    (B) to fight
    (C) having fought
    (D) being fought

28. On_____our village, we asked him for chocolate.
    (A) him to reach
    (B) his to reach
    (C) for him to reach
    (D) his reaching

29. An old friend of mine came near_____by the train.
    (A) to kill
    (B) killing
    (C) being killed
    (D) to being killing

30. There is no_____the fact that he was innocent.
    (A) to deny
    (B) denying
    (C) being denied
    (D) denial

31. She makes a point of_____to him once a week.
    (A) writing
    (B) having written
    (C) being written
    (D) having been written

32. J. F. Kennedy liked_____many questions at the press conference.
    (A) being asked
    (B) asking
    (C) of asking
    (D) ask

33. It goes without_____that Isaac Stern is among the greatest violinists.
    (A) saying
    (B) say
    (C) to say
    (D) to have said

34. She is very busy_____for a journey.
    (A) to prepare   (B) preparing
    (C) to be preparing   (D) being prepared

35. He went _____ in the river nearby.
    (A) fish
    (B) fishing
    (C) to fishing
    (D) having fish

36. _____ one's work properly may be worse than not doing it at all.
    (A) Not do
    (B) Do
    (C) Not doing
    (D) Doing

37. The one job my husband does not like is _____.
    (A) to taking out the garbage
    (B) taking out the garbage
    (C) to be taking out the garbage
    (D) out taking the garbage

38. She didn't seem to mind _____ TV while she was trying to study.
    (A) their watching
    (B) them to watch
    (C) their watch
    (D) for them to watch

39. Jennifer said in her letter that she'd anticipate _____ from you some time.
    (A) to hear
    (B) hearing
    (C) having heard
    (D) to hearing

40. Mark, scolded by his teacher, finally confessed to _____ the book.
    (A) have stolen
    (B) steal
    (C) stealing
    (D) having stolen

41. He prided himself on _____ at chess.
    (A) having never been beaten
    (B) having been never beaten
    (C) have never been beaten
    (D) having never beaten

42. The bus was so crowded that he had a hard time _____.
    (A) got off
    (B) getting off
    (C) to get off
    (D) get off

43. We had trouble _____ the obscure path through the forest.
    (A) to find
    (B) for finding
    (C) finding
    (D) with finding

44. When I walked along the street, I saw a poor old lady and _____.
    (A) couldn't help sympathizing her
    (B) couldn't but sympathize her
    (C) couldn't hardly sympathize to her
    (D) couldn't help sympathizing with her

45. The purpose of this essay is that of giving some informa-
    tion and _____.
    (A) to present the author's opinions on flying saucers
    (B) on flying saucers
    (C) the author's opinions presented on flying saucers
    (D) presenting the author's opinions on flying saucers

Ⅱ. 請根據句意和文法，選出一個錯誤的答案。

46. (A) He insisted on marrying her.
       = He insisted that he should marry her.
    (B) I don't object to going with you.
       = I have no objection to going with you.
    (C) Remember to see him this afternoon.
       = Don't forget to see him this afternoon.
    (D) He stopped talking.
       = He stopped to talk.

47. (A) He tried kicking the ball.
       = He tried to kick the ball.
    (B) I don't care about going.
       = I do not care to go.
    (C) We agreed on going back.
       = We agreed to go back.
    (D) He decided on leaving school.
       = He decided to leave school.

48. (A) He admitted stealing the money.
       = He admitted that he had stolen the money.
    (B) I am sure of his coming on time.
       = I am sure that he will come on time.
    (C) There is no hope of his being set free.
       = There is no hope that he will be set free.
    (D) He repents of having been idle in his youth.
       = He repents that he had been idle in his youth.

49. (A) It is no use my going there.

    = It is of no use for me to go there.

    (B) On reading the letter, he turned pale.

    = As soon as he read the letter, he turned pale.

    (C) This is a picture of his own painting.

    = This is a picture he paints himself.

    (D) She was scolded for not coming.

    = She was scolded because she did not come.

50. (A) Needless to say, man is mortal.

    = It goes without saying that man is mortal.

    (B) Do you mind my reading it aloud?

    = Do you mind if you read it aloud?

    (C) What's the use of arguing with him?

    = It's quite useless to argue with him.

    (D) She is above telling a lie.

    = She is not so mean as to tell a lie.

Ⅲ. 選出下列各句中錯誤的部分。

51. Continue <u>reading</u> and the meaning of these sentences will
    (A)

    become clear to you, and <u>finally</u>, try to <u>avoid</u> going back
    (B)　　　　　　(C)

    and <u>to reread</u> words and phrases.
    (D)

52. The human ribs are capable <u>to move</u> <u>so as</u> to allow room
    (A)　　(B)

    for the lungs <u>to expand</u> <u>during</u> breathing.
    (C)　　　(D)

53. The student <u>had difficulty</u> <u>to write</u> <u>a short paragraph</u>
　　　　　　　　　　(A)　　　　　(B)　　　　　　(C)

　　<u>correctly</u>.
　　　(D)

54. <u>More and more</u> Americans are planning to stop <u>to smoke</u>
　　　(A)　　　　　　　　　　　　　　　　　　　　　　(B)

　　<u>since</u> the government <u>required</u> health warnings on cigarette
　　　(C)　　　　　　　　　(D)

　　packages.

55. Livy was <u>the</u> only great <u>historian of the time</u>, and he de-
　　　　　　(A)　　　　　　(B)

　　voted his attention <u>to give</u> the world <u>splendid</u> pictures.
　　　　　　　　　　　(C)　　　　　　　(D)

Ⅳ. 在下列各空格中，填入適當的字。

56. When I pass over the bridge, I always think of the accident.
　　= I can _____ pass over the bridge_____ thinking of
　　the accident.

57. It is impossible to know how old she is.
　　= There is_____ knowing her_____.

58. I felt like _____ at the sad news.
　　= I was <u>i</u>_____ to cry at the sad news.

59. I could not go on the trip because I was ill.
　　= Illness p_____ me _____ _____ on the trip.

60. She is proud that he was so rich.
　　= She is proud of _____ _____ _____ so rich.

61. There was no doubt that he had forgotten my birthday.

   = There was no doubt of ＿＿＿＿ ＿＿＿＿ ＿＿＿＿ my birthday.

62. Let's take a walk in the park.

   = What do you say ＿＿＿＿ ＿＿＿＿ a walk in the park?

63. This diamond is not only valuable but also very rare.

   = B＿＿＿＿ ＿＿＿＿ valuable, this diamond is very rare.

64. I reminded him that he had promised it.

   = I reminded him ＿＿＿＿ his ＿＿＿＿ ＿＿＿＿ it.

65. I don't know the reason why I should believe his words.

   = I don't know the reason ＿＿＿＿ ＿＿＿＿ his words.

66. He lives here and I don't object to it.

   = I don't mind ＿＿＿＿ ＿＿＿＿ here.

67. The grass needs cutting.

   = The grass needs ＿＿＿＿ ＿＿＿＿ ＿＿＿＿.

68. This is a profession which I have chosen myself.

   = This is a profession of ＿＿＿＿ ＿＿＿＿ ＿＿＿＿.

69. In learning a foreign language, it is necessary to advance step by step.

   = ＿＿＿＿ you ＿＿＿＿ a foreign language, it is necessary to advance step by step.

70. Exercise doesn't weaken the body, but strengthens it.

   = ＿＿＿＿ ＿＿＿＿ weakening the body, exercise strengthens it.

3. 分詞 (Participles)

Points of Grammar

1. 分詞的形式

時\語\式\態\例	write（及物動詞）		rise（不及物動詞）	
	主　　動	被　　動	主　　動	被　動
現在分詞　簡單	writing	being written	rising	無
現在分詞　完成	having written	having been written	having risen	無
過去分詞	無	written	risen	無

2. 分詞的用法

(1) 作為主要動詞的一部分。

He is **doing** some work.

He has **done** the work.

The work was **done**.

She was **elected** President.

The stars are **shining** brightly.

(2) 作形容詞用。

She opened the letter with her **trembling** hands.

In the parlor there was a lady **reading** a magazine.

I looked at the **fallen** leaves.

A letter **sent** by air-mail should arrive sooner than one **sent** by regular mail.

(3) 作補語用。

The baby lay **sleeping** in the cradle.

He went out of the classroom **unobserved**.

I saw a boy **running**.

I saw a whale **caught**.

I had (*or* got) a new suit **made**.

I had (*or* got) my right leg **broken**.

(4) 作副詞用。

It is **boiling** (*or* burning) hot.

It is **biting** (*or* cutting) cold this morning.

It is **shocking** bad.

(5) 作介詞用。

What's your opinion **regarding** (=about) his punishment?

They had long talks **concerning** (= about) religion.

Considering (*or* For) his age, he is very wise.

(6) 作連接詞用。

Supposing (= If) it rains, what shall we do?

Granting that (= Though) he has spoken the truth, I can hardly believe it probable.

He will do the work **provided that** (= if) you pay him.

Seeing that (=Since) we know nothing of the truth, it is best to wait for further information.

3. 分詞構句的形成

(1) 先將引導副詞子句的連接詞去掉。

(2) 副詞子句的主詞與主要子句的主詞相同時，則再把副詞子句的主詞去掉；如不相同時則保留。

(3) 任何動詞（包括 be 動詞）均改爲現在分詞。（如進行式,則須把 be 動詞去掉）

(4) 分詞爲 being 和 having been 時，可把它省略掉。

(5) 如遇到否定詞則放在分詞前（否定詞＋分詞）。

(6) 其餘照抄。

> As he is ill, he cannot attend the meeting.
> = **Being** ill, he cannot attend the meeting.

> If you turn to the right, you will find the bank.
> = **Turning** to the right, you will find the bank.

(**Having been**) praised too much, he became too proud.

School (**being**) over at last, they ran to their games.

Not having found his key, he still had the money with him.

4. 分詞構句的含意

(1) 表時間：相當於 when, while, as, after 等所引導的副詞子句。

Sleeping (=While he was sleeping) on the bank of a stream, he dreamed a strange dream.

My work **finished** (=When my work was finished), I went out for a walk.

(2) 表原因、理由：相當於 because, as, since 等所引導的副詞子句。

(**Being**) A wise boy (= As he was a wise boy), he listened to his father.

She smiled, not **being** able to help it. (=, for she was not able to help it)

(3) 表條件：相當於 if, unless 等所引導的副詞子句。

Seen from the plane (= If they are seen from the plane), these islands are really beautiful.

(4) 表讓步：相當於 though, even if 等所引導的副詞子句。

Admitting what you say (= Though I admit what you say), I can not consent.

Wounded (= Though he was wounded), the brave soldier continued to fight.

(5) 表連續或附帶狀態。

The train starts here at 5, **arriving** there at 11. (=, and it arrives there at 11.)

Taking off his hat, he smiled at me. (=He took off his hat, and smiled at me.)

＊表示附帶狀況的獨立分詞構句，有時以「with ＋受詞＋ V-ing」的形式出現；being 省略後則以「with ＋受詞＋ p.p. 或形容詞」的形式出現。

She rushed out of the room with her eyes **shining**. (= and her eyes were shining)

An old man stood there, with his arms **folded**. (=, and his arms were folded. = folding his arms.)

(6) 獨立分詞構句：當分詞構句的意義上的主詞和主要子句的主詞不同，則分詞前必須加上主詞，稱之。

The sun **having set**, (=As the sun had set,) we started for home.

It **being** fine (= If it is fine) tomorrow, we will go on a picnic.

＊若副詞子句的主詞為人稱代名詞 (we, you, he, I 等) 時，分詞片語的主詞可以省略。

Generally speaking, (=If we speak generally,) all the world loves justice.

EXERCISE 3

I. 請根據句意和文法選出一個最正確的答案。

1. That is Mary _____ over there.
   (A) sitting
   (B) to sit
   (C) to be sat
   (D) being sat

2. The police caught him _____ a car.
   (A) to steal
   (B) stealing
   (C) stolen
   (D) to be stolen

3. These are the facts _____ by the committee.
   (A) to gather
   (B) gathering
   (C) gathered
   (D) being gathered

4. They got their car _____ at the garage.
   (A) to wash
   (B) washing
   (C) being washed
   (D) washed

5. I had my suit _____ yesterday.
   (A) to press
   (B) pressing
   (C) press
   (D) pressed

6. The language_____in Canada is English.
   (A) to speak
   (B) speaking
   (C) spoken
   (D) speaks

7. I am sorry to have kept you_____so long.
   (A) to wait
   (B) waiting
   (C) be waiting
   (D) be waited

8. She kept her eyes_____all the time.
   (A) to close
   (B) closing
   (C) close
   (D) closed

9. Can Mary make herself _____ in English?
   (A) understood
   (B) understand
   (C) to understand
   (D) understanding

10. A noise that disturbs someone is a_____noise.
    (A) disturb
    (B) disturbance
    (C) disturbed
    (D) disturbing

11. A worker on an exhausting job is an_____worker.
    (A) exhaust
    (B) exhausting
    (C) to exhaust
    (D) exhausted

12. The dog, _____, will make a good watch dog.
    (A) to train properly
    (B) training properly
    (C) properly to train
    (D) trained properly

13. I started the clock _____.
    (A) to go
    (B) going
    (C) gone
    (D) to be gone

14. Before _____ to the college, he had to go through an examination.
    (A) admitting
    (B) to admit
    (C) being admitted
    (D) having been admitted

15. A beggar was dragging his weary feet with many kids _____ behind.
    (A) following
    (B) to follow
    (C) followed
    (D) being followed

16. _____ with mine, your audio components are rather expensive.
    (A) Comparing
    (B) To compare
    (C) To be compared
    (D) Compared

17. " How was the concert last night?" " It was _____."
    (A) disappointing
    (B) disappointed
    (C) disappoint
    (D) disappointment

18. The room is crowded, but there are _____.
    (A) a few seats to leave
    (B) few seats left
    (C) a few seats left
    (D) few seats to leave

19. All the students felt _____ listening to his lecture.
    (A) bored
    (B) boring
    (C) to bore
    (D) bore

20. The President was sitting on the chair _____ by his supporters.
    (A) surrounding
    (B) to surround
    (C) surrounded
    (D) surround

21. A _____ man will catch at a straw.
    (A) drowned
    (B) to drown
    (C) drowning
    (D) being drowning

22. The concert conducted by Karajan proved very _____.
    (A) exciting
    (B) excited
    (C) to excite
    (D) being excited

23. The gentleman sitting with his arms _____ was my boss.
    (A) folding
    (B) to fold
    (C) folded
    (D) being folded

24. Beethoven wasted too much time_____his symphony No. 9.
    (A) composed
    (B) being composed
    (C) compose
    (D) composing

25. _____all things into consideration, his life is a happy one.
    (A) Taking
    (B) Having taken
    (C) Take
    (D) To take

26. I saw Professor Lee_____in the library last night.
    (A) works
    (B) to work
    (C) working
    (D) worked

27. " A man was killed." " Where is the body of the _____ man ?"
    (A) murder
    (B) murdered
    (C) murdering
    (D) having murdered

28. The name Nebraska comes from the Oto Indian word " nebrathka,"_____flat water.
    (A) to mean
    (B) meaning
    (C) it means
    (D) by meaning

29. _____ his answer, she sent the second letter.
    - (A) Receiving not
    - (B) Not to receive
    - (C) Not being received
    - (D) Not having received

30. Our school, _____ on a hill, commands a fine view.
    - (A) located
    - (B) locating
    - (C) having located
    - (D) to locate

31. We will go for a walk in the Grand Park tomorrow, weather
    _____.
    - (A) permitting
    - (B) to permit
    - (C) permitted
    - (D) having permitted

32. _____ that the train is gone, it is useless to wait.
    - (A) Seen
    - (B) Seeing
    - (C) Having seen
    - (D) To see

33. My letter, _____ to the wrong number, reached him late.
    - (A) to have addressed
    - (B) being addressed
    - (C) having been addressed
    - (D) to have been addressed

34. He wanted a basket of flowers _____ to his wife
    - (A) sending
    - (B) sent
    - (C) to send
    - (D) to have sent

35. When I returned home, I found the window open and some-
thing _____.
(A) to steal
(B) stealing
(C) stolen
(D) stole

36. My father encouraged me in my painting, but never lived
to see any of my works _____ in public.
(A) exhibiting
(B) exhibited
(C) having exhibited
(D) exhibit

37. Standing, _____ on a hill, his villa commands a fine view.
(A) as it is
(B) as it was
(C) as he does
(D) as it does

38. Hidden _____ by a big tree, his house was not to be
seen.
(A) as it was
(B) as it is
(C) as it did
(D) as he did

39. Walking along the riverside path, _____.
(A) I met several groups of hikers
(B) the river met several groups of hikers
(C) it was several groups of hikers
(D) we met by several groups of hikers

40. Asked if he could come to the party that night,_____.
    (A)   nobody said anything.
    (B)   they did not get an answer from him.
    (C)   nothing was said by him.
    (D)   Tom nodded his head and left the room.

41. _____, Tom jumped into the river and saved the drowning girl.
    (A)   Being a good swimmer
    (B)   Good swimmer as he is
    (C)   He can swim very well
    (D)   Being that he was a good swimmer.

42. The same thing, _____, would amount to disaster.
    (A)   happen in crowded places
    (B)   happening in crowded places
    (C)   it happened in crowded places
    (D)   it has happened in crowded places.

43. Eva,_____born in Canada, lived and practiced law in America.
    (A)   was
    (B)   he was
    (C)   although
    (D)   who he was

44. The water of a hot spring carries many dissolved minerals,
    usually _____ us an unusual taste and smell.
    (A)   give
    (B)   gives
    (C)   to be given
    (D)   giving

45. While attempting to break into their third bank in one week,
    _____.
    (A)   the police finally managed to catch the robbers
    (B)   the robbers were finally caught.
    (C)   it happened at last that they were captured.
    (D)   the capture of the robbers was finally done.

Ⅱ. 選出下列句子中錯誤的部分。

46. <u>After searching</u> the house for evidence the police <u>concluded</u>
    　　　(A)　　　　　　　　　　　　　　　　　　　　　　　(B)

    that someone must have come <u>in through</u> the kitchen window
    　　　　　　　　　　　　　　　　　　(C)

    and <u>stole</u> the silver while the family was asleep.
    　　　　(D)

47. Baroque <u>has been</u> the term <u>using</u> by art <u>historians</u> for
    　　　　　(A)　　　　　　　(B)　　　　　　(C)

    almost a century <u>to designate</u> the dominant style of the
    　　　　　　　　　　(D)

    period 1600-1750.

48. <u>After finishing</u> Roots, the <u>one-hundred-year</u> history of a
    　　(A)　　　　　　　　　　(B)

    black American family, the Nobel Prize Committee <u>awarded</u>
    　　　　　　　　　　　　　　　　　　　　　　　　　　　(C)

    author Alex Haley a special citation <u>for</u> literary excellence.
    　　　　　　　　　　　　　　　　　(D)

49. Knowing <u>little</u> <u>about</u> algebra, <u>it was difficult</u> to <u>solve</u> the
    　　　　(A)　　(B)　　　　　　　(C)　　　　　　(D)

    equation.

50. Having <u>hit</u> more home runs <u>than</u> <u>any other player</u> in the
    　　　　(A)　　　　　　　　(B)　　(C)

    history of baseball, <u>Hank Aaron's record</u> is famous.
    　　　　　　　　　　(D)

Ⅲ. 根據括號中所提示的字，做適當的變化後，填入空格內。

51. This is the conclusion_____at between them. ＜arrive＞

52. _____ from a distance, it looked like a human face.＜see＞

53. Mr. Wang is the most _____speaker I have ever heard. ＜bore＞

54. Of those_____all but him came to the party. ＜invite＞

55. I sent her a letter_____ that I was ill. ＜say＞

56. The end of the movie was_____. ＜surprise＞

57. I saw the poor child_____ in the accident. ＜kill＞

58. He sat in the chair, with his mouth_____. ＜open＞

59. He could not make his voice_____. ＜hear＞

60. His parents_____last week, the child has no one to look after him. ＜die＞

61. It is_____how many foreigners are now taking up the study of Taiwanese. ＜surprise＞

62. So far as I am _____, your suggestion leaves nothing to be desired. ＜concern.＞

63. Some books,_____carelessly, will do us harm rather than good. ＜read＞

64. Have you ever heard Beethoven's violin concerto_____ by Hsu Chiao-Liang? ＜perform.＞

65. _____ _____, students do not like English grammar. ＜speak generally.＞

Ⅳ. 在下列空格中填入適當的字，使上下意思可以成立。

66. _____ my purse stolen, I could not but feel helpless.
    = As my purse was stolen, I could not _____ feeling helpless.

67. The old man's only son was killed in the war.
    = The old man _____ his only son _____ in the war.

68. There was not a vacant seat in the bus, and I kept standing.
    = _____ not _____ a vacant seat in the bus, I kept standing.

69. I have never read the book, so I can not criticize it.
    = _____ _____ read the book, I can not criticize it.

70. If we grant that this is true, what follows?
    = _____ that this is true, what follows?

Ⅴ. 將下列各分詞構句改為子句的形式。

71. <u>Taken by surprise</u>, he lost his presence of mind.

72. <u>Taken by surprise</u>, he did not give up the contest.

73. <u>Brought up in a better family</u>, he would not have gone bad.

74. People <u>living in towns</u> do not know the pleasure of country life.

75. The man <u>respected by all the villagers</u> was imprisoned yesterday.

4. 被動語態(Passive Voice)

1. **S＋V＋O**

   He paints a picture. →A picture **is painted** by him.

   She has been writing a letter since this morning.

   →A letter has been **being written** by her since this morning.

2. **S＋V＋IO＋DO**

   He gave me a book.

   →I **was given** a book by him.　→A book **was given** (*to*) me by him.

   ＊write, read, make, get, buy, sing 等動詞，通常用直接受詞做為被動語態的主詞。

   He wrote me a letter.

   →A letter **was written** (*to*) me by him.（正）

   →I *was written* a letter by him.（誤）

3. **S＋V＋O＋C**

   We call him a fool. →He **is called** a fool (*by us*).

   I saw him enter the building. →He **was seen to** enter the building by me.

   He made his daughter marry the rich merchant.

   →His daughter **was made to** marry the rich merchant by him.

4. **S＋V＋O**（＝**that** -子句）

   They say that he was innocent.

   ＝ It **is said** that he was innocent. →He **is said** to have been innocent.

5. **動詞＋受詞＋介副詞**

   We can not carry it out in practice.

   → It can not **be carried out** in practice.

6. **不及物動詞＋介詞**

   The bus ran over a child.

   →A child **was run over** by the bus.

7. 不及物動詞＋副詞＋介詞

They looked forward to his arrival eagerly.

→His arrival **was eagerly looked forward to**.

8. 及物動詞＋名詞＋介詞

You must take good care of the child.

→The child must **be taken good care of**.

→Good care **must be taken of** the child.

9. 祈使句

Do it at once. → **Let it be done** at once.

Don't forget me. → **Don't let me be forgotten**. → **Let me not be forgotten**.

10. have (or get)＋受詞＋過去分詞

* have (or get)＋受詞＋過去分詞表「被動經驗」和「使役」,但 get 是出自本身的意願，have 則出於無奈或自願。

I **had** my umbrella **blown** out.

I **had** my purse **stolen**.

I *got* my purse stolen.（誤）

I **got** my watch repaired.

11. be ＋過去分詞表「狀態」,通常不用 *by* ～

He **is known to** all the villagers.

12. 動詞＋反身代名詞

She dressed herself in black. → She **was dressed in** black.

Seat yourself. ＝ **Be seated**.

13. 有些及物動詞沒有被動語態

He **reached** Taiwan yesterday.

→Taiwan *was reached* yesterday by him.（誤）

14. 有些及物動詞作不及物動詞用時，形式上雖然爲主動，但表被動意義

The scientific papers **read** easily.

The door will not **open**.

Who is to **blame** for starting the fire?

EXERCISE 4

I. 請根據句意和文法選出一個最正確的答案。

1. Peace _____by everybody.
   - (A) desires
   - (B) is desiring
   - (C) has desired
   - (D) is desired

2. By whom_____this paper written?
   - (A) has
   - (B) was
   - (C) ought
   - (D) should

3. Taiwan is becoming _____.
   - (A) Americanize
   - (B) Americanizing
   - (C) Americanized
   - (D) Americanization

4. When all the students _____, the professor began his lecture.
   - (A) sit
   - (B) were seated
   - (C) seat
   - (D) seated

5. "Where is your money?" "My money was_____."
   - (A) robbed
   - (B) lose
   - (C) not here no more
   - (D) stolen

6. He said that his teeth needed _____.
   (A) to be repaired
   (B) to being repaired
   (C) repaired
   (D) being repaired

7. He was named Robert _____ his father by mother.
   (A) to
   (B) upon
   (C) after
   (D) under

8. He was _____ to go out with his girl friend by his teacher.
   (A) allow
   (B) allowed
   (C) let
   (D) letted

9. Next time the Olympic Games _____ here.
   (A) is held
   (B) will hold
   (C) will be held
   (D) are about to be held

10. The fact that he stole the money _____ everybody.
    (A) is known to
    (B) is known by
    (C) is known with
    (D) is known at

11. A man _____ the company he keeps.
    (A) is known to
    (B) is known by
    (C) is known with
    (D) is known as

12. The poor girl is to _____ a rich businessman.
    (A) marry with
    (B) be married with
    (C) marry to with
    (D) be married to

13. Yesterday I was _____ an Englishman.
    (A) spoken to by
    (B) spoken by to
    (C) spoken to
    (D) spoken by

14. Let this poem _____.
    (A) to remember
    (B) remembering
    (C) remember
    (D) be remembered

15. Mr. Lin asked me if these islands _____ to America.
    (A) belong
    (B) are belonging
    (C) are belonged
    (D) have been belonged

16. Tom is _____ the lectures.
    (A) interested to attend
    (B) interesting to attend
    (C) interested in attending
    (D) interesting in attending

17. She had her hat _____ off.
    (A) blow
    (B) blowing
    (C) blew
    (D) blown

18. He was very_____with the news.
    (A) pleased
    (B) to please
    (C) pleasing
    (D) please

19. Betty has never been heard_____ill of others.
    (A) speak
    (B) spoke
    (C) to speak
    (D) spoken

20. He tried not to_____mixed up in politics.
    (A) make
    (B) take
    (C) have
    (D) get

21. No attention was _____to his warning.
    (A) taken
    (B) paid
    (C) made
    (D) done

22. He was_____thought and didn't hear me call him.
    (A) lost after
    (B) losing after
    (C) lost in
    (D) losing in

23. The president_____to have delivered the speech on this platform.
    (A) said
    (B) says
    (C) is said
    (D) was told

24. Don't _____ it be forgotten.
   (A) make
   (B) let
   (C) get
   (D) cause

25. The teacher is said to _____ his students before.
   (A) scold
   (B) scolded
   (C) have scolded
   (D) be scolded

26. He is _____ by everybody.
   (A) spoken well
   (B) spoken well of
   (C) well spoken
   (D) well spoken of

27. He had his wife _____ on him a few years ago.
   (A) die
   (B) to die
   (C) dead
   (D) be died

28. He is engaged _____ writing a novel.
   (A) by
   (B) in
   (C) at
   (D) to

29. We were delighted _____ the news of his success.
   (A) at
   (B) by
   (C) to
   (D) about

30. We were caught _____ a shower on our way home.
    (A) by
    (B) with
    (C) at
    (D) in

31. He is quite satisfied _____ his income.
    (A) to
    (B) at
    (C) with
    (D) in

32. The sky was covered _____ dark clouds.
    (A) with
    (B) by
    (C) of
    (D) to

33. He was devoted _____ the study of archaeology.
    (A) by
    (B) to
    (C) with
    (D) at

34. He was born _____ a noble family.
    (A) at
    (B) of
    (C) from
    (D) among

35. She is absorbed _____ the practice of the violin.
    (A) at
    (B) with
    (C) by
    (D) in

Ⅱ. 選出錯誤的句子。

36. (A) A rise of salaries was asked for by the workmen.
    (B) She was cured from her sickness by her family doctor.
    (C) It was biting cold. The poor orphan was frozen to death.
    (D) Nobody likes being looked at in public.

37. (A) He was thought to be innocent.
    (B) What language is spoken in Canada?
    (C) They were made stay at home.
    (D) She was never heard to speak ill of others.

38. (A) His father was resembled by the little boy.
    (B) By whom has this letter been written?
    (C) The house was being built by him.
    (D) Good care must be taken of our health.

39. (A) What can not be cured must be endured.
    (B) Get the luggage carry to the station.
    (C) A stranger was seen to go into the garden.
    (D) A doctor must be sent for at once.

40. (A) The girl was seized with terror while reading the mystery.
    (B) The widow is possessed of a large farm.
    (C) At school he was informed about his mother's illness.
    (D) They were convinced of the truth of their theory.

41. (A) The country is now involved in the war.
    (B) The village is still isolated from civilization.
    (C) He was satisfied with the result of the experiment.
    (D) Mother was relieved with his safety.

Ⅲ. 選出正確的句子。

42. (A) He was laughed by all his classmates.
    (B) So far as I am concerned, I can see no reason why she should not be allowed to go.
    (C) I never see the photograph without reminding of my early life.
    (D) The next war will be more cruel than can be imagine.

43. (A) I was blown off my hat.
    (B) I became acquainted with the singer at the party.
    (C) He was stolen his watch on his way to school.
    (D) Water is consisted of hydrogen and oxygen.

Ⅳ. 選出下列句子中錯誤的部分。

44. When I was grown up, I spent every summer helping out
                    (A)   (B)
    on my grandparents' farm.
    (C)   (D)

45. She was said by the women that they had husbands to
              (A)
    protect their rights and that what she needed was a husband.
    (B)   (C)   (D)

46. Poor Cinderella was made live in the kitchen, where she
    (A)   (B)   (C)
    had to do all the dirty work dressed in rags.
                                  (D)

47. Let wealth <u>regard</u> by some society of the future as a
　　　　　　　(A)

　　<u>means</u> to the proper ends of human life, and <u>its wealth</u>
　　　(B)　　　　　　　　　　　　　　　　　　　　　　　(C)

　　will be <u>fairly distributed</u>.
　　　　　　　(D)

V. 將下列各句改爲被動語態。

48. Let us do away with all the ceremony.

49. Everybody knows him.

50. It seems that they imprisoned the student.

51. We have painted the house white.

52. What do you call this flower in English?

53. We suppose that he made great progress.

54. You should pay particular attention to the handling of the engine.

55. Admit that honesty is the best policy.

56. No one has ever solved this problem.

57. He took no notice of my presence.

5. 語法 (Mood)

Points of Grammar

1. 假設法 (Subjunctive Mood)

(1) 與現在事實相反的假設

If he **had** the book, he **could lend** it to you.

Were I rich, I **could go** abroad.

I **wish** it were true. (I wish = If only ～ = Would that ～ = O that ～)

$$\begin{cases} \text{It is time he went to bed.} = \text{It's time he } \textbf{should go} \text{ to bed.} \\ = \text{It's time for him to go to bed.} \end{cases}$$

He talks **as if** he **knew** everything.

He talked **as if** he **knew** everything.

(2) 與過去事實相反的假設

You **could have done** it better, if you **had tried**.

I **wish** I **had followed** his advice.

I **wished** I **had read** the book.

He talks **as if** he **had read** the fiction.

He talked **as if** he **had read** the fiction.

(3) 與未來事實相反的假設

If I **should** lose my sight, what **shall** (*or* **should**) I do?

If you **would** succeed, you **would have** to work harder.

Even if the sun **were to** rise in the west, I **would never** change my mind.

(4) If 的省略:假設法中的 If 可以省略,但主詞、動詞必須調換位置。

Had he helped me, I might have succeeded.

Should it rain, he would (*or* will) not go out.

(5) If 子句以外的假設法 (詳見文法寶典 p. 366)

To hear him talk, we would take him for a fool.

$$\begin{cases} \textbf{But for} \text{ (= Without) } \textbf{water}, \text{ nothing } \textbf{could live}. \\ = \textbf{If it were not for water}, \text{ nothing could live}. \\ = \textbf{If there were no water}, \text{ nothing could live}. \end{cases}$$

> **Without your help,** she could not have escaped death.
> = **If it had not been for your help,** she ~ .
> = **If you had not helped her,** she ~ .

> **With** a little more care, you could succeed.
> = **If you had a little more carefulness**, you could succeed.
> = **If you were a little more careful**, you could succeed.

I am engaged, otherwise (= or = if I were not engaged) I would accept.

He can not be honest, **or**(= if he were honest) he would not say so.

> **A true sales girl** would not say so.
> = If she were a true sales girl, she would not say so.

I would not say so **in your place.** (= **if I were in your place**)

　＊ 相當於 if 的其他連接詞: unless, in case, suppose, provided, on condition that, etc.
　　In case I forget , please remind me about the incident.

2. 祈使法 (Imperative Mood)

(1) 對第二人稱 you 的祈使，通常省略其主詞，用原形動詞。

Go at once. Be kind to old people.

　＊ 以 Don't 或 Never 來表否定的祈使句。

Don't be lazy. Don't read the book.

(2) 間接命令句，用 let 表命令或依賴；此種祈使句通常用於第一或第三人稱。

Let me go there. Let us know the time of your arrival.

Don't let her stay up too late. = Let her not to stay up too late.

(3) 祈使句表條件，可與直說法的條件句互換。

> Get up earlier, **and** you will be on time.
> = If you get up earlier, you will be on time.

> Work hard, **or** you will fail the examination.
> = If you don't work hard, you will fail the exam.

(4) 祈使句可表讓步。

> **Be it true or not,** it does not concern me.
> =**Whether it is** (*or* **may be**) **true or not,** it does not concern me.

> **Say what you will,** I will not go with you.
> =**Whatever you may say,** I will not go with you.

> **Be he ever so rich** (=Let him be ever so rich), he must not be proud.
> =**However rich he may be,** he must not be proud.

> **Try as he would,** he could not remember the meaning.
> =**However hard he might try,** he could not remember the meaning.

EXERCISE 5

I. 請根據句意和文法選出一個最正確的答案。

1. He suggested that the newcomer_____his medical report soon.
   - (A) submit
   - (B) submitted
   - (C) has submitted
   - (D) would submit

2. "What did the girl look like?" "She wore a wedding dress _____she were a bride."
   - (A) like
   - (B) so
   - (C) so that
   - (D) as if

3. "As a matter of fact, I don't like the lady." "If the lady_____actually a bother, I'll take her home."
   - (A) are
   - (B) was
   - (C) is
   - (D) were

4. "I didn't catch the train." "You _____ the train if you had hurried."
   - (A) would catch
   - (B) had caught
   - (C) could have caught
   - (D) could catch

5. " The teacher demands that everyone _____ in his seat at nine o'clock.
   (A) will be
   (B) be
   (C) were
   (D) shall be

6. If the car _____ no good, I would have to buy another one.
   (A) were
   (B) is
   (C) was
   (D) are

7. " Did you work yesterday?" " I wish yesterday _____ a holiday."
   (A) is
   (B) was
   (C) were
   (D) had been

8. " You didn't go to the party, did you?" " I do wish I _____ there."
   (A) was
   (B) were
   (C) had been
   (D) went

9. I would have gone swimming, if I _____ a swimming suit.
   (A) had had
   (B) have had
   (C) had
   (D) have

10. What would you have done if you_____to work yesterday?
   (A) didn't have
   (B) hadn't had
   (C) didn't
   (D) didn't have had

11. He required that Alice_____the meeting.
   (A) would attend
   (B) attends
   (C) attended
   (D) attend

12. If you _____see Mr. Allen, give him my regards.
   (A) should
   (B) would
   (C) shall
   (D) will

13. She is not supposed to play with us until the teacher recommends that she_____allowed to do so.
   (A) is
   (B) be
   (C) were
   (D) will be

14. "You should have been to your sister's home!" "Yes, I _____."
   (A) should
   (B) ought to be
   (C) must
   (D) should have

15. If it_____tomorrow, we will put off our picnic.
   (A) rains
   (B) will rain
   (C) would rain
   (D) rained

16. If you _____ help me, I should be very grateful to you.
    (A) should
    (B) would
    (C) will
    (D) can

17. If a man doesn't remain content with what he has, ill
    _____ him.
    (A) will befall
    (B) befall
    (C) hardly befall
    (D) tell

18. If you_____me, I could find Jane is unaware of the
    fact.
    (A) would have told
    (B) told
    (C) have told
    (D) tell

19. Helen doesn't know how much I spent in repairing the house;
    if she ever found out, I am sure _____.
    (A) she'd never forgive me
    (B) she never forgives me
    (C) she'll never forgive me
    (D) she does not forgive me

20. _____out of season, I would have ordered some from
    the fruit stand.
    (A) If oranges would have been
    (B) If oranges have not been
    (C) Had oranges not been
    (D) Should oranges not have been

21. If the United States had build more homes for poor people in 1955, the housing problems now in some parts of this country_____so serious.
   (A) wouldn't be
   (B) will not have been
   (C) wouldn't have been
   (D) would have not been

22. _____that the time will soon be ripe for intervention in Iran, they would be faced by a large army.
   (A) It is believed
   (B) Should they believe
   (C) They would believe
   (D) If they had believed

23. I wish we_____with my brother when he flies to England next week.
   (A) could go
   (B) had gone
   (C) will go
   (D) are going

24. Sandra says that she wishes she_____in New York now.
   (A) have been
   (B) be
   (C) is
   (D) were

25. I wish I were as smart as you_____.
   (A) have been
   (B) had been
   (C) are
   (D) were

26. William wishes now that he _____ English instead of French when he was in high school.
    - (A) have had studied
    - (B) studies
    - (C) had studied
    - (D) studied

27. I would rather she _____ tomorrow than today.
    - (A) come
    - (B) came
    - (C) should come
    - (D) has come

28. "What will you do during the winter vacation?"
    " I don't know, but it's about time _____ on something.
    - (A) I'm deciding
    - (B) I'll decide
    - (C) I'd decided
    - (D) I decided

29. " He would go to see you." "_____ he did not come?"
    - (A) What if
    - (B) Where if
    - (C) What come
    - (D) Why whether

30. I would buy that book but I _____ enough money.
    - (A) do not have
    - (B) did not have
    - (C) will not have
    - (D) had not had

31. I would wear my red dress if it _____ a stain in the front.
    - (A) had
    - (B) didn't have
    - (C) would have
    - (D) has

32. Mary might have come to school in time for Professor Smith's lecture_____.
    (A) if she got up earlier
    (B) unless she had got up earlier
    (C) but she got up rather late
    (D) but she had gotten up so late

33. We would have arrived sooner except we_____a flat tire.
    (A) had
    (B) would have
    (C) has not
    (D) has

34. I hope that you_____all right.
    (A) will be
    (B) should be
    (C) were
    (D) would be

35. How happy I_____, if you had been with me then.
    (A) could be
    (B) would have been
    (C) should have been
    (D) were

36. _____their assistance, he would have to lead a very miserable life; he might even starve to death.
    (A) With
    (B) But for
    (C) Without for
    (D) If not

37. He might have led a life quite different from the one he lived _____ this event which happened all of a sudden.
    (A) were it not for   (B) had it not been for
    (C) if it were not for   (D) if there were not

38. As you know, I am a disabled man, but I should be very happy if I _____ of service to you.
    (A) am
    (B) have been
    (C) could be
    (D) would be

39. It is proposed by some that the new method _____ adopted at once, but others say that they may be criticized if it _____ a failure.
    (A) should be, were to prove
    (B) is, would prove
    (C) shall be, proved
    (D) be, should prove

40. " He is already on the wrong side of the forties." " It's necessary that he _____ himself a wife and settled down."
    (A) finds
    (B) should find
    (C) found
    (D) had found

41. She is little, _____ at all, better than a beggar.
    (A) though
    (B) when
    (C) unless
    (D) if

42. _____ water, no living things could exist.
    (A) Unless it were not for
    (B) Had it not been for
    (C) If it were not for
    (D) If it had not been for

43. I _____ it to her if I had thought she would understand.
    (A) would explain
    (B) explained
    (C) will explain
    (D) would have explained

44. He lives a luxurious life as if he _____ a millionaire.
    (A) is
    (B) was
    (C) were
    (D) will be

45. If it had not rained yesterday, the ground _____ muddy now.
    (A) is not
    (B) will not be
    (C) would not be
    (D) would not have been

46. _____ if you had studied the problem carefully last week.
    (A) You won't find any difficulty now,
    (B) You would not find any difficulty now,
    (C) You would not have found any difficulty now,
    (D) You have not found any difficulty now,

47. It has been raining for several weeks, I wish _____.
    (A) it would stop raining before tomorrow
    (B) I could stop it raining before tomorrow
    (C) it will stop it raining before tomorrow
    (D) it would stop to rain before tomorrow

48. The judge assented to the suggestion that _____.
    (A) both of the criminals will soon be set freedom
    (B) some of the criminals there are of guilt only
    (C) the girl was to be paroled in the custody of a welfare society
    (D) the prisoner be sentenced to death

49. He did his best in everything; _____ he would not have been what he was.
    (A) and
    (B) but
    (C) otherwise
    (D) but that

50. There is no living plant or animal, _____, that will not repay the study of it, and provide, if intelligently observed, quite an interesting story.
    (A) it be ever so common
    (B) be it ever so common
    (C) however it be ever so common
    (D) be it however common

Ⅱ. 選出下列句子中錯誤的部分。

51. Our guide <u>requested</u> that <u>we all are</u> as attentive as
                (A)   (B)

    <u>possible</u> when we <u>visit</u> the observatory this afternoon.
      (C)   (D)

52. If you <u>knew</u> how many pieces John <u>ate</u> for breakfast this
           (A)   (B)

    morning, you would never have <u>doubted</u> why <u>he</u> is overweight.
                       (C)   (D)

53. I sometimes wish that my university <u>is</u> <u>as large as</u> State
                              (A) (B)

    University because our facilities are <u>more</u> limited <u>than</u>
                          (C)   (D)

    theirs.

54. It was our neighbor's opinion that if Kennedy was alive
              (A)   (B)

    today, the country would have fewer problems than it has
                                  (C)   (D)

    now.

55. If I have learned the phonetic system of reading when I
           (A)   (B)

    was in college, I would be a better reader today.
          (C)   (D)

Ⅲ. 請根據句意和文法，選出一個錯誤的答案。

56. (A) Should you find him, please bring him back to me
        = If you should find him, please bring him back to me.
    (B) He worked hard; otherwise he would have failed.
        = He worked hard; if he didn't work hard, he would
          have failed.
    (C) We should have arrived earlier but that we met with an
        accident.
        = We should have arrived earlier, if we had not met
          with an accident.
    (D) A man of sense would not have done such a thing.
        = If he had been a man of sense, he would not have
          done such a thing.

57. (A) How delightful it would be for us to work together!
        = How delighful it would be, if we could work together!
    (B) To hear him speak Chinese, you would take him for a
        Chinese.
        = If you were to hear him speak Chinese, you would
          take him for a Chinese.

(C) The same thing, happening in Taiwan, would amount to disaster.

= The same thing, if it should happen in Taiwan, would amount to disaster.

(D) Left to herself, she would have been ruined.

= If she were left to herself, she would have been ruined.

58. (A) Take a rest sometimes, or you will fall ill.

= If you do not take a rest sometimes, you will fall ill.

(B) Go where you will, you will find human nature the same.

= Wherever you may go, you will find human nature the same.

(C) It is my judgement, be it good or bad.

= It is my judgement, whether it is good or bad.

(D) Try as he would, he could not remember a word of the sermon.

= Though he would try, he could not remember a word of the sermon.

59. (A) A little more effort would have made him pass the test.

= If he made a little more effort, it would have made him pass the test.

(B) Let the world be what it will, the American does not doubt the fact.

= Whatever the world may be, the American does not doubt the fact.

(C) Would that I were young again.

= I wish I were young again.

(D) Any boy who should do such a thing would be scolded.

= Any boy, if he should do such a thing, would be scolded.

60. (A) It is time for you to go to bed.
     = It is time you went to bed.
   (B) What would you do in my place?
     = What would you do if you were in my place?
   (C) One more effort, and you will succeed.
     = If you made one more effort, you will succeed.
   (D) Seen from a distance, it would look like a huge animal.
     = If it were seen from a distance, it would look like
        a huge animal.

Ⅳ. 在下列各句的空格中填入適當的字。

61. My mother's illness prevented me from going to school.
   → If it _____ _____ _____ _____ my
     mother's illness, I could have gone to school.
   → If my mother _____ _____ _____ _____,
     I could have gone to school.

62. With your help, we could have passed the examination.
   → If we _____ _____ your help, we could have passed
     the examination.
   → If you _____ _____ us, we could have passed the
     examination.

63. With a little more care, she could have escaped death.
   → If she _____ _____ a little more care, she could
     have escaped death.
   → If she _____ _____ a little more careful, she
     could have escaped death.

64. I do not tell you, because I do not know it.
   → _____ I _____ it I would tell you.

65. I am sorry I could not meet your requirements.

→ I _____ I could _____ _____ your requirements.

66. It would be better for you not to overwork yourself.

→ You _____ _____ not overwork yourself.

67. Without your kind help, I could not have succeeded.

→ I _____ my success _____ your kind help.

68. He is not a baby, but he cries like one.

→ He cries _____ _____ _____ _____ a baby.

69. It is a _____ that the car is too expensive.

→ I wish the car _____ not so expensive.

70. A closer examination of it might have revealed a new fact.

→ If you _____ _____ it more closely, it might have revealed a new fact.

6.　基本動詞句型 (Verb, Sentence Patterns)

Points of Grammar

1. 五種基本句型

(1) S＋V（主詞＋動詞）

The sun **rises** in the east.

There **is** a vase on the desk.

(2) S＋V＋SC（主詞＋動詞＋主詞補語）

We **are** students. He **remained** silent.

＊用於此種句型的動詞有：be, stand, sit, lie, remain, keep, look, seem, appear, sound, get, grow, become, fall, taste, etc.

(3) S＋V＋O（主詞＋動詞＋受詞）

We **learn** English.

(4) S＋V＋IO＋DO（主詞＋動詞＋間接受詞＋直接受詞）

He **gave** me a book.

> ◎ S＋V＋IO＋DO→S＋V＋DO＋Prep.＋IO
> ① 介詞用 to 的動詞有：
> 　　give, offer, bring, lend, pay, send, show, teach, tell, write, do, render, afford, etc.
> ② 介詞用 for 的動詞有：
> 　　make, buy, choose, cook, get, gain, leave, order, sing, etc.
> ③ 介詞用 of 的動詞有：
> 　　ask, inquire, demand, require

(5) S＋V＋O＋OC（主詞＋動詞＋受詞＋受詞補語）

I **made** her happy.

I **painted** the roof red.

I **had** him do it. ＝ I **got** him to do it.

I **saw** a girl cross the street.

I **watched** the boys playing baseball.

I **found** the window broken.

She didn't **expect** him to help her.

I **had** my purse stolen.

2. 間接受詞（IO）和直接受詞（DO）間要有介詞的動詞

(1) | supply, provide, furnish, present, charge, etc. | ＋ sb. ＋ | with | ＋ sth.

The cow **supplies** (*or* provides) us **with** milk→The cow **supplies** milk **for** us.

present sb. **with** sth. → **present** sth. **to** sb.

charge sb. **with** sth. → **charge** sth. **to** *or* **into** sb.

They **charged** him **with** an important task.

→They **charged** an important task **to** him.

(2) | rob, rid, deprive, clear, cure (break), relieve, strip, etc. | ＋ sb. ＋

| of | ＋ sth.

The robber **rob**bed (*or* relieved) me **of** my belongings.

He **cured** (*or* broke) me **of** my bad habit.

(3) | suggest, propose, explain, say, relate, introduce, mention, speak,

confess, demonstrate, etc. | ＋ sth. ＋ | to | ＋ sb.

She **suggested** the plan **to** me.

She **confessed** her sin **to** her friend.

He **explained to** us that the earth is round.

3. 直接受詞（DO）和間接受詞（ID）間不需有介系詞的動詞

| envy, save, take, answer, forgive, strike, deny, cost, grudge, etc. |

＋ sb. ＋ sth.

I **envy** you your good memory.

That **saved** me much trouble.

It **takes** me two hours to go there on foot.

It **cost** me lots of labor.

I **grudge** such a stupid fellow his fine house and family.

EXERCISE 6

I. 請根據句意和文法選出一個最正確的答案。

1. John _____ his father.
   (A) looks like
   (B) looking like
   (C) like to
   (D) is liking

2. Up till then, these problems had been _____ for centuries.
   (A) laying dormant
   (B) laying dormantly
   (C) lying dormant
   (D) lain dormantly

3. "What happened?" "The situation is _____."
   (A) embarrassed
   (B) embarrass
   (C) much embarrassed
   (D) embarrassing

4. "I hear that you are having a house built. Is it finished yet?" "No, but it is _____ completion."
   (A) nearly to
   (B) almost at
   (C) close to
   (D) must about it

5. The reason I didn't go to France was _____ a new job.
   (A) because I got
   (B) because of getting
   (C) due to
   (D) that I got

6. I saw the coach on the field after the game, and he seemed
   _____.

   (A) real angry
   (B) very angrily
   (C) maddening
   (D) angry

7. I like Mozart's music very much because his music sounds
   _____.

   (A) sweet and soothing
   (B) sweetly and soothingly
   (C) sweetingly and soothingly
   (D) sweetingly and soothing

8. It seemed to Mary that the butter smelled somewhat
   _____.

   (A) bad
   (B) badly
   (C) worse
   (D) worsely

9. John Joseph Pershing _____ in 1919, the first highest
   rank held by any American citizen except George Washington.
   (A) to be a full general
   (B) he made a full general
   (C) made a full general
   (D) was being made a full general

10. Controversial matters involving the two groups were dis-
    cussed; nevertheless, most of the representatives _____.
    (A) remaining calm
    (B) remained calmly
    (C) remain calmly
    (D) remained calm

11. "How about him?" "He came home _____."
    (A) safe
    (B) safely
    (C) with safety
    (D) with safeness

12. "What did you do with the door?" "The door was painted _____."
    (A) whitely
    (B) white
    (C) with white
    (D) with white hands

13. Though she didn't feed her baby milk or foods, he could _____.
    (A) feed by himself
    (B) feed of himself
    (C) eat by himself
    (D) eat for himself

14. If we hurry we can _____ there in time for the opening speech.
    (A) go to
    (B) get to
    (C) go
    (D) get

15. "What do you have to do tomorrow?" "I have to _____ in a conference."
    (A) join
    (B) taking part
    (C) attend
    (D) participate

16. In the stillness of the night the sound _____ very loudly.
    (A)　resounded
    (B)　sounded
    (C)　listened
    (D)　heard

17. " Who is responsible for sending out misinformation? "
    " Most of the fault _____ with the administration."
    (A)　has laid
    (B)　lays
    (C)　is laying
    (D)　lies

18. At last day _____ and it began to get light.
    (A)　broke
    (B)　lighted
    (C)　rose
    (D)　lightened

19. " All the people in this village have black hair." " Yes,
    they all _____ each other."
    (A)　resemble as
    (B)　resemble with
    (C)　resemble
    (D)　resemble from

20. We all survived _____.
    (A)　from the war
    (B)　during the war
    (C)　after the war
    (D)　the war

21. " Were you able to contact John ? " " Yes, and he _____
    me of a good place to eat here."
    (A)　said   (B)　suggested
    (C)　recommended   (D)　told

22. " I think I understand his point." " Then _____."
    (A) explain me it
    (B) explain it to me
    (C) explain it for me
    (D) explain for me it

23. " How does she manage it?" " She asks _____."
    (A) to the students for help
    (B) the students for help
    (C) for help to the students
    (D) to students for help

24. Even if no violation of law is discovered, it _____
    troubling questions of political ethics.
    (A) rises
    (B) raises
    (C) has risen
    (D) arises

25. Eva laid her glasses on the desk and _____ in a chair
    beside her sister.
    (A) seated down
    (B) seated herself
    (C) set down
    (D) sit herself down

26. " You look very tired." " I had to _____ all the dishes
    after dinner."
    (A) make
    (B) settle
    (C) get
    (D) do

27. " It's time to leave." " Yes, the clock _____ two o'clock."
    (A) says   (B) indicates
    (C) tells   (D) marks

28. " Do I have to _____ trains at the next station ? "
    " Yes, you will see the train for Taipei."
    (A) change
    (B) get off
    (C) depart
    (D) take

29. " What happened ? " " As you know, my schoolmates never
    _____ their clothes well. "
    (A) hanging
    (B) hanged
    (C) hung
    (D) hang

30. " How can we settle the problem? " " Well, we must _____
    it to her own judgement. "
    (A) believe
    (B) express
    (C) leave
    (D) depend

31. " Why does everybody like Mrs. Rose ? " " Because she al-
    ways _____ good after-dinner jokes. "
    (A) says
    (B) speaks
    (C) to tell
    (D) tells

32. While in his college days he used to _____ long hair.
    (A) have
    (B) wear
    (C) reserve
    (D) grow

33. " Did you see her ? " " She_____her hair in curls. "
   (A) have
   (B) wear
   (C) set
   (D) reserve

34. " These two girls are very popular in town. " " Every boy here wants _____. "
   (A) to date them
   (B) a date with them
   (C) dating
   (D) and dates them

35. " You seem to have a lot of money with you. " " Yes, the store_____. "
   (A) cashed a check at me
   (B) cashed a check to me
   (C) cashed me a check
   (D) cashed to me a check

36. The professor_____us we could leave.
   (A) said
   (B) asked
   (C) told
   (D) spoke

37. " How did you get that green album ? " " It was _____ from my father. "
   (A) gift for me
   (B) gift to me
   (C) a gift to me
   (D) a gift for me

38. The university owed_____for the construction of the
    laboratory.
    (A) to the builders thirty million dollars
    (B) thirty million dollars on the builders
    (C) for the builders thirty million dollars
    (D) the builders thirty million dollars

39. "What did you do?" " I mailed_____."
    (A) at him the letter
    (B) the letter on him
    (C) the letter to him
    (D) the letter at him

40. "Yesterday was my birthday." "My mother_____."
    (A) made a cake to me
    (B) made a cake me
    (C) made for me a cake
    (D) made me a cake

41. "What is your opinion of Mark?" " I _____him a
    genius."
    (A) consider
    (B) say
    (C) understand
    (D) look at

42. I believe_____due to mistaken views of the world.
    (A) this unhappiness are
    (B) to be this unhappiness
    (C) this be unhappiness
    (D) this unhappiness to be

43. Are you going to leave_____?
    (A) the open windows   (B) the windows opened
    (C) open the windows   (D) the windows open

44. " Is dinner ready ? " " No, mother is_____it ready now."
    (A) doing
    (B) cooking
    (C) getting
    (D) preparing

45. Last night, in a radio address, the President urged us _____the Red Cross"
    (A) to support
    (B) support
    (C) supporting
    (D) supported

46. The president was very angry because Mr. Lin_____.
    (A) had permitted the students to use the instruments
    (B) had let the students to use the instruments
    (C) allowed the students use the instruments
    (D) had allowed the students using the instruments

47. A later phase of land reform, called " Land to the Tiller," enables peasants_____up to 17.5 acres of the land.
    (A) to buy
    (B) to buying
    (C) buying
    (D) buy

48. I like Nancy but I do not like_____.
    (A) her sing
    (B) her singing
    (C) she sing
    (D) she singing

49. " Isn't that our plane ? " " Yes, let's go. Maybe we'll find Tom _____ at the gate."
    (A) to have waiting for us
    (B) to have waited for us
    (C) waited for us
    (D) waiting for us

50. When I returned home, I found the window _____ and something _____ .
    (A) break, steal
    (B) broken, stolen
    (C) breaking, stealing
    (D) to break, to steal

51. The people in general looked upon the situation _____ .
    (A) as critical
    (B) to be critical
    (C) being critical
    (D) critical

52. Teaching and learning are part of the same educational experience, but unfortunately they are often thought of _____ .
    (A) to be separate
    (B) as separate
    (C) separate
    (D) as to be separate

53. You would become irritated if you watched the correspondence _____ on your desk day by day.
    (A) to pile up
    (B) pile up
    (C) to be piling up
    (D) pile down

54. "Where did you see him?" " I saw him_____downtown last night."
    (A) had worked
    (B) had been working
    (C) worked
    (D) working

55. "What did you do yesterday?" " I saw a whale_____."
    (A) to catch
    (B) catch
    (C) caught
    (D) having caught

56. " Has Helen decided to argue with the instructor about her grades?" "No, she said she would _____."
    (A) let the matter resting
    (B) let rest the matter
    (C) let the matter rest
    (D) let matter to rest

57. "What does he wish?" " He wishes_____."
    (A) he would cut his hair
    (B) to have his hair cut
    (C) cutting his hair
    (D) to cut his hair

58. " I don't understand that sentence." " Let's get Tom _____that sentence again."
    (A) explain
    (B) explained
    (C) explaining
    (D) to explain

59. "What can I do?" " Please get the lawn_____."
    (A) to be mowed   (B) to mow
    (C) mowing   (D) mowed

60. "What should we do now?" "Let's tell the taxi driver
    _____ for us here."
    (A) waiting
    (B) waited
    (C) to wait
    (D) to waited

61. He will flatly_____that he is responsible for the acci-
    dent.
    (A) decline
    (B) deny
    (C) refuse
    (D) reject

62. "What did Peter do?" "He _____asleep all morning."
    (A) lay
    (B) laid
    (C) lain
    (D) lying

63. "Will eighty dollars be enough?" "Another twenty_____."
    (A) will do
    (B) will cover
    (C) will fix
    (D) will fine

64. They, having many children, want to_____a servant.
    (A) let
    (C) rent
    (B) hire
    (D) lend

65. I couldn't afford to_____a house like that.
    (A) rent
    (B) borrow
    (C) spend
    (D) use

66. He always _____ his dictionary when he comes across a difficult word.
    (A) consults
    (B) opens
    (C) looks
    (D) seeks

67. The president _____ a good income.
    (A) pleases
    (B) asks
    (C) enjoys
    (D) satisfies

68. What has _____ of him?
    (A) been
    (B) become
    (C) got
    (D) done

69. A wooden building can easily _____ fire.
    (A) reach
    (B) spreads
    (C) burn
    (D) catch

70. We can _____ seats for you only if you pay in advance.
    (A) take
    (B) reserve
    (C) acquire
    (D) cancel

71. Rumor _____ it that he was killed in the accident.
    (A) does
    (B) says
    (C) has
    (D) makes

72. Clara wanted to buy the coat, but it cost more than she could _____.
    (A) afford
    (B) affect
    (C) assent
    (D) assume

73. Please_____yourself to the refreshments.
    (A) make
    (B) reach
    (C) save
    (D) help

74. " Hello. I'd like to speak to Tom." " Sorry. He isn't in now." " Can I _____a message for him?"
    (A) write
    (B) leave
    (C) send
    (D) tell

Ⅱ. 在下列各空格中填入適當的字，使上下兩句意思相同。

75. I was so astonished that I could hardly speak.
    = _____ almost d_____me of my power of speech.

76. They did not understand what I meant.
    = I could not make myself _____.

77. This watch keeps good time.
    = This watch neither g_____ nor l_____.

78. He can lift the rocks because he is a man of power.
    = His power_____ him _____lift the rocks.

7. 時式 (Tense)

Points of Grammar

1. 現在式

(1) They **live** in the suburbs.

(2) We **go** to school by subway.

(3) The earth **moves** round the sun.

(4) The plane **starts** for New York tomorrow morning.

(5) I shall go out if the rain **stops** immediately.

(6) Caesar **crosses** the Rubicon and **enters** Italy.

(7) Dryden **says** that none but the brave deserve the fair.

2. 過去式

(1) World War II **broke out** in 1939.

(2) We **met** him very often during our stay in New Zealand. I **used to get up** early in the morning.

She **would often sit up** till late at night.

(3) I **was** there during the summer of 1972. He **sold** insurance for ten years.

3. 未來式

(1) I **shall be** late for school if I miss the train.

We hope you **will soon get** well.

He **will be** glad to hear it.

(2) **Shall** I **be able** to pass the examination?

Shall you **be** free tomorrow? **Will** it **be** fine tomorrow?

(3) I will go there. = I intend to go there.

You shall go there. = I will send you there.

He shall go there. = I will let him go there.

(4) Shall I go there? = Do you want me to go there?

Will you go there? = Do you intend to go there?

Shall he go there? = Will you send him there?

4. 進行式

(1) He **is reading** a novel. 〔現在進行式〕

(2) She **was reading** a novel when I entered the room. 〔過去進行式〕

(3) Jim **will be reading** a novel when we go to bed. 〔未來進行式〕

(4) John **has been waiting** for you since noon. 〔現在完成進行式〕

(5) She **is** always **finding** fault with me.

　　＊現在進行式與 always, usually, constantly, continually 等表「連續」的時間副詞連用，通常表示現在說話者認爲 不良習慣或不耐煩之意。

(6) Where **are** you **spending** your next winter vacation?

5. 現在完成式

(1) I **have** just **finished** my homework.

(2) **Have** you ever **climbed** Mt. Ali ?

(3) He **has been** in bed since last week.

(4) He **has lost** his watch. She **has gone** to America.

(5) I'll lend him the book as soon as I **have done** with it.

6. 未來完成式

(1) I **shall have finished** the task by tomorrow.

(2) I **shall have read** it three times if I read it again.

(3) He **will have lived** in Taipei for five years by next September.

7. 過去完成式

(1) We **had** just **finished** our breakfast when he came.

(2) I recognized Mrs. Kim at once, for I **had seen** her several times before.

(3) No sooner **had** he **seen** a policeman come than he **ran** away.
　　Hardly (＝Scarcely) **had** the airplane **taken** off before (＝when) it
　　began to blow hard. (*or* No sooner ～ than, Scarcely (Hardly)～ before
　　(when ～).

EXERCISE 7

I. 請根據句意和文法選出一個最正確的答案。

1. " Has he found a new house?" " Yes, he will move_____.
   (A) in those days
   (B) on Sunday last
   (C) already
   (D) one of these days

2. " Did you wait for him very long?" " Yes, I _____to bed until five in the morning."
   (A) did go
   (B) didn't go
   (C) had gone
   (D) went

3. " How long have you been here?" " I _____here three weeks ago."
   (A) came
   (B) I'd be
   (C) I have been
   (D) I'd have been

4. " Did Mary come here and visit?" " She_____ twice since March 1969."
   (A) visited here
   (B) was visiting here
   (C) has visited
   (D) visits

5. " Do you mean George?" " Yes, he _____ a note to me yesterday.
   (A) had written   (B) wrote
   (C) was written   (D) writes

6. "What happened in that new area?" "New houses _____ recently over there."
   - (A) are built
   - (B) build
   - (C) have built
   - (D) have been built

7. "How long?" "Peter_____for you since noon."
   - (A) waits
   - (B) is going to wait
   - (C) has been waiting
   - (D) had waited

8. "What will happen?" "By next June we _____ a million refrigerators."
   - (A) will have sold
   - (B) sell
   - (C) shall sell
   - (D) will sell

9. "When will Richard be home?" "Richard _____ one-fourth of his ROTC services by this time next year."
   - (A) will complete
   - (B) will have completed
   - (C) is completing
   - (D) completes

10. "Do you know Professor Lee?" "Of course I do. I _____ him long ago in Taipei."
    - (A) had met
    - (B) have met
    - (C) would meet
    - (D) met

11. " My English isn't good." " How many years ago _____ English ? "
    (A) did you study
    (B) do you study
    (C) have you studied
    (D) had you studied

12. " How is Jane ? " " She has been sick _____ last Monday.
    (A) on
    (B) since
    (C) in
    (D) during

13. " Is Nancy living here ? " " Yes, _____ here for the last four years.
    (A) she lived
    (B) she lives
    (C) she's living
    (D) she's been living

14. " How often has Miss Lin come to visit you recently ? "
    " She _____ here twice in 1986."
    (A) was
    (B) be
    (C) is
    (D) has

15. I _____ to the tennis club of my school.
    (A) am belong
    (B) am belonged
    (C) am belonging
    (D) belong

16. In those days people _____ without chopsticks.
    (A) eat
    (B) ate
    (C) were eating
    (D) had been eating

17. Mr. Blake _____ to Switzerland, so he is not here.
    (A) has gone
    (B) has been
    (C) will have been
    (D) will have gone

18. The teacher told us that Watt _____ the steam engine.
    (A) invented
    (B) has invented
    (C) had invented
    (D) had been inventing

19. After she _____ the package, she took it to the railway station.
    (A) wrap
    (B) was wrapped
    (C) has wrapped
    (D) had wrapped

20. Let's go for a walk, _____?
    (A) aren't we
    (B) shall we
    (C) will we
    (D) do we

21. Please have a seat, _____?
    (A) are you
    (B) won't you
    (C) will you
    (D) shall you

22. " Shall I give you a hand ? " " _____."
    (A) Yes, thank you
    (B) Yes, you may
    (C) That's wonderful
    (D) You are welcome

23. " Shall we eat now? " "_____."
    (A) Yes, you shall
    (B) It's very kind of you
    (C) Yes, thank you
    (D) Yes, let's eat now

24. If you _____ lend me your fountain pen, I'll be very much obliged.
    (A) will
    (B) shall
    (C) may
    (D) do

25. Let's go out for a drink when we _____ this work.
    (A) will finish
    (B) will have finished
    (C) finished
    (D) have finished

26. I should think the corn crop _____ by next weekend.
    (A) was gathered in
    (B) will have gathered in
    (C) has been gathered in
    (D) will have been gathered in

27. I _____ there nowadays, as it has become a very noisy place.
    (A) never go
    (B) never went
    (C) am never going
    (D) have never gone

28. " Have you ever been to Scandinavia? " "_____."
    (A) Yes, I've ever
    (B) Yes, ever
    (C) No, I have
    (D) Yes, I have

29. John has been a teacher since he _____ the army.
    (A) has left
    (B) left
    (C) had left
    (D) leaving

30. I recognized him at once, for I _____ him before.
    (A) have seen
    (B) saw
    (C) had seen
    (D) would have seen

31. London has been an important city for centuries, and it
    _____ important.
    (A) is still being
    (B) has still been
    (C) had still been
    (D) is still

32. I enjoy Shakespeare's works. Up to now I _____ three
    of his plays.
    (A) had read
    (B) have read
    (C) was reading
    (D) am reading

33. " Did you see Betty yesterday?" " Yes, at five o'clock she
    _____."
    (A) has written a letter
    (B) had written a letter
    (C) was writing a letter
    (D) is writing

34. How long _____ there by next week?
    (A) are you working　　　　(B) will you be working
    (C) will you work　　　　(D) will you have been working

35. Every morning he_____ten and then jumps out of bed.
    (A) counts to
    (B) is counting
    (C) counted
    (D) has counted

36. A man's dignity_____on his wealth but on what he is.
    (A) is depended
    (B) depends
    (C) does not depend
    (D) is depending

37. At this moment somebody in the world is dying and another
    _____.
    (A) being born
    (B) is born
    (C) born
    (D) is being born.

38. On September 16,1620, the Mayflower, a sailing vessel of
    about 180 tons,_____ a memorable voyage from England.
    (A) starting
    (B) started
    (C) was started
    (D) had started

39. Do you remember the incident that_____at our first
    meeting?
    (A) took place
    (B) has taken place
    (C) had taken place
    (D) had place

40. When she entered the room, he_____beside the center table grinning expectantly.
    (A) stands
    (B) standed
    (C) was standing
    (D) standing

41. _____to Japan, her father has not heard from her.
    (A) Since she went
    (B) Because she went
    (C) After she went
    (D) When she went

42. It _____ every day so far this month.
    (A) is raining
    (B) rained
    (C) rains
    (D) has rained

43. I _____twice to Russia since the Revolution and I was there several times before it.
    (A) was
    (B) have been
    (C) was gone
    (D) had been

44. By the time we got to the airport, our plane_____.
    (A) has already left
    (B) had already left
    (C) left
    (D) had already been left

45. The cost of living _____ by ten percent before the government took any action.
    (A) was going   (B) went up
    (C) had gone up   (D) has gone up

46. This morning's earthquake was one of the most severe that we _____ for the past twenty years.
    (A) experienced
    (B) experiencing
    (C) have experienced
    (D) had experienced

47. When you visit Boston, _____.
    (A) it will be raining
    (B) it will be rain
    (C) it is rain
    (D) it is raining

48. The students _____ anything by the end of the term if the teacher goes on like this.
    (A) not taught
    (B) were not taught
    (C) will not have been taught
    (D) used not to be taught

49. It will not be long before _____ to the moon.
    (A) we will have a trip
    (B) we can have a trip
    (C) we shall be able to have a trip
    (D) we be able to have a trip

50. No sooner _____ he seen me than he ran away.
    (A) is
    (B) did
    (C) has
    (D) had

51. Seven years _____ since he died.
    (A) passed
    (B) have passed
    (C) is passing
    (D) had passed

52. She bought me a book and_____ me that I _____kind
    to her friend.
    (A) advised, be
    (B) would advise, am
    (C) had advised, was
    (D) had been advising, would be

53. Immediately after breakfast the prisoners were sent on
    their way to Savannah, under the guard of a sergeant and
    a corporal, with eight men. They _____ long before
    Jasper took leave of his brother, and set out on some
    pretended errand.
    (A) would not go
    (B) have not gone
    (C) had not gone
    (D) was not going

54. It _____ not till 1838, on reading Thomas Malthus'
    Essay on Population that Darwin got the answer to the
    problem of how and why living things change from genera-
    tion to generation. Malthus held that the human population
    tended to increase faster than its food supply.
    (A) is
    (B) would be
    (C) had been
    (D) was

Ⅱ. 選出不正確的用法。

55. (A) Girls <u>will</u> be curious.
    (B) Boys <u>will</u> be noisy.
    (C) When he <u>will come</u>, please give him this book.
    (D) A drowning man <u>will</u> catch a straw.

56. (A) The sun rises in the <u>east</u> and sets in the west.
    (B) I <u>am hearing</u> you are married.
    (C) The earth <u>moves</u> round the sun once a year.
    (D) Plants <u>breathe</u> just as animals do.

57. (A) By the time you <u>graduate</u> from college, he will return to Taiwan.
    (B) I will talk over the matter with him when he <u>comes</u> back.
    (C) They will help you if you <u>ask</u> them nicely.
    (D) Mother is cooking some food at present; she always <u>cook</u> in the mornings.

58. (A) We <u>have been</u> married for fifteen years.
    (B) When <u>have you returned</u> from Germany ?
    (C) Steve <u>has been</u> ill since last month.
    (D) How long <u>have you been</u> here ?

59. (A) I <u>had hoped</u> to see him at the meeting tonight.
    (B) I <u>had expected</u> to pass the examination.
    (C) I <u>had known</u> him for many years before he became a teacher.
    (D) We <u>had intended</u> to call on Dave.

Ⅲ. 選出錯誤的句子。

60. (A) Have you ever been to the Hyde Park ?
    (B) Did you ever go to the park?
    (C) When have you been to the park?
    (D) Where have you come from ?

61. (A) He is always thinking of going abroad.
    (B) He is resembling his father.
    (C) I am leaving here tomorrow.
    (D) We are having a good time.

62. (A) When he will come, I will have left here.
    (B) I don't know when he will have finished his work.
    (C) If you will do it, you will be praised.
    (D) The day will come when we will be able to travel in outer space.

63. (A) I don't know if it will rain tomorrow, but if it rains, I shall not go.
    (B) We had hardly walked five minutes when we were caught in a shower.
    (C) He has been waiting for an hour, and so have I.
    (D) I have gone to Chiang Kai-Sheik Airport to see a friend of mine off.

64. He has not been home a week. 與下列何者相同？
    (A) It is more than a week since he left home.
    (B) It is not yet a week since he came home.
    (C) It is just one week since he came home.
    (D) He has been away from home for less than a week.

Ⅳ. 選出下列句子中錯誤的部分。

65. No doubt you would like to know how I have been getting
        (A)   (B)

    along since I have left school.
        (C)   (D)

66. When Columbus discovered America, he thought that he
                     (A)

    arrived in India, so he called the people he met "Indians."
      (B)   (C)   (D)

67. Immanuel Kant was so regular in his habits that until the day
                    (A)   (B)

    he died people have been able to set their watches by his actions.
               (C)   (D)

68. The detective told us in his talk that every human being had
                 (A)   (B)   (C)

    a distinctive set of finger prints.
             (D)

69. There is no returning on the road of life. The frail bridge
             (A)

    of Time, on which we tread, sinks back into eternity at
           (B)

    every step we take. The past is gone from us forever. It
                         (C)

    is belonging to us no more.
           (D)

Ⅴ. 根據括號中所提示的字，做適當的變化後，填入空格內。

70. I lost the watch which my aunt_____me. < give >

71. By the time you get back, I _____all my correspondence.
    < finish >

72. I _____a lot about him before I finally met him. <hear>

73. It will not be long before spring_____around. < come >

74. He thanked me for what I _____. < do >

75. I _____a mile before it began to rain. < not go >

76. Jane _____the book for two hours when I visited her.
    < read >

77. Mother_____out shopping; she is not at home now. < go >

78. He _____ill for a long time, when the doctor was sent for.<be>

79. It_____three years since we celebrated our wedding. < be >

8. 助動詞 (Auxiliary Verbs)

Points of Grammar

1. must

(1) He **must** be out to lunch.

* It **must** be true. →〔肯定的推測〕It can not be true. →〔否定的推測〕

  Can it be true?→〔疑問的推測〕

* must 的過去式用 had to 來表示；未來式則是 will (shall) have to。

(2) must 可當名詞，作「不可不看（聽）的東西；必需品」解。

The temple is a real **must** for tourists.

A car is a **must** in America.

(3) must 還可表示過去不巧的事，作「偏偏」解。

Just as I was busiest, he **must** come in and worry me with silly questions.

2. ought to (＝ should) 表「應該」

(1) You **ought to** go there. ＝ You should go there.

* must, ought to, should 皆可用來表示肯定的推測。

(2) It **ought to** be warmer inside. ＝ It should be warmer inside.

3. can

(1) 表能力 (＝ be able to)

He **can** swim very well but he **cannot** skate.

(2) 表推測（常用於否定和疑問句）

Can it be true?

It **cannot** be true.

(3) 表許可 (can ＝ may; can't ＝ must not)

You **can** go home as soon as you have finished it.

4. might

(1) 表許可。

You **might** post this letter for me.

(2) 表現在或未來的推測。

It **might** be true.

(3) 表請求。

Might I ask your name?

5. would

She **would** often go swimming in the river. 〔表過去不規則的習慣〕

Would you like to have some tea？〔表謙恭的請求〕

Would that I were a bird. 〔would 代替 I wish, 表決心、意向或祈望〕

6. used to ＋原形動詞：表過去（規則）的習慣

She **used to** go shopping.

→〔否定〕She **used not to** go shopping.

　　　　＝She **didn't use**（ *or* used）**to** go shopping.

→〔疑問〕**Used** she **to** go shopping？

　　　　＝**Did** she **use**（ *or* used）to go shopping？

→〔回答〕Yes, she **used to**.（也可以回答 Yes, she **did**.）

7. may well （理所當然；有足夠的理由～）

He **may well** be surprised. ＝It is natural that he should be surprised.

What he says **may well** be false.

8. should

(1) 表義務。

　　You **should** obey your parents.

(2) 表明顯的結果或合理的推論。

　　My friends **should**（＝ought to）be there by now, I think.

(3) 用於委婉的說法。

　　I **should**（**would**）**like to** know about Taiwan.

(4) 疑問句中 should 表驚訝、不合理、難以相信或不應該之事。

　　How **should** I know that？

(5) It is (strange, necessary, natural, important, a pity, right, surprising, etc.) that ～ should 在名詞子句中表感情，說話者認為有「應該如此」或「不合理、難以相信、不應如此」的意思。

　　It is surprising that she **should** marry a brute of a man.

(6) 欲望動詞 propose, demand, insist, suggest, recommend, etc. 之後所接的 that -子句中, 用 should 表「應該」。

　　I insisted that she (**should**) marry him.

9. **need**

Need he work so hard? He **need not** do such a silly thing.

He **needs to** work hard.

注意：(1) 回答 need 或 must 的問句時，肯定一律是 must，否定是 need not。

　　　　　Need he go there? Yes, he **must**. 或 No, he **needn't**.

　　　(2) needs must 或 must needs 中之 needs 為副詞，用來加強語氣，作「必要地；一定地；偏偏」解。

　　　(3) need 做助動詞時，只用於否定句和疑問句中，但如果肯定句中有否定副詞 hardly, scarcely, never, no 等，或是含有否定、疑問的意味，仍可用 need。

　　　　　He told me that I **need** not pay so much money.

10. **dare**

I **dare not** go to the bar.

How **dare** you say such a thing to my face?

She **dares to** insult me.

* I **dare say** = probably. I **dare say** that she is still alive.

11. **助動詞＋ have ＋ p.p.**（表對過去的推測）

(1) can not have ＋ p.p. → She can not have said so.

(2) can ～ have ＋ p.p. ? → Can she have told a lie?

(3) may have ＋ p.p. → She may have been ill.

(4) must have ＋ p.p. → She must have lost her way.

(5) should have ＋ p.p. ＝ ought to have ＋ p.p. 〔表過去該做而未做的事〕

You ought to have come a little earlier.

They ought to have arrived there.

(6) need not have ＋ p.p. 〔表過去不必做而已經做的事〕

She need not have hurried.

EXERCISE 8

I. 請根據句意和文法選出一個最正確的答案。

1. "Must I finish all this work in an hour?" "No, you _____."
   (A) must not
   (B) won't
   (C) should not
   (D) need not

2. My sister never used to oppose me, but my brother occasionally_____.
   (A) did
   (B) used to
   (C) usedn't
   (D) didn't

3. "Why didn't you answer when I called to you?" "I_____, but you didn't hear me."
   (A) couldn't
   (B) didn't answer
   (C) did
   (D) had to

4. Paul lives in London, and so_____his parents.
   (A) are
   (B) do
   (C) don't
   (D) live

5. She used to go shopping on Sundays,_____?
   (A) used she
   (B) didn't she
   (C) usedn't she to
   (D) did she

6. Oh, Jane, you've broken still another glass. You ought
   _____ when you washed it.
   (A) be careful   (B) to careful
   (C) to be careful   (D) to have been careful

7. He is as poor as poor_____be.
   (A) can
   (B) may
   (C) must
   (D) should

8. "Will the weather clear up this afternoon?" "No, I'm
   afraid it _____."
   (A) may not
   (B) won't
   (C) mustn't
   (D) shouldn't

9. I_____the book, but I hardly remember it.
   (A) can read
   (B) may read
   (C) can have read
   (D) may have read

10. You might_____advise me to give up my fortune as
    spend it in gambling.
    (A) as good
    (B) as well
    (C) well
    (D) as well as

11. We_____hardly believe it.
    (A) won't
    (B) ought
    (C) can't
    (D) can

12. " Can you play basketball ? " " I _____ play basketball."
   (A) am used to
   (B) am used for
   (C) used to
   (D) used of

13. " I was late again this morning." "Well, I think you had
   better _____ on time."
   (A) start being
   (B) to start to be
   (C) started being
   (D) to be

14. " I am sorry. I broke your glasses." " It _____ ."
   (A) matters not
   (B) has no matter
   (C) doesn't matter
   (D) isn't matter

15. " Do you mind closing the window ? " " _____ . We have
   enough fresh air. "
   (A) No, I don't mind
   (B) Yes, I don't
   (C) No, I do
   (D) No, I don't

16. " I usually go dancing at night." " _____ do that."
   (A) You had not better
   (B) You had better not
   (C) You had better not to
   (D) You have better not

17. His advice _____ not be taken.
   (A) was needed
   (B) needs
   (C) need
   (D) is needed

18. " Do you speak French ? " " No, I don't speak French, but I _____ speak Chinese. "
    (A) do
    (B) must
    (C) ought
    (D) have to

19. " John smokes too much. " " Well, he used to smoke more than he _____ now. "
    (A) did
    (B) does
    (C) could
    (D) has

20. _____ you like to join us for supper ?
    (A) Did
    (B) Don't
    (C) Will
    (D) Would

21. " Doesn't Mary want to go to that movie? " " Yes, but she says _____ tonight. "
    (A) she'd not rather go
    (B) she'll rather not go
    (C) she'd rather not go
    (D) she won't rather go

22. " Did you criticize him for his mistakes ? " " Yes, but _____ it. "
    (A) I'd not rather
    (B) I'd rather not have done
    (C) I'd better not do
    (D) I'd rather not doing

23. In fact, Mary would rather have left for San Francisco
    _____ in Los Angeles.
    (A) by staying
    (B) than stay
    (C) to stay
    (D) than have stayed

24. "Are you going to be there?" " If I_____ , I'll let
    you know."
    (A) am
    (B) will be
    (C) would be
    (D) do there

25. "Who's taken away my cookies ? " " I_____ ."
    (A) won't
    (B) do
    (C) have
    (D) am

26. It is natural that an employee_____ his work on time.
    (A) finishes
    (B) finishs
    (C) can finish
    (D) finish

27. It is extremely necessary that you _____ that honesty
    is the best policy.
    (A) realizing
    (B) realize
    (C) will realize
    (D) can realize

28. It is important that he_____his reservations before Friday.
    (A) confirm   (B) confirms
    (C) will confirm   (D) must confirm

29. It is great pity that she _____ have done such a thing
    (A) would
    (B) must
    (C) should
    (D) didn't

30. I am sorry that Tom _____ be so weak.
    (A) can
    (B) would
    (C) may
    (D) should

31. I wonder my uncle _____ commit such an error.
    (A) shall
    (B) should
    (C) will
    (D) must

32. I should insist that he _____ accepted as a member,
    since he is very bad-tempered.
    (A) be
    (B) will not be
    (C) not be
    (D) must being

33. It was recommended that the students _____ their
    reports as soon as they could.
    (A) finish writing
    (B) finished writing
    (C) should finish written
    (D) finished the writing

34. He ignored his doctor's advice that he _____ a vacation.
    (A) takes
    (B) took
    (C) would take
    (D) take

35. They yielded to her request that they _____ to the result of their experiment.
    (A) paid attention
    (B) pay attention
    (C) paying attention
    (D) had paid attention

36. " The streets are all wet. It _____ during the night."
    (A) must be raining
    (B) must have been rain
    (C) had to rain
    (D) must have rained

37. The first thing which a student should bear in mind is that a book _____ for mere amusement.
    (A) ought not to be read
    (B) ought to not be read
    (C) not ought to be read
    (D) ought to be not read

38. I'm not used _____ in such a rude way.
    (A) being talked to
    (B) to being talked to
    (C) to be talked to
    (D) be talked to

39. I want to go to the dentist, but you _____ with me.
    (A) need not to go
    (B) do not need go
    (C) need not go
    (D) need go not

40. Since Oriental ideas of woman's subordination to man prevailed in those days, she _____ meet with men on an equal basis.
    (A) did dare
    (B) dare not
    (C) dare not to
    (D) did dare not to

41. Few people in our village_____ afford to buy a car.
    (A) must
    (B) need
    (C) may
    (D) can

42. Take an umbrella with you lest it_____ rain.
    (A) should
    (B) would
    (C) did
    (D) might

43. He stepped aside so that the fat lady_____ pass by.
    (A) will
    (B) can
    (C) might
    (D) used to

44. It is one of the most tragic facts in the recent develop-
    ment of science that the conquest of the air, which on all
    grounds _____ towards the unification of the world and
    the harmony of mankind, has actually become our most
    threatening danger.
    (A) would have worked
    (B) could have worked
    (C) should have worked
    (D) will have worked

Ⅱ. 選出下列句子中錯誤的部分 。

45. The first dog-like creatures <u>probably</u> looked more like bears
                                    (A)

    <u>than</u> the dogs we <u>are used</u> to <u>see</u> now.
    (B)   (C)   (D)

46. Carbon-14 analysis <u>is not able to</u> be used <u>to date</u> such
    (A)   (B)

    inorganic materials as pottery shards <u>or</u> rock and metal
                                          (C)

    artifacts, <u>often</u> the only traces of early man.
               (D)

47. We requested the superintendent of the building <u>to clean</u>
                                                      (A)

    up the storage room <u>in</u> the basement <u>so that</u> the children
                        (B)   (C)

    <u>had</u> enough space for their bicycles.
    (D)

48. <u>To become</u> a member of the civic association, one <u>need only</u>
    (A)   (B)

    attend two meetings and <u>to pay</u> his fees <u>regularly</u>.
                            (C)   (D)

49. <u>It was</u> Leopold Mozart who suggested <u>to his son</u> that he
    (A)   (B)

    <u>writes</u> <u>a number of</u> violin concertos.
    (C)   (D)

Ⅲ. 在下列各句的空格中，填入適當的字。

50. _____ you live long and die happy！

51. Who are you that you <u>s_____</u> speak like this?

52. Little _____ I dream that I could get the highest scores
    in the national examination for college entrance.

53. We _____ be too careful about our health.

54. I gave him no answer for fear that I _____ annoy him.

55. Who _____ come in but the very man we were talking of?

56. His father is now in Washington, and so the man you saw this morning _____ not have been he.

57. "I have a sore throat." "You _____ have seen a doctor yesterday."

58. He who _____ search for pearls must dive deep.

59. Soldiers must wear uniforms, but farmers _____ have to.

Ⅳ. 在下列各句的空格中填入適當的字，使上下兩句意思相同。

60. It is certain that he told a lie.
= He _____ have told a lie.

61. It is impossible that she killed herself.
= She _____ have killed herself.

62. Perhaps she didn't catch the first train.
= She _____ _____ have caught the first train.

63. It is wrong that you did not go to the concert.
= You _____ have gone to the concert.

64. He did not need to write to her, but he did.
= He _____ have written to her.

9. 敍述法 (Narration)

Points of Grammar

直接敍述改爲間接敍述的方法

1. 直述句

⑴ 主要動詞爲 say to 時，要改爲 tell, observe, answer 等。

⑵ 連接詞用 that。

⑶ 刪去引號及其前面的逗點。

⑷ 改變名詞子句的動詞時態。

⑸ 適當地改變代名詞和表地方及時間的副詞。

He **says**, " **I am** too tired to walk."

→He **says** that **he is** too tired to walk.

She **said to** me, " I **took your** pen by mistake."

→She **told** me that **she had taken my** pen by mistake.

He said, " Tom **was here** a minute **ago**."

→He said that Tom **had been there** a minute **before**.

⑹ 直接敍述中的 will, shall 在間接敍述時，也須將時態加以適當地改變。

He said, " I **shall** soon recover."

→He said that he **would** soon recover.

Bob said to her, " I **will** be back **tomorrow**."

→Bob told her that he **would** be back **the next day**.

⑺ 直接敍述改爲間接敍述時，表不變的眞理、歷史的事實和假設法時，動詞時式不變。

He said, " The earth **goes** round the sun."

→He said that the earth **goes** round the sun.

＊ 引句中表時間和場所的副詞，須予以適當的改變。

this (these) → that (those), here → there, now → then,

ago → before, today → that day, next → the next

tomorrow → (*the*) next day, the following day,

yesterday → the day before, the previous day,

last night → the night before, the previous night.

2. 疑問句

(1) 直接敍述中的主要動詞 say（to）於間接敍述時，須改為 ask, inquire 等。

(2) 無疑問詞時，加 whether 或 if, 不可用 that。

(3) 主詞要放在動詞前；問號（？）改為句點（。）。

I **said to** him, " Where are you going now ? "

→ I **asked** him where he was going then.

" Are you busy ? " he said to me. " **No,**" I said.

→He **asked** me **if** I was busy. I said I **wasn't.**

3. 祈使句

(1) 主要動詞 say（to）要改成 tell, order, command, ask, beg, request, advise 等。

(2) 原祈使句改為不定詞的形式。

He said to me, " Start at once." →He **told** me **to start** at once.

He said to us, " Let's go swimming."

→He **suggested** (*to us*) that **we** (*should*) **go** swimming.

Father said to us, " Don't be noisy."

→Father **told** us **not to be** noisy.

She said to me, " Will you wait for a moment ? "

→She **requested** me **to wait** for a moment.

4. 感嘆句

(1) 主要動詞 say 可改成 cry, shout。

(2) 加上適當的修適語，如：with delight, with joy, with regret, with a sigh 等。

She said, " How beautiful the full moon is ! "

→She said that the full moon was **very beautiful.**

→She cried **how beautiful** the full moon was.

He said, " Good heavens ! The bus has left."

→He cried **with regret** that the bus had left.

5. 祈願句

主要動詞 say 要改成 pray, wish, 名詞子句中的動詞前面加上助動詞 may（might）。

He said, " God bless this child !"

→He **prayed that** God **might** bless that child.

6. 合句

直接敍述中的名詞子句,如果是由 and 或 but 連接對等子句而成的合句, 改爲間接敍述時, 兩個對等子句前面都要加 that; 表原因、理由時, 連接詞用 for。

He said, " The watch is very expensive **and** I can not buy it."

→He said (*that*) the watch was very expensive, **and that** he could not buy it.

He said, " I will say no more, **for** I hate explanation."

→He said (*that*) he would say no more, **for** he hated explanation.

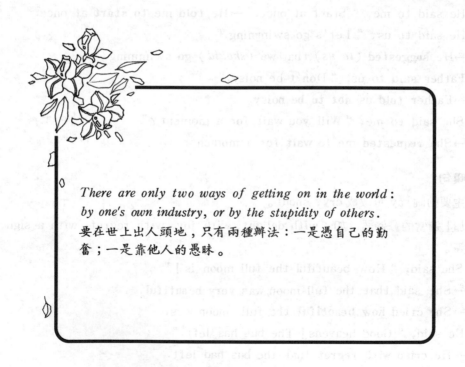

There are only two ways of getting on in the world :
by one's own industry, or by the stupidity of others.
要在世上出人頭地, 只有兩種辦法:一是憑自己的勤奮;一是靠他人的愚昧。

EXERCISE 9

I. 請根據句意和文法選出一個最正確的答案。

1. She said, "I was studying in the library."
   = She said that _____ in the library.
   (A) I was studying
   (B) I had been studying
   (C) she was studying
   (D) she had been studying

2. He said to us, "American schools begin in September."
   = He told us that American schools _____ in September.
   (A) begin
   (B) begun
   (C) has begun
   (D) had begun

3. Jim said, "I have been to New York."
   = Jim said that _____ to New York.
   (A) he has been
   (B) he had been
   (C) I had been
   (D) I have been

4. He said, "I am going to leave here tomorrow."
   = He said that he _____ _____ to leave there _____
   following _____.
   (A) is, going, the, day
   (B) is, going, a, day
   (C) was, going, the, day
   (D) was, going, a, day

5. He said, "The earth moves round the sun."
   = He said that the earth _____ round the sun.
   (A) move
   (B) moves
   (C) moved
   (D) would move

6. Jane said, "I wish I were rich enough to buy this."
   = Jane said that _____ rich enough to buy that.
   (A) she wish she were
   (B) she wished she had been
   (C) she wish she had been
   (D) she wished she were

7. He said to me, "I will come if you send for me."
   = He told me that _____ if _____ .
   (A) he will come, I send for him
   (B) he would come, I sent for him
   (C) he shall come, I sent for him
   (D) he should come, I send for him

8. Last night Mary met Jane here and said, "My brother will
   see you here tomorrow afternoon."
   = Last night Mary met Jane here and said that her brother
      would see her _____ .
   (A) there the following afternoon
   (B) there this afternoon
   (C) here this afternoon
   (D) here the following afternoon

9. He said to me, "You will pass the exam next year."
   = He told me that I _____ the next year.
   (A) should pass the exam
   (B) would be pass the exam
   (C) should have passed the exam
   (D) shall pass the exam

10. I said to her, "What are you doing now?"
   = I asked her what _____ doing then.
   (A) is she
   (B) she is
   (C) she was
   (D) was she

11. He said to me, "Is Susan in a black dress?"
   = He asked me _____ Susan was in a black dress.
   (A) that
   (B) if
   (C) if that
   (D) that if

12. The teacher said to me, "What do you have in your hands?"
   = The teacher asked me _____ in my hands.
   (A) if I had
   (B) what I have
   (C) what I had had
   (D) what I had

13. He said to me, "Which do you like better, this or that?"
   = He asked me _____ I liked better.
   (A) if this or that
   (B) whether that or this
   (C) which of the two
   (D) whether which of the two

14. She said to us, "Don't tell a lie."
   = She told us _____ a lie.
   (A) not to tell
   (B) to not tell
   (C) not tell
   (D) tell not

15. The doctor said to the patient, "Don't smoke."
    = The doctor_____the patient not to smoke.
    (A) forced
    (B) believed
    (C) expected
    (D) advised

16. I said to him yesterday, "Please come early tomorrow morning."
    = Yesterday I_____him to come early_____morning.
    (A) told, the next
    (B) asked, this
    (C) begged, the following
    (D) advised, that

17. He said to me, "Let's go on a picnic next Sunday."
    = He_____that_____go on a picnic next Sunday.
    (A) suggested, they
    (B) told, we
    (C) suggested, we
    (D) told, they

18. He said to her, "Let's go swimming in the river."
    = He _____that_____ swimming in the river.
    (A) suggested to her, they should go
    (B) suggested her, we should go
    (C) said to her, they should go
    (D) told her, we would go

19. He said to me, "Don't smoke any more. It is very harmful to your health."
    = He told me not to smoke any more_____it_____
    very harmful to my health.
    (A) that, is   (B) because, was
    (C) so, was   (D) saying, is

20. He said to me, "Would you show me the way to the station
    = He _____ me _____ to show _____ the way to
        the station.
    (A) told, calmly, me
    (B) asked, abruptly, him
    (C) asked, politely, him
    (D) told, with goodness, me

21. Jane said, " Excuse me."
    = Jane excused _____.
    (A) her
    (B) me
    (C) myself
    (D) herself

22. He never said, " Help me."
    = He never cried _____ help.
    (A) for
    (B) over
    (C) up
    (D) against

23. She said, " Good-bye, friends！"
    = She _____ her friends good-bye.
    (A) asked
    (B) advised
    (C) told
    (D) bade

24. The students said to me, " How kind of you！"
    = The students _____ me for my kindness.
    (A) shouted
    (B) exclaimed
    (C) thanked
    (D) asked

25. I said to her, " What are you looking for?"
    = I asked her what _____ looking for.
    (A) she is
    (B) she was
    (C) is she
    (D) was she

26. She said to me, " What do you say to having a date with me tonight? "
    = She proposed that we _____ have a date that night.
    (A) would
    (B) should
    (C) might
    (D) could

27. " Hurrah! I've passed the exam!" he said.
    = He exclaimed _____ that he had passed the exam.
    (A) in delight
    (B) in joy
    (C) with joy
    (D) for delight

28. He said to me, " Hello! Where are you going?"
    = He _____ me and asked where I was going.
    (A) told
    (B) shouted
    (C) asked
    (D) greeted

29. The priest said, " God save my country!"
    = The priest _____ that God might save his country.
    (A) prayed
    (B) hoped
    (C) worshipped
    (D) shouted

30. The man said to her, "Do you know where the post office is?"

= The man asked her _____ where the post office was.

(A) that she knows

(B) that she knew

(C) if she knows

(D) if she knew

31. I said to him, "If I were in your place, I would do other-wise."

= I told him that if I _____ in his place, I _____ otherwise.

(A) were, would do

(B) had been, would do

(C) were, would have done

(D) had been, would have done

32. I said to him, "Please go."

= I _____ him to go.

(A) pleased

(B) said to

(C) ordered

(D) begged

33. Tom suggested to us that we should play soccer from then on.

= Tom said to us, "_____ play soccer from now on."

(A) We should

(B) We must

(C) Let's

(D) We will

34. The doctor advised Mary not to overwork herself.

= The doctor said to Mary, "You _____ overwork yourself."

(A) must not   (B) had better not

(C) don't have to   (D) don't

35. He said, " I shall be eighteen next year."
    = He said that he _____ be eighteen _____.
    (A) would, the next year
    (B) would, next year
    (C) will, next year
    (D) shall, the next year

36. The teacher said, " The Civil War broke out in 1861."
    = The teacher said that the Civil War_____ out in 1861.
    (A) breaks
    (B) broke
    (C) has broken
    (D) had broken

37. He said to me, " I have lost my pen. May I use yours?"
    = He told me he had lost his pen, and _____ he might
    use mine.
    (A) that
    (B) if
    (C) asked me if
    (D) questioned if

38. She said, " Yes."
    = She answered in the _____.
    (A) yes
    (B) right
    (C) agreement
    (D) affirmative

39. She said, " Will you go there?" I said, " Yes."
    = She asked if I would go there, and I said _____.
    (A) yes
    (B) in affirmative
    (C) I wouldn't
    (D) I would

40. She said, "May God bless this baby of mine ! "
   = She _____ that God might bless her baby.
   (A) wished
   (B) hoped
   (C) prayed
   (D) suggested

41. She said, " Alas, how foolish I have been!"
   = She cried with _____ that she had been very foolish.
   (A) a roar
   (B) a sigh
   (C) a shout
   (D) an exclamation

42. He said to me, " Thank you."
   = He _____ his thanks.
   (A) expressed
   (B) said
   (C) offered
   (D) gave

43. "Work hard, and you will succeed in the project." he said.
   = He told me to work hard, _____ that I should succeed
      in the project.
   (A) and
   (B) or
   (C) adding
   (D) hoping

44. He said to the new boys, "Where do you live? Have you
      any family connections at the school ?"
   = He asked the new boys where they lived and _____ any
      family connections at the school.
   (A) they had   (B) had they
   (C) if had they   (D) if they had

45. Tom said, "Hello, Jane! Where has your brother been?"
    = Tom _____ to Jane and asked where her brother _____.
    (A) greeted, has been
    (B) called, had been
    (C) said, has been
    (D) told, has been

Ⅱ. 選出下列句子中錯誤的部分。

46. He said to me yesterday, "Are you leaving for Taipei
    tomorrow."

    = He <u>asked</u> me yesterday <u>if</u> I <u>was leaving</u> for Taipei <u>the</u>
           (A)   (B)   (C)

    <u>following day</u>.
        (D)

47. He said to her, "Do you remember the time we liked each
    other?"

    = He <u>asked</u> her <u>if</u> she <u>remembered</u> the time they <u>liked</u> each
           (A)   (B)   (C)   (D)

    other.

48. She said to us, "Let's camp here."
    = She <u>suggested</u> <u>us</u> that <u>we</u> should camp <u>here</u>.
            (A)   (B)   (C)   (D)

49. She said, "Would that I were young again!"
    = She <u>exclaimed</u> <u>that</u> she <u>wishes</u> she <u>were</u> young again."
            (A)   (B)   (C)   (D)

50. I said to him, " You look pale. What is the matter with you?"
= I <u>told</u> him that he <u>looked</u> pale, and <u>told</u> him what was the
    (A)   (B)   (C)

   <u>matter</u> with him.
   (D)

51. He said, " The camera is too expensive, and I can't buy it."
= He said that camera <u>was</u> so expensive <u>and that</u> he <u>couldn't</u>
                (A)   (B)   (C)

   buy <u>it</u>.
    (D)

52. He said, " I bought a book, but it was too difficult for me
to read."
= He said that he <u>had bought</u> a book, <u>but</u> it <u>had been</u> too
              (A)   (B)   (C)

   difficult for <u>him</u> to read.
           (D)

53. Mother said to her, " Don't make a noise, Jane. We are
playing a record."
= Mother told Jane <u>to not make</u> a noise <u>because</u> <u>they were</u>
                (A)   (B)   (C)

   <u>playing a record</u>.
     (D)

54. She said to me, " Make haste, and you will be in time."
= She <u>told</u> me <u>that</u> I <u>would be</u> in time if I <u>make</u> haste.
    (A)   (B)   (C)   (D)

10. 名詞 (Noun)

Points of Grammar

1. 名詞的種類

(1) 普通名詞 (Common Noun)

① **A dog** (＝ The dog) is a faithful animal.

   ＝ Dogs are faithful animals. 〔一般用法〕

② **The pen** is mightier than the sword. 〔普通名詞的抽象用法〕

③ **All the village** were delighted at the news. (指村人)

    ＊ all England, all Europe

④ **That fool of** a John has forgotten to clean my boots. (＝ foolish)

    ＊ an angel of a wife, a mountain of a wave

(2) 集合名詞 (Collective Noun)

① { **The public is** the best judge.

     { **The public are** divided in their opinions.

② **The police** are on the track of the robber.

③ Some **furniture** was bought for the new house.

(3) 專有名詞 (Proper Noun)

① Everyone cannot be **a Shakespeare** or **a Beethoven**.

② There is **a Mr. Adams** who wants to see you.

③ In the party there were **three Marys**.

④ **The Woods** are our best friends.

⑤ I saw **a genuine Rodin** in this museum.

(4) 物質名詞 (Material Noun)

① Several **glasses** tumbled from the table.

② They deal in **teas and coffees**.

③ I saw **a light** in the distance.

(5) 抽象名詞 (Abstract Noun)

① **Youth** should have respect for **age**.

② The King **had the generosity to spare** the guilty. 〔 have the ＋抽象名詞＋ to ～ 〕

③ He is a man **of learning**. 〔of ＋抽象名詞＝形容詞〕

④ I can read the book **with ease**. 〔with（in, by）＋抽象名詞＝副詞〕

⑤ She was **kindness itself**. 〔＝all kindness ＝ very kind〕

2. 名詞的數

(1) 複數變化的例外情形：

① 字尾若為子音＋o 時，加 es，但有例外，如：

pianos, kilos, photos, dynamos（發電機）, etc.

② 字尾是 f 或 fe 時，變為 ves，但有例外，如：

roofs, griefs, chiefs, beliefs, safes（保險箱）, cuffs（袖口）, etc.

(2) 單複數同形的一些名詞：

salmon, trout, carp, sheep, deer, Japanese, Chinese, corps, means（手段）, series, species（種類）, etc.

(3) 複合名詞的複數：

① 將主要字變複數→passers-by, fathers-in-law, etc.

② 合成字的前後兩個元素都要變成複數形→men-servants.

③ 如果合成字中沒有可數名詞時，把最後一個字加 s → go-betweens.

(4) 外來名詞的複數：

datum（資料）→ data, radius（半徑）→ radii, oasis（綠洲）→ oases, etc.

3. 複數名詞的慣用語

make friends with, be on good terms, shake hands with, change cars（trains, buses, seats, etc.）, change hands

4. 有些名詞的單複數意義不同

air（空氣）→airs（裝腔作勢）, arm（臂）→ arms（武器）, letter（信）→ letters（文學）

5. 名詞做形容詞表示單位

a ten-dollar note（10 元鈔票）

6. **head, dozen, hundred, thousand** 等字表確定數目時，不必加 s；如表不定數目，則要加 s

① 表確定數目：twenty head of cattle（二十頭牛）, three dozen（of）pencils（三打鉛筆）

② 表不定數目：a few dozens（幾打）, thousands of people（好幾千人）

7. 名詞的性

① 陽性名詞和陰性名詞各使用不同的字→nephew: niece, bachelor: spinster, etc.

② 將陽性名詞字尾略加改變後再加 " ess " 而成陰性名詞→master: mistress, prince: princess, etc.

③ 加表示性別的字來區分陰陽性→he-goat: she-goat, man-servant: maid-servant, etc.

8. 名詞的所有格

① 無生命（包括植物）名詞的所有格，不可在字尾加（'s）或（'），必須用 of 表示
→ *this table's legs*（誤）, → the legs of this table（正）

② 獨立所有格：所有格單獨存在，沒有名詞尾隨其後，稱爲獨立所有格。
(i)所有格後面的名詞因重複而省略。
My father's farm is larger than my uncle's.
(ii)所有格所修飾的名詞爲 house, shop 等建築物時，可省略。
a butcher's (*shop*), at **my uncle's** (*house*), etc.

③ 當 this (these), that (those), which, what, some (any), a(an), no 與所有格修飾同一名詞時，兩者不能同時放在該名詞的前面，一定要用雙重所有格的形式，即 a (this, that …)＋名詞＋ of ＋所有格名詞。
→ *this my mother's overcoat*（誤）
→ this overcoat of my mother's （正）

EXERCISE 10

I. 請根據句意和文法選出一個錯誤的答案。

1. (A) Mrs. Lin was a beauty.
   = Mrs. Lin was a beautiful lady.
   (B) They sell various wines at that store.
   = They sell a variety of wines at that store.
   (C) He bought a 1987 Ford.
   = He bought a 1987 Ford automobile.
   (D) Waiter, two black coffees, please.
   = Waiter, two glasses of coffee without milk, please.

2. (A) Youth should respect age.
   = Young people should respect aged persons.
   (B) He is all ears.
   = He is listening eagerly.
   (C) He has done me many kindnesses.
   = He has done me very kindly.
   (D) The pen is mightier than the sword.
   = The power of the pen is stronger than the military power.

3. (A) He wishes to be an Edison in the future.
   = He wishes to become a great inventor like Edison in the future.
   (B) He was a failure as a violinist.
   = He was a person who failed as a violinist.
   (C) He forgot the judge in the father.
   = He forgot the duty of being a judge in paternal love.
   (D) All the world are good.
   = All the countries of the world are good.

4. (A) A Mr. Smith wants you on the phone.
       = One of Messrs. Smiths wants you on the phone.

   (B) He is attention itself.
       = He is very attentive.

   (C) The Bakers loved each other dearly.
       = Mr. and Mrs. Baker loved each other dearly.

   (D) Lend me your Webster.
       = Lend me your Webster dictionary.

5. (A) All the village remember the story.
       = All the villagers remember the story.

   (B) His wife is a Lincoln.
       = His wife is a member of the Lincoln family.

   (C) Temperance is a virtue.
       = Temperance is a kind of virtue.

   (D) Even a word of advice will be helpful to me.
       = Even an advice will be helpful to me.

Ⅱ. 請根據句意和文法選出一個最正確的答案。

6. "What do you want?" "I want _____ that is on the table."
   (A) the loaf of bread
   (B) some bread
   (C) a loaf of bread
   (D) a bread

7. "Is his house beautiful?" "There isn't _____ in the house."
   (A) much furniture
   (B) many furniture
   (C) a lot furniture
   (D) very many furniture

8. "What's new?" "There is not _____ news in the paper.
   (A) lot of
   (B) many
   (C) much
   (D) many of

9. "Mrs. Baker went to the store to buy three _____ of toothpaste.
   (A) pieces
   (B) brushes
   (C) loaves
   (D) tubes

10. "Mary went to the library because she wanted _____.
   (A) the informations
   (B) some information
   (C) an information
   (D) one piece of an information

11. He spent all his _____ on that car.
   (A) safe
   (B) saving
   (C) safety
   (D) savings

12. "Mary, where is my hat?" "It's on _____."
   (A) the hall table
   (B) the hall's table
   (C) the table of the hall
   (D) the table of hall

13. I am going to go to the _____.
   (A) shoe's store
   (B) shoes' store
   (C) shoes store
   (D) shoe store

14. " Is Alice a very good actress?" "Yes, she is_____."
   (A) a favorite to me
   (B) a favorite of mine
   (C) a favorite of me
   (D) mine favorite

15. " Is she very helpful?" " She is only a_____ girl."
   (A) ten-years-old
   (B) ten-years-olds
   (C) ten-year-old
   (D) ten-old-years

16. "What have you finished?" " I have finished _____."
   (A) a day's work
   (B) a day work
   (C) day's working
   (D) a-day work

17. The activities of the Tennessee Valley Authority have aided the economic rehabilitation of the Tennessee Valley,_____ of some 40,000 square miles.
   (A) an area
   (B) its area
   (C) area
   (D) areas

18. "How old is he?" "_____."
   (A) He is thirty-four years
   (B) He has thirty-four
   (C) He is thirty-four years old
   (D) He is thirty-four old

19. " How about the walls?" "The walls are _____ thick."
   (A) third inches
   (B) three inches
   (C) three inch
   (D) third inch

20. "What authors do you like?" "Hemingway is_____."
    (A) favorite for me
    (B) the favorite of mines
    (C) for me the favorite
    (D) my favorite

21. "Would you like to hear classical music or contemporary music?" "Classical music is my_____."
    (A) preferring
    (B) preference
    (C) one preferring
    (D) one prefer

22. He had to balance his account very carefully because he had _____.
    (A) a few moneys
    (B) few moneys
    (C) little money
    (D) a little money

23. _____police were acting upon the information they received.
    (A) The
    (B) Many
    (C) Much
    (D) Little

24. The victim of the accident sued the bus company for_____.
    (A) the damage
    (B) a damage
    (C) damages
    (D) damage

25. The representatives of the party took great_____ in reaching a final agreement.
    (A) a pain   (B) pains
    (C) pain   (D) the pain

26. _____is one of my favorite subjects.
    (A) A mathematic
    (B) The mathematic
    (C) The mathematics
    (D) Mathematics

27. _____is a five-cent coin in America.
    (A) A nickel
    (B) Nickel
    (C) Nickels
    (D) The Nickel

28. There are four_____in our class.
    (A) Mary
    (B) Maries
    (C) Mary's
    (D) Marys

29. Where are the_____magazines?
    (A) women's
    (B) women
    (C) womens
    (D) woman

30. His house is within _____from the post office.
    (A) stone's throw
    (B) a throw of a stone
    (C) a stone's throw
    (D) the stone's throw

31. I saw_____at the barber's.
    (A) my sister's a boy friend
    (B) a boy friend of my sister's
    (C) boy friend of my sister
    (D) my sister boy friend

32. " Who are those boys ? " " Those boys are friends of _____ . "
    (A) them
    (B) they
    (C) their
    (D) theirs

33. _____ twelve can be divided by 2, 3, 4 and six.
    (A) Number
    (B) A number
    (C) The number
    (D) Numbers

34. The teacher advised Jane to read the passage at the end of _____ .
    (A) chapter seven
    (B) the seven chapter
    (C) seventh chapter
    (D) chapter the seventh

35. When I got to the theater, they were already playing _____ .
    (A) second act
    (B) the act two
    (C) act two
    (D) the act second

36. Do you happen to know _____ insulin is ?
    (A) what kind of a substance
    (B) what kind of substance
    (C) what kind a substance
    (D) of what kind of substance

37. _____ should be planted in the shade.
    (A) This kind of flowers
    (B) These kind of flowers
    (C) These kinds of flowers
    (D) This kind flower

38. I'd like to make_____with you.
    (A) friend
    (B) a friend
    (C) the friend
    (D) friends

39. That fact is of great scientific_____.
    (A) interest
    (B) interesting
    (C) interested
    (D) interests

40. The teacher gave me_____.
    (A) many good advice
    (B) many good pieces of advice
    (C) many good advices
    (D) many pieces of good advice.

41. She was almost killed. The car missed her by a hair's
    _____.
    (A) breadth
    (B) length
    (C) width
    (D) thickness

42. You should always keep a close_____on the small chil-
    dren playing outdoors.
    (A) care
    (B) warning
    (C) heed
    (D) eye

43. His visit saved me _____of writing to him.
    (A) the habit
    (B) the occasion
    (C) the opportunity
    (D) the trouble

44. He must be near-sighted, for he wears _____ .
    (A) spectacle
    (B) spectacles
    (C) a spectacle
    (D) a pair of spectacle

45. He was in _____ when he got married.
    (A) thirties
    (B) the thirties
    (C) thirty age
    (D) his thirties

46. _____ birthdays both come in October.
    (A) My brother and sister's
    (B) My brother and my sister
    (C) My brother's and sister's
    (D) My brother's sister's

47. The concert should have started two hours ago. I don't know
    what could have caused the _____ .
    (A) delay
    (B) detail
    (C) demand
    (D) discount

48. The prevalence of smog over the city is both a _____
    to the citizens and a danger to their health.
    (A) surprise
    (B) pleasure
    (C) nuisance
    (D) noise

49. The law makes no _____ between the rich and the poor.
    (A) agreement
    (B) difference
    (C) sense
    (D) connection

50. Most scientists retain a special _____ for the first discovery or theory they produce in their own field.
    (A) impression
    (B) fault
    (C) sign
    (D) affection

51. In Japan today a fierce _____ is going on about primary schools between traditionalists and progressives.
    (A) contest
    (B) debate
    (C) fighting
    (D) battle

52. The United States was founded on the _____ that all men are created equal. Even in colonial New England, and, later, on the Western frontier, class lines were by no means as rigid as in Europe.
    (A) distinction
    (B) permission
    (C) philosophy
    (D) principle

53. He was poor, given to drinking, and always in debt. He would have been totally forgotten, had he not gone mad. But his madness released _____ that was in him. He was born again. A fountain of song rose up from the depth of his spirit.
    (A) a hidden poet
    (B) the hidden poet
    (C) hidden poets
    (D) the hidden poets

54. Whether_____is an Englishman, a Frenchman, or a German is a matter of no real importance. His discoveries are open to all, and nothing but intelligence is required in order to profit by them.
    (A) a man of science
    (B) a man of the science
    (C) the man of the science
    (D) a man of a science

55. The famous painter Picasso was having some friends to lunch in his house in the south of France. One of them looked around and said, " I notice you don't have any_____on your walls. Why is that? Don't you like them? " " On the contrary," Picasso replied, " It is just that I can't afford them. "
    (A) Picasso
    (B) member of the Picassos
    (C) Picassos
    (D) one of Picasso

Ⅲ 選出下列各句中錯誤的部分。

56. <u>Classification</u> is a useful approach to the <u>organization</u> of
      (A)   (B)

    <u>knowledges</u> in <u>any</u> field.
       (C)   (D)

57. The buffalo was <u>wantonly</u> killed, until <u>they</u> became <u>almost</u> <u>extinct</u>.
                      (A)   (B)   (C)   (D)

58. When Rhodesia declared <u>their</u> independence from England, <u>few</u>
                            (A)   (B)

    thought that the new government <u>would last</u> <u>even a month</u>.
                                       (C)   (D)

59. Nicholas finds <u>these kind of assignments</u> <u>unpleasant</u>, but
                         (A)   (B)

    he does say that he <u>has had</u> little <u>practice</u> writing about
                         (C)   (D)

    the books he read.

60. In order to make people <u>change</u> <u>their feelings</u> about this
                             (A)   (B)

    writer <u>he</u> has to write another <u>books</u> regarding this problem.
           (C)   (D)

Ⅳ. 在下列各句的空格中填入適當的字，使上下兩句意思相同。

61. He speaks English fluently.
    = He is a _____ _____ of English.

62. Jack smokes very much.
    = Jack is a _____ _____.

63. To my great astonishment, I found her dead.
    = I was greatly _____ to find her dead.

64. They have come to Taiwan on business.
    = Business has _____ them to Taiwan.

65. He could not go to the concert because it rained.
    = The rain p<u>_____</u> him from going to the concert.

66. As he is honest, he is beloved by every girl.
    = His _____ makes him beloved by every girl.

67. If you wear these glasses, you will be able to see the letters.

= These glasses will _____ you to see the letters.

68. Whenever I see the orphan, I am reminded of his parents.

= The _____ of the orphan always _____ me of his parents.

69. If you take this medicine, you will feel better.

= This medicine will _____ you feel better.

70. Compare them carefully, and you will see the difference.

= A careful _____ of them will show you the difference.

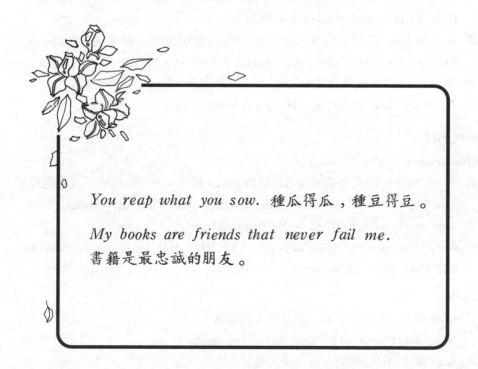

You reap what you sow. 種瓜得瓜，種豆得豆。

My books are friends that never fail me.
書籍是最忠誠的朋友。

11. 代名詞 (Pronoun)

Points of Grammar

1. 人稱代名詞

(1) 複合人稱代名詞

① 反身用法：主詞和受詞為同一人或物時，就用反身代名詞。

Monroe killed **herself**. She prided **herself** on her beauty.

The door opened **of itself**.

② 加強語氣的用法：用來強調主詞、受詞或補語的語氣，省略後對句意無影響。

The president **himself** gave the medal. He did it **himself**.

(2) it 的用法

① 非人稱的 it 可做主詞，指天氣、時間、季節、距離等。

It is fine today. 〔天氣〕 What time is **it** now? 〔時間〕

It is two miles from here to my house. 〔距離〕

How is **it** in the market? 〔情形〕

② it 可做形式主詞或形式受詞，代替後面所說的不定詞、動名詞或名詞子句。

It matters little **who** goes there. I felt **it** my duty to help the poor.

③ it is (was)＋加強的部分＋ that ＋其餘部分，用來表加強語氣。

It is he **that** is wrong. **It** was a window **that** Tom broke.

2. 指示代名詞

(1) this (these), that (those)

① this, that 可用來代替前面所提過的名詞、片語、子句或句子，以避免重覆。

The population of Japan is much larger than **that** of Taiwan.

② this ＝ the latter, that ＝ the former

Work and play are both necessary to life; **this** gives us recreation, and **that** gives us energy.

(2) such

① such 做代名詞用時，指「如此的人或事物」

→He isn't well off, only he seems **such**.

② such 做主詞補語用時，表示前文提及之內容

→My bullet killed him, but **such** was not my intention.

3. 不定代名詞

(1) one（任何人、某人、某事），複數形 ones

One should obey **one's** parents. If you need a pen, I'll lend you **one**.

This story is more interesting than the preceding **ones**.

(2) another; one ～ the other (s); others; some ～ others

① another = one more → I don't like this. Show me **another**.

② one 代替二人或二物中的一個，the other 代替剩下來的一個；the others（= the rest）是指「其餘的」。

I have two sisters; **one** is in New York, **the other** in Washington.

③ others（他人）→ Be kind to **others**.

④ some ～ others → **Some** people like classical music; **others** do not.

4. 否定構句

(1) 部分否定 → I **don't** know **both** of them.（他們兩個我並沒有都認識。）

All that glitters is **not** gold.（閃亮的東西未必都是金子。）

(2) 全部否定 → I know **neither** of them. **None** of them were present.

5. 其他

(1) something（某物），everything（每一物），nothing（無一物）

He wants to do **something**.（= something important）

My wife means **everything** to me.

Money is **nothing** to women.

(2) ～ , and that = ～ at that, 作「而且」解，具有加強語氣的作用

It began to rain, **and that** in earnest.

He has lost his watch, a new one **at that**.

(3) …one thing ～ another（…是一回事，～是另一回事）

To know is **one thing**, to teach is **another**.

It is **one thing** to enjoy listening to good music, but it is quite **another** to perform skillfully yourself.

EXERCISE 11

I. 請根據句意和文法選出一個最正確的答案。

1. Everybody should do＿＿＿＿＿＿best.
   (A) their
   (B) his
   (C) one's
   (D) our

2. ＿＿＿＿＿＿but peace can save the world.
   (A) Anyone
   (B) Someone
   (C) Anything
   (D) Nothing

3. ＿＿＿＿＿＿but the brave deserve the fair.
   (A) None
   (B) Anyone
   (C) Anything
   (D) Nothing

4. I don't know＿＿＿＿＿＿of them.
   (A) none
   (B) any
   (C) neither
   (D) someone

5. Some students speak English slowly, but there are＿＿＿＿＿＿
   students.
   (A) the others
   (B) others
   (C) other
   (D) another

6. Airplanes have made_____.
   (A) easy and comfortable for us to travel
   (B) us to travel easily and comfortably
   (C) it easy and comfortable for us to travel
   (D) themselves easy and comfortable for us to travel

7. If you do not go, I shall not_____.
   (A) either
   (B) neither
   (C) too
   (D) also

8. My friends hope you will come back again soon and_____.
   (A) so I do
   (B) so do I
   (C) I do so
   (D) I too do

9. The construction work will be finished in_____three weeks.
   (A) the other
   (B) other
   (C) some
   (D) another

10. He cares so little about his meals that_____will do so long as it fills his stomach.
    (A) anything
    (B) everything
    (C) nothing
    (D) something

11. This is as good a map as_____.
    (A) any   (B) neither
    (C) never   (D) none

12. It is one thing to enjoy listening to good music, but it is
    quite _____ to perform skillfully.
    (A) other
    (B) another
    (C) some
    (D) any

13. Jane is _____ of a musician.
    (A) anybody
    (B) anyone
    (C) somebody
    (D) something

14. Mr. Wang has four brothers; one is in Taipei, but _____
    are in Kaoshiung.
    (A) another
    (B) other
    (C) the other
    (D) the others

15. I thought it was _____ who went with her last night.
    (A) they
    (B) their
    (C) them
    (D) theirs

16. I believe the pickpocket to be _____.
    (A) he
    (B) his
    (C) him
    (D) one

17. The climate of Taiwan is milder than _____ of Japan.
    (A) one   (B) that
    (C) this   (D) it

18. Work and play are both necessary to health;_____gives us rest, and_____gives us energy.
    (A) that, this
    (B) one, the other
    (C) one, another
    (D) this, that

19. To some life is pleasure, to_____it is suffering.
    (A) ones
    (B) other
    (C) others
    (D) those

20. My watch is out of order; I want to buy_____.
    (A) a new one
    (B) good one
    (C) new one
    (D) accurate one

21. Scrooge had often heard_____said that Marley had no money.
    (A) ones
    (B) another
    (C) it
    (D) this

22. He found_____difficult to support his family.
    (A) this
    (B) it
    (C) that
    (D) such

23. _____was her bravery that they were all frightened.
    (A) So   (B) This
    (C) That   (D) Such

24. He lived in poverty, and he could not help_____.
    (A) so
    (B) such
    (C) it
    (D) that

25. Let me see the picture. This is Mr. Lin, isn't_____?
    (A) it
    (B) this
    (C) he
    (D) that

26. You must help him, and _____ immediately.
    (A) so
    (B) such
    (C) it
    (D) that

27. I asked mother to let Lucy and _____ help her in the
    kitchen.
    (A) I
    (B) myself
    (C) me
    (D) my

28. "Do you have my passport, Joe?" "Yes, I have _____
    right here."
    (A) one
    (B) it
    (C) this
    (D) one passport

29. "Do you have a job?" "Yes, _____."
    (A) I have it   (B) I have one
    (C) I have   (D) I certainly have

30. "Harry and I have a lot in common." "Yes, your ideas, _____ somewhat unusual to me."
   (A) like his, are
   (B) like him, is
   (C) like he, are
   (D) like his, is

31. "Will she come tomorrow?" "We believe _____."
   (A) her
   (B) it
   (C) so
   (D) that

32. "Is Prof. Lee very sick?" "I'm afraid _____."
   (A) so
   (B) that
   (C) this
   (D) to

33. "Are the products of Taiwan _____?
   (A) somewhat like Japan
   (B) something like Japan
   (C) somewhat like that of Japan
   (D) somewhat like those of Japan

34. Love of power is a strong element in normal human nature, and _____.
   (A) is to be accepted such as
   (B) is to be accepted as such
   (C) such as is to accept
   (D) as such is to accept

35. "Anything wrong?" "There was no objection on the part of _____ present."
   (A) these   (B) that
   (C) those   (D) who

36. "What color is your suitcase?" "My suitcase is the same color_____yours."
    (A) with
    (B) from
    (C) like
    (D) as

37. "I was born in Chicago?" "_____."
    (A) So did my parents
    (B) So were my parents
    (C) So was my parents
    (D) My parents were, either

38. "What is the difference?" "This bread is different from _____."
    (A) that
    (B) that one
    (C) that ones
    (D) those ones

39. Women treat_____ men in a rather unsportsman-like manner, don't you think so?
    (A) we
    (B) our
    (C) us
    (D) me

40. Please see to it_____the door is locked.
    (A) and
    (B) but
    (C) that
    (D) if

41. What happened is not his responsibility, but yours. This
    means _____ responsible for what happened.
    (A) it is not you but he who is
    (B) it is not he but you who are
    (C) it is not only you but he who are
    (D) it is not he but you who is

42. I have two brothers. One is an engineer; _____ is a
    chemist.
    (A) the other
    (B) other
    (C) another
    (D) any other

43. Reading is to the mind what exercise is to the body. As
    by the one health is preserved and strengthened, so by the
    other, virtue is kept alive and cherished. " The one " refers
    to _____.
    (A) mind
    (B) body
    (C) reading
    (D) exercise

44. We hold a meeting every two weeks; on every _____
    Thursday evening, in fact.
    (A) both
    (B) odd
    (C) other
    (D) following

45. He asked me _____ to the party tomorrow.
    (A) if I went
    (B) who was going
    (C) if going
    (D) who went

46. She didn't understand _____ .
    (A) what he was talking about
    (B) what was he talking about
    (C) why he is talking
    (D) how was he talking about

47. Do you know _____ ?
    (A) how much it costs
    (B) how cost it is
    (C) how much does it cost
    (D) how much to cost

48. The main facts in human life are five; birth, food, sleep,
    love and death. One could increase the number—add breathing
    for instance—but these five are the most obvious. Let
    us briefly ask ourselves _____ our lives.
    (A) they play in what part
    (B) they play what part in
    (C) what part they play in
    (D) in what part they play

49. "_____ in this town?" "I think Mr. Lin is the richest
    man."
    (A) Whom do you think is the richest man
    (B) Who do you think is the richest man
    (C) Do you think who is the richest man
    (D) Who you think is the richest man

50. _____ of the clerks was instructed to do his own work.
    (A) All
    (B) Some
    (C) Several
    (D) Each

51. " How did he like the city? " " In the city, he was always being annoyed by noise of one sort or _____ .
(A) all
(B) others
(C) another
(D) kind

52. He feels, _____ , that he must do for himself many household jobs which, before the war, he would have hired professional help.
(A) for one reason or another
(B) for one reason or other
(C) for one reason or the other
(D) for another reason or the other

53. Teaching is one thing when it addresses itself to the average student, quite _____ when it addresses itself to a gifted few. The basic difference between school and university is that in schools the teacher must teach all the students entrusted to him. In the university, however, he has no such obligation.
(A) the other
(B) the others
(C) other
(D) another

54. Just as it is impossible to see the shape of a woods when you are journeying through the middle of it, so it is as impossible for us to see _____ . Till we have got out of the woods, and can see it as a whole, can we judge which of the trees are most essential to its general shape.
(A) how our own age is like
(B) what our own age is like
(C) what is our own age like
(D) how is our own age like

55. Although not a strong boy, there was _____the coward about him, and at an early age he showed the spirit of absolute fearlessness which in later years enabled him to do such great services for the nation.
    (A) anything of
    (B) something of
    (C) nothing of
    (D) everything of

Ⅱ. 選出下列各句中錯誤的部分。

56. It was her who represented her country in the United Nations
    (A)   (B)   (C)

    and later became ambassador to the United States.
        (D)

57. If we finish all of our business as planned, Helen and me
            (A)   (B)

    will leave for New York on Monday morning.
            (C)   (D)

58. If you ask you what you really want to do, you can solve
            (A)   (B)   (C)

    your problem quickly.
               (D)

59. There can be no change in policy if the person in charge is
    (A)   (B)   (C)

    him.
    (D)

60. It is difficult for a political leader to accept any criticism.
                                                     (A)
    Yet, the good statesman, like all sensible human beings,
                    (B)   (C)
    always learns more from their opponents than from sup-
                            (D)
    porters.

61. The professor said he liked Tom's style a lot but he felt
                          (A)   (B)
    that John's style was better than him.
                        (C)   (D)

62. Everybody is having an enjoyable time at the party, isn't he?
              (A)   (B)   (C)   (D)

63. Let me give you two of the consequences of which I would
                             (A)   (B)
    guess that one will shock you, while another may perhaps
                                          (C)
    surprise you more favorably.
                      (D)

64. Nobody ever has the complete freedom to do nothing that
                    (A)   (B)
    he wants when he wants to.
             (C)   (D)

65. The boss threatened that unless the workers went back to
                            (A)   (B)
    work immediately he would discharge all them.
                          (C)   (D)

66. When I asked him <u>who</u> he was <u>inviting</u>, he refused <u>to tell</u>
                 (A)   (B)   (C)

    me, and changed the subject <u>instead</u>.
                          (D)

67. The Taiwan standard of living will be <u>much</u> higher <u>than most</u>
                                         (A)   (B)

    of <u>the other</u> countries <u>in Asia</u>.
        (C)   (D)

68. It was <u>not until</u> he was <u>graduated from</u> National Taiwan
            (A)   (B)

    University in 1975 <u>when</u> he made up his mind <u>to become</u>
                      (C)   (D)

    a teacher.

69. <u>Anybody never</u> wants to <u>be without</u> money <u>during</u> a period
         (A)   (B)   (C)

    that necessitates a lot of extra <u>spending</u>.
                                    (D)

70. Numerous efforts have been made <u>to promote</u> the laws
                                        (A)

    <u>governing</u> air pollution, but none have been <u>as successful</u>
     (B)   (C)

    as <u>them</u> devised by the state of Oregon.
        (D)

Ⅲ. 在下列各句的空格中填入適當的字。

71. Some were praised, _____ were scolded.

72. To say is one thing and to do is quite_____ .

73. Heaven helps_____who help themselves.

74. See to_____that I do not have to complain to you about this matter.

75. Musical ability often shows i_____ early in life.

76. _____was his anxiety that he lost his health.

77. I called out for help but I could not make_____heard.

78. May I avail_____ of this chance?

79. If you want a true friend, you will find_____in him.

80. Do unto_____as you would have them do unto you.

12. 關係代名詞 (Relatives)

Points of Grammar

1. 關係代名詞的用法

(1) which

　① 可用來代替前面敘述事實的整個句子。

　　You say so, **which** is a clear proof of your honesty.

　② 可用來代替前面的名詞。

　　He is a professor, **which** I am not.

(2) that

　① 可用來代替 who, whom, which。

　② 下列情形通常只能用 that:

　　(i) 先行詞之前有 the only, the last, the same… 或 all, any, no 時;

　　(ii) 前面有疑問代名詞時; (iii) 先行詞中含有「人」和「非人」時。

　　Jane is the only girl friend **that** I have.

　　He is the last man **that** will do such a thing.

　　Who **that** has common sense can believe such a thing?

　　A truck ran over a boy and his dog **that** were crossing the street.

　　I have nothing **that** I have to tell you.

(3) what

　　what 是本身兼做先行詞的關係代名詞,相當於 that (*or* those) which 或 the thing(s) which; 但有時也用作 all that 的意思。

　What is beautiful is not always good.

　I have sold **what** few books I had.

(4) 準關係代名詞

　① as 的用法:前面有 as, such, the same 時,引導形容詞子句的關代用 as。

　　Avoid such friends **as** will do you harm.

　② but 的用法:but 本身含有否定的意思,其作用相當於 " that … not ",但其前面的主要子句須有否定的字(如 no, not, hardly …等)。

　　There is no rule **but** has exceptions.

　③ than 的用法:先行詞有比較級形容詞修飾時,關係代名詞應該用 than。

　　He has more money **than** is needed.

2. 關係代名詞的省略

(1) 關係代名詞作及物動詞或介詞的受詞時，可被省略。

This is the boy (*whom*) I saw yesterday.

There is a lady (*who*) wants to see you.

(2) ① 如果句首或句中有 there is, here is, that is, it is 時，主格關代可省。

② that 做主詞補語時，亦可省。

It was Wilson (**that**) told me this.

He is not the man (**that**) he was. 〔主詞補語〕

3. 關係代名詞的二種用法

(1) 限定用法：

She had four sons **who** became doctors. (她有四個當醫生的兒子。)

(2) 補述用法：

She had four sons, **who** became doctors. (她有四個兒子，他們都是醫生。)

4. 關係副詞

(1) where (＝ in (on,at) which)──表地方

This is the house **where** (＝ in which) he lives.

(2) when (＝ in (on,at) which)──表時間

Monday is the day **when** (＝ on which) we are busiest.

(3) why (＝ for which)──表理由

There is no reson **why** you should go.

(4) how (＝ the way in which)──表方法

This is **how** (＝ the way in which) he did it.

(5) that ──在口語中亦可用 that 代替關係副詞 when, why, how 等字，或省略。

Is that the reason (**that**) you went there ?

5. what 的慣用法

(1) what is (*or* was) ＋ $\begin{cases} 比較級 \\ 最高級 \end{cases}$ (而且，更有甚者)。

I was tired, and **what was still worse**, it began to rain.

(2) what with ～ and (what with)…(半因～半因…)

What with drink **and** (**what with**) fright, he did not know much about the facts.

(3) what by ～ and（what by）…（半靠～半靠…）。

What by threats **and**（**what by**）entreaties he could finally persuade her.

(4) He is **what we call** a self-made man.（所謂的）

(5) A is to B what C is to D（A之於B猶C之於D）。

Reading is to the mind **what** food is to the body.

(6) I owe **what I am** to my father.（＝My father has made me **what I am**.）——（現在的某人，今日的成就）。

6. 複合關係代名詞

(1) Give it to **whoever**（＝ anyone who）wants the book.

Give it to **whomever**（＝ anyone whom）you like.

Return the book to **whosever**（＝ anyone whose）name is on it.

(2) **Whatever** you have is mine.（＝Anything that ～）

Whatever happens, you are safe.（＝No matter what）

(3) You may take **whichever**（＝ either of the two that *or* any one of them that）you like.

Whichever（＝No matter which）you take, I will give it to you.

(4) Take **whichever** shovel is not in use.

Whatever results follow, I will pursue the beaten track.

7. 複合關係副詞

(1) **Wherever**（＝No matter where）you may go, you will be respected.

(2) **Whenever**（＝No matter when）you start, you will not catch up with her.

(3) **However**（＝No matter how）hard you may try, you can not do it.

EXERCISE 12

I. 請根據句意和文法選出一個最正確的答案。

1. John was the only one _____ I had invited.
   (A) which
   (B) that
   (C) whom
   (D) who

2. He arrived half an hour late, _____ annoyed us very much.
   (A) that
   (B) as
   (C) which
   (D) what

3. They are the boys _____ I went to school with.
   (A) what
   (B) where
   (C) when
   (D) whom

4. " Who is it ? " " This is the actress _____ his father claims seduced his son！ "
   (A) who
   (B) whom
   (C) whose
   (D) which

5. " Do you like this tie ? " " I prefer the one _____ . "
   (A) which is on the counter
   (B) is on the counter
   (C) which it is on the counter
   (D) which on the counter

6. Thank you very much for _____ you have done for my sister.
   (A) that
   (B) which
   (C) it
   (D) what

7. He had no other desire _____ to make a fortune.
   (A) but
   (B) than
   (C) except
   (D) as

8. Most of his rich acquaintances ignored him, _____ is the way of their world.
   (A) so
   (B) as
   (C) that
   (D) what

9. Joe believed without question _____ in his daily newspaper.
   (A) about what he read
   (B) of what he read
   (C) whatever he read
   (D) whenever he read

10. The doctor will speak to _____ comes in first.
    (A) whoever
    (B) whomever
    (C) whichever
    (D) whatever

11. He was in a traffic jam, _____ made him late for his appointment.
    (A) that
    (B) which
    (C) what
    (D) how

12. Choose _____ you think is suitable.
    (A) which
    (B) that
    (C) whom
    (D) what

13. I gave him a warning, _____ he turned a deaf ear.
    (A) of what
    (B) for which
    (C) to that
    (D) to which

14. This dictionary, the few pages _____ are missing, is of no use.
    (A) among which
    (B) of which
    (C) in which
    (D) to which

15. The audience were utterly astonished at the fluency _____ the little girl made her first English speech.
    (A) with which
    (B) by which
    (C) of which
    (D) in what

16. The sick man _____ sake you are doing all this work ought to be very grateful to you.
    (A) for whom
    (B) for whose
    (C) of whom
    (D) of whose

17. I was so eager to go away that when I stood in the hall, ready to leave, I did not even think of saying good-bye to the boys and girls _____ I had eaten and slept and lived for so many weeks.
    (A) by whom
    (B) of whom
    (C) with whom
    (D) with which

18. _____ comes back first is supposed to win the prize.
    (A) Those who
    (B) Anyone
    (C) No one
    (D) Whoever

19. Give this prize to _____ composition is thought excellent.
    (A) whoever
    (B) whosever
    (C) whomever
    (D) whatever

20. This is the very boy _____ parents were killed last year.
    (A) who
    (B) that
    (C) whose
    (D) whom

21. Mr. Brown is intelligent, and _____ he's very handsome.
    (A) what is more
    (B) what is worse
    (C) as is often the case
    (D) which is better

22. There is no one _____ wishes peace.
    (A) who   (B) but
    (C) that   (D) whom

23. There is not one of us_____hopes to help you.
    (A) which
    (B) whose
    (C) whoever
    (D) but

24. " How destructive we are nowadays！" " The next war will be more cruel_____can be imagined."
    (A) that
    (B) as
    (C) than
    (D) which

25. There is_____at the news.
    (A) no man but who would be surprised
    (B) no man but would be surprised
    (C) not no man who would be surprised
    (D) not any man would be surprised

26. She is one of the few girls who_____passed the examination.
    (A) was
    (B) were
    (C) has
    (D) have

27. All history confirms the doctrine that_____rely upon the sword shall perish by it.
    (A) those who
    (B) if we
    (C) however we
    (D) during we

28. The subject_____I am most interested is English.
    (A) in that   (B) in what
    (C) in which   (D) in where

29. One _____ desires and impulses are not his own has no character.
    (A) who
    (B) whose
    (C) whom
    (D) of whom

30. She has been suffering from a kind of disease _____ .
    (A) the cure for which is now possible
    (B) whose cure is a recent recovery
    (C) whose cure is unable
    (D) the cure which is now be done

31. He is my son, _____ a better son does not exist.
    (A) but
    (B) than who
    (C) against whom
    (D) than whom

32. The teacher _____ is at that desk over there.
    (A) you should talk to
    (B) you are talk to
    (C) whom you talking to
    (D) you to whom will talk

33. _____ is more time.
    (A) That what we need
    (B) What we are needing
    (C) What we need
    (D) Which we need

34. President Lee greeted Chen Yi-an, _____ a gold medal at the Olympic Games.
    (A) by winning   (B) the winning
    (C) she was the winner of   (D) who was the winner of

35. Mac-Arthur controls a thousand men, _____ must obey his orders in both war and peace.
    (A) all of whom
    (B) all of who
    (C) all them
    (D) all of which

36. Insulin is perhaps the drug _____ more lives than any other in the history of medicine.
    (A) which saved
    (B) who saves
    (C) which has saved
    (D) what has saved

37. As many members _____ were present agreed to the plan.
    (A) who
    (B) that
    (C) which
    (D) as

38. Avoid such insects _____ will do you harm.
    (A) as
    (B) but
    (C) who
    (D) which

39. He was a foreigner, _____ they perceived from his accent.
    (A) that
    (B) what
    (C) as
    (D) whom

40. _____ , he played truant from school yesterday.
    (A) That is often the case with an idle boy
    (B) As is often the case with an idle boy
    (C) Which is often the case for an idle boy
    (D) What is often the case for an idle boy

41. I would like to do_____I can do for you.
  (A) what little service
  (B) what few service
  (C) which little service
  (D) which few service

42. Who_____has common sense can believe such a superstition?
  (A) who
  (B) which
  (C) but
  (D) that

43. My father has made me_____I am.
  (A) who
  (B) which
  (C) what
  (D) that

44. That is the town_____he was born.
  (A) which
  (B) where
  (C) when
  (D) why

45. She does not see the reason_____he would like to join them.
  (A) why
  (B) when
  (C) how
  (D) where

46. The day will soon come_____man will set foot on another planet.
  (A) which   (B) when
  (C) why   (D) where

47. We travelled together as far as Chicago,_____we parted.
   - (A) when
   - (B) which
   - (C) why
   - (D) where

48. I was about to leave,_____she came in.
   - (A) where
   - (B) which
   - (C) when
   - (D) how

49. _____the children sleep.
   - (A) That's where
   - (B) There's
   - (C) There's in which
   - (D) That's

50. I will invite_____my daughter loves.
   - (A) whoever
   - (B) whomever
   - (C) whichever
   - (D) whatever

51. A man has a right to spend his money_____he pleases.
   - (A) how
   - (B) in which
   - (C) why
   - (D) for which

52. She was rich,_____unfortunately I was not.
   - (A) that
   - (B) what
   - (C) which
   - (D) who

53. The doctor told me to take a few days' rest,_____
    advice I did not follow.
    (A) that
    (B) what
    (C) this
    (D) which

54. _____business you may be engaged in, you must do
    your best.
    (A) Whatever
    (B) However
    (C) Whoever
    (D) Wherever

55. _____clever you may be, you will not make out the
    meaning.
    (A) Whichever
    (B) Whoever
    (C) However
    (D) Wherever

56. You may come_____it is convenient to you.
    (A) however
    (B) whenever
    (C) wherever
    (D) whatever

57. You can not succeed without perseverance,_____you may
    go.
    (A) whenever
    (B) whatever
    (C) however
    (D) wherever

58. Rice is to the Chinese _____ potatoes are to many Europeans.
    (A) whose
    (B) that
    (C) what
    (D) which

59. _____ working too hard and taking too little care of himself, he was taken ill.
    (A) The thing that
    (B) What is
    (C) That which is with
    (D) What with

60. _____ might have been expected, he refused our request.
    (A) What
    (B) As
    (C) That which
    (D) Which

61. From the standpoint of daily life, however, there is one thing we do know; that man is here for the sake of other men — above all, for those upon _____ smile and well-being our own happiness depends.
    (A) whom
    (B) who
    (C) whose
    (D) that

62. Democracy has another merit. It allows criticism, and if there is not public criticism there are bound to be hushed-up scandals. That is _____ I believe in the Press, despite all its lies and vulgarity.
    (A) why
    (B) how
    (C) where
    (D) when

63. There was once a poor tailor who killed seven flies with a single blow. He made himself a belt on which he printed in large letters " seven at a blow."_____he went, people reading these words greatly feared this tailor, for they thought that he had killed seven with one blow.
    (A) Whenever
    (B) However
    (C) Wherever
    (D) Whatever

64. Perhaps dissatisfaction with government is due to failure to establish and maintain close contact with elected representatives. Ideally, each voter feels obligated to know both the character and policies of the man _____he votes, but in actuality the relationship between a voting public and its representatives is sometimes distant.
    (A) of whom
    (B) to whom
    (C) in whom
    (D) for whom

65. Growing plants take their nourishment from the soil, and unless the materials that they use are replaced, the soil loses its fertility. If the plants decay _____they were grown, the materials are replaced; but if they are taken away, the soil will become sterile.
    (A) when
    (B) where
    (C) in which
    (D) how

Ⅱ. 選出下列句子中錯誤的部分。

66. He is one of those men whom, I am sure, always do their
                             (A)   (B)
    best, even in the most trying circumstances.
          (C)   (D)

67. <u>Contrary</u> to the opinion of the members, the president
(A)

should appoint <u>whomever</u> he thinks <u>can do</u> the job the most
(B)　　　　　　　　(C)

<u>adequately</u>.
(D)

68. The shore patrol <u>has found</u> the body of a man <u>who</u> they
(A)　　　　　　　　　　　　(B)

believe <u>to</u> be the <u>missing</u> marine biologist.
(C)　　　(D)

69. Miami, Florida, is <u>among</u> the few cities in the United States
(A)

<u>which</u> <u>has been</u> awarded official status <u>as</u> a bilingual municipality.
(B)　　(C)　　　　　　　　　(D)

Ⅲ. 在下列各句的空格中填入適當的字。

70. There is no one in the world ＿＿＿＿＿commits errors.

71. He offers a helping hand to ＿＿＿＿ is in need of help.

72. He is ＿＿＿＿ is called a walking dictionary.

73. Don't trust such friends＿＿＿＿ praise you to your face.

74. Reading is to the mind ＿＿＿＿food is to the body.

75. I said nothing,＿＿＿＿ made him still more furious.

76. There is scarcely a man ＿＿＿＿ has his weak side.

77. Great men are too often unknown, or ＿＿＿＿ is worse, misknown.

78. They robbed him of＿＿＿＿ little money he had.

79. ＿＿＿＿＿is always the case with success, the last efforts
were the greatest.

13. 冠詞 (Article)

Points of Grammar

1. 不定冠詞

(1) We consider him **a** fool.

(2) Rome was not built in **a** day. (= one)

(3) In **a** sense it is true. (= a certain)

(4) Birds of **a** feather flock together. (= the same)

(5) **A** cat is not so faithful as **a** dog. (a 相當於 any, every)

(6) Take this medicine three times **a** day. (= per, each)

(7) She will stay here for **a** time. (= some)

(8) at **a** distance (稍遠一些),〔參考: in the distance (在遠處)〕,
   in **a** hurry, be at **a** loss, etc.〔慣用語〕

2. 定冠詞

(1) I lost a pen but found **the** pen.〔前面已提過的名詞,再度提到時,前面加 the 〕

(2) Open **the** door.〔所指的東西已非常明顯,或已有了一定的範圍時,該名詞前應加 the 〕

(3) **The** earth moves round **the** sun.〔用在宇宙間獨一無二的天體名詞之前〕

(4) We are paid by **the** month.〔表示單位的名詞前要加 the 〕

(5) Mr. Wang is **the** principal *of our school*.〔用於片語或子句所修飾的特定的人或物之前〕

(6) **The** rich are not always happier than **the** poor.〔 the ＋形容詞＝形容詞＋ people 〕

(7) He was **the** only man that solved the problem.〔在 only, first, last, same 等限制語前面要加 the 〕

(8) in **the** morning, in **the** wrong, on **the** way, etc.〔慣用語〕

3. 有關冠詞應注意的事項

(1) We keep **a** black and white dog. (一隻黑白花狗。)
   We keep **a** black and **a** white dog. (一隻黑狗和一隻白狗。——兩隻狗)

(2) Give me **a** knife and fork, please〔兩個名詞並列而不可能指同一人或物時，第二個名詞之前的冠詞就可以省略〕

A needle and thread was found on the floor.〔同上〕

a cup and saucer, a watch and chain, etc.〔一件東西附屬於其他東西上，而成爲一件東西時，冠詞只用一個〕

4. 冠詞的省略

(1) **Waiter!** Bring me a glass of water.〔稱呼用語前不加冠詞〕

(2) **Father** has gone out and **mother** is ill.〔家庭稱謂前不加冠詞〕

(3) They elected him **chairman**.〔表官職、身份、頭銜的名詞當補語，或作同位語時，不加冠詞〕

Bush, **President** of America.

(4) **School** is over at 11.〔school, church, hospital 等字，指原有的用途時，不加冠詞；若指建築物本身或場所時，則要加冠詞〕

(5) **Summer** is gone and **autumn** has come.〔季節名稱前不加冠詞〕

(6) I have **breakfast** at 6.〔三餐名稱前不加冠詞〕

(7) **Girl** as she was, she was not afraid.〔as 用於表讓步的副詞子句中，在倒裝時冠詞省略〕

(8) Both **husband and wife** are to blame〔兩個相對的名詞並用時，不用冠詞〕，from door to door, face to face, day and night, etc.

(9) She went to Taipei **by train**.〔交通工具前不加冠詞〕

(10) make room, on purpose, give way to, take place, etc.〔慣用語〕

5. 下列專有名詞前須加定冠詞 the

(1) 海洋、河流、港灣名詞——the Red Sea, the Pacific Ocean, the English Channel, the Panama Canal, etc.

(2) 朝代及國家名稱——the Chin Dynasty, the United States of America, etc.

(3) 經典、書籍、報章、雜誌等——the New York Times, the Bible, etc.

(4) 山脈、群島、半島——the Alps, the West Indies, the Netherlands, the Scandinavian Peninsula, etc.

(5) 複數姓氏之前（指某家的夫婦、兄弟或全家人）——the Smiths, the Changs,etc.

6. 其他

(1) such（what, many）a ～→ such an honest man

(2) all（both, double, half）the ～→ all the students

(3) so（as, too, how）＋形容詞＋a ～→ so honest a man, too good an opportunity to lose

EXERCISE 13

I. 請根據句意和文法選出一個最正確的答案。

1. _____ is a very old political system.
   (A) Democracy
   (B) A democracy
   (C) The democracy
   (D) Such a democracy

2. _____ of West Germany visited America a few years ago.
   (A) President
   (B) A President
   (C) The President
   (D) Such the President

3. _____ the official residence of the President of the USA.
   (A) White House is
   (B) A White House is
   (C) White Houses are
   (D) The White House is

4. "What on earth is that?" "Don't you know? That's a whale, _____."
   (A) largest world's mammal
   (B) a largest mammal in the world
   (C) the world's largest mammal
   (D) largest mammal of the world

5. _____ he was, he was not afraid at all.
   (A) Child as   (B) A child as
   (C) A child though   (D) The Child though

6. _____ is a most widely used language.
   (A) The English
   (B) The English language
   (C) An English
   (D) English language

7. _____ was created to be the companion, not the slave, of man.
   (A) Woman
   (B) A woman
   (C) The woman
   (D) Women

8. At the sight of the orphan, she felt _____ rise in her heart.
   (A) a mother
   (B) mother
   (C) the mother
   (D) mothers

9. _____ in the hand is worth two in the bush.
   (A) Bird
   (B) Birds
   (C) The bird
   (D) A bird

10. My uncle comes here twice _____ week.
    (A) a
    (B) in
    (C) the
    (D) by

11. Two of _____ seldom agree.
    (A) trade
    (B) a trade
    (C) the trade
    (D) trades

12. There is＿＿＿＿in the back room of my house.
    (A) a picture
    (B) the another picture
    (C) my picture
    (D) more two pictures

13. "What is your nationality?" "I am ＿＿＿＿."
    (A) America
    (B) an American
    (C) Americans
    (D) the American

14. "How did you pay the workers?" "As a rule, they were paid ＿＿＿＿."
    (A) by a hour
    (B) by an hour
    (C) by the hour
    (D) by hours.

15. "Did you see a channel? " " Yes, I've been to ＿＿＿＿ Channel."
    (A) English
    (B) an English
    (C) the English
    (D) England

16. "Did Miss Wang enjoy her trip on the ocean liner?" "No, she stayed in her cabin while the ship was＿＿＿＿."
    (A) over the sea
    (B) in the sea
    (C) to sea
    (D) at sea

17. I bought a pair of shoes ＿＿＿＿.
    (A) at the half price   (B) half at the price
    (C) at half the price   (D) the half at price

18. " Did Sylvia fly across the Caspian Sea?" " No, she crossed both ways by _____ . "
    (A) a ship
    (B) the ship
    (C) ships
    (D) ship

19. The chance to enter _____ came and she took it.
    (A) college
    (B) for college
    (C) in college
    (D) to college

20. None but _____ deserve the fair.
    (A) brave
    (B) a brave
    (C) braves
    (D) the brave

21. Adventure allows _____ to happen to us.
    (A) the unexpected
    (B) a unexpected
    (C) an unexpected
    (D) unexpected

22. Will you pass me _____ , please?
    (A) salt
    (B) the salt
    (C) a salt
    (D) salts

23. He caught me _____ .
    (A) by my hand
    (B) in my hand
    (C) by the hand
    (D) in the hand

24. I patted him _____.
    (A) by the back
    (B) on the back
    (C) in the back
    (D) of the back

25. She looked him _____.
    (A) by the eye
    (B) on the eye
    (C) in the eye
    (D) to the eye

26. He had _____ to show me the way to the station.
    (A) kindness
    (B) a kindness
    (C) a kind
    (D) the kindness

27. She plays _____very well.
    (A) the piano
    (B) a piano
    (C) on piano
    (D) pianos

28. I have not taken_____ yet.
    (A) supper
    (B) a supper
    (C) the supper
    (D) suppers

29. I had _____this morning.
    (A) heavy breakfast
    (B) a heavy breakfast
    (C) the heavy breakfast
    (D) heavy breakfasts

30. He was _____ to discover the land.
    (A) first man
    (B) the first man
    (C) a first man
    (D) the man first

31. You must get off at _____.
    (A) a second stop
    (B) the stop second
    (C) the second stop
    (D) second stop

32. I have to buy _____ pair of shoes.
    (A) a second
    (B) second
    (C) the second
    (D) second the

33. He was brought up for _____.
    (A) church
    (B) a church
    (C) churches
    (D) the church

34. _____ was a broad-minded person.
    (A) Deceased
    (B) A deceased
    (C) The deceased
    (D) Decease

35. Let's play _____, shall we?
    (A) baseball
    (B) a baseball
    (C) the baseball
    (D) baseballs

36. What species of_____is this?
 (A) lily
 (B) a lily
 (C) the lily
 (D) lilies

37. I put_____on the table.
 (A) cup and saucer
 (B) a cup and saucer
 (C) a cup and a saucer
 (D) cup and a saucer

38. _____was running behind the cat.
 (A) Black and white dog
 (B) A black and a white dog
 (C) The black and a white dog
 (D) A black and white dog

39. I paid_____price for this camera.
 (A) a double
 (B) double a
 (C) double the
 (D) the double

40. I have never seen _____.
 (A) so brave a boy
 (B) so a brave boy
 (C) a so brave boy
 (D) so brave boy

41. Jack is as _____as his brother.
 (A) a tall man
 (B) tall man
 (C) tall a man
 (D) taller a man

42. She was _____ girl that they all loved her.
    - (A) a such nice
    - (B) such a nice
    - (C) such nice
    - (D) such nice a

43. London Bridge over _____ is very famous.
    - (A) Thames
    - (B) a Thames
    - (C) The Thames
    - (D) one Thames

44. It is better to tell _____ than to tell a lie.
    - (A) the truth
    - (B) a truth
    - (C) truths
    - (D) truth

45. Of the two this is _____ .
    - (A) very more useful
    - (B) much more useful
    - (C) the more useful
    - (D) most useful

46. My father was appointed _____ of the city last year.
    - (A) mayor
    - (B) a mayor
    - (C) the mayor
    - (D) one mayor

47. _____ Kennedy is still very much loved by many people in the world.
    - (A) Late President
    - (B) A late President
    - (C) The late President
    - (D) Late a President

48. _____ a democratic revolution took place in Korea.
    (A) In Spring of 1980
    (B) In a Spring of 1980
    (C) In the Spring of 1980
    (D) In Springs of 1980

49. It is_____to collect old records.
    (A) fun
    (B) a fun
    (C) the fun
    (D) any fun

50. Taiwan is a small country, but it has_____.
    (A) large population
    (B) a large population
    (C) the large population
    (D) large populations

51. She is always off_____on Saturdays and Sundays.
    (A) duty
    (B) a duty
    (C) the duty
    (D) duties

52. The young girls were sitting _____.
    (A) a hand in a hand
    (B) the hand in a hand
    (C) the hand in the hand
    (D) hand in hand

53. When she was charged with murder, she set up_____.
    (A) a alibi
    (B) an alibi
    (C) the alibi
    (D) alibi

54. Our teacher is a subscriber to _____.
    (A) a New York Times
    (B) the New York Times
    (C) New York Times
    (D) one New York Times

55. When I was absorbed in listening to Mozart, there was _____ on the door.
    (A) knock
    (B) a knock
    (C) the knock
    (D) knocking

56. We Americans are taught to be very conscious of the passage of time. Such slogans as " Time is Money " can often be seen hanging on the walls of many of our factories. Work - men are paid _____, and they are constantly reminded that " every minute counts."
    (A) by an hour
    (B) by hour
    (C) by the hour
    (D) by the hours

57. To understand the African, one must get to know him _____. To a greater or lesser degree he will seem to us strange and unattractive, but one must overlook all that and understand his essential nature.
    (A) man to man
    (B) a man to a man
    (C) the man to the man
    (D) the man to a man

58. A soldier, stationed at the entrance of a picture gallery, had strict orders to allow no one to pass without first depositing his walking stick. A gentleman came in with his hands in his pockets. The soldier, taking him _____, said: "Stop, where is your stick?" "I have no stick." "Then you will have to go back and get one before I can allow you to pass."
    (A) in his arm
    (B) by his arm
    (C) by the arm
    (D) in the arm

59. Many people know that Ben Franklin's kite experiment helped to prove that lightning is electricity. Kites have been used for scientific purposes since _____ for testing weather conditions, taking aerial photographs, etc.
    (A) middle 1700's
    (B) the middle 1700's
    (C) middle the 1700's
    (D) a middle 1700's

II. 選出下列句子中錯誤的部分。

60. Jane felt that she was as good swimmer as he was, if not
        (A)   (B)   (C)
    better.
    (D)

61. American manufactures depend on ocean shipping for most
                             (A)   (B)
    of trade with other countries.
    (C)   (D)

62. This kind of an article can make a reader of even the most
         (A)   (B)   (C) (D)
    reluctant.

63. Mr. Brown, the son of <u>an</u> wealthy merchant, <u>became</u> <u>an</u>
    (A)   (B)   (C)

    important <u>military</u> leader.
              (D)

64. After <u>the church</u> <u>the men</u> stood together <u>in the churchyard</u>
          (A)   (B)   (C)

    <u>saying</u> he must be crazy.
    (D)

III. 在下列各句的空格中填入適當的冠詞，若無須冠詞則打× 。

65. The dealer has just bought_____used car from her.

66. Did you take in _____ film?

67. Girls of _____ age are not always of _____mind.

68. Because I had _____ heavy lunch, I have no appetite.

69. Let me know the result by _____ telephone.

70. A child was run over by_____bus and killed while
    crossing the street.

71. _____ Smiths pay their servant by _____ week.

72. All _____ students of our school went on a picnic.

73. How glad we were when we saw_____light in the dis-
    tance !

74. John make it_____rule to go to_____movies once
    _____ week for fear of being behind _____times.

14. 形容詞 (Adjective)

===={ Points of Grammar }====

1. 形容詞的限定用法和敘述用法

It is an **interesting** book. 〔限定用法〕

I found the book **interesting**. The book is **interesting**. 〔敘述用法〕

(1) 只用於限定用法的形容詞—— elder, inner, utter, mere, former, latter, wooden, etc.

(2) 只用於敘述用法的形容詞—— alone, afraid, alive, asleep, awake, ashamed, content, unable, worth, liable, well, etc.

　　This brige is *wooden*. （誤）　　This is a **wooden** bridge. （正）

　　This bridge is made of wood. （正）

　　Latin is not a **living** （不可用 *alive*）language.

　　We catch animals **alive** （不可用 *living*）.

(3) 有些形容詞雖有限定、敘述兩種用法，但意思各不相同—— ill（壞的；生病的），late（已故的；遲的），present（現在的；出席的）。

(4) 限定用法的形容詞通常放在（代）名詞之前，但下列情形，應置於被修飾字之後。

　① a dictionary **useful for us**. ——名詞＋形容詞片語。

　　She was a girl **twelve years old**. ——數詞＋名詞＋old。

　② He is the greatest conductor **alive**, We tried every means **imaginable**.
　　——名詞前有限定最高級或 all, every, only, alive, 等形容詞時，則以 -ible 或 -able 作字尾的形容詞，要放在名詞後。

　③ Please give me **something cold**. I saw **somebody strange**. ——-ing, -body ＋形容詞。

　④ the sum **total**（總計），Asia **Minor**（小亞細亞），from time **immemorial**（太古）——形容詞置於後位的常用語。

2. 常用的非人稱形容詞

　非人稱形容詞不能用來修飾人，只能修飾事物。

easy, hard, difficult, dangerous, pleasant, impossible etc.

It is **difficult** for them to solve the problem. （正）

They are *difficult* to solve the problem. （誤）

The problem is **difficult** for them to solve.（正）

It is **hard** to please him. ＝He is **hard** to please.（正）

3. 形容詞作準介詞的用法

worth, like, near 這三個形容詞均具有介詞性質，後面可直接加受詞。

A bird in the hand is **worth two** in the bush.

He looks **like his father**.

His villa is **near the lake**.

4. 不定數量形容詞

(1) **Many** talk of democracy, but **few** understand it in the true sense.

〔many, few 可代替複數可數名詞〕

(2) She has **much** skill in teaching, but **little** patience with her students.

〔much, little 可用以修飾不可數名詞〕

* quite a few ＝ not a few ＝ a good many

  quite a little ＝ not a little ＝ a good deal of

The liar's punishment is not in the least that he is not believed, but he cannot believe anyone else.

騙子的懲罰一點也不是在於沒人相信他，而是在於他無法相信任何人。

EXERCISE 14

I. 請根據句意和文法選出一個最正確的答案。

1. Latin is not＿＿＿＿＿＿ language.
   (A) live
   (B) alive
   (C) an alive
   (D) a living

2. There is＿＿＿＿＿＿ about Mr. Lee, my teacher.
   (A) anything noble
   (B) noble something
   (C) something noble
   (D) noble anything

3. Miss Wang is ＿＿＿＿＿ her mother in many respects.
   (A) alike
   (B) similar
   (C) like with
   (D) like

4. Don't eat too＿＿＿＿＿＿sugar lest it should do you harm.
   (A) much
   (B) a little
   (C) many
   (D) few

5. She has failed this time, but there is still＿＿＿＿＿hope.
   (A) few
   (B) a few
   (C) little
   (D) a little

6. We should be polite to _____.
   (A) older
   (B) elder
   (C) an old
   (D) the old

7. Mary had enough time to go to France, but she had _____ money to go.
   (A) too few
   (B) too little
   (C) enough
   (D) enough of

8. You _____ to drop by my house any time you like.
   (A) are welcomed
   (B) welcome
   (C) are welcome
   (D) are welcoming

9. There were _____ people watching the football game.
   (A) seven thousands
   (B) seven millions
   (C) thousands of
   (D) thousands

10. The man is always complaining that he can't live on a _____ salary.
    (A) small
    (B) cheap
    (C) trivial
    (D) inexpensive

11. There are _____ children attending school in our village than in your village.
    (A) a few   (B) few
    (C) less   (D) fewer

12. School being over, there were only a _____ number of
    students in the playground.
    (A) little
    (B) small
    (C) few
    (D) short

13. "Are they able to start on time?" "No, they are _____
    to do so."
    (A) impossible
    (B) incapable
    (C) unable
    (D) inable

14. The prisoner remained _____ throughout the questioning.
    (A) silence
    (B) silently
    (C) silent
    (D) silencing

15. I don't think that his watch is _____.
    (A) worth the price
    (B) worthy the price
    (C) worthy to buy
    (D) worth of the price

16. The bookstore did not prepare _____ books for all of
    the students in the class.
    (A) plenty
    (B) enough
    (C) enough of
    (D) as many

17. "What do they eat there in Honolulu?" "_____ eat rice
    rather than potatoes."
    (A) Most of people   (B) The most of people
    (C) Most of the people (D) The most people

18. " What's for dinner? " " I don't know. There isn't _____ food left in the house."
    (A) none
    (B) no
    (C) some
    (D) any

19. An invertebrate is an animal with _____ spine.
    (A) any
    (B) no
    (C) not
    (D) none

20. Scientists are searching for the oldest _____ because it can teach them a great deal about many matters.
    (A) tree alive
    (B) tree lively
    (C) tree live
    (D) alive tree

21. Many women and children were walking down the street, but _____.

    (A) scanty men
    (B) little of men
    (C) few men
    (D) a little number of men

22. _____ of us will wait here.
    (A) A fewer
    (B) Some
    (C) Much
    (D) A little

23. She spent _____ on her new coat.
    (A) quite a little money   (B) money quite a little
    (C) quite little money   (D) little money quite

24. This club has a large_____of girls.
    (A) lot
    (B) amount
    (C) number
    (D) many

25. I weigh 65kg and you weigh 65kg. We are_____weight.
    (A) same heavy
    (B) as heavy as
    (C) as heavy
    (D) of the same

26. A _____reader does not understand science books written for experts.
    (A) young
    (B) foolish
    (C) lay
    (D) careless

27. " That's a very nice skirt you're wearing." " Thank you. I'm glad_____."
    (A) liked it by you
    (B) you to like it
    (C) to be liked by you
    (D) you like it.

28. The men at the lunch counter ordered_____and two platters of fried shrimp.
    (A) three black coffees
    (B) some three black coffee
    (C) black three coffees
    (D) black three coffee

29. He was surprised to read the passage at the end of_____.
    (A) five chapter   (B) chapter five
    (C) fifth chapter   (D) chapter the fifth

30. "Is this camera cheap?" "It is not＿＿＿＿what we paid."
    (A) value
    (B) cost
    (C) worthy
    (D) worth

31. It is easy＿＿＿＿her.
    (A) for us to get on with
    (B) that we get on with
    (C) our getting on with
    (D) get on with

32. Is it necessary＿＿＿＿the book immediately?
    (A) his returning
    (B) that he returns
    (C) for him to return
    (D) to him return

33. It is certain ＿＿＿＿the examination.
    (A) for her to pass
    (B) her passing
    (C) her to pass
    (D) that he will pass

34. She was very＿＿＿＿when I told her my pet dog died.
    (A) sympathetic
    (B) helpful
    (C) pitiful
    (D) friendly

35. Palm trees are native to ＿＿＿＿climates.
    (A) cold
    (B) warm
    (C) cool
    (D) wet

36. We felt _____ when we realized that perhaps we had offended Mr. Lee.
    (A) uncomfortable
    (B) uncomfortably
    (C) comfortably
    (D) comfort

37. Coffee mixed with chicory is likely to taste _____ to a person not used to it.
    (A) well
    (B) bitter
    (C) sweetly
    (D) bitterly

38. "Has your lost Ford been located?" "It was found _____ on the highway."
    (A) to be abandoned
    (B) to be abandoning
    (C) abandoned
    (D) abandon

39. "Are you going to the concert with me?" "That's a good idea, but I'm afraid it _____ expensive."
    (A) much too
    (B) too much
    (C) very greatly
    (D) seems

40. "Do you think the news is true?" "Yes, _____."
    (A) I am sure of its being true
    (B) I am sure of being true
    (C) I am not sure it to be true
    (D) I am sure it not to be true

41. " Do you read very many books ? " " Yes, _____ ."
    (A) very little
    (B) quite a few
    (C) just a little
    (D) very few of them

42. " Did you tell Ted and Mary about our change in plans ? "
    " Yes, I told them we'd be _____ ."
    (A) a little late
    (B) a few late hours
    (C) late several hours
    (D) to some late

43. " Glad to see you again. " " Would you like _____ hot coffee ? "
    (A) any
    (B) any more
    (C) some
    (D) some any

44. You should be _____ towards seniors.
    (A) respectable
    (B) respectful
    (C) respective
    (D) respecting

45. The solution of the problem is very _____ to the development of our economy.
    (A) momentary
    (B) momently
    (C) momentous
    (D) momental

46. Any unilateral action is a _____ undertaking.
    (A) world-wide   (B) cooperative
    (C) one-sided   (D) malicious

47. He was an ＿＿＿＿＿ statesman and diplomat; his record
    was untarnished by scandals or rumors, and the public
    treated him with great respect.
    (A) imminent
    (B) eminent
    (C) envious
    (D) immediate

48. Men, since they are by nature ＿＿＿＿＿, necessarily die.
    (A) moral
    (B) immoral
    (C) immortal
    (D) mortal

49. ＿＿＿＿＿ more to be pitied than blamed.
    (A) The uneducated are
    (B) The uneducated is
    (C) Uneducated are
    (D) Uneducated is

50. " I hear that you're having a house built. Is it finished
    yet? " " No, but it's ＿＿＿＿＿ completion."
    (A) nearly to
    (B) almost at
    (C) close to
    (D) about at

51. The weather is good today, except in the ＿＿＿＿＿.
    (A) west-north
    (B) south-west
    (C) east-south
    (D) south-north

52. To keep ＿＿＿＿＿ hours makes you healthy, wealthy and wise.
    (A) small   (B) little
    (C) some   (D) good

53. One dollar is roughly _____ to twenty-seven New Tai-
    wanese dollars.
    (A) worthy
    (B) equivalent
    (C) necessary
    (D) available

54. I can't get a good picture on my TV set. There is some-
    thing _____ with it.
    (A) bad
    (B) matter
    (C) wrong
    (D) untrue

55. Susan began looking for a winter job in September; she
    knows that the _____ bird catches the worm.
    (A) wise
    (B) shrewd
    (C) thoughtful
    (D) early

56. The salary increase proposed by the company fell _____
    of what we had expected.
    (A) short
    (B) equal
    (C) behind
    (D) down

57. He is the _____ man to be influenced by power.
    (A) most healthy
    (B) last
    (C) weak
    (D) hardly

58. She had _____ reason to be satisfied.
    (A) any
    (B) each
    (C) every
    (D) all

59. I never dreamed that his statement would lead to such a _____ situation.
    (A) selfish
    (B) grave
    (C) punctual
    (D) capable

60. Poverty is _____ to dishonesty.
    (A) better
    (B) worse
    (C) less
    (D) preferable

61. Goethe placed before me a landscape by Rubens. " You have already seen this picture, " said he, " but nobody can look often enough at _____ . "
    (A) anything really excellent
    (B) really excellent anything
    (C) really anything excellent
    (D) excellent anything really

62. If anyone wishes to learn a foreign language, the normal way that has been customary since _____ is to spend as much time as possible with someone who talks that language, to imitate that person's way of talking, and to learn the language by reproducing it as well as possible.
    (A) immemorial time
    (B) memorial time
    (C) time immemorial
    (D) immemorial times

63. Among the greatest discoveries of science _____ have been made by accident. Setting out to reach a certain goal, the investigator chances on his way upon a law, or an element, that had no place in his purpose. The discovery is a by-product of his activity.
    - (A) not few
    - (B) not a few
    - (C) not little
    - (D) not a little

64. Language teaching and language learning are fields of activity which are engaging a great amount of human attention and energy. _____ people make a living by teaching languages.
    - (A) Ten millions
    - (B) Tens million
    - (C) Million of
    - (D) Millions of

65. Mountain-climbing involves many risks, and the climber must be alert at all times. Reckless climbers soon meet with an accident. The job is really one for a man who is _____.
    - (A) bold
    - (B) strong
    - (C) frightened
    - (D) prudent

Ⅱ. 選出下列句子中錯誤的部分。

66. It was very <u>considerable</u> <u>of</u> you <u>not to play</u> the violin <u>while</u>
　　　　　　　　(A)　　　　(B)　　　　(C)　　　　　　(D)

the baby was sleeping.

67. <u>Born and raised</u> in Austria, Mary <u>became</u> interested <u>in</u>
    　　　(A)　　　　　　　　　　　　　(B)　　　　　　　　　(C)

    music and opera at <u>a very little age</u>.
    　　　　　　　　　　　　(D)

68. It is <u>indeed</u> an artistic little home, but more by far it is
    　　　　(A)

    <u>because of</u> her good <u>taste</u> rather than expensiveness of the
    　　(B)　　　　　　　　(C)

    <u>furniture</u>.
    　　(D)

69. Few of us <u>realizes</u> what a vast <u>amount</u> of information has
    　　　　　　(A)　　　　　　　　　　(B)

    <u>been</u> gathered about our <u>feathered</u> friends, the birds.
    　(C)　　　　　　　　　　　(D)

70. There <u>is</u> a number of things <u>that</u> will be discussed <u>at</u> <u>the</u>
    　　　(A)　　　　　　　　　(B)　　　　　　　　　　(C)　(D)

    policy council meeting tomorrow.

Ⅲ. 在下列各句的空格中填入適當的字，使上下兩句意思相同。

71. You have guessed wrong.

    ＝ Your guess is w_____ of the mark.

72. He doesn't depend on his parents for money.

    ＝ He is economically _____ of his parents.

73. There is nobody who has not his faults.

    ＝ Nobody is _____ from his faults.

74. He is a talkative person.

= He is man of _____ words.

75. He is practically dead.

= He is as g_____ as dead.

76. He is a student from Holland.

= He is a _____ student.

77. He will never betray me.

= He is the _____ man to betray me.

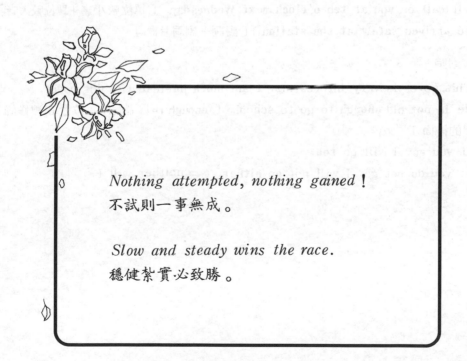

Nothing attempted, nothing gained !
不試則一事無成。

Slow and steady wins the race.
穩健紮實必致勝。

15. 副詞 (Adverb)

| Points of Grammar |

1. 副詞的位置

(1) It is **awfully** good of you to offer to help. 〔be 動詞＋副詞〕

(2) He wrote the letter **carefully**. 〔及物動詞＋受詞＋副詞〕

(3) Put **on** your raincoat. Put your raincoat **on**. Put it **on**. *Put on it*. （誤）
〔動詞＋介副詞的位置有三：動詞＋介副詞＋受詞（＝名詞），動詞＋受詞（＝名詞）＋介副詞，動詞＋受詞（＝代名詞）＋介副詞。〕

(4) He **always** travels third class. 〔always, usually, often, seldom 等頻率副詞，通常放在一般動詞之前，be 動詞之後。〕

2. 副詞的排列順序

(1) I drove **downtown quickly this morning**. 〔地點＋狀態（或方法）＋時間〕

(2) I'll call on you **at ten o'clock next Wednesday**. 〔單位較小者＋單位較大者〕

(3) We arrived **safely at the station**. 〔副詞＋副詞片語〕

3. 程度副詞

(1) This novel is **very** interesting. I am **much** interested in this novel.

(2) He is not old **enough** to go to school. 〔enough 作爲副詞時，位置在被修飾字的後面〕

(3) If you go, I will go **too**.

If you do not go, I will not go **either**. （＝neither will I.）

EXERCISE 15

I. 請根據句意和文法選出一個最正確的答案 。

1. She looks _____ than she is.
   - (A) more younger
   - (B) very younger
   - (C) more young
   - (D) much younger

2. Jane liked her new hat so much that she wouldn't _____.
   - (A) take it off
   - (B) take off it.
   - (C) put it off
   - (D) put off it

3. Breakfast is ready. Let's go _____.
   - (A) downstairs
   - (B) the downstairs
   - (C) to downstair
   - (D) to downstairs

4. "Where is he going ?" "He is going _____."
   - (A) to home
   - (B) home
   - (C) at home
   - (D) for home

5. "Do you know your results ?" "No, I don't know them _____."
   - (A) already
   - (B) since
   - (C) before
   - (D) yet

6. He does not like a child, _____ a baby.
   - (A) much less
   - (B) still more
   - (C) much worse
   - (D) more

7. The actuality is _____ stern a thing for sentiment.
   - (A) as
   - (B) much
   - (C) too
   - (D) so

8. My brother _____ alone at night.
   - (A) seldom go out
   - (B) seldom goes out
   - (C) goes seldom out
   - (D) goes out seldom

9. He was too tired to go _____ farther.
   - (A) still
   - (B) some
   - (C) any
   - (D) no

10. " Don't be long." " _____ ."
    - (A) Yes, please do so
    - (B) Yes, I am
    - (C) No, I am not
    - (D) No, I won't

11. " Aren't you tired?" " _____ ."
    - (A) Yes, little
    - (B) Yes, a little
    - (C) No, a little
    - (D) No, not a little

12. Tom said that he had come back three years _____.
    - (A) ago
    - (B) before
    - (C) once
    - (D) never

13. Several days _____, I saw the girl again on the street.
    - (A) late
    - (B) later
    - (C) latter
    - (D) last

14. "Do you mind if I smoke here?" "_____. You can smoke here."
    - (A) Yes, I do
    - (B) Yes, please
    - (C) Please not
    - (D) No, not at all

15. _____ have a chance to meet the great musician.
    - (A) Not until then I did
    - (B) Not until then did I
    - (C) Until then did I
    - (D) Until then did I not

16. How _____ can you finish them?
    - (A) fast
    - (B) soon
    - (C) long
    - (D) quick

17. The students are _____ for the test.
    - (A) study hard
    - (B) hard study
    - (C) hardly studying
    - (D) studying hardly

18. Having worked hard for several years, Mr. Lin _____.
   (A) finally decided to take a trip to Europe
   (B) decided finally to take a trip to Europe
   (C) decided to take a trip to Europe finally
   (D) decided to finally take a trip to Europe

19. I think Mary will _____ to see her parents.
   (A) arrive early enough
   (B) arrive enough early
   (C) enough early arrive
   (D) early enough arrive

20. I really believed there was no danger _____.
   (A) no matter what
   (B) what
   (C) nevertheless
   (D) whatever

21. What _____ is the matter with him?
   (A) on earth
   (B) in world
   (C) does
   (D) more

22. "Tom, why did you come so early for lunch today?" "I thought the bell _____."
   (A) already had rung
   (B) has already rung
   (C) had already rung
   (D) already rang

23. "Michael has lived in Taiwan for ten years." "Yes, but he _____ doesn't understand Chinese."
   (A) yet
   (B) still
   (C) already
   (D) any more

24. " Are the days getting colder ? " "_____."
    (A) Yes, it is
    (B) No, it isn't
    (C) Yes, they are
    (D) No, they don't

25. " I have to leave now." " Well, I hope we see each other again _____."
    (A) before many days
    (B) before some time
    (C) in few days
    (D) before long

26. Jackson put the plants _____ the show window.
    (A) near
    (B) close
    (C) nearly
    (D) next

27. You _____ go out lest it should rain.
    (A) had not better
    (B) had better not
    (C) not had better
    (D) better had not

28. Susie arrived here a week _____, and has been here ever _____.
    (A) before, ago
    (B) before, since
    (C) ago, before
    (D) ago, since

29. Kennedy did not get up until nine that morning and he arrived at the meeting _____.
    (A) too late much
    (B) too much late
    (C) much too late
    (D) late too much

30. Winnie married_____ she graduated from college.
    (A) soon
    (B) immediately
    (C) early
    (D) fast

31. The first, second, and third prizes went to Dora, Esther, and Jennie _____.
    (A) partially
    (B) equally
    (C) differently
    (D) respectively

32. The new medicine rescued David from the illness; _____ it might have been desperate.
    (A) otherwise
    (B) whatever
    (C) if
    (D) therefore

33. " Are you going to the concert? " " No, the ticket is _____ expensive for me."
    (A) so much
    (B) lots of
    (C) far too
    (D) very much

34. _____Emily's mother is a charming woman.
    (A) For most the part
    (B) For the most part
    (C) Mostly part
    (D) Part for the most

35. This plant is _____big that it should really be moved outside.
    (A) so   (B) too
    (C) such   (D) very

36. Most foreign students don't like American coffee, and
_____ .

   (A) I don't too

   (B) either don't I

   (C) neither don't I

   (D) neither do I

37. Doctoral students who are preparing to take their qualifying
examinations have been studying in the library every night
_____ the last three months.

   (A) since

   (B) for

   (C) ago

   (D) before

38. " Christina is going skiing tomorrow." "_____ ."

   (A) So am I

   (B) So I am

   (C) So David is

   (D) So does Edmond

39. " I haven't turned in papers yet." "_____ ."

   (A) So has Kitty

   (B) Neither have Kitty

   (C) Neither has Kitty

   (D) Neither Kitty has

40. " I slipped on the stairs. I think my leg is broken." "Oh!
I _____ ."

   (A) do not hope so

   (B) do not hope

   (C) hope not so

   (D) hope not

41. _____had we got into the building than it began to rain.
    (A) No sooner
    (B) The moment
    (C) Hardly
    (D) Directly

42. Let a man be _____so rich, he should not live an idle life.
    (A) however
    (B) ever
    (C) no matter
    (D) whatever

43. Should a world war break out, no country would be able to _____ a crushing blow.
    (A) shut itself off from
    (B) shut off itself to
    (C) shut itself off upon
    (D) shut on itself against

44. Maurice could not so_____as write his own name.
    (A) little
    (B) few
    (C) much
    (D) more

45. We can no _____live without sleep than without food.
    (A) little
    (B) much
    (C) most
    (D) more

46. "How often did you give her money?" "_____than I can remember."
    (A) More time   (B) More times
    (C) The more time   (D) The more times

47. The poor old man was so ill that he died_____
    last month.
    (A) sometime
    (B) sometimes
    (C) some times
    (D) some time

48. "Are you going so soon? Won't you stay with us_____
    longer?"
    (A) a little
    (B) little
    (C) just
    (D) a just

49. "What time is it now?" "It is five o'clock_____."
    (A) just
    (B) yet
    (C) sharp
    (D) on time

50. It is_____cold here in this classroom.
    (A) much and
    (B) very nice
    (C) more and
    (D) nice and

51. The manners of a child are of more or less importance,
    according to his station in life; his moral can not be
    attended to_____early, let his station be what it may
    be.
    (A) so
    (B) too
    (C) such
    (D) more

52. The influence of imitation in human society _____ . It is assuredly not always a bad thing that men imitate one another. Without imitation, there can be no civilized life.
    (A) can hardly be overestimated
    (B) hardly can be overestimated
    (C) can be hardly overestimated
    (D) can be overestimated hardly

53. Many an unfortunate elementary-school child in our age has never been exposed to the reading habit and can not, therefore, read without effort. Some modern children seldom _____ read for fun. Like muscles that are almost never used, their concentration and interest give way quickly.
    (A) do not
    (B) if any
    (C) if ever
    (D) can hardly

54. The dog prefers negotiation to fighting, and _____ since he is very bad at fighting. But he is a good watch dog — has a roar like a lion, designed to conceal from night-wandering strangers the fact that he is a great coward.
    (A) equally so
    (B) properly so
    (C) otherwise so
    (D) scarcely so

55. I did not at all like Mr. Smith. I made my way into the smoking-room. I called for a pack of cards and began to play patience. I had _____ started _____ a man came up to me and asked me if he was right in thinking my name was so-and-so.
    (A) no sooner, when
    (B) hardly, than
    (C) immediately, that
    (D) scarcely, when

Ⅱ. 選出下列句子中錯誤的部分。

56. The purpose <u>of</u> the United Nations, <u>broad speaking</u>, <u>is</u> to
    (A)   (B)   (C)

    maintain peace and security and <u>to encourage</u> respect for
                                        (D)

    human rights.

57. Jessica <u>always</u> gets <u>to work</u> <u>no later than</u> 8:00 but Eli-
            (A)   (B)   (C)

    zabeth <u>does seldom</u>.
              (D)

58. When the war broke out <u>over</u> thirty-seven years <u>before</u>, we
                              (A)   (B)

    found <u>ourselves</u> unprepared <u>for</u> it.
             (C)   (D)

59. Rain clouds and smoke caused by pollution look <u>so much</u>
                                                      (A)

    alike that one <u>can not hardly</u> tell <u>the difference between</u>
                      (B)   (C)

    the two <u>of them</u>.
               (D)

60. Margaret thinks she is a <u>more better</u> singer than <u>anybody</u>
                                (A)   (B)

    <u>else</u> in the chorus <u>but</u> she usually sings <u>off key</u>.
       (C)   (D)

Ⅲ. 在下列各句的空格中填入適當的字。

61. ＿＿＿＿＿ seemed to be no chance of his recovery.

62. They worked hard＿＿＿＿＿ to fail.

63. He can not so＿＿＿＿＿ as spell his name.

64. You can not be ＿＿＿＿＿ careful in choosing your friends.

Ⅳ. 在下列各句的空格中填入適當的字，使上下兩句意思相同。

65. Her pride will not allow her to ask such questions.
    ＝ She is ＿＿＿＿＿ proud to ask such questions.

66. She is all but dead.
    ＝ She is a＿＿＿＿＿ dead.

67. I think he is not so much a scholar as a novelist.
    ＝ I think he is a novelist＿＿＿＿＿ than a scholar.

68. It is already out of date.
    ＝ It is no longer＿＿＿＿＿ to date.

69. If he had not studied hard, he would have failed.
    ＝ He studied hard;＿＿＿＿＿ he would have failed.

16.　比較 (Comparison)

Points of Grammar

1. 形容詞的比較方式

(1) 原級：

He is **as** busy **as** a bee. This tree is half **as** tall **as** that. She is **not so** old **as** she looks.

(2) 比較級：

She is three years **older** than I. (= She is older than I by three years.)

She is **more** beautiful than her sister.

Which do you like **better,** this **or** that?

He is **less** interested in sports than you are.

① 比較級＋and＋比較級 (越來越～)——

The sky grew **darker and darker**.

② the＋比較級——

The more (we are together), **the merrier** (we shall be).

She is **the more** diligent **of the two**.

You are **all the better for** your failure.

③ more ～ than … (與其說…毋寧說～)——

She is **more kind than wise**.

(3) 最高級：

This is **the most** beautiful picture that I have ever seen.

She is **happiest** when she is with her mother.

2. 用原級或比較級表示最高級

Kaoshiung is the largest city in Taiwan. ＝Kaoshiung is the largest of all (the) cities in Taiwan. ＝Kaoshiung is larger than any other city in Taiwan. ＝Kaoshiung is as large a city as any in Taiwan. ＝No other city in Taiwan is so large as Kaoshiung. ＝No other city in Taiwan is larger than Kaoshiung.

3. 不及——劣等比較

(1) 原級：

He can **not so much as** write his own name. (= even)

He is **not so much** a teacher **as** a writer.

(2) 比較級：

He has **no more than** ten dollars. (= only)

He has **not more than** ten dollars. (= at most)

He has **no less than** ten dollars. (= as much as)

He has **not less than** ten dollars. (= at least)

He is **no more** mad **than** you are. (= He is **not** mad **any more than** you are.)

She is **no less** beautiful **than** her sister. (= quite as ~ as)

She is **not less** beautiful **than** her sister. (= more ~ than)

(3) 最高級：

He stayed in Taipei **at least** ten days.

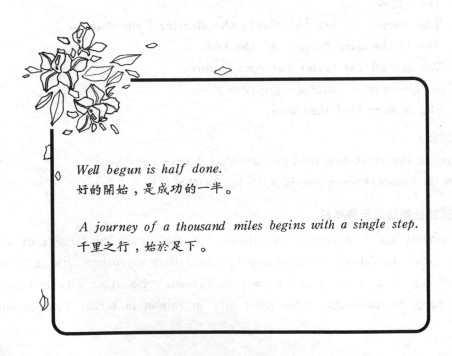

Well begun is half done.
好的開始，是成功的一半。

A journey of a thousand miles begins with a single step.
千里之行，始於足下。

EXERCISE 16

Ⅰ. 請根據句意和文法選出一個最正確的答案。

1. Christopher is taller than _____ in his class.
   (A) any other boy
   (B) all the boys
   (C) any other boys
   (D) every other boy

2. My sister is _____ than wise.
   (A) smarter
   (B) more smart
   (C) more smarter
   (D) smartest

3. Which do you like _____ , summer _____ winter?
   (A) good, and
   (B) better, and
   (C) better, or
   (D) best, or

4. Jonathan is _____ of the two boys.
   (A) the wiser
   (B) wiser
   (C) more wise
   (D) the wisest

5. _____ we have, the more we want.
   (A) The more
   (B) More
   (C) The most
   (D) The much

6. He is _____ for his poverty.
   (A) happier
   (B) all the happier
   (C) happiest
   (D) the happiest

7. America is _____ Taiwan in natural resources.
   (A) superior of
   (B) superior to
   (C) more superior than
   (D) superior than

8. He knows _____ than to quarrel.
   (A) more
   (B) less
   (C) better
   (D) worse

9. He can not speak French, still _____ English.
   (A) more
   (B) better
   (C) less
   (D) not

10. Nothing is more precious than time, yet nothing is _____ valued.
    (A) much
    (B) less
    (C) so
    (D) far

11. I have _____ records as he has.
    (A) four times as
    (B) four times many
    (C) four times as many
    (D) four times many as

12. Learning to play tennis well is not_____it seems when you are a spectator.
    (A) as easy so
    (B) so easy as
    (C) as easily as
    (D) more easy as

13. A child in the first grade tends to be_____all of the other children in his class.
    (A) the same old to
    (B) the same age than
    (C) as old like
    (D) the same age as

14. Perhaps_____thirty million Indians were living in America when the Europeans arrived.
    (A) that many
    (B) very many
    (C) as many as
    (D) many more

15. It is not the words that matter_____the way you say them.
    (A) too much as
    (B) as far as
    (C) not as much as
    (D) so much as

16. Of gold and silver,_____.
    (A) the former is much more precious than the latter.
    (B) the former is precious than the latter.
    (C) the former is the more precious.
    (D) the former is more precious than any other thing.

17. " I don't like to ride in a car." " I think most people prefer riding＿＿＿＿＿."
　　(A) to walking
　　(B) than walking
　　(C) more than walking
　　(D) better than walking

18. Catherine is as miserable as miserable＿＿＿＿＿be.
　　(A) can
　　(B) may
　　(C) will
　　(D) must

19. I like black coffee so much because the stronger it is, ＿＿＿＿＿.
　　(A) I like it better
　　(B) the more I like
　　(C) the better I like it
　　(D) I like it more

20. The more Jonathan tried to help her, ＿＿＿＿＿she seemed to appreciate it.
　　(A) the lesser
　　(B) less
　　(C) lesser
　　(D) the less

21. Karl's term paper is inferior＿＿＿＿＿.
　　(A) than mine
　　(B) to me
　　(C) to mine
　　(D) than I

22. Did you read＿＿＿＿＿of the story?
　　(A) later half　　　　　(B) the latter half
　　(C) latter half　　　　(D) the later half

23. Peter arrived in America＿＿＿＿＿＿Jack did.
    (A) much later than
    (B) much latter than
    (C) as later than
    (D) very later than

24. A good tale is＿＿＿＿＿＿for being twice told.
    (A) none the worse
    (B) no worse
    (C) none worse
    (D) never worst

25. It is none the ＿＿＿＿＿＿true because it sounds strange.
    (A) better
    (B) less
    (C) more
    (D) farther

26. Jessica was＿＿＿＿＿＿most brave girl.
    (A) a
    (B) so
    (C) far
    (D) one of

27. "What do you think about Joe?" "He is wiser than＿＿＿＿＿ in his class."
    (A) any else ones
    (B) else any one
    (C) anyone else
    (D) any other one

28. "Why did you choose the lion as your symbol?" "Because he is considered the＿＿＿＿＿＿."
    (A) most nobility of beasts
    (B) noble beast of all
    (C) beast of all the most noble
    (D) noblest of beasts

29. " Someone hit my car in the parking lot and didn't attempt to let me know."
   " It seems that honest people are becoming _____ these days."
   (A) less and fewer
   (B) more and more
   (C) less and less
   (D) fewer and fewer

30. If the teacher's life is hard, the doctor's is even _____.
   (A) harder
   (B) more hard
   (C) the hardest
   (D) more hardly

31. Compared to the others Mark is _____.
   (A) more diligent student
   (B) the more diligent student
   (C) the most diligent student
   (D) the most diligent student of all

32. She feels _____ when she is cooking.
   (A) the happiest
   (B) happiest
   (C) the happier
   (D) happily

33. Everyone has a right to enjoy his liberty, and _____ his life.
   (A) much more
   (B) much less
   (C) indeed
   (D) so

34. " Where is Jane?" " I haven't the _____ idea."
   (A) better   (B) least
   (C) little   (D) less

35. This is＿＿＿＿＿＿ sight I've ever seen.
    (A) the beautiful
    (B) a more beautiful
    (C) the most beautiful
    (D) more beautiful

36. When you run, you must go as＿＿＿＿＿＿.
    (A) possible as you can
    (B) possible as fast
    (C) possible fast as you can
    (D) fast as possible

37. Johnson has only one sister, but I have＿＿＿＿＿＿eleven
    brothers and sisters.
    (A) no more than
    (B) not more than
    (C) no less than
    (D) not less than

38. ＿＿＿＿＿＿man in the world does not know everything.
    (A) The wise
    (B) Wise
    (C) Wisest
    (D) The wisest

39. He is so idle. He is＿＿＿＿＿＿man to succeed in the attempt.
    (A) the last
    (B) a last
    (C) the later
    (D) a later

40. They were＿＿＿＿＿＿content that it should be like that.
    (A) more
    (B) better
    (C) more than
    (D) less

41. Mary went out without _____ saying good-bye.
    (A) much as
    (B) so much as
    (C) as much as
    (D) as many as

42. To _____ of my knowledge, there are no adequate books on the subject.
    (A) the best
    (B) the good
    (C) the better
    (D) the most

43. If he continues drinking, _____ he will lose his job.
    (A) less or more
    (B) less and less
    (C) more and more
    (D) sooner or later

44. The New York Philharmonic is the second _____ symphony orchestra in America.
    (A) good
    (B) better
    (C) best
    (D) well

45. American collectors have worked feverishly to uncover and preserve as much of the national folklore _____ before it is all forgotten.
    (A) as possible
    (B) so possible
    (C) as possible can
    (D) as possible as can

46. Houses should be built so as to admit plenty of light as
    well as of fresh air. The former is _____ necessary
    _____ the latter to a healthy condition of body. Just
    as plants, when deprived of light, become white in their
    stalks and leaves, so man becomes pale and unhealthy when
    he lives under ground.
    (A) no more, than
    (B) not less, than
    (C) not more, than
    (D) less, than

47. Forty-two years _____ , on a soft spring night when the
    tulips were blooming on the campus, this man, Sir William
    Osler, addressed the students of Yale University.
    (A) after
    (B) latter
    (C) later
    (D) last

48. Effort is painful, it may be very painful: and yet, while
    making it, we feel that it is _____ the work it results
    in, because, thanks to it, we have drawn from ourselves
    not only all that was there, but more than was there: we
    have raised ourselves above ourselves.
    (A) so precious, and perhaps precious than
    (B) as precious as, and perhaps as more precious than
    (C) more precious than, and perhaps as precious as
    (D) as precious as, and perhaps more precious than

49. If the sun were to be extinguished, in a day or two, the
    whole earth would be fast bound in a frost so terrible, that
    every animal, every plant would die; we could _____ live
    in such a frost _____ we could live in boiling water.
    (A) no less, than
    (B) no more, than
    (C) not more, than
    (D) less, than

Ⅱ. 選出下列句子中錯誤的部分。

50. <u>Even though</u> Miss Colombia lost the beauty contest, she
    (A)

    <u>was</u> still <u>more prettier</u> <u>than</u> the other girls in the pageant.
    (B)   (C)   (D)

51. The more the relative humidity reading <u>rises</u>, <u>the worst</u>
                                            (A)   (B)

    the heat <u>affects</u> <u>us</u>.
             (C)   (D)

52. <u>Of the three plants</u> Amy <u>had</u> in her apartment, only the
    (A)   (B)

    ivy, which is <u>the hardier</u>, lived through <u>the winter</u>.
                  (C)   (D)

53. <u>The Chinese</u> were the first and <u>large</u> ethnic group <u>to work</u>
    (A)   (B)   (C)

    on the construction <u>of</u> the transcontinental railroad system.
                        (D)

54. The songs of John Denver are very popular <u>among young</u>
                                              (A)

    girls, <u>who regard</u> him as <u>more superior</u> <u>to other musicians</u>.
           (B)   (C)   (D)

Ⅲ. 在下列各句的空格中填入適當的字，使上下兩句意思相同。

55. She is as industrious as her brother.

    = She is no_____industrious than her brother.

56. No other teacher was more enthusiastic than Mr. Lee.
= Mr. Lee was more enthusiastic than_____ _____
   teacher.

57. It's quite a surprise to see you here.
= You are the_____man I expected to meet here.

58. He is too wise to do such things.
= He knows _____than to do such things.

59. He is a better speaker of English than I.
= He is_____to me in speaking English.

60. Karajan is the greatest conductor that ever lived.
= Karajan is_____great a conductor_____ever
   lived.

61. David is three years younger than I
= David is my j_____ _____three years.

62. Helen has four times the number of my records.
= Helen has four times_____ _____records as I
   have.

63. This problem is not so easy as that.
= This problem is_____easy _____that.

64. This is the most interesting book that I have ever read.
= I have _____read a _____interesting book than
   this.

IV. 在下列各句的空格中填入適當的字。

65. Time is more valuable than anything _____ .

66. Whitman is_____to none in playing tennis.

67. I would_____stay at home than go out in the rain.

68. To the _____ of my knowledge, he is honest and reliable.

69. Alice is as p_____ as a peacock.

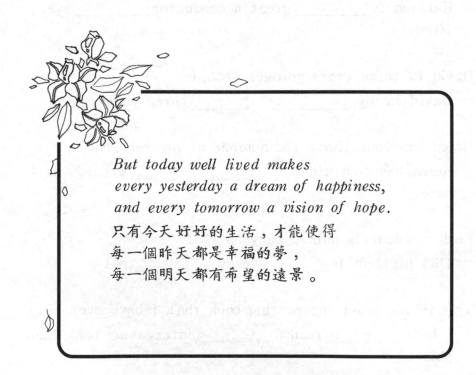

But today well lived makes
every yesterday a dream of happiness,
and every tomorrow a vision of hope.
只有今天好好的生活，才能使得
每一個昨天都是幸福的夢，
每一個明天都有希望的遠景。

17.　一致 (Agreement)

=[Points of Grammar]=

1. 主詞為集合名詞時，若指一個集合整體，用單數動詞；若指組成集合的份子時，則用複數動詞

(1) My family **is** a large one. My family **are** all well.

(2) The police **are** on the murderer's track.

2. 有些名詞雖為複數形式，但為單數意義時，用單數動詞

(1) The United States **is** a big country. (Ex. the United Nations, the Netherlands, etc.)

(2) The Times **is** read all over the country. (Ex. Gulliver's Travels, the Dialogues of Plato, etc.)

(3) Physics **is** my favorite subject. Measles **is** a very bad disease.
The news **says** that Senator Gary Hart will run for the presidency.

(4) Five hours **is** a long time to wait. 〔表一個數目〕
cf. Three years **have** passed since she died. 〔表一天天的過去〕

3. $\left\{\begin{array}{l}\text{all, half, part, some, a lot, most, the rest, }\cdots\end{array}\right\}$ + of + $\left\{\begin{array}{l}\text{可數複數名詞 ——}\\ \text{不可數名詞}\\ \text{可數單數名詞}\end{array}\right\}$

—— **用複數動詞**

—— **用單數動詞**

Three-fourths of the earth's surface **is** covered with snow.
Three-fourths of the sailors **were** drowned.

4. 不定代名詞的一致

(1) All : All **is** well that **ends** well. All **were** agreed to start early. 〔 all 後面沒有 of 片語，若代表「人」或「動物」，則用複數動詞；若表「事物」，則用單數動詞〕

(2) both : Both the brothers **were** invited.

(3) each, every: Every boy **has his** own right.

(4) either, neither: Neither of them **is** right.

(5) no one 做主詞時，用單數動詞，而 none 做主詞時，用單、複數動詞均可，但若 none 代表可數的名詞做主詞時，用複數動詞比較普遍。

5. 複合主詞的情況

(1) A and B 的情形。

① Bread and butter **is** my usual breakfast.〔A，B 為不可分的東西時，用單數動詞，如：a needle and thread, a watch and chain, etc.〕

② The captain and goal-keeper **has** saved the game.〔表同一人〕

③ Every boy and every girl **arrives** on time.〔every + every, each + each〕

(2) A with B, A as well as B, A no less than B，動詞與 A 一致。

The captain of the team, as well as most players, **was** opposed to the decision.

(3) A or B
either A or B
neither A nor B
not only A but also B

動詞與靠近者一致。

Not only you but also I **am** to blame.

Either you or he **is** wrong.

Is the child or the parents to be blamed?

(4) 其他

① one of A that (which, who …)：關係代名詞 who, that, etc. 作子句的主詞時，其後動詞須與先行詞一致。

He is one of those **people** who **believe** in God.

② a number of (= many) 用複數動詞，the number of 用單數動詞。

③ more than one + 單數動詞，more than one of + 複數動詞。

EXERCISE 17

I. 請根據句意和文法選出一個最正確的答案。

1. The French_____a very polite people.
   (A) is
   (B) was
   (C) are
   (D) has been

2. Ten years _____a long time to wait.
   (A) is
   (B) were
   (C) are
   (D) have been

3. A pair of trousers_____hanging in the room.
   (A) is
   (B) are
   (C) have been
   (D) have

4. The number of casualties_____unknown.
   (A) have
   (B) has
   (C) are
   (D) is

5. My sisters as well as I _____happy in those days.
   (A) are
   (B) were
   (C) is
   (D) was

6. Bacon and eggs_____his favorite breakfast.
   (A) are
   (B) were
   (C) is
   (D) have been

7. Henry with his friends_____on a trip to France.
   (A) has left
   (B) are left
   (C) have left
   (D) have been leaving

8. The United Nations _____the old League of Nations.
   (A) has been replaced
   (B) have replaced
   (C) have been replaced
   (D) has replaced

9. A list of the names of all survivors_____available.
   (A) are
   (B) is
   (C) have
   (D) has

10. Early to bed and early to rise_____a man healthy,
    wealthy, and wise.
    (A) is made
    (B) have made
    (C) makes
    (D) make

11. More than one person_____interested in the problem.
    (A) were
    (B) was
    (C) has
    (D) have

12. _____the rest of the audience refuse to go out?
    (A) Does
    (B) Have
    (C) Has
    (D) Do

13. What annoys me about them_____their constant com-
    plaints.
    (A) is
    (B) are
    (C) has
    (D) have

14. Neither the Giants nor the Tigers_____to win the
    pennant.
    (A) have gone
    (B) has gone
    (C) is going
    (D) are going

15. A number of people_____for a train at the station.
    (A) is waiting
    (B) are waiting
    (C) have been waited
    (D) has waiting

16. Mathematics _____a very difficult subject for me.
    (A) have
    (B) has
    (C) are
    (D) is

17. It is mosquitoes which _____malaria.
    (A) has caused
    (B) causes
    (C) cause
    (D) is causing

18. Eighty dollars _____a small sum for my pocket money.
    (A) has
    (B) have
    (C) are
    (D) is

19. Every boy and every girl_____ to church every Sunday.
    (A) goes
    (B) go
    (C) are going
    (D) have gone

20. Romeo and Juliet _____one of my favorite plays.
    (A) is
    (B) are
    (C) have been
    (D) were

21. The use of credit cards in place of cash_____rapidly in recent years.
    (A) have increased
    (B) has increased
    (C) were increased
    (D) have been increasing

22. Advertisements on television_____more competitive than ever before.
    (A) is become
    (B) are becomed
    (C) are becoming
    (D) is becoming

23. Mr. Jones, accompanied by some members of the committee, _____ some changes in the election law.
    (A) has been proposed   (B) have been proposed
    (C) has proposed   (D) have proposed

24. Anything_____than doing nothing.
    (A) is good
    (B) are good
    (C) are better
    (D) is better

25. There_____little change in the patient's condition since he was moved to the intensive care unit.
    (A) have been
    (B) is had
    (C) are having
    (D) has been

26. Never before_____ so many people in Taiwan been interested in baseball.
    (A) has
    (B) have
    (C) is
    (D) are

27. He wanted to make his son receive a good education, travel extensively, and_____.
    (A) to other advantages are many more
    (B) many other advantages
    (C) enjoy many other advantages
    (D) many other advantages are stored by him

28. Robert didn't know whether to sell his books or_____.
    (A) to keep them for reference
    (B) if he should keep them for reference
    (C) keeping them for reference
    (D) kept for reference

29. Everybody who_____a fever must see a doctor immediately.
    (A) is   (B) has
    (C) are   (D) have

30. Each student_____the first three questions.
    - (A) have answered
    - (B) have been answered
    - (C) has been answered
    - (D) has answered

31. All work and no play_____Jack a dull boy.
    - (A) is made
    - (B) are made
    - (C) makes
    - (D) make

32. A watch and chain _____on the floor of the room.
    - (A) was found
    - (B) were found
    - (C) have found
    - (D) has found

33. The editor and publisher of the magazine_____something strange since this morning.
    - (A) is doing
    - (B) are doing
    - (C) has been doing
    - (D) have been doing

34. The fear of robbery and kidnapping_____many people to flee Lebanon.
    - (A) has been caused
    - (B) has caused
    - (C) have been caused
    - (D) have caused

35. Conditions in Red China_____so severe that many refugees have risked death to escape.
    - (A) has grown
    - (B) is growing
    - (C) have been grown
    - (D) have grown

36. No one but nurses and doctors_____the fact that the child will die of cancer.
    (A) knows
    (B) know
    (C) knew
    (D) have known

37. I didn't know lots of money_____on this experiment.
    (A) have been spent
    (B) had been spent
    (C) has been spent
    (D) has spent

38. It is better to lose one's life than_____.
    (A) if you lose your spirit
    (B) losing your spirit
    (C) to lose one's spirit
    (D) your spirit getting lost

39. Mailing a letter a few days early is better than _____.
    (A) run the risk of late arrival
    (B) running the risk of its arriving late
    (C) to run the risk of its arriving late
    (D) to run the risk of late arriving

40. The new stores will operate in thirty cities around the country and_____.
    (A) five executives running them
    (B) run by five executives
    (C) five executives to run them
    (D) be run by five executives

41. Six of the players from the Tigers_____to participate in the All Star Game.
    (A) have been chosen   (B) has been chosen
    (C) have chosen   (D) have been choosing

42. Neither the students nor the teacher_____to smoke in the classroom.
    (A) allows
    (B) is allowed
    (C) allow
    (D) have been allowed

43. When a person needs to take this medicine, _____directions first.
    (A) you will have to read
    (B) you must to read
    (C) you have to read
    (D) he has to read

44. When we approached the campus,_____.
    (A) we saw the tower
    (B) one saw the tower
    (C) the tower was seen
    (D) we were seeing the tower

45. Collecting coins was his favorite pastime, but _____.
    (A) he also enjoy music listening
    (B) listening to music also gave him great pleasure
    (C) also listening to music
    (D) to listen to music was enjoyed by him also.

46. He did not sleep all night, and as happens to many and many a man who_____the Bible, he understood for the first time the full meaning of the words read often before but passed by unnoticed.
    (A) are reading
    (B) have been reading
    (C) reads
    (D) have read

47. Education is not only a preparation for later life; it is an aspect of life itself. The great bulk of the young now _____ a minimum of twelve years in school; with kindergarten attendance becoming more widespread, more and more of the young will have spent thirteen to fifteen years attending school by the time they have finished high school.
    (A) spend
    (B) spends
    (C) has spent
    (D) has been spending

48. Among the greatest discoveries of science not a few_____ by accident. Setting out to reach a certain goal, the investigator chances in his way upon a law, or an element, that had no place in his purpose. The discovery is a by-product of his activity.
    (A) have made
    (B) have been made
    (C) has made
    (D) had made

49. Everything we shut our eyes to, everything we run away from, everything we deny or despise, _____ to defeat us in the end. What seems nasty, painful, evil, can become a source of beauty, joy and strength, if faced with open mind.
    (A) serve   (B) serves
    (C) are served   (D) have been serving

II. 選出下列句子中錯誤的部分。

50. The president, with his wife and daughter, <u>are</u> returning
                                                (A)

    <u>from</u> a brief vacation at Sun Valley in order <u>to attend</u> a
    (B)   (C)

    press conference <u>this afternoon</u>.
                     (D)

51. A good artist <u>like</u> a good engineer learns <u>as</u> much from
    (A)   (B)

    <u>their</u> mistakes as <u>from</u> successes.
    (C)   (D)

52. Economists have tried <u>to discourage</u> <u>the use</u> of the phrase
    (A)   (B)

    "underdeveloped nation" and <u>encouraging</u> <u>the more</u> accurate
    (C)   (D)

    phrase "developing nation" in order to suggest an ongoing

    process.

53. The registrar has requested that each student and teacher

    <u>sign</u> <u>their name</u> on the grade sheet before <u>submitting</u> <u>it</u>.
    (A)   (B)   (C)   (D)

54. <u>Historically</u> <u>there</u> <u>has been</u> <u>only</u> two major factions in the
    (A)   (B)   (C)   (D)

    Republican Party- the liberals and the conservatives.

55. Neither of the two candidates <u>who</u> <u>had applied</u> for admission
                                  (A)   (B)

    <u>to</u> the college <u>were</u> eligible for scholarships.
    (C)   (D)

56. Jane is the only student in the class who never <u>admit</u>
                                                    (A)

    <u>making</u> a mistake, even when <u>it</u> is <u>pointed</u> out to her.
    (B)   (C)   (D)

57. If one <u>had read</u> all of the committee's report, <u>you</u> <u>would</u>
        (A)   (B)   (C)

    not have been <u>so quick</u> to disagree.
                   (D)

58. <u>Either</u> David or one of his friends <u>have taken</u> the car and
    (A)   (B)

    <u>driven</u> to the airport <u>to meet</u> her.
     (C)   (D)

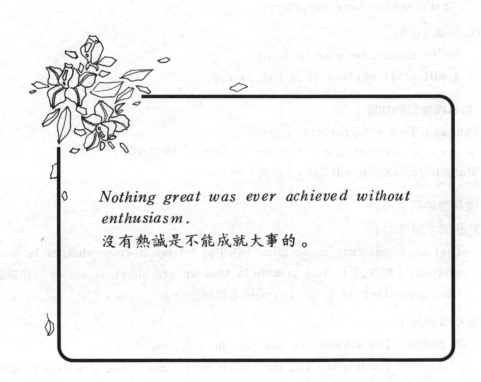

Nothing great was ever achieved without enthusiasm.

沒有熱誠是不能成就大事的。

18. 連接詞 (Conjunction)

Points of Grammar

1. 連接詞的種類

(1) 對等連接詞。

We have not yet decided where to go on a trip **and** when to leave.

Which do you like better, tea **or** coffee?

I gave him a present, **but** he gave me nothing in return.

I asked her to stay for tea, **for** I had something to say to her.

This book is **both** (at once, alike) agreeable **and** instructive.

He can speak **not only** English **but also** French.

Either John **or** I am to blame.

That's neither here nor there.

(2) 從屬連接詞。

He is absent, **because** he is ill.

I will start **whether** it is fine or not.

2. 對等連接詞的功用

Tom **and** Jack are brothers. 〔連接單字〕

He lived an earnest life in war **and** in peace. 〔連接片語〕

Study hard, **or** you will fail. 〔連接子句〕

3. 從屬連接詞

(1) 引導名詞子句。

That he is innocent is certain. 〔作主詞〕I don't know **whether** he has arrived. 〔作受詞〕 The trouble is **that** we are short of money. 〔作補語〕 The rumor **that** he is ill is true. 〔作同位語〕

(2) 引導副詞子句。

① 表時間：**The moment** he saw me, he ran away.

I will show you the sample **next time** I see you. (the moment, as soon as, etc.)

As I grew richer, I grew more ambitious.

② 表地點：**Where** there is a will, there is a way.

③ 表原因：**Now that** we have got liberty, we may do anything.

④ 表條件：Any book will do **so long as** (＝ if only) it is interesting.

⑤ 表讓步：**Even though** I were starving, I would not ask a favor of him.

　　　　　Granted (*or* Granting) that this is true, he is still in the wrong. (seeing, providing, provided, supposing, suppose etc.)

⑥ 表目的：They died **that** we **might** live.

　　　　　He is going early, **so that** he will get a good seat.

⑦ 表狀態：Don't touch the vase. Leave it **as** it is.

⑧ 表比較：The woman is not **so** old **as** she looks.

* 在從屬連接詞 if, when, while, though, as 等所引導的子句中，句義明確時，可省略主詞和 be 動詞。

When (*I was*) a boy, I had a great longing for the sea.

I'll drop in if (*it is*) possible.

We'd like you to pay this bill as soon as (*it is*) convenient.

Correct the errors if (*there are*) any.

He seldom, if (*he*) ever (*does*), goes to church.

She opened her lips as if (*she were*) to speak.

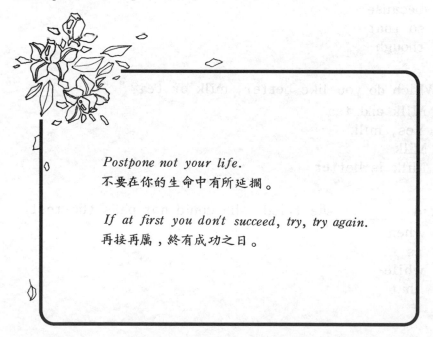

Postpone not your life.
不要在你的生命中有所延擱。

If at first you don't succeed, try, try again.
再接再厲，終有成功之日。

EXERCISE 18

I. 請根據句意和文法選出一個最正確的答案

1. It is spring now,_____the birds are singing.
   (A) because
   (B) though
   (C) for
   (D) unless

2. Cows must eat grains,_____they will not grow fat.
   (A) or
   (B) but
   (C) when
   (D) though

3. I have never spoken ill of him,_____I don't like him.
   (A) if
   (B) because
   (C) so that
   (D) though

4. "Which do you like better, milk or tea?" "_____."
   (A) Milk and tea
   (B) Yes, milk
   (C) Milk
   (D) Milk is better

5. Hard_____she tried, she could not pass the test.
   (A) when
   (B) as
   (C) while
   (D) that

6. She hadn't reached the top of the stairs＿＿＿＿＿he caught her round the waist.
   (A) because
   (B) if
   (C) although
   (D) before

7. ＿＿＿＿＿it rains, what shall we do?
   (A) Supposing
   (B) Imagining
   (C) Considering
   (D) Thinking

8. The dense fog will have cleared away＿＿＿＿＿day breaks.
   (A) by the time
   (B) till the time
   (C) even if
   (D) though

9. Excuse me, ＿＿＿＿＿which is the way to the station?
   (A) and
   (B) because
   (C) but
   (D) so

10. Truth is not true＿＿＿＿＿it applies to everyone everywhere.
    (A) how
    (B) when
    (C) if
    (D) unless

11. ＿＿＿＿＿he opened the window, a sparrow flew in.
    (A) Though
    (B) The moment
    (C) If
    (D) Unless

12. You should not despise others_____ you are rich.
    (A) while
    (B) when
    (C) because
    (D) that

13. The world always will be the same_____ men are men.
    (A) though
    (B) unless
    (C) that
    (D) so long as

14. _____he is no more, we have no one to fear.
    (A) Now that
    (B) So that
    (C) Unless
    (D) When

15. _____ Jackson is industrious is well known to us.
    (A) That
    (B) Which
    (C) So
    (D) What

16. Such was her beauty_____everybody admired her.
    (A) as
    (B) that
    (C) which
    (D) what

17. You should study hard_____you should fail in the examination.
    (A) lest
    (B) but
    (C) that
    (D) when

18. It will not be long _____ we can have a trip to the moon.
   (A) that
   (B) after
   (C) until
   (D) before

19. Because of the snow the cars couldn't move, _____ could the buses.
   (A) so
   (B) also
   (C) nor
   (D) either not

20. We had not gone far _____ we saw a great crowd of people.
   (A) before
   (B) after
   (C) as soon as
   (D) while

21. It is not _____ we lose our health that we realize its value.
   (A) because
   (B) after
   (C) until
   (D) that

22. I wanted to know _____ all the members had arrived.
   (A) because
   (B) if
   (C) till
   (D) while

23. It is three years _____ he died.
   (A) when   (B) after
   (C) since   (D) that

24. You can read a magazine＿＿＿＿＿you are waiting.
   (A) until
   (B) during
   (C) unless
   (D) while

25. The report＿＿＿＿＿President Kennedy had been killed gave me quite a shock.
   (A) which
   (B) that
   (C) what
   (D) when

26. Do you mind＿＿＿＿＿I open the window?
   (A) if
   (B) that
   (C) whether
   (D) because

27. We do not necessarily grow wiser＿＿＿＿＿we grow older.
   (A) that
   (B) as
   (C) though
   (D) than

28. No man is so old＿＿＿＿＿he can learn.
   (A) that
   (B) as
   (C) when
   (D) but

29. I did not know＿＿＿＿＿he had arrived or not.
   (A) why
   (B) whether
   (C) when
   (D) how

30. Some people want to go hunting,＿＿＿＿＿others want to go fishing.
    (A) or
    (B) because
    (C) while
    (D) since

31. She had no sooner heard the news＿＿＿＿＿she turned pale.
    (A) when
    (B) that
    (C) as
    (D) than

32. Bad habits,＿＿＿＿＿formed, are difficult to give up.
    (A) and
    (B) once
    (C) or
    (D) but

33. Everett did not get the letter in time＿＿＿＿＿.
    (A) since it was delivered late.
    (B) since it was late delivered
    (C) because of it was delivered late
    (D) because it was late delivered

34. It was not until the night was far advanced＿＿＿＿＿the crowd dispersed.
    (A) when
    (B) before
    (C) that
    (D) though

35. The reason Virginia did not attend the concert is＿＿＿＿＿ the violinist was unpopular with the young.
    (A) because   (B) since
    (C) what   (D) that

36. We kept quiet _____ we would disturb the patients.
    (A) for fear
    (B) so as to
    (C) that
    (D) so that

37. He is ahead of me not in English, _____ in German.
    (A) when
    (B) but
    (C) so
    (D) or

38. _____ are fed into a tape recorder, they magnetize the particles on the tape in varying patterns.
    (A) Electric waves
    (B) Electric waves that
    (C) Because of electric waves
    (D) When electric waves

39. Take an umbrella with you _____ it should rain.
    (A) in time
    (B) in case
    (C) unless
    (D) even if

40. Matt was absent from school yesterday _____.
    (A) because his fever
    (B) because of he had a fever
    (C) because he had a fever
    (D) because with a fever

41. They seem to eat well; _____ they always look hungry.
    (A) except
    (B) until
    (C) nevertheless
    (D) unless

42. Kitty studied all afternoon. She was _____studying that she couldn't go to the restaurant with us.
    (A) so busy
    (B) very busy
    (C) too busy
    (D) much busy

43. As you treat me,_____will I treat you.
    (A) and
    (B) like
    (C) as
    (D) so

44. Mr. Chung came to work today_____he sprained his ankle last night.
    (A) unless
    (B) despite
    (C) although
    (D) because

45. _____grammar is concerned, there is nothing to be desired in this composition.
    (A) So far as
    (B) So that
    (C) According as
    (D) As well as

46. Duncan will accept the post_____the salary is satisfactory.
    (A) unless
    (B) though
    (C) on condition that
    (D) for fear that

47. Most writers speak of their fame_____it were quite a worthless matter.
 (A) although
 (B) as if
 (C) according as
 (D) so far as

48. He is said to have won the first prize, but I doubt_____ it is true.
 (A) when
 (B) what
 (C) which
 (D) whether

49. Knowledge is certainly not wisdom_____are the more knowledgeable the more wise. If knowledge alone could save the world, we would be in a far happier condition than we are, since knowledge has been vastly extending its range.
 (A) and
 (B) that
 (C) so
 (D) nor

50. Disobedient and independant _____ John was, he never-theless had a clear sense of right and wrong. He developed, before he was ten, a deep religious feeling which prevented his doing anything seriously wrong. For all his mischief he never did anything mean or deceitful.
 (A) as
 (B) so
 (C) but
 (D) whether

51. Newly acquired power is something like newly acquired riches; it needs watching closely_____a man should become the victim of his own power as, for example, Hitler did.
   (A) so that
   (B) lest
   (C) till
   (D) as

52. Just as we appreciate warmth because we've experienced cold,_____we appreciate what love means all the more because we know what it is to have feelings of hate.
   (A) as
   (B) that
   (C) so
   (D) nor

Ⅱ. 選出下列句子中錯誤的部分。

53. <u>While</u> he was <u>in Taiwan</u>, he <u>learned</u> both Chinese <u>as well as</u> French.
    　(A)　　　　　(B)　　　　　　(C)　　　　　　　(D)

54. Professor Duncan <u>teaches</u> <u>both</u> <u>anthropology</u> as well as
    　　　　　　　　　(A)　　(B)　　　(C)

    sociology <u>each fall</u>.
    　　　　　(D)

55. I don't know <u>that</u> you <u>can recognize</u> her <u>from here</u>, but
    　　　　　　　(A)　　　　(B)　　　　　　(C)

    the girl <u>reading</u> the newspaper is Susan.
    　　　　　(D)

56. <u>Neither Emily has mentioned</u> the time <u>nor</u> the place <u>where</u>
    　　　(A)　　　　　　　　　　　　　　(B)　　　　　(C)

    the wedding <u>will be held</u>.
    　　　　　　　(D)

57. Eugene was in <u>so</u> terrible hardships that <u>it</u> seemed impossible
          (A)   (B)

   <u>for him</u> to live <u>a rich and useful</u> life.
     (C)   (D)

Ⅲ. 在下列各句的空格中填入適當的字。

58. You should not look down upon a man _____ he is poor.

59. I stepped aside _____ the fat lady might pass by.

60. Make hay _____ the sun shines.

61. One more effort, _____ you will attain it.

62. _____ or not he is coming hasn't been decided yet.

63. Not a day passed by _____ he repented of what he had done.

64. She seldom, _____ ever, goes shopping.

65. It will not be long _____ he is sorry for what he has done.

66. He did not think of his future job _____ he went to
   college.

67. The rich are not always happy, _____ are the poor always
   miserable.

68. _____ I grew richer, I grew more ambitious.

69. Don't touch my desk. Leave it _____ it is.

70. She's not only an excellent housewife, _____ a first
   class mathematician.

71. He had not gone far _____ he was caught in a shower.

72. Not that I hate this kind of work, _____ that I have no
   time.

19. 介系詞 (Preposition)

Points of Grammar

1. 介系詞的種類

(1) 由分詞轉用者：concerning, during, regarding, except, past, etc.

(2) 由形容詞或副詞轉用者：like, near, opposite

(3) 片語介系詞：according to, as for, because of, owing to, etc.

According to today's newspapers, the rumor is groundless.

2. 介系詞的受詞

(1) 形容詞：Things went **from** bad **to** worse.

(2) 副詞：I have received a letter **from** abroad.

(3) 動名詞：He succeeded **in** solving the problem.

(4) 不定詞：She was **about** to leave.

(5) 介系詞片語：The moon appeared **from** behind the clouds.

(6) 子句：Your success will largely depend **upon** what you do and how you do it.

3. 介系詞片語

(1) 作名詞：**From three o'clock** will do.

(2) 作形容詞：He is a man **of wisdom**. (= a **wise** man)

(3) 作副詞：You should handle the vase **with care**. (= carefully).

4. 介系詞的位置

原則上，介系詞要放在受詞前。但下列情況中，受詞常和介系詞分離而放到前面去。

(1) 受詞為疑問詞時：What are you looking **for**?

(2) 位於當形容詞的不定詞之後：He has no friend to talk **with**.

(3) 含有介系詞的動詞片語用於被動態時：The child must be taken care **of**.

EXERCISE 19

I. 請根據句意和文法選出一個最正確的答案。

1. We really need to start _____ ten o'clock sharp.
   (A) in
   (B) with
   (C) at
   (D) on

2. Every year _____ October 10th the Chinese have a celebration.
   (A) in
   (B) on
   (C) at
   (D) by

3. "When will Mr. Carpenter come back?" "He will be back _____."
   (A) on next Friday
   (B) about next Friday
   (C) in next Friday
   (D) next Friday

4. You must finish the work _____ seven o'clock.
   (A) by
   (B) till
   (C) until
   (D) to

5. I haven't seen my wife _____ last spring.
   (A) for
   (B) until
   (C) yet
   (D) since

6. We have been waiting for many hours to see the movie star, but the plane must have been _____.
   (A) on time
   (B) punctual
   (C) on schedule
   (D) behind schedule

7. My uncle has not been here _____ seven years.
   (A) during
   (B) for
   (C) since
   (D) by

8. Helen has met many friends _____ the four years she has been in America.
   (A) for
   (B) from
   (C) during
   (D) in

9. I will visit you _____ the week.
   (A) at the beginning of
   (B) at the middle of
   (C) in the end of
   (D) during the middle of

10. The opening speech of the meeting will be _____.
    (A) in a while little
    (B) after a little while
    (C) in little a while
    (D) after a while little

11. A man who leads orchestra must have, in _____ to great energy, head, heart, and charm.
    (A) order   (B) addition
    (C) respect   (D) search

12. Robert called me up_____Sunday morning.
    (A) at
    (B) in
    (C) on
    (D) to

13. Some Africans were starved _____ death.
    (A) to
    (B) by
    (C) because of
    (D) through

14. Milk is made _____ butter and cheese.
    (A) of
    (B) from
    (C) into
    (D) with

15. Mr. Lee laid down his own life_____ the cause of democracy.
    (A) on
    (B) of
    (C) in
    (D) to

16. The Pacific Ocean is_____the east of Taiwan.
    (A) by
    (B) of
    (C) at
    (D) to

17. The boy jumped into the pond_____his eyes closed.
    (A) through
    (B) with
    (C) at
    (D) by

18. Flowers have begun to appear_____the earth.
    (A) from under
    (B) beneath
    (C) above
    (D) over

19. We can do nothing_____these circumstances.
    (A) at
    (B) for
    (C) under
    (D) to

20. I'm_____duty from 8 in the morning to 6 in the afternoon today.
    (A) on
    (B) in
    (C) for
    (D) at

21. The money was divided _____the three robbers.
    (A) between
    (B) on
    (C) among
    (D) for

22. His house is _____a stone's throw from the school.
    (A) within
    (B) to
    (C) on
    (D) of

23. In those days there were no lamps which they could read books _____.
    (A) for
    (B) with
    (C) at
    (D) by

24. _____her surprise and relief, her husband arrived.
    (A) With
    (B) On
    (C) To
    (D) From

25. "Why do you ask if I've been smoking?" "Because you smell_____cigarettes."
    (A) by
    (B) of
    (C) with
    (D) to

26. Taking him_____the well-known movie star, they gave him a hearty welcome.
    (A) upon
    (B) to
    (C) into
    (D) for

27. Your carelessness resulted_____the accident.
    (A) for
    (B) from
    (C) in
    (D) at

28. He has every reason_____not accepting her offer.
    (A) for
    (B) at
    (C) in
    (D) from

29. "Is Jessica older than you?" "Yes, she is older than _____three years."
    (A) me for   (B) me by
    (C) I for   (D) I by

30. The girls danced _____ the music of Paul Mauriat's band.
   - (A) with
   - (B) to
   - (C) by
   - (D) of

31. We went on a picnic _____ the heavy rain.
   - (A) although
   - (B) in spite of
   - (C) because of
   - (D) when

32. Patricia got seriously hurt _____ a car accident.
   - (A) by
   - (B) with
   - (C) in
   - (D) for

33. You should look in the dictionary _____ .
   - (A) for the new word
   - (B) on the new word
   - (C) to knowing the new word
   - (D) to acquaint the new word

34. Let's do away with the new laws depriving many people _____ the most elementary freedoms.
   - (A) for
   - (B) of
   - (C) off
   - (D) upon

35. _____ helping me with my homework, I thank you.
   - (A) By
   - (B) With
   - (C) At
   - (D) For

36. The child died _____cancer at the age of seven.
    (A) of
    (B) by
    (C) in
    (D) with

37. In this company we are paid_____the month.
    (A) on
    (B) at
    (C) by
    (D) for

38. It is impossible to know whether she has anything to do
    _____ the matter.
    (A) with
    (B) for
    (C) about
    (D) of

39. Africa is now reported to be entirely_____of new cases
    of this disease.
    (A) far
    (B) free
    (C) among
    (D) lacking

40. Oxford has a famous library named the Bodleian _____
    Sir Thomas Bodley, who constituted it in 1602.
    (A) of
    (B) with
    (C) to
    (D) after

41. "What does that building look like?" "That is similar in
    shape _____mine."
    (A) to   (B) with
    (C) as   (D) for

42. I reminded him_____what he had promised.
    (A) to
    (B) with
    (C) of
    (D) for

43. She did not resort _____punishment in any case.
    (A) of
    (B) to
    (C) by
    (D) for

44. In reading stories you should read_____ the lines.
    (A) by
    (B) to
    (C) with
    (D) between

45. The watch he sent me last year keeps good time _____
    the minute.
    (A) to
    (B) by
    (C) for
    (D) with

46. I ordered the book directly_____the publisher.
    (A) to
    (B) from
    (C) of
    (D) for

47. She made up her mind to leave the school_____ the
    grounds of marriage.
    (A) by
    (B) to
    (C) on
    (D) with

48. She did not distinguish _____ barley and wheat.
    (A) of
    (B) from
    (C) among
    (D) between

49. The automobile went _____ the direction of the post office.
    (A) to
    (B) in
    (C) by
    (D) for

50. Both of my sisters are looking forward _____ next week.
    (A) to going on vacation
    (B) to go on vacation
    (C) to be going on vacation
    (D) to have gone on vacation

51. "What is Jack doing there?" "I don't know. He is going _____ all fours."
    (A) about
    (B) with
    (C) on
    (D) by

52. I can not concentrate my attention _____ reading in a noisy room.
    (A) about
    (B) on
    (C) at
    (D) to

53. I congratulate you _____ your promotion.
    (A) for
    (B) of
    (C) to
    (D) on

54. Thanks _____ his timely rescue, the child escaped death.
    (A) to
    (B) by
    (C) for
    (D) with

55. " Why aren't you happy ? " " I don't like the idea _____. "
    (A) in getting up early
    (B) of getting up early
    (C) for getting up early
    (D) to get up early

56. Mr. Lin is _____ the faculty of our school.
    (A) in
    (B) with
    (C) on
    (D) at

57. Please lend me a hand _____ this trunk.
    (A) on
    (B) about
    (C) for
    (D) with

58. It goes _____ saying that sometimes we have to turn to some amusement or other to refresh ourselves.
    (A) with
    (B) without
    (C) on
    (D) about

59. Besides being able to go for three days without drinking, the camel can also live for a long time _____ small quantities of food. Since ancient times the camel has been called " the ship of the desert."
    (A) with　　　　　　　　　(B) on
    (C) by　　　　　　　　　　(D) to

60. I never walk into my tailor's _____ feeling apologetic. I know I am unworthy of their efforts. I am the kind of man who can make any suit of clothes look shabby after about a fortnight's wear.
    (A) by
    (B) on
    (C) of
    (D) without

61. A soldier, stationed at the entrance of a picture gallery, had strict orders to allow no one to pass _____ first depositing his walking stick. A gentleman came in with his hands in his pocket. The soldier, taking him by the arm, said: " Stop, where is your stick?" " I have no stick." " Then you will have to go back and get one before I can allow you to pass."
    (A) with
    (B) about
    (C) without
    (D) on

62. We ourselves have binocular vision. That is, we bring both our eyes to bear on an object. The same is true _____ certain mammals besides ourselves-monkeys, dogs, and cats for instance.
    (A) of
    (B) with
    (C) to
    (D) without

63. The basic difference _____ a school and a university is that in schools the teacher must teach all the students entrusted to him. In the university, however, he has no such obligation.
    (A) for   (B) about
    (C) with   (D) between

Ⅱ. 選出下列句子中錯誤的部分。

64. Despite of the increase in air fares, most people still prefer
    (A)   (B)   (C)
    to travel by plane.
    (D)

65. People with an exceptionally high intelligence quotient may
                      (A)
    not be the best employees since they become bored of their
           (B)   (C)
    work unless the job is constantly changing.
                                     (D)

66. Stern just walked out of the classroom, went down the
          (A)   (B)
    stairs and got on a taxi.
     (C)   (D)

67. Katherine always does whatever she pleases, without regard
                          (A)   (B)
    of the feelings of others.
    (C)   (D)

Ⅲ. 在下列各句的空格中填入適當的字。

68. His death had a great influence _____ us.

69. Having succeeded in saving the country, he could succeed
    _____ the throne.

70. At last she got an occupation _____ her taste.

71. He was chosen a representative irrespective _____ age.

72. The new railway is still _____ construction.

73. _____ all appearances she was a lady.

74. They discussed the matter o_____ a bottle of wine.

75. He is _____ selling his country.

76. It is _____ your dignity to do such a mean thing.

77. He was taken ill _____ drinking too much.

78. He lost his commission _____ neglect of duty.

79. Mr. Lee is not very popular _____ his students.

80. I have been familiar _____ him for years.

81. Life is often compared _____ a voyage.

82. Human life consists _____ a succession of small events.

83. He is now independent _____ his parents.

84. He saved the child _____ the risk of his own life.

85. The flower is going to die _____ want of water.

86. He left school _____ a view to becoming a movie star.

87. I am not at all _____ favor of the proposition.

88. The ship was drifting _____ the mercy of the waves.

89. I don't blame you _____ not inviting her again.

90. This medicine will relieve you _____ your pain.

20. 特殊構句 (Constructions of Other Kinds)

Points of Grammar

1. 倒裝句（ inversion ）

What is your brother？〔疑問句的倒裝〕

How brave a boy he is！〔感嘆句的倒裝〕

May you live long and die happy！〔祈願句的倒裝〕

Poor as he is, he is happy．〔讓步子句裏的倒裝〕

Should it rain tomorrow, we will not go on a picnic．〔假設法之條件子句的倒裝〕

2. 強調構句（ emphasis ）

Never have I seen such a sight．

No thought did you give to my distress．

Such is the way of the world．

3. 省略句（ ellipsis ）

⑴ Must I go now？——Yes, you must (*go now*)．——在疑問句的回答中，本動詞多省略。

⑵ I won't do that．——Why not？(＝Why won't you do that？)

⑶ What a big house (*it is*)！——感嘆句中主詞與動詞句義明確時，常省略。

⑷ I came here because I wanted to (*come*)．——動詞爲避免重複常省略。

⑸ When (*I was*) a boy, I liked to play baseball．——從屬連接詞 if, when, while, as, though 所引導的子句中，句義明確時，可省略主詞和 be 動詞。

⑹ Breakfast (*being*) over, we hurried to the station．——分詞 being 和 having been 當其前面無主詞，或名詞爲其意義上的主詞時，常省略。

4. 否定構句（ negation ）

① 否定構句的形成：加上否定字詞，如 not, no, …等。

No many of them were present at the meeting．

He decided **not to go** to the party．

Will he fail？I hope **not** (＝ I hope he will not fail)．

② 加上有否定含義的字詞，如 few, hardly…等。

I have **few** acquaintances in town.

He **hardly** ever goes to bed before midnight.

(2) 全部否定與部分否定。

No man can be free from faults. 〔全部否定〕

I do **not** know **both** of them. 〔部分否定〕

(3) 雙重否定。

There is **nobody but** has his fault. = There is **nobody** that **does not** have his fault. = Everybody has his fault.

No man is **so** old **but** he can learn. = No man is so old **that** he can **not** learn. = However old a man may be, he can learn.

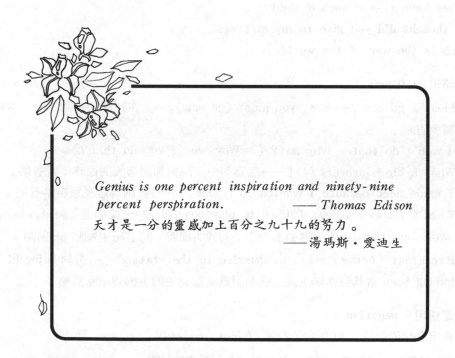

Genius is one percent inspiration and ninety-nine percent perspiration.　　——　*Thomas Edison*

天才是一分的靈感加上百分之九十九的努力。

——湯瑪斯‧愛迪生

EXERCISE 20

I. 請根據句意和文法選出一個最正確的答案。

1. Down_____.
   (A) came the shower in torrents
   (B) the shower came in torrents
   (C) the shower in torrents came
   (D) in torrents the shower came

2. Here_____.
   (A) the bus goes
   (B) the bus is running
   (C) comes the bus
   (D) the bus coming

3. Hardly_____entered the building before it began to rain.
   (A) I had
   (B) had I
   (C) did I
   (D) I was

4. _____ I would see you here.
   (A) Little I dreamed
   (B) Little do I dream
   (C) I dreamed little
   (D) Little did I dream

5. Under no circumstances _____ be left on.
   (A) do the switch
   (B) the switch must
   (C) the switch will
   (D) must the switch

6. At no point of the river _____ the enemy advanced more than a mile.
   (A) have
   (B) did
   (C) were
   (D) could

7. Then _____ a beautiful sight.
   (A) saw
   (B) will see
   (C) was seen
   (D) had seen

8. "May I use your pen?" "Sure, _____."
   (A) Here are you
   (B) Here you are
   (C) You are here
   (D) Are you here

9. How many people _____ the concert last night?
   (A) did attend
   (B) was attending
   (C) did they attend
   (D) attended

10. Only by doing the work themselves _____.
    (A) the students will get experience
    (B) the students will to get experience
    (C) will the students get experience
    (D) will the students to get experience

11. _____, you would have seen the movie star.
    (A) You had come earlier
    (B) If you come earlier
    (C) Had you come earlier
    (D) Earlier coming

12. _____ was his diligence that everyone praised him.
    (A) So
    (B) Such
    (C) It
    (D) What

13. Who _____ composed this violin concerto?
    (A) was it that
    (B) did it
    (C) was it which
    (D) was it be

14. "Do you think she is coming tomorrow?" "I am afraid _____."
    (A) she is coming
    (B) she will come
    (C) she did not come
    (D) not

15. Don't speak until _____.
    (A) you speak to
    (B) spoken to
    (C) you will speak to
    (D) you will have to speak to

16. _____ they set out on a journey.
    (A) Although raining
    (B) Although there is raining
    (C) Although having rained
    (D) Although it was raining

17. Most of us would rather be found fault with, _____, to our face.
    (A) if ever
    (B) if any
    (C) if not
    (D) if at all

18. Agatha spent more than half the money,_____ .
   (A) if ever
   (B) if any
   (C) if not all
   (D) if possible

19. Peter, _____ born in Canada, lived and practiced law in America.
   (A) although
   (B) he was
   (C) was
   (D) who he was

20. You can not have your cake _____ eat it, too.
   (A) but
   (B) and
   (C) to
   (D) without

21. It is _____ violence but good that overcomes evil.
   (A) without
   (B) no
   (C) not
   (D) less

22. More often than _____ , he had to go in person.
   (A) not
   (B) rarely
   (C) hardly
   (D) less

23. Most foreign students don't like American coffee, and
   _____ .
   (A) I don't too
   (B) either don't I
   (C) neither don't I
   (D) neither do I

24. How kind _____ of you to show me the way to the con-
    cert hall !
    (A) were
    (B) it is
    (C) are
    (D) they are

25. You had to read the first chapter more carefully, _____?
    (A) didn't you
    (B) shouldn't you
    (C) don't you
    (D) did you

26. Jackson hardly has anything nowadays, _____?
    (A) has he
    (B) doesn't he
    (C) hasn't he
    (D) does he

27. This is the second time this week Jenny was late for school,
    _____?
    (A) hasn't it
    (B) hasn't she
    (C) isn't it
    (D) isn't she

28. Let's ask her to go swimming with us, _____?
    (A) will you
    (B) shall we
    (C) don't we
    (D) do we

29. " Have a glass of beer, _____?" " Yes, please."
    (A) won't you
    (B) shall we
    (C) would you
    (D) wouldn't you

30. Only after food has been dried or canned _____.
  - (A) that it should be stored for later consumption
  - (B) should be stored for later consumption
  - (C) should it be stored for later consumption
  - (D) it should be stored for later consumption

31. Not until a monkey is several years old _____ to exhibit signs of independence from its mother.
  - (A) it begins
  - (B) does it begin
  - (C) and begin
  - (D) beginning

32. Closely tied to the population problem _____. The world's total supply of food, and particular protein, has at last come to be seen as a massive problem.
  - (A) is the problem of food
  - (B) the problem of food is
  - (C) the problem is of food
  - (D) food is the problem of

II. 選出下列句子中錯誤的部分。

33. Nobody ever <u>has</u> the complete freedom to do <u>nothing</u> that he
          (A)   (B)

  wants <u>when</u> he <u>wants to</u>.
        (C)   (D)

34. <u>Not only</u> <u>they lost</u> all their money, but they <u>also</u> came
    (A)   (B)   (C)

  close to <u>losing</u> their lives.
           (D)

Editorial Staff

- 企劃・編著 / 王怡華
- 英文撰稿 / David Bell・Bruce S. Stewart
  Edward C. Yulo・John C. Didier
- 校訂 / 劉　毅・王慶銘・陳瑠琍・陳怡平
  陳威如・許碧珍・劉馨君・林佩汀
  林順隆・程文嬌・陳麒永
- 校閱 / Larry J. Marx・Lois M. Findler
  John H. Voelker・Keith Gaunt
- 封面設計 / 張鳳儀
- 插畫 / 林惠貞
- 版面設計 / 張鳳儀・林惠貞
- 版面構成 / 蘇淑玲・王孝月・張端懿
- 打字 / 黃淑貞・倪秀梅・蘇淑玲
  吳秋香・徐湘君

文法練習 1000 題
English Grammar Drills 1000

售價：220 元

編　　著／王怡華

發 行 所／學習出版有限公司　　☎ (02) 2704-5525

郵 撥 帳 號／05127272 學習出版社帳戶

登 記 證／局版台業 2179 號

印 刷 所／裕強彩色印刷有限公司

台 北 門 市／台北市許昌街 17 號 6F　　☎ (02) 2331-4060

台灣總經銷／紅螞蟻圖書有限公司　　☎ (02) 2795-3656

本公司網址　www.learnbook.com.tw

電 子 郵 件　learnbook0928@gmail.com

2023 年 9 月 1 日新修訂

ISBN 957-519-124-2

人人必讀

文法練習
1000題

教師手冊

王怡華　編著
David Bell　校閱

ENGLISH GRAMMAR DRILLS

●學習出版有限公司●

習題解答

Exercise 1

Ⅰ. 1.（ B ）　can not but ＋原形動詞 「不得不～」。

2.（ B ）　see ＋受詞＋原形動詞（ or V-ing ）。

3.（ C ）　make ＋受詞＋原形動詞。

4.（ B ）　what ＋不定詞＝名詞片語；在此，what 兼作with 的受詞。

5.（ A ）　let ＋受詞＋原形動詞。

6.（ C ）　order ＋ *sth.* ＋ to be ＋ p.p.，其中不定詞的 to 不可省。

7.（ A ）　It is true that～ 「的確～」，(B)(C)(D)的形容詞通常用於「 It ＋ be動詞＋ *adj.* ＋ for ＋受詞＋ to-V」的句型。

8.（ C ）　It is hard for ＋受詞＋ to-V；(A) false 應用「 It is ＋ false ＋ of ＋受詞＋ to-V」的句型；(B) likely 和 (D) certain 應用「 It ＋ be動詞＋ *adj.* ＋ that 子句」的句型。

9.（ B ）　對受詞稱讚或責備時，用「 It is ＋ *adj.* ＋ of ＋受詞＋ to-V」的句型。

10.（ B ）　whether ～ or not 「是否～」。

11.（ D ）　expect 可接（代）名詞作受詞，再接不定詞作受詞補語；suggest，hope，propose 則否。（ 詳見文法寶典 p.438 ）

12.（ A ）　finish ＋ V-ing 「完成～」。

13.（ C ）　be about to-V 「即將～」。

14.（ A ）　to begin with 「首先」。

15.（ A ）　be sorry to-V 「爲～感到抱歉」。

16.（ C ）　enable ＋受詞＋ to-V 「使～能夠…」；選(A) to have gone 就變成 go 的動作比 enable 先發生，不合句意。

17.（ B ）　make it a rule to-V 「照例～；經常～」。

18.（ B ）　lead ＋受詞＋ to-V 「導致～」。

19.（ D ）　to put things in 是不定詞片語，當形容詞用，修飾 pocket。而 pocket 是介系詞 in 意義上的受詞，故 in 不可省。（詳見文法寶典 p.412 ）

20.（ A ）　help ＋ *sb.* ＋原形動詞（ or to-V ）。

21.（ B ）　would（ or had ）rather ＋原形動詞＋ than ＋原形動詞 「寧願～而不願…」。

22.（ D ）　stop ＋ to-V 「停下來，開始去做～」。（ 詳見文法寶典 p.435 ）

23.（ C ）　need＋to be＋p.p.（＝need V-ing），表被動。（詳見文法寶典 p.430）

24.（ C ）　enough＋to-V「足夠～」。　　＊ *let alone* 違論

25.（ A ）　be afraid＋to-V「害怕～」；(C) to have lost 表該動作發生在 were afraid 之前，不合句意。

26.（ D ）　It is difficult＋to-V「～是困難的」；make conversation with *sb.*「和某人交談」。

27.（ C ）　fail＋to-V「不能夠～」

28.（ B ）　find it difficult＋to-V「發現～是困難的」。
　　　　　　＊ rampant〔'ræmpənt〕*adj.* 猖獗的
　　　　　　accustomed〔ə'kʌstəmd〕*adj.* 習慣的

29.（ A ）　have no alternative but＋to-V（＝cannot but＋原形動詞）「不得不～」。　＊ alternative〔ɔl'tɝnətɪv〕*n.* 選擇

30.（ B ）　what clothes *to take*＝what clothes should be taken（「疑問詞＋不定詞＝名詞片語」的句型，詳見文法寶典 p.147，418）

31.（ D ）　to insist … behavior 是不定詞片語，當形容詞用，修飾 the first men；先行詞之前有 the first 時，關係代名詞用 that；(C) *who insists → that insist* 。（詳見文法寶典 p.153）
　　　　　　＊ pragmatist〔'prægmə,tɪst〕*n.* 實用主義者

32.（ A ）　capability to-V「做～的能力」

33.（ C ）　be used＋to-V「被做為～」。注意：be used to＋V-ing「習慣於～」。

34.（ A ）　be free＋to-V「直率地～」。

35.（ A ）　adj.＋enough to-V「足夠可以～」。

36.（ C ）　To be quite honest「老實說」。

37.（ D ）　不定詞中的原形動詞與前面的動詞重複時，原形動詞可省略；(A) *to do → to be or to become* 。

38.（ A ）　根據句意，應用不定詞片語 to keep up my courage 當副詞用，修飾 muttered，表目的。

39.（ B ）　it is time to-V「是～的時候了」。　＊ molar〔'molɚ〕*n.* 臼齒

40.（ B ）　ask *sb.* to-V ⇒ *sb.* be asked to-V。　＊ exhibition game 表演賽

Ⅱ. 41.（ C ）　It is likely＋that＋S＋will＋V 表現在或未來，故(C)應改為 It is likely … *will* … 。

42.(A)　be sure ＋ to-V，表說話者或其他人對主詞的確信（詳見文法寶典 p.587）。所以：He is sure to pass the examination.（他一定會通過考試。意即「我確信他會通過考試。」）╪ He is sure that he will pass the examination.（他確信自己會通過考試。）

43.(C)　It's time that you *could start*. → It's time that you *started*.（詳見文法寶典 p.374）

44.(C)　This river is dangerous to *swim*. → This river is dangerous to *swim in*.（詳見文法寶典 p.411）

45.(D)　根據前句的句意，You are too *old* to drink. 應改爲 You are too *young* to drink.

46.(D)　I can not but *to admire* her. → I can not but *admire* her. can not but ＋原形動詞「不得不～」。

47.(D)　He was to have dined with us yesterday.（他昨天原本要和我們共進晚餐。意即「他昨天並沒有和我們共進晚餐。」）╪ He had been with us to dine yesterday.（他昨天和我們共進晚餐。）

48.(D)　This bed is comfortable to *sleep*. → This bed is comfortable to *sleep in*.

49.(B)　It is said that he was very generous.（據說他從前很慷慨。）╪ He is said to be very generous.〔據說他（現在）很慷慨。〕（詳見文法寶典 p.422－423）

50.(C)　Nobody was to be seen in the house.（屋內沒見到有人。）╪ Nobody should be seen in the house.（屋內不可有人。）

Ⅲ. 51.(D)　*to be avoiding* → *to avoid*　用簡單式不定詞表發生在主要動詞（came to a stop）之後的動作。（詳見文法寶典 p.422）

52.(C)　*protesting* → *to protest*　decide ＋ to-V「決定～」。

53.(D)　*of* → *for*　too ～ for ＋（動）名詞＋ to-V「太～而不能…」。

54.(D)　*it* → *you*　表條件之不定詞置於句首時，句子的主詞須是該不定詞意義上的主詞。（詳見文法寶典 p.414）

55.(A)　*to have learned* → *to learn*　had hoped ＋ to ＋原形動詞（＝ hoped ＋ to have ＋ p.p.）表過去未實現的願望。

Ⅳ. 56. there　57. very　58. It　59. dare　60. to　61. happened to　62. as to　63. too, for　64. to have　65. no, to deny　66. of, to sign　67. lest, as not　68. to have been　69. too dirty, see through　70. to have

Exercise 2

I. 1. (A) admit ＋V-ing「承認～」。

2. (D) decide ＋ to-V「決定～」；(A)(B)(C)後只可接動名詞為受詞。
   * *lay down* 舖設

3. (B) 根據句意，此題應選(B) failed。fail ＋ to-V「無法～」

4. (C) appreciate ＋V-ing *or* N.「感激～」。此處的 your 為動名詞
   pointing out 的意義上主詞。

5. (C) consider ＋V-ing「認為～」。

6. (A) allow ＋V-ing「允許～」。注意：allow *sb*. to-V「允許某人～」。

7. (C) avoid ＋V-ing「避免～」。

8. (A) by ＋V-ing「藉著～」。

9. (B) mind ＋V-ing「介意～」。

10. (D) deny ＋V-ing「否認～」，此題 V-ing 須用完成式，表比主要動詞
    denied 先發生的動作。　* practical joke 惡作劇

11. (B) object to ＋V-ing「反對～」。

12. (C) be accustomed to ＋V-ing「習慣於～」。

13. (C) a good way of ＋V-ing「～的好方法」。

14. (A) look forward to ＋V-ing「期盼～」；watch 是感官動詞，其後須
    接原形動詞。

15. (D) (be) worth ＋V-ing「值得～」。

16. (C) remember ＋V-ing 表「記得曾做過～」；keep *sb*. ＋V-ing「使
    某人～」。

17. (A) What do you say to ＋V-ing ?「你認為～如何？」
    * *go on a hike* 遠足

18. (C) can not help ＋V-ing「不得不～」；be satisfied with「對～感
    到滿意」。

19. (C) *sb*. ＋ spend ＋時間＋(in) ＋V-ing。（詳見文法寶典 p.299）

20. (D) be capable of ＋V-ing「能夠～」。

21. (A) never ～without ＋V-ing（每～必…）。根據題意，本題中的 V-ing
    應用被動語態，故選(A)。　* impress〔ɪmˊprɛs〕*v*. 使感動

22. (A) There is no ＋V-ing「～是不可能的」。

23.（ B ）　repent of ＋V-ing「後悔～」；V-ing 用完成式表比主要動詞
　　　　　　repented 先發生的狀態或動作。

24.（ A ）　forget ＋ to-V 表 to-V 的動作尚未發生。（詳見文法寶典 p.435 ）

25.（ B ）　want（需要）後接主動形式的動名詞，表示被動的意思。（詳見文法
　　　　　　寶典 p.430 ）

26.（ C ）　It is no use ＋V-ing「～是沒有用的」。

27.（ A ）　stop ＋V-ing「停止～」。　　＊ *call in* 延請（醫生…）

28.（ D ）　on ＋V-ing「一～就」。

29.（ C ）　come near（ *to* ）＋V-ing「幾乎要～」。

30.（ B ）　There is no ＋V-ing「～是不可能的」。

31.（ A ）　make a point of ＋V-ing「必定～」。

32.（ A ）　like ＋V-ing「喜歡～」；根據句意，本題的 V-ing 應用被動語態。

33.（ A ）　It goes without saying that 子句「不用說～」。

34.（ B ）　be busy ＋（ *in* ）＋V-ing「忙於～」。

35.（ B ）　go ＋V-ing「去～」（ V-ing 大部分指運動或遊戲）。

36.（ C ）　動名詞具有名詞的性質，可作主詞，根據句意，應選(C)。

37.（ B ）　動名詞具有名詞性質，可作補語。

38.（ A ）　mind ＋V-ing「介意～」。

39.（ B ）　anticipate ＋V-ing「期待～」。

40.（ D ）　confess to ＋V-ing「供認～」；V-ing 用完成式表發生在主要動詞
　　　　　　confessed 前的動作。

41.（ A ）　完成式的動名詞，表示比主要動詞 prided 先發生的動作，而根據句意，
　　　　　　應用被動語態。　＊ *pride oneself on* ～以～自傲

42.（ B ）　have a hard time（ *in* ）＋V-ing「～很費力」。

43.（ C ）　have trouble（ *in* ）＋V-ing「～有困難」。
　　　　　　＊ obscure〔 əb'skjur 〕 *adj.* 偏僻的

44.（ D ）　cannot help ＋V-ing ＝ cannot but ＋原形動詞「不得不～」；
　　　　　　sympathize with ～「同情～」。

45.（ D ）　and 是對等連接詞，在此連接文法作用相同的片語，故選(D) present-
　　　　　　ing …和 giving …形成對稱。

Ⅱ. 46.（ D ）　stop ＋V-ing 表「停止做～」；stop ＋ to-V 表「停下來，開始去
　　　　　　做～」，故等號不能成立。

47.（ A ）　try＋V-ing 表「試驗～」；try＋to-V 表「設法～」，故等號不能成立。

48.（ D ）　He repents that he *had been* …→ He repents that he *was* idle …。

49.（ C ）　This is a picture of his own painting.（這是他自己畫的圖畫。）≒ This is a picture he painted himself.（這是他的自畫像。）

50.（ B ）　Do you mind if *you* …→ Do you mind if I …

Ⅲ. 51.（ D ）　*to reread → **rereading***　　avoid＋V-ing「避免～」。

52.（ A ）　*to move → **of moving***　　be capable of＋V-ing「能夠～」。

53.（ B ）　*to write → （**in**）**writing***　　have difficulty（in）＋V-ing「～有困難」。

54.（ B ）　*to smoke → **smoking***　　根據句意，應用 stop＋V-ing 表「停止做～」。

55.（ C ）　*to give → **giving***　　devote ～ to＋V-ing「以～從事…」

Ⅳ. 56. never, without　　57. no, age　　58. crying, inclined　　59. prevented, from going　　60. his having been　　61. his having forgotten　　62. to taking　　63. Besides being　　64. of, having promised　　65. for believing　　66. his living　　67. to be cut　　68. my own choosing　　69. when, learn　　70. Instead of

---

Exercise 3

Ⅰ. 1.（ A ）　用現在分詞表主動及進行的意思，sitting over there 作形容詞片語，修飾Mary。

2.（ B ）　catch *sb*.＋V-ing「撞見某人在～」。

3.（ C ）　過去分詞表被動，用來修飾 facts；本題是指既成的事實，故(D) being gathered 不合句意。

4.（ D ）　get＋受詞＋p.p.「使～被…」。（詳見文法寶典 p.454）

5.（ D ）　have＋受詞＋p.p.「使～被…」。（詳見文法寶典 p.454）

6.（ C ）　過去分詞作形容詞，表被動，用來修飾 language。

7.（ B ）　keep＋受詞＋V-ing「使～繼續…」。

8.（ D ）　過去分詞表被動。

9.（ A ）　make *one*self understood「使人了解自己的想法」。

10.（ D ）　現在分詞 disturbing 作形容詞，修飾 noise，表主動。（詳見文法寶典 p.448）

11.（ D ）　過去分詞 exhausted 作形容詞，修飾 worker，表被動。（詳見文法寶典 p.448）

12.（ D ）　trained properly 由形容詞子句 which is trained properly 簡化而來，修飾 dog。

13.（ B ）　start＋受詞＋V-ing「使～開始…」。

14.（ C ）　Before being admitted …是由 Before he was admitted … 簡化而來：將主詞 he 去掉，be 動詞改爲現在分詞。

15.（ A ）　with＋受詞＋V-ing，表伴隨主要動詞的情形，此處表主動意義，故 V-ing 用主動語態。（詳見文法寶典 p.462－463）

16.（ D ）　compared with「與～比較起來」。

17.（ A ）　表情緒的動詞，在「非人」作主詞時，常以現在分詞形式作形容詞用，表主動。（詳見文法寶典 p.390）

18.（ C ）　根據句意，應以 a few（＝ some）來表肯定意味；left 之前省略了 being，修飾 seats。

19.（ A ）　表情緒的動詞，在「人」作主詞時，通常以過去分詞形式作形容詞用，表被動。（詳見文法寶典 p.390）

20.（ C ）　surrounded by … 是由形容詞子句 which is surrounded by … 簡化而來，修飾 chair。

21.（ C ）　現在分詞 drowning 表進行的意思，在此作「快要淹死的」解。本句是諺語，意爲「溺者攀草求援；急不暇擇」。

22.（ A ）　理由同第 17 題。

23.（ C ）　with＋受詞＋p.p. 表伴隨主要動詞的情形，當受詞是「非人」時，表被動含意，要用過去分詞（p.p.）。

24.（ D ）　waste time＋（in）＋V-ing「浪費時間在～上」。

25.（ A ）　Taking all things into consideration「從各方面來說」，本句是由 If we take … into consideration 變成的獨立分詞片語，其主詞不是 he，而是「一般人」。（詳見文法寶典 p.463）

26.（ C ）　感官動詞 see 之後接現在分詞或原形動詞表主動。

27.（ B ）　過去分詞修飾名詞時，是由「動詞是被動的形容詞子句」轉變而來。故 the murdered man 可改成 the man who was murdered。

28.（B） meaning flat water 是由形容詞子句which means flat water 簡化而來，修飾 “ nebrathka ”。

29.（D） 分詞構句的否定詞要放在分詞前；用完成式分詞表分詞動作發生在主要子句動詞 sent 之前。

30.（A） located on a hill 是由形容詞子句which is located … 簡化而來。
* command〔kəˊmænd〕v. 俯視

31.（A） weather permitting（天氣許可的話）是由 if weather permits 簡化而來。

32.（B） seeing that「因為；既然」。（分詞可當連接詞用者詳見文法寶典 p.456）

33.（C） having been addressed … number 是由which had been addressed … 簡化而來。

34.（B） want ＋受詞＋ p.p.「要～被…」。（詳見文法寶典 p.454）

35.（C） 感官動詞 find ＋受詞＋ p.p.「發現～被…」。（詳見文法寶典 p.454）

36.（B） 感官動詞 see ＋受詞＋ p.p.「看見～被…」。

37.（D） Standing, $\overbrace{as\ it\ does}$ on a hill, 此句是表原因的副詞子句的倒裝，相當於 As it stands on a hill, 其中 as one does（or is）是插入語。（詳見文法寶典 p.530）　* villa〔ˊvɪlə〕n. 別墅

38.（A） 理由同上。

39.（A） 本題原句是由副詞子句When *I* walked along … 簡化而來，所以主要子句的主詞要用 I 。（詳見文法寶典 p.458）

40.（D） 當副詞子句改為分詞構句時，如果其主詞和主要子句的主詞相同，可把副詞子句的主詞去掉。根據句意，主要子句的主詞須用 Tom 。

41.（A） Being a good swimmer 是由表原因的副詞子句Because he was a good swimmer 簡化而來。(B) Good swimmer as he is「雖然他很會游泳」，不合句意。（此句型詳見文法寶典 p.529）

42.（B） 理由同第 28 題。

43.（C） although（or though）所引導的子句，在句意明確時，可省略主詞和 be 動詞。（詳見文法寶典 p.462）

44.（D） usually *giving* people …是由對等子句 *and* usually *gives* people …簡化而來的分詞構句。　* dissolved〔dɪˊzɑlvd〕adj. 溶解的　mineral〔ˊmɪnərəl〕n. 礦物

45.（B） 根據句意，主要子句的主詞是 the robbers 。

Ⅱ. 46.（ D ）　*stole* → **have stolen**　　and 兩邊所連接的時式通常必須一致，故 stole 應改爲完成式。

47.（ B ）　using → **used**　　used by …是由形容詞子句which is used … **簡化而來**。　＊ designate〔ˈdɛzɪɡˌnet〕*v*. 標明
dominant〔ˈdɑmənənt〕*adj*. 顯著的；有支配力的

48.（ A ）　*After finishing* → **He having finished**　　副詞子句中動詞的動作時間比主要子句動詞 awarded 的動作先發生，所以應改成完成式分詞；**He** 不可省略，因子句彼此主詞不同。
＊ citation〔saɪˈteʃən〕*n*. 褒揚

49.（ C ）　*it was difficult* → **I found it difficult**　　分詞構句意義上的主詞和主要子句的主詞須一致。而 knowing little about algebra 是由 Because I knew little about algebra 簡化而來的，因此主要子句的主詞應是 I。　＊ algebra〔ˈældʒəbrə〕*n*. 代數學

50.（ D ）　*Hank Aaron's record* → **Hank Aaron**　　理由同上。

Ⅲ. 51. *arrived*　　arrived at between them 是由形容詞子句which is arrived … 簡化而來；arrive at a conclusion「達成結論」。

52. *seen*　　本句原是由副詞子句 If it was seen … 簡化而來的分詞構句。
（ 副詞子句改爲分詞構句的方法，詳見文法寶典 p.458 ）

53. *boring*　　根據句意，用 boring 表「令人厭煩的」。

54. *invited*　　those invited 是由 those who were invited 簡化而來的，故 invite 應用過去分詞。

55. *saying*　　saying … 是由which said … 簡化而來的。

56. *surprising*　　表情緒的動詞，在「非人」作主詞時，常以現在分詞形式作形容詞用，表主動。（ 詳見文法寶典 p.390 ）

57. *killed*　　感官動詞 see 之後接過去分詞，表被動。

58. *open*　　with ＋受詞＋形容詞，表附帶狀態的獨立分詞構句。（ 詳見文法寶典 p.462 ）

59. *heard*　　make ＋受詞＋ p.p.「使～被…」。

60. *having died*　　His parents having died … 是由 After his parents have died … 簡化而來。〔詳見文法寶典 p.459（註 2 ）〕

61. *surprising*　　理由同第 56 題。

62. *concerned*　　so far as I am concerned「就我而言」。

63. ***read***   read〔rɛd〕carelessly 是由 which are read〔rɛd〕carelessly 簡化而來，read 的三態為 read〔rid〕, read〔rɛd〕, read〔rɛd〕。

64. ***performed***   performed by … 是由 which was performed by … 簡化而來。

65. ***Generally speaking***   generally speaking 「一般說來」。

Ⅳ. 66. Having, help   67. had, killed   68. There, being   69. Never having
70. Granting *or* Granted

Ⅴ. 71. As he was taken by surprise   72. Though he was taken by surprise
73. If he had been brought up in a better family   74. who live in towns
75. who was respected by all the villagers

Exercise 4

Ⅰ. 1.（ D ） be 動詞＋p.p., 表被動。

2.（ B ） 理由同上。

3.（ C ） become ＋p.p. 表「轉變」之被動語態。（詳見文法寶典 p.387）
    ＊ Americanize〔ə'mɛrəkən͵aɪz〕*v*. 美國化。

4.（ B ） be seated ＝ sit down 「坐下」。

5.（ D ） 本題應選(D)，不可選(A) robbed ，rob 的句型應該是 *sb*. be robbed of *sth*.「某人的東西被搶了」。

6.（ A ） need to be ＋p.p.（＝need ＋主動形式的 V-ing ）「需要被～」。
    （詳見文法寶典 p.430）

7.（ C ） be named ＋補語＋ after 「被以～的名字命名為～」。

8.（ B ） 依句意，本題應用被動語態；let 作「允許；讓」解時，通常不用被動語態。

9.（ C ） 依句意，用未來式及被動語態。

10.（ A ） be known to ～「為～所熟知」。

11.（ B ） be known by ～「根據～而知道」；A man is known by the company he keeps. 「〔諺語〕觀其友知其人」。

12.（ D ） be married to（＝marry）「嫁；娶」。（詳見文法寶典 p.389）

13.（ A ） 此題原句是 Yesterday an Englishman spoke to me. 改為被動語態則變成 Yesterday I was spoken to by an Englishman.

14.（ D ） 依句意，此題用 let 的被動語態：Let ＋受詞＋ be（原形）＋p.p. 。
    （詳見文法寶典 p.385）

15.（ A ）　belong to 「屬於」，沒有被動語態和進行式。

16.（ C ）　*sb*. be interested in *sth*.「某人對某事感興趣」。

17.（ D ）　have ＋受詞＋p.p.「使～被…」。

18.（ A ）　be pleased with 「對～感到高興」。

19.（ C ）　感官動詞的被動語態：be 動詞＋感官動詞的 p.p. ＋ to ＋原形動詞。
（詳見文法寶典 p.381 ）

20.（ D ）　get mixed up 「與（不良的事）有關係」。

21.（ B ）　此題用被動語態；pay attention to 「注意」。（「及物動詞＋名詞＋
介詞」的被動語態，詳見文法寶典 p.383 ）

22.（ C ）　be lost in thought 「沈思」。

23.（ C ）　S. ＋ be said to ＋原形動詞（ ＝ It be said that ＋S. ＋原形動詞）
「據說某人～」。（詳見文法寶典 p.386 ）

24.（ B ）　第三人稱的否定祈使句，其被動語態句型為：Don't let ＋受詞＋ be
（原形）＋p.p. 。（詳見文法寶典 p.386 ）

25.（ C ）　用完成式不定詞來表示發生在主要動詞（ is said ）之前的動作。

26.（ B ）　speak well of 「讚揚」，改為被動時，of 不可省。

27.（ A ）　have 在本題中為使役動詞，其後動詞須原形，這句話的意思是「他幾
年前慘遭喪妻之痛。」

28.（ B ）　be engaged in ～「從事於～」。

29.（ A ）　be delighted at ～「對～感到高興」。

30.（ D ）　be caught in 「被（暴風雨等）襲擊；遇上」。

31.（ C ）　be satisfied with ～「對～感到滿足」。

32.（ A ）　be covered with 「佈滿」。

33.（ B ）　be devoted to ＋N. *or* V-ing 「致力於～」。
　＊ arch（a）eology〔ˌɑrkɪˈɑlədʒɪ〕*n*. 考古學

34.（ B ）　be born of 「出身於」。

35.（ D ）　be absorbed in 「專心於」。

Ⅱ. 36.（ B ）　(B)→ She was cured *of* …　　cure *sb*. of ～「治癒某人的～」。

37.（ C ）　(C)→ They were made *to stay* at home.　　S ＋ be ＋使役動詞
的 p.p. ＋ to ＋原形動詞。

38.（ A ）　resemble （和～相像）不可用被動語態。

39. (B) (B) → Get the luggage *carried* …　　get ＋受詞＋ p.p.「使～被…」。

40. (C) (C) → At school he was informed *of* …　　inform *sb.* of *sth.*「通知某人某事」。

41. (D) (D) → Mother was relieved *to* …　　be relieved to ～「對～感到放心」。

Ⅲ. 42. (B) (A) → He was laughed *at* by …。laugh at「嘲笑」；
(C) → … without being reminded of。remind *sb.* of *sth.*「使某人想起某事」；(D) → … than can be *imagined*。be 動詞＋ p.p. 表被動。

43. (B) (A) → *My hat was blown off*。(C) → *His watch was stolen* …。
(D) → Water *consists of* hydrogen and oxygen. consist of（＝be made up of）「由～組成」。

Ⅳ. 44. (A)　*grown* → *growing*　　be growing up「漸漸長大」。

45. (A)　*said* → *told*　　say *sth.* to *sb.* ＝ *sb.* ＋ be 動詞＋ told ＋ *sth.*「告訴某人某事」。

46. (B)　*was made live* → *was made to live*　　使役動詞make 的被動語態句型與感官動詞相同，請參考第 19 題。

47. (A)　*regard* → *be regarded*　　依句意，本題應用被動語態；let ＋受詞＋ be（原形）＋ p.p. 表被動。

Ⅴ. 48. Let all the ceremony be done away with（by us）.

49. He is known to everybody.

50. The student seems to have been imprisoned（by them）.

51. The house is painted white.

52. What is this flower called in English?

53. It is supposed that he made great progress.
＝ He is supposed to have made great progress.

54. Particular attention should be paid to the handling of the engine.
＝ The handling of the engine should be paid particular attention to.

55. Let it be admitted that honesty is the best policy.

56. This problem has never been solved.

57. No notice was taken of my presence by him.

Exercise 5

Ⅰ.
1. (A)　suggest that … (should) ＋原形動詞，should 可以省略。(詳見文法寶典 p.372)

2. (D)　as if (好像) ＋ S. ＋ were (或過去式)，指與現在事實相反的假設。(詳見文法寶典 p.371)

3. (C)　此題陳述事實，故用直說法。

4. (C)　由 if you had hurried 可知，是表與過去事實相反的假設，故選(C)。

5. (B)　demand 屬慾望動詞，句型同第 1 題。

6. (A)　由 I would have to … 可知，是表與現在事實相反的假設。

7. (D)　由 yesterday 可知，本題是表與過去事實相反的假設，故子句中須用過去完成式；子句動詞的時態不受 wish 時態的影響。(詳見文法寶典 p.368)

8. (C)　理由同上一題。

9. (A)　由 I would have gone … 可知，是表與過去事實相反的假設，故選(A)。

10. (B)　由 … would you have done … 和 yesterday 可知，是表與過去事實相反的假設，故選(B)。

11. (D)　require 也是慾望動詞，句型同第 1 題。

12. (A)　If ＋ S. ＋ should ＋原形動詞，should 作「萬一」解，表可能性極小。(詳見文法寶典 p.363)

13. (B)　recommend 也是慾望動詞，句型同第 1 題。

14. (D)　should ＋ have ＋ p.p. 表過去應做而未做的事；回答問句時，應根據問句的時態來回答。

15. (A)　依句意，此句陳述一項事實，故用直說法；而 if 引導副詞子句，表條件時，其未來的動作要以現在式表示。(詳見文法寶典 p.356，327，354)

16. (B)　假設法的 if 子句中，可用 would 來表示「客氣的請求」；(A) should 「萬一」，不合句意；(C)(D)須改成過去式。

17. (A)　由 If a man doesn't remain … 可知，本題是直說法，故選(A)。
　　　＊ befall〔bɪˋfɔl〕v. 降臨。

18. (B)　由 I could find 可知，本題是與現在事實相反的假設，故選(B)。

19. (A)　由 if she ever found out 可知，本題是與現在事實相反的假設，故選(A)。

20. (C)　由 I would have ordered … 可知，本題是與過去事實相反的假設，
Had oranges not … season ＝ If oranges had not … season。
（ if 的省略，詳見文法寶典 p.365 ）

21. (A)　雖然 if 子句是與過去事實相反的假設，但主要子句出現 now，所以必
須改用與現在事實相反的假設。〔詳見文法寶典 p.364（注意 3 ）〕

22. (B)　should they believe 是由 If they should believe 省略而來。（詳見
文法寶典 p.365 ）

23. (A)　由 next week 可知，本題是與未來事實相反的假設，所以 wish 的子句
的動詞要用「過去式助動詞＋原形動詞」的句型。（詳見文法寶典 p.368 ）

24. (D)　由 now 可知，是與現在事實相反的假設，故選(D)。

25. (C)　依句意，as 所引導的子句是敘述現在的事實，故用直說法。

26. (C)　由 when he was in high school 可知，that 子句是與過去事實相反
的假設，故選(C)。

27. (B)　S₁＋would rather（ that ）＋S₂＋過去式（指與現在或未來事實相
反的假設）。（詳見文法寶典 p.370 ）

28. (D)　It is（ high , about ）time（ that ）＋S.＋過去式動詞（ or were ）
「是～的時候」。（詳見文法寶典 p.374 ）

29. (A)　What if（＝What would happen if ）「如果～怎麼辦」，表一種強
烈的情緒。（詳見文法寶典 p.367 ）

30. (A)　由 but 可知是敘述事實，故用直說法。

31. (B)　由 I would wear … 可知，是與現在事實相反的假設。
＊ stain〔sten〕n. 污點

32. (C)　由 Mary might have come … 可知，是與過去事實相反的假設。

33. (A)　except that ＋子句（直說法）「除～之外」。

34. (A)　hope 表示「能實現的願望」，故 that 子句用直說法。

35. (B)　由 then 可知，是與過去事實相反的假設。(C) should have been「應
該會」，不合句意。

36. (B)　But for＋名詞片語，主要子句（假設法）「如果不是因為～，…」。

37. (B)　由 He might have led … 可知是與過去事實相反的假設，故選(B) had
it not been for（＝if it had not been for ）「如果不是因為」。

38. (C)　根據句意，could 是表客氣的請求；would 表謙恭的請求時，通常用
於疑問句，在本題中(D) would be 不合句意。

39.(D) propose 是慾望動詞，句型同第 1 題。 if it should prove a failure 是與未來事實相反的假設，should 作「萬一」解，表可能性極小。

40.(B) It is necessary＋that＋主詞＋should＋原形動詞（表現在或未來）。（詳見文法寶典 p.374）
* be on the wrong side of～「（人）已過～歲」。

41.(D) little , if at all 「即使有，也很少」。

42.(C) 由… could exist 可知，本題是與現在事實相反的假設。 if it were not for 「如果不是因為」。

43.(D) 由 if I had thought … 可知是與過去事實相反的假設。

44.(C) 由 He lives … 可知， as if 引導與現在事實相反的假設法子句，句型同第 2 題。

45.(C) 由 now 可知，主要子句是與現在事實相反的假設，請參照第 21 題的說明。

46.(B) 理由同上一題。

47.(A) 由 before tomorrow 可知，本題是與未來事實相反的假說，句型請參照第 23 題；而 stop＋V-ing 「停止～」， stop to-V 「停下來去做～」，根據句意，選(A)。

48.(D) 本題中， that 子句是 suggestion 的同位語，表示「應該做而尚未做的事」，故屬於慾望動詞句型。句型請參照第 1 題。
* assent〔ə'sɛnt〕v. 同意　　parole〔pə'rol〕v. 假釋
custody〔'kʌstədɪ〕n. 監護

49.(C) 依句意，應選(C) otherwise 「否則」；(D) but that 「如果不是因為」之後的子句須用直說法；(A)(B)則不合句意。

50.(B) be＋S.＋ever so＋形容詞 「無論～多麼…」。（詳見文法寶典 p.634）

Ⅱ. 51.(B) *we all are → we all（should）be*　　理由同第 13 題。

52.(A) *knew → had known*　　由主要子句中的 you would never have doubted … 可知，是與過去事實相反的假設。

53.(A) *is → were*　　依句意，是與現在事實相反的假設。

54.(B) *was → were*　　由 today 可知，是與現在事實相反的假設。

55.(A) *have learned → had learned*　　由 if 子句的 when I was in college 可知，是與過去事實相反的假設。

II. 56.(B) (B)… ; if he *didn't work* hard, …→… ; if he **hadn't worked** hard, … 由 he would have failed 可知，此題應用與過去事實相反的假設法句型。

57.(D) (D) If she *were* left …→ If she **had been** left … 由 she would have been ruined 可知，應用與過去事實相反的假設法句型。

58.(D) (D) Though he would try → However hard he might try。

59.(A) (A) If he *made* …→ If he **had made** … 由 it would have made …可知，應用與過去事實相反的假設法句型。

60.(C) (C) If you *made* … → If you **make** one … 本題是以事實為條件，說話者心中並未存有與事實相反之意，故用直說法。

IV. 61. had not been for , had not been ill   62. had had , had helped

63. had had , had been   64. if , knew   65. wish , have met

66. had better   67. owe to   68. as if he were   69. pity , were

70. had examined

Exercise 6

I. 1.(A)   look like「長得像」，表事實狀態，不能用進行式。

2.(C) 根據句意，應用過去完成進行式 had been + V-ing ; lie + adj.（作補語用）「在（某種狀態中）」。（ lie 和 lay 的區別，詳見文法寶典 p.295）
   * dormant〔'dɔrmənt〕*adj*. 潛伏的

3.(D) 表情緒的動詞，在「非人」作主詞時，常以現在分詞形式作形容詞用，表主動。

4.(C)   be close to「接近」；(A)(B)皆無此種用法。

5.(D)   The reason … is + that 子句「～的理由是…」；但口語中有時也用 The reason … is + because 子句，此種用法並不正式。

6.(D)   seem + adj.（作補語用）「看起來～」。

7.(A)   sound + adj.（作補語用）「聽起來～」。

8.(A)   smell + adj.（作補語用）「聞起來～」。

9.(C) 本題是考 S + V + SC 的句型；the first …Washington 是主詞補語 a full general 的同位語。

10.(D)   remain + adj.（作補語用）「依然是～」。
   * controversial〔,kɑntrə'vɝʃəl〕*adj*. 爭論的

11.（ A ）　safe 通常放在 come , arrive , keep , bring 等動詞之後作補語。

12.（ B ）　be painted＋adj.（作補語用）「被漆成～」。

13.（ D ）　for oneself「自己；親自」；by oneself「獨自；獨力」；
　　　　　　of oneself「獨自」。

14.（ D ）　get to（＝arrive at＝reach）「抵達」。其後接地方副詞 there
　　　　　　時，to 必須省略。

15.（ D ）　have to＋原形動詞「必須～」；participate in＝take part in
　　　　　　＝attend（vt.）「參加」；參加會議不可用 join。

16.（ A ）　此題是 S＋V 句型。　＊resound〔rɪˈzaʊnd〕v. 起回聲

17.（ D ）　lie with（＝lie in）「在於」
　　　　　　＊administration〔ədˌmɪnəˈstreʃən〕n. 政府

18.（ A ）　由…get light 可知，應選(A) broke（原形 break）「（天空）破曉」。

19.（ C ）　resemble（和～相像）是及物動詞，後面直接接受詞。

20.（ D ）　survive（由～中生還）是及物動詞，後面直接接受詞。

21.（ D ）　tell *sb*. of *sth*.「告訴某人某事」。

22.（ B ）　explain *sth*. to *sb*.「向某人解釋某事」。

23.（ B ）　ask *sb*. for help「向某人求助」。

24.（ B ）　依句意，本題應選一及物動詞，除 raise「增加」以外，其餘皆為不
　　　　　　及物動詞。　＊violation〔ˌvaɪəˈleʃən〕n.（對法律的）違反
　　　　　　ethics〔ˈɛθɪks〕n.（作複數用）道德

25.（ B ）　seat oneself＝sit down「坐下」。

26.（ D ）　do the dishes「洗碟子」。

27.（ A ）　say 與 tell 均可表時間，但意思不同：The clock says two o'clock.
　　　　　　「時鐘是二點」；而 tell 則有「辨認」的意思，The child can tell
　　　　　　time.「那小孩能辨認鐘錶的時間。」

28.（ A ）　change trains「換火車」；(C) depart〔dɪˈpɑrt〕vi. 出發。

29.（ C ）　hang（掛，吊）的動詞變化為 hang hung hung；hang（吊死）的動
　　　　　　詞變化為 hang hanged hanged。（詳見文法寶典 p.296）

30.（ C ）　leave *sth*. to one's own judgement「讓某事由某人判斷」。

31.（ D ）　tell a joke「說笑話」。

32.（ B ）　wear hair「蓄髮」。

33.（ C ）　set *one's* hair in curls「把頭髮弄捲」。

34.(B) date with *sb*. 「和某人約會」。

35.(C) cash *sb*. a check ＝ cash a check for *sb*. 「替某人兌現支票」。

36.(C) tell ＋ *sb*. ＋ that 子句「告訴某人～」;(A) say 的句型是 say ＋ that 子句;(D) speak 的句型是 speak to *sb*. about *sth*.。(詳見文法寶典 p.299－300)

37.(C) My father gave a gift *to* me. ＝ It was a gift *to* me from my father. cf. a gift for ～「有～的才能」。

38.(D) owe *sb*. *sth*. ＝ owe *sth*. to *sb*. 「欠某人某物」。

39.(C) mail *sth*. to *sb*. 「寄某物給某人」。

40.(D) make *sb*. *sth*. ＝make *sth*. for *sb*. 「為某人做某物」。

41.(A) consider *sb*. ＋ (*to be*) ＋受詞補語「認為某人是～」。

42.(D) believe ＋受詞＋ to be ＋受詞補語「認為～是…」，其中 to be 可省略。

43.(D) leave *sth*. open 「使某物打開著」。

44.(C) get *sth*. ready 「準備好某物」。

45.(A) urge *sb*. to-V 「促使某人～」。

46.(A) (B) let 是使役動詞，之後必須接原形動詞;(C)(D) allow *sb*. to-V 「允許某人～」。

47.(A) enable *sb*. to-V 「使某人能夠～」。
　　　　 ＊ phase〔fez〕*n*. 階段　　　 tiller〔ˈtɪlɚ〕*n*. 耕者;農夫
　　　　 peasant〔ˈpɛzn̩t〕*n*. 農夫　　　 acre〔ˈekɚ〕*n*. 英畝

48.(B) but 連接文法作用相同的單字、片語或子句，故由 Nancy 可知，應選 (B) her singing。

49.(D) find ＋受詞＋ V-ing (*or* p.p.)「發現～」，根據句意，應用 V-ing 形式。

50.(B) find ＋ *sth*. ＋ p.p. 「發現某物被～」。

51.(A) look upon ～ as …「認為～是…」。

52.(B) be thought of as 「被認為是」。

53.(B) watch ＋受詞＋原形動詞 (*or* V-ing)「看著～」。
　　　　 ＊ correspondence〔ˌkɔrəˈspɑndəns〕*n*. 信件

54.(D) 感官動詞 see，之後接現在分詞，表當時正在進行的動作。

55.(C) 感官動詞 see，之後接過去分詞，表被動。

56.（ C ）　使役動詞 let，之後須接原形動詞。

57.（ B ）　have *one's* hair cut「剪頭髮」。

58.（ D ）　get ＋受詞＋ to-V「要～做…」。

59.（ D ）　get ＋受詞＋ p.p.「使～被…」。
　　　　　　＊ lawn〔lɔn〕*n*. 草地　　mow〔o〕*v*. 割

60.（ C ）　tell *sb.* ＋ to-V「告訴某人～」。

61.（ B ）　依句意應選(B) deny「否認」；(A) decline「婉拒」；(C) refuse「拒絕」；(D) reject「拒絕」皆不合句意。

62.（ A ）　由 did 可知，本題應用過去式，lie（ lie asleep「躺著睡覺」）的過去式為 lay，故選(A)。

63.（ A ）　do 在本題中，表「可；可用」，不是助動詞，如 That will do.「可以」。

64.（ B ）　依句意，除(B) hire「雇用」外，其餘皆不合句意。

65.（ A ）　依句意，除(A) rent「租」外，其餘皆不合句意。

66.（ A ）　consult a dictionary「查字典」。

67.（ C ）　除(C) enjoy「享有」外，其餘皆不合句意。

68.（ B ）　become of「（以疑問詞 what 為主詞）使遭遇」。

69.（ D ）　catch fire「著火」。

70.（ B ）　依句意，應選(B) reserve「保留」。

71.（ C ）　Rumor has it that 子句「謠傳～」。

72.（ A ）　依句意，應選(A) afford「付得起」；(B) affect「影響」；(C) assent「同意」；(D) assume「假設」，皆不合。

73.（ D ）　help oneself to「自行取用」。

74.（ B ）　leave a message「留言」。

Ⅱ. 75. Astonishment，deprived　76. understood　77. gains，loses
　　78. enables，to

Exercise 7

Ⅰ. 1.（ D ）　由 will 可知，本題應用未來式，選(D) one of these days「幾天內，不久」；(A) in those days「當時」；(B) on Sunday last「上周日」用於過去式；(C) already 通常用於完成式。

　2.（ B ）　用過去式問，則用過去式回答；not ～ until …「直到…才～」。

3.（A）　ago 與簡單過去式連用。（詳見文法寶典 p.247）

4.（C）　since 通常與現在完成式連用。

5.（B）　由 yesterday 可知，本題應用過去式。

6.（D）　recently 常與現在完成式連用；因為 New houses 作主詞，所以要用被動語態。

7.（C）　由句意可知，動作從過去某時（since noon）開始，一直繼續到現在仍在進行，故用現在完成進行式。（詳見文法寶典 p.349）

8.（A）　依句意，應用未來完成式，表在另一未來動作前，已經完成的動作。

9.（B）　理由同上一題。

10.（D）　long ago（很久以前）與簡單過去式連用。

11.（A）　理由同第 3 題。

12.（B）　理由同第 4 題。

13.（D）　由前後句意可知，應用現在完成進行式，表從過去某時間開始，一直繼續到現在仍在進行的動作。

14.（A）　由 in 1986 可知，應用簡單過去式。

15.（D）　belong to「屬於」沒有被動語態和進行式。

16.（B）　in those days「當時」，與簡單過去式連用。

17.（A）　have gone 表「已經到～去了」，只用於第三人稱；have been 則表「曾經去過」（詳見文法寶典 p.336）。由 he is not here 可知，應選(A) has gone。

18.（A）　主要子句的動詞為過去式時，其後名詞子句的動詞也要用過去式。
（詳見文法寶典 p.351）

19.（D）　after 所引導的子句，是在主要子句之前先完成的動作，故用過去完成式。（詳見文法寶典 p.338，③）

20.（B）　Let's … 後的附加問句用 shall we？

21.（C）　肯定祈使句之後，表示「請求」的附加問句用 will you。

22.（A）　Shall I …？（＝Do you want me to …？）用以徵求對方意見，故回答(A)最為恰當。

23.（D）　回答 Shall we …？時，若包括現在說話者，要用 let's …。

24.（A）　表主詞（You）的意志，助動詞用 will；You will …「你願…」。

25.（D）　表時間（或條件）的副詞子句，不能用 shall，will 表示未來，本題要用現在完成式來代替未來完成式。（詳見文法寶典 p.354）

26.（ D ） 依句意，須用未來完成式，又 corn crop 作主詞，故須用被動語態。

27.（ A ） 從 nowadays 可知，本題是敘述現在的事情，故用現在式來表示。

28.（ D ） 用現在完成式問，則用現在完成式回答；Yes 之後用肯定，No 之後用否定。

29.（ B ） since 所引導的子句，動詞用過去式。

30.（ C ） 依句意，應用過去完成式，表該動作比 recognized 先發生。

31.（ D ） 依句意，應用現在簡單式。

32.（ B ） 由 Up to now 可知，本題是表從過去某時到現在的經驗，用現在完成式。

33.（ C ） 依句意，用過去進行式表過去某時（ at five o'clock ）正在進行的動作。

34.（ D ） 敘述動作將繼續進行到未來某時，用未來完成進行式。

35.（ A ） 由 every morning 可知，表現在的習慣，用現在簡單式。

36.（ C ） not ～ but …「不～而…」。

37.（ D ） and 連接文法作用相同的子句，由 is dying 可知，空格應填現在進行式，而且依句意，應用被動語態。

38.（ B ） 由 On September 16 , 1620 可知，用過去式。

39.（ A ） 依句意，表過去所發生的事，用過去式。

40.（ C ） 依句意，表過去某時正在進行的動作，用過去進行式。
　　　　　 * grin〔grɪn〕v. 露齒而笑

41.（ A ） since 所引導的子句，動詞通常用過去式；(C) after 所引導的副詞子句是過去式時，其主要子句也應用過去式，故主要子句中的 *has not heard → did not hear*。

42.（ D ） so far「到目前為止」，依句意，表過去繼續到現在的動作，用現在完成式。

43.（ B ） since 通常與現在完成式連用。

44.（ B ） 過去兩個不同時間發生的動作，先發生的用過去完成式，後發生的用過去式。

45.（ C ） 理由同上一題。

46.（ D ） 依句意，表過去某時已有過的經驗，用過去完成式。

47.（ A ） 依句意，表未來某段時間將要進行的動作，用未來進行式。

48.(C) 依句意，表在未來某時之前，已經完成之動作，用未來完成式，而且要用被動語態。

49.(B) 表時間（或條件）的副詞子句，其未來動作要用現在式表示。

50.(D) no sooner ～ than …（一～就…）連接兩個過去的動作時，先發生的動作，通常用過去完成式表示。

51.(B) since 通常與現在完成式連用。

52.(A) and 通常連接兩個時態相同的動詞；而 advise（勸告）屬慾望動詞，故 that 子句中的動詞要用原形。

53.(C) 理由同第44題，not ～ long before「～不久，就」。本句意思爲「吃過早飯後不久，囚犯們在一名中士，一名下士和八名士兵的看守下，立刻上路前往沙瓦邦；在他們走後不久，傑斯波便向他的哥哥告別，假裝出去辦事。」
* sergeant〔'sɑrdʒənt〕 n.（陸軍）中士
corporal〔'kɔrp(ə)rəl〕 n.〔軍〕下士
take leave of 向～告別　　errand〔'ɛrənd〕 n. 差事

54.(D) 本題是「It is（or was）＋所強調的部份＋ that ＋其餘部份」的公式，not till … Population 即爲所要強調的部分，根據句意，It 的動詞應用過去式。
* Malthus〔'mælθəs〕 n. 馬爾薩斯（1766－1834，英國經濟學家）

Ⅱ. 55.(C) *will come → comes*　　表時間或條件的副詞子句，其未來的動作要用現在式表示。（詳見文法寶典 p.327, 354）

56.(B) *am hearing → heard*　　感官動詞（hear，feel 等）沒有進行式。

57.(D) *cook → cooks*　　從 always 可知，本句是表習慣動作，用現在式。

58.(B) *have you returned → did you return*　　疑問副詞when不能與現在完成式連用。（詳見文法寶典 p.336）

59.(C) *had known → knew*　　know（認識）是一時性動詞，不可用現在完成式。

Ⅲ. 60.(C) → When *did* you *go* to the park? 現在完成式不與疑問副詞when連用。

61.(B) → He *resembles* his father. resemble「像」，沒有進行式。
（詳見文法寶典 p.343）

62.(A) → When he *comes*, … 表時間的副詞子句，其未來的動作要用現在式表示。

63.（ D ）　→ I have **been to** … have gone 表「已經到～去了」，只可用在第
三人稱。

64.（ B ）　He has *not* been home (*for*) *a week.* 當 not 修飾副詞片語（for）
two years，for 可以省略，全句意思爲「他回家還不到一星期。」
（ not～ for ＋時間，詳見文法寶典 p.657 ）

Ⅳ. 65.（ D ）　*have left* → *left*　　理由同第 29 題。

66.（ B ）　*arrived* → *had arrived*　　主要子句的動詞爲過去式時，名詞子句
的動詞要用過去完成式。

67.（ C ）　*have been able* → *had been able*　　依句意，應用過去完成式表過
去某時（ until the day he died ）之前的繼續動作。

68.（ C ）　*had* → *has*　　名詞子句說的是眞理或不變的事實，一律用現在式。

69.（ D ）　*is belonging to* … → *belongs to* …　　belong to（屬於）沒有進
行式。

Ⅴ. 70. had given　　71. shall（＝will）have finished　　72. had heard
73. comes　　74. had done　　75. had not gone　　76. had been reading
77. has gone　　78. had been　　79. is *or* has been

Exercise 8

Ⅰ. 1.（ D ）　回答 must 的疑問句，肯定用 must，否定用 need not。（詳見文法寶典
p.318 ）

2.（ A ）　本題所強調的是 oppose，而非 used to，故可用 do 來代替前面已出
現過的 oppose；由前面子句的 never 可知，but 後面的子句是肯定
的，故選(A)。

3.（ C ）　回答問句時，可用 do 來代替問句中提過的動詞，以避免重複。

4.（ B ）　用 do 代替 live，以避免重複。

5.（ B ）　used to 的附加問句要用 didn't ＋主格代名詞？（ *or* usedn't ＋主格
代名詞？）

6.（ D ）　ought to ⎫
　　　　　　should ⎭ ＋ have ＋ p.p. 表「（過去）該～而未…」。

7.（ A ）　as ～ as ～ can be「非常～」。

8.（ B ）　回答 will 的疑問句，否定用 won't。

9.（D）　may have＋p.p. 表對過去的推測，肯定句中若表示 " perhaps "「也許」時，須用 may，could，might，故選(D)。

10.（B）　might as well ～ as …「與其…不如～」。（詳見文法寶典 p.317）

11.（D）　hardly「幾乎不」，本身已具有否定意味，助動詞不須再用否定。

12.（C）　used to＋原形動詞，表過去（規則）的習慣；be used to＋V-ing「習慣於～」。

13.（A）　had better＋原形動詞「最好～」。

14.（C）　It doesn't matter.「沒關係。」

15.（D）　Do you mind…？的回答句通常是 No，I don't。

16.（B）　had better not＋原形動詞「最好不～」。

17.（C）　need 在此當助動詞，不必加 s。（need 的用法，詳見文法寶典 p.321）

18.（A）　do 加在原形動詞前，表加強語氣，作「一定；的確」解。

19.（B）　由 now 可知，than 引導的子句須用現在式，又爲了避免重複，以助動詞 does 代替 smokes。

20.（D）　would like「願意；想」。（詳見文法寶典 p.310）

21.（C）　would rather＋原形動詞「寧願～」，否定則是 would rather not。

22.（B）　由 Did…可知是過去式，故應用 would rather＋have＋p.p.，表過去時間的寧願，又依句意，要用否定的形式。（詳見文法寶典 p.310）

23.（D）　would rather ～ than …「寧可～而不願…」，than 前後的動詞時式要一致，由 have left 可知，應選(D)。

24.（A）　依句意，本題是直說法。If I am＝If I am *going to be there*。

25.（C）　用現在完成式問，要用現在完成式回答。

26.（D）　It is natural（自然的）＋that＋S.＋（*should*）＋原形動詞，此句型表說話者認爲有「應該如此」的意思，所以 that 子句中的 should 是假設法，但在美語中常省略。（詳見文法寶典 p.312，374）

27.（B）　necessary 的句型，在本題中與第 26 題相同。

28.（A）　important 的句型，在本題中與第 26 題相同。

29.（C）　It is a great pity（很可惜）＋that＋S.＋should＋have＋p.p.（表過去），should 在此作「居然，竟然」解。（詳見文法寶典 p.375）

30.（D）　用 should 來表示「驚愕，惋惜」之意。（詳見文法寶典 p.375，（註3 ）〕

31.（B）　理由同第 30 題。

32.(C)　insist（堅持）是慾望動詞，其句型如下： insist＋that＋S＋
　　　　　（ should ）＋原形動詞。

33.(A)　recommend（建議）也是屬慾望動詞，句型同第 32 題。

34.(D)　advice 是慾望動詞 advise（勸告）的名詞，所以 that 子句的動詞形
　　　　　式也是「（ should ）＋原形動詞」。〔詳見文法寶典 p.373，（註3 ）〕

35.(B)　request（要求）是慾望動詞 request 的名詞，所以 that 子句的句型
　　　　　同第 34 題。

36.(D)　must have＋p.p. 表對過去的推測。（詳見文法寶典 p.319 ）

37.(A)　ought to 的否定是 ought not to。

38.(B)　be used to＋V-ing「習慣於～」。

39.(C)　need 具有助動詞和動詞兩種功能，但句型不同：〔助動詞〕need not
　　　　　＋原形動詞＝〔動詞〕don't need to＋原形動詞。

40.(B)　dare 也具有助動詞和動詞的性質，句型如下〔助動詞〕dare not＋
　　　　　原形動詞＝〔動詞〕don't dare to＋原形動詞。
　　　　　＊oriental〔‚orɪ'ɛntḷ〕adj. 東方的
　　　　　　subordination〔sə‚bɔrdṇ'eʃən〕n. 從屬；次要
　　　　　　prevail〔prɪ'vel〕v. 盛行

41.(D)　afford（～得起）常與 can 連用。

42.(A)　lest＋S.＋should＋原形動詞「以免～」。（詳見文法寶典 p.514 ）

43.(C)　so that＋S.＋may（ or might ）＋原形動詞「以便～」，如果主
　　　　　要子句為過去式，that 子句要用 might。（詳見文法寶典 p.513 ）

44.(C)　根據句意，應用 should＋have＋p.p. 表過去應該做而未做的事。
　　　　　（詳見文法寶典 p.311 ）
　　　　　＊conquest〔'kɑŋkwɛst〕n. 征服
　　　　　　unification〔‚junəfə'keʃən〕n. 統一

Ⅱ.45.(D)　*see → seeing*　　be used to＋V-ing「習慣於～」。

46.(A)　*is not able to → **cannot***　　「非人」作主詞時，不可以用 be
　　　　　able to。
　　　　　＊inorganic〔‚ɪnɔr'gænɪk〕adj.〔化〕無機的
　　　　　　pottery〔'pɑtəɪ〕n. 陶器　　shard〔ʃɑrd〕n. 碎片
　　　　　　artifact〔'ɑrtɪ‚fækt〕n. 加工品

47.(D)　*had → **might have***　　理由同第 43 題。
　　　　　＊superintendent〔‚suprɪn'tɛndənt〕n. 管理員

48. (C) *to pay* → **pay**　　need 在本句中作助動詞，後面須接原形動詞，故 pay 之前不可有 to 。

49. (C) *writes* → **write**　　suggest 屬慾望動詞，其後所接的 that 子句中，動詞形式是「(should)＋原形動詞」。

Ⅲ. 50. May　　51. should　　52. did　　53. cannot　　54. should　　55. should
　 56. can　　57. should　　58. would　　59. don't

Ⅳ. 60. must　　61. can't　　62. may not　　63. should　　64. needn't

Exercise 9

Ⅰ. 1. (D) 直接敘述改為間接敘述時，過去進行式要變為過去完成進行式。

2. (A) 直接敘述改為間接敘述時，若名詞子句說的是不變的事實，一律用現在式。

3. (B) 直接敘述改為間接敘述時，代名詞須做適當改變，現在完成式則改為過去完成式。

4. (C) 直接敘述改為間接敘述時，am going to → was going to；時間副詞 tomorrow → the following day 。

5. (B) 直接敘述改為間接敘述時，若名詞子句指不變的眞理、歷史的事實或假設法，子句動詞不變。

6. (D) 直接敘述改為間接敘述時，代名詞須做適當改變，現在式改為過去式，而 wish 之後 that 子句的時態，不受 wish 的影響。

7. (B) 直接敘述改為間接敘述時，代名詞須做適當改變，現在式改為過去式。

8. (C) 根據句意，地方副詞 here 不變，tomorrow afternoon 改為 this afternoon（今天下午）。

9. (A) 直接敘述改為間接敘述時，主要子句動詞為過去式時，that 子句中用 should 代替 shall 表"過去未來"。

10. (C) 直接敘述改為間接敘述時，代名詞須做適當改變，現在進行式改為過去進行式。

11. (B) 疑問句由直接敘述改為間接敘述時，如果沒有疑問詞，須用 if 或 whether 當連接詞。

12. (D) 疑問句由直接敘述改為間接敘述時，如果有疑問詞（what, who …），就以疑問詞作連接詞，現在式改為過去式。

13.（ C ） 理由同上一題 。

14.（ A ） 祈使句由直接敘述改爲間接敘述時，原祈使句要改爲不定詞形式，否
定字則要放在不定詞之前 。

15.（ D ） 祈使句由直接敘述改爲間接敘述時，動詞 say（ *sth.* to *sb.*）要依句
意適當改成 advise , order , tell , ask 等 。

16.（ B ） 動詞部分，更改理由同上題； tomorrow morning 依句意應改爲 this
morning 。

17.（ C ） Let's …由直接敘述改爲間接敘述時，動詞 say（ *sth.* to *sb.*）應改
爲 suggest（ to *sb.*）＋ that 子句，而 that 子句的主詞，根據句意，
要用 we 。

18.（ A ） 理由同上一題，但 that 子句的主詞，應用 they 。

19.（ B ） 依句意，連接詞應用 because，動詞則由現在式改爲過去式 。

20.（ C ） Would you …？（請您…好嗎？）是表謙恭的請求，由直接敘述改爲
間接敘述時，應在主要動詞之後加上 politely（客氣地），以保留原
句禮貌的語氣 。

21.（ D ） 直接敘述改爲間接敘述時，代名詞須加以適當的改變 。

22.（ A ） cry for help 「呼救」 。

23.（ D ） bid〔bɪd〕*v.* 說（問候話），其過去式爲 bade〔bæd〕。

24.（ C ） 感嘆句由直接敘述改爲間接敘述，動詞 say 要依情況改成適當的動詞，
How kind of you！（你眞好心！）有感謝之意，故選(C) 。

25.（ B ） 疑問句由直接敘述改爲間接敘述時，以疑問詞作連接詞，主詞要放在
動詞之前，問號改爲句點 。

26.（ B ） propose 屬於慾望動詞， that 子句中的助動詞須用 should 。

27.（ C ） with joy 「高興地」； in delight 「喜悅地」 。

28.（ D ） hello 是打招呼用語，故選(D) greeted 「向（某人）打招呼」比較恰
當 。

29.（ A ） 祈願句由直接敘述改爲間接敘述時，動詞須加以適當改變，依句意，
應選(A) prayed（祈求）。

30.（ D ） 理由同第 11 題，而子句的動詞應用過去式 。

31.（ A ） 假設法由直接敘述改爲間接敘述時，其時式不變 。

32.（ D ） Please go. 有祈求的意味，故選(D) 。

33.（ C ）「 suggest＋that 子句」由間接敘述改爲直接敘述時，that 子句應
改用 Let's …的句型。

34.（ B ）　advise 表勸告、建議，故選(B)。

35.（ A ）" I shall … "是單純未來，改爲間接敘述時，shall 必須根據主詞人
稱作變化（詳見文法寶典 p.333）：主詞是 he，子句時式爲過去式，故用
would 。

36.（ B ）理由同第 5 題。

37.（ C ）直接敘述中，若有兩個以上的單句，改爲間接敘述時，用 and 或 but
連接，其餘改法則參照直述句、疑問句等的改法。

38.（ D ） in the affirmative「肯定地」。

39.（ D ）原句中" Yes. "是" Yes, I will（ go there ）. "的省略，改爲間接
敘述時，應爲 I would 。

40.（ C ）理由同第 29 題。

41.（ B ）感嘆句由直接敘述改爲間接敘述時，可加上適當的修飾語，依句意，
應選(B) with a sigh「嘆息」。

42.（ A ）　express one's thanks「道謝」。

43.（ C ）依句意，應選(C) adding（＋that 子句）「接著說；補充說」。（這
裡的 adding … 是由 and added … 簡化而來的分詞構句。）

44.（ D ）疑問句由直接敘述改爲間接敘述時，沒有疑問詞者，要以 if 或
whether 當連接詞，「（助）動詞＋主詞」的次序改爲「主詞＋（助）
動詞」。

45.（ B ）　call to「叫喊」；直接敘述改爲間接敘述時，現在完成式要變爲過去
完成式。

I. 46.（ D ）　*the following day →* ***today*** 。

47.（ D ）　*liked →* ***had liked***　　直接敘述改爲間接敘述時，過去式要變成過
去完成式。

48.（ B ）　*us →* ***to us***　　suggest to *sb.* ＋ that 子句「向某人建議～」，
其中的 to 不可省。

49.（ C ）　*wishes →* ***wished***　　直接敘述是與（當時）現在事實相反的假設，
改爲間接敘述時要用過去式。

50.（ C ）　*told →* ***asked***　　疑問句由直接敘述改爲間接敘述時，動詞須用 ask,
inquire 等。

51.（ B ）　*and that* → **that**　　so … that ～「如此…以致於～」。

52.（ B ）　*but* → **but that**　　直接敍述中的名詞子句如果是由 but 或 and 連接對等子句而成的合句，改為間接敍述時，兩個對等子句前面都要加 that。

53.（ A ）　*to not make* → **not to make**　。否定字要放在不定詞 to 之前。

54.（ D ）　*make* → **made**　　直接敍述是現在式，改為間接敍述要用過去式。

Exercise 10

Ⅰ. 1.（ D ）　Waiter, two *glasses* of … → Waiter, two **cups** of … 計量 coffee（或 tea）的單位名詞，多用 cup。（詳見文法寶典 p.57）

　 2.（ C ）　He has done me many kindnesses.（他幫過我很多忙。）
　　　　　　　≒ He has done me very kindly.（他對我很仁慈。）

　 3.（ D ）　All the world *are* good. → All the world *is* good.　all the world「全世界（的人）；萬物」作主詞，後面要用單數動詞。

　 4.（ A ）　A Mr. Smith … phone. = Someone named Mr. Smith … phone.（一位名叫史密斯的先生打電話給你。）；One of … phone. 在美語中，無此用法。

　 5.（ D ）　兩句不等，advice 作為不可數名詞時表「忠告」，作為可數名詞時表「消息」。

Ⅱ. 6.（ A ）　物質名詞須用單位名詞來表數的觀念，a loaf of bread「一條麵包」。（詳見文法寶典 p.57－58）

　 7.（ A ）　furniture 是各種家具的總稱，屬集合名詞，但用法相當於物質名詞，須用 much，(a) little 等來表示量。（詳見文法寶典 p.59）

　 8.（ C ）　news 雖以 -s 結尾，却是單數意義，用法上相當於物質名詞，須用 much，(a) little 等來表示量。

　 9.（ D ）　a tube of toothpaste「一管牙膏」。

　10.（ B ）　information 用法上相當於物質名詞，須用 some，much 等來表示量，用 one（*or* a）piece of 來表示數。

　11.（ D ）　savings「儲金」。

　12.（ A ）　hall table「大廳的桌子」，hall 作形容詞，修飾 table。（名詞作形容詞的用法，詳見文法寶典 p.100）

13.(D) shoe store「鞋店」；(A)(B)指的是「鞋子所擁有的店」；(C)名詞修
飾名詞，應用單數形（詳見文法寶典 p.100 ）。

14.(B) 冠詞 a(n) 和所有格代名詞修飾同一個名詞時，要用「雙重所有格」
的句型：

$$\boxed{\text{a(n)} + \text{名詞} + of + \text{所有格代名詞}}$$ （詳見文法寶典 p.108 ）

15.(C) 名詞作形容詞來表單位，應該取單數形。（詳見文法寶典 p.87, 100 ）

16.(A) 表「時間」的名詞常用（'s）或（'）來表示所有格。（詳見文法寶典 p.95）

17.(A) 根據句意，應選(A)，an area of some 40,000 square miles（一
塊大約四萬平方英哩的地區）。

18.(C) 表數量的名詞，應放在 old，thick 等形容詞之前。

19.(B) 理由同上一題。

20.(D) one's favorite「某人最受喜愛的人（或物）」。

21.(B) one's preference「某人的偏好」。

22.(C) $\begin{cases} \text{little「很少」} \\ \text{a little「一些」} \end{cases}$ ＋不可數名詞，依句意，應選(C) little money。

23.(A) the police「警方」，用複數動詞。（詳見文法寶典 p.53 ）

24.(C) $\begin{cases} \text{damage「損失」} \\ \text{damages「賠償損失費」} \end{cases}$ ，依句意，應選(C) damages。

25.(B) $\begin{cases} \text{pain「痛苦」} \\ \text{pains「辛勞」} \end{cases}$ ，依句意，應選(B) pains。take pains「費力」。

26.(D) mathematics「數學」，雖看起來是複數，但其意義為單數，它屬於
學科的名稱，所以前面不加冠詞。（詳見文法寶典 p.223 ）

27.(A) nickel「五分鎳幣」，是可數名詞。在此用 A nickel 來表同類全體。

28.(D) 專有名詞作普通名詞用，可以有複數形，Mary 的複數形，直接在字
尾加上 s。（詳見文法寶典 p.60 ）

29.(A) 字尾無 s 的複數名詞，形成所有格時，要加（'s）。（詳見文法寶典 p.94）

30.(C) 表「距離」的名詞，常用（'s）或（'）來表示所有格，a stone's
throw「一石之遙」。

31.(B) 「雙重所有格」的句型：a（this，that，…）＋名詞＋of＋所有格
名詞。

32.(D) they 的所有格代名詞為 theirs。

33.（ B ）　表同位格常用 the ＋單數普通名詞＋名詞，如 the word peace（和平這個字）。

34.（ A ）　chapter seven ＝ the seventh chapter 。〔詳見文法寶典 p.178,（17）〕

35.（ C ）　act two ＝ the second act（第二幕）。

36.（ B ）　What kind of 後面的單數普通名詞不加冠詞。（詳見文法寶典 p.223）

37.（ C ）　of 可表同格關係，故前後名詞的單複數須對稱。（詳見文法寶典 p.588－589）

38.（ D ）　make friends with ～「和～做朋友」。

39.（ A ）　interest 在此作「重要性」解，of great interest「非常重要」；(D) interests「利益」。

40.（ B ）　advice「忠告」為抽象名詞，必須用單位名詞來表數的觀念，如 a piece of advice「一項忠告」。

41.（ A ）　a hair's breadth「千鈞一髮」。

42.（ D ）　keep a close eye on「注意」。

43.（ D ）　save *sb*. the trouble of「省了某人～的麻煩」。

44.（ B ）　spectacles（＝ a pair of spectacles）「一副眼鏡」，但在美語中，較少使用 a pair of spectacles 。

45.（ D ）　in one's thirties「在某人三十幾歲時」。

46.（ C ）　表個別所有，要把（'s）加在各名詞之後（詳見文法寶典 p.96），依句意，可知哥哥、妹妹生日雖在十月，但不同天，故選(C)。

47.（ A ）　依句意應選(A) delay「延誤」。

48.（ C ）　依句意應選(C) nuisance「討厭的東西（或人）」。

49.（ B ）　make no difference「一視同仁；沒有差別」。

50.（ D ）　依句意應選(D) affection「情感」。

51.（ B ）　依句意應選(B) debate「辯論」。

52.（ D ）　on the principle that 子句「依照～的原則」。

53.（ B ）　從 that was in him，可知已限定了範圍，名詞前要加定冠詞 the，由 him 可判斷出空格中的名詞須用單數形，故選(B)。

54.（ A ）　a man of science「科學家」。

55.（ C ）　專有名詞可作為普通名詞，空格中的 Picassos 作「畢卡索的作品」解，故須加上 s 。

Ⅱ. 56.（ C ）　*knowledges* → **knowledge**　　knowledge 是抽象名詞，沒有複數形。

57.（ B ）　*they* → **it**　　由 the buffalo 可知，(B)應改成 it，使前後主詞一致。

58.（ A ）　*their → **its***　　Rhodesia 是國名，代名詞所有格用通性的 its 。

59.（ A ）　*these kind of assignments → **these kinds of assignments***
　　　　　由 these 可知，kind 應用複數 。

60.（ D ）　*books → **book***　　another ＋單數名詞 。

Ⅲ. 61. fluent , speaker　　62. heavy , smoker　　63. astonished　　64. brought
　65. prevented　　66. honesty　　67. enable　　68. sight reminds　　69. make
　70. comparison

Exercise 11

Ⅰ. 1.（ B ）　everybody 之後的代名詞所有格多用 his 。

2.（ D ）　nothing but（ ＝ only ）「只有」。

3.（ A ）　none 可用來指人或物，nothing 多半指物，none but ＝ only 。本句
　　　　　是諺語：「只有勇士才配得美女 。」

4.（ B ）　not … any 是全部否定，本句意思是「他們我一個也不認識 。」；而(A)
　　　　　none ，(C) neither 本身已具有否定的意味，故不可再加上 not ；(D)
　　　　　someone 只可用在肯定句 。

5.（ C ）　other 在本題中作形容詞用，字尾不能加 s 。(D) another 多半接單數
　　　　　名詞 。

6.（ C ）　用 it 作形式受詞，代替後面的不定詞（ for us ）to travel 。

7.（ A ）　either 在此作副詞用，表否定的「也」。

8.（ B ）　so ＋助動詞＋主詞「～也是」。

9.（ D ）　another 在此作「再過～」解 。

10.（ A ）　依句意應選(A)「只要能填飽肚子，任何東西都可以」。

11.（ A ）　as ～ as any「不亞於任何一個的～」。

12.（ B ）　one thing ～ , another（ thing ）…「～是一回事 ，…是另一回事」。

13.（ D ）　be something of ＋名詞「稍有～之風」。（詳見文法寶典 p.132）

14.（ D ）　the others「其餘的人（物）」。（詳見文法寶典 p.141）

15.（ A ）　it was … night 是名詞子句，作 thought 的受詞，it 在子句中是主
　　　　　詞，故其後的代名詞要用主格，選(A) they 。

16.（ C ）　pickpocket 是 believe 的受詞，故 to be 之後應用受格 him ，以和
　　　　　pickpocket 形成同格關係 。（詳見文法寶典 p.108）

17.（ B ）　that 代替前面所提過的 the climate ，以避免重覆。（詳見文法寶典 p.122）

18.（D）　this ～ that …＝ the latter ～ the former …「後者～前者…」。
　　　（詳見文法寶典 p.123 ）

19.（C）　some ～ others …「有些人～有些人…」。

20.（A）　one 代替前面所提過的 watch，所以在形容詞 new 之前要加上冠詞 a。

21.（C）　it 作形式受詞，代替後面的 that 子句。

22.（B）　find it ＋受詞補語（多為形容詞）＋ to-V「發現～很…」。
　　　（詳見文法寶典 p.114 ）

23.（D）　such ～ that … 和 so ～ that … 都作「如此～以致於」解，但只有
　　　such 是形容詞，可與 be 動詞連用，作主詞補語。（詳見文法寶典 p.516）

24.（C）　it 代替 He … poverty. 整句話，以避免重複。

25.（A）　用 it 代替 This is Mr. Lin. 整句話。

26.（D）　and that ＋副詞或副詞片語「而且～」，that 代替前面提過的子句。
　　　（詳見文法寶典 p.122 ）

27.（C）　作 let 的受詞，故用 me。

28.（B）　it 用來代替 my passport，以避免重複。

29.（B）　one ＝ a job，指同類中的任何一個。

30.（A）　his 是所有代名詞，相當於 his ideas；因為主詞 ideas 是複數，所以
　　　動詞用 are。

31.（C）　so 代替 she will come tomorrow，作 believe 的受詞。（詳見文法寶
　　　典 p.128 ）

32.（A）　so 代替 Prof. Lee is very sick，作 I'm afraid 的受詞。

33.（D）　those 代替 the products，以避免重複。

34.（B）　such 在此作代名詞，相當於 a strong … nature，且本題應用被動語
　　　態，故選(B)。（詳見文法寶典 p.124）such as 之後應接（代）名詞，在
　　　此句型不合。

35.（C）　those present ＝ those who are present「凡是出席者」。

36.（D）　the same ～ as …「和…同樣的～」。

37.（B）　So ＋（助）動詞＋主詞「～也是」，因為問句中的 be 動詞，所以也
　　　必須以 be 動詞來回答。

38.（A）　one 不可代替不可數名詞（物質名詞和抽象名詞）（詳見文法寶典
　　　p.140），故選(A)。

39.（C）　用 us 當 men 的同位語，作為 treat 的受詞。

40.(C) that 子句是 it 的同位語，作為 see to「留意；照料」的受詞。

41.(B) 依句意應選(B)，not A but B（不是A而是B），動詞與靠近者一致。

42.(A) one ～ the other …「（兩者中）一個～另一個…」。

43.(D) 依句意，the one 指的是 exercise；the one ～ the other …「前者～後者…」。
　　　　　* preserve〔prɪ'zɝv〕n. 保持　　cherish〔'tʃɛrɪʃ〕v. 珍愛

44.(C) every other「每隔一個」。

45.(B) 由 asked 和 tomorrow 可知，應用 was going to-V 來表「過去即將做～」。

46.(A) what 作疑問代名詞，引導名詞子句，作 understand 的受詞，名詞子句要用「主詞＋動詞」的形式。（詳見文法寶典 p.146）

47.(A) 間接疑問句要用敘述句的形式，即「主詞＋動詞…」。

48.(C) what 在此作疑問形容詞，其所引導的名詞子句，也必須用「主詞＋動詞」的形式。

49.(B) 在「疑問詞＋do you think …」的疑問句中，do you think 是主要子句，但名詞子句的疑問詞卻須放在句首，根據句意，應用主格的 who。（詳見文法寶典 p.147）

50.(D) 由 was 可知，應選(D) each。其餘答案，皆不可用單數動詞。

51.(C) one ～ or another。

52.(A) for one reason or another「無論如何」。

53.(D) ～ one thing, … another（thing）「～是一回事，…是另一回事」。
　　　　　* obligation〔,ɑblə'geʃən〕n. 義務

54.(B) 疑問代名詞 what 引導名詞子句，作 see 的受詞，而 what 又在子句中作 like 的受詞；該名詞子句則須用「主詞＋動詞」的形式。

55.(C) nothing of the ＋名詞「絕不是～」。

Ⅱ.56.(B) *her → she*　　she 是 it 的同位語，由於 it 是主詞，故其後的代名詞要用主格。　* ambassador〔æm'bæsədɚ〕n. 大使

57.(B) *me → I*　　I 在本題中，作為主要子句中的主詞，故不能用受格。

58.(A) *you → yourself*　　及物動詞的受詞和主詞一樣時，用複合人稱代名詞。

59.(D) *him → he*　　he 是 the person 的同位語，由於 the person 在副詞子句中是主詞，所以其後的代名詞要用主格。　* *in charge* 負責

60. (D)　*their opponents* → **his opponents**　主詞 statesman 是單數，所以其後的所有格要用 his 。　* opponent〔ə'ponənt〕n. 對手

61. (D)　*him* → **his**　應用所有代名詞 his 來代替 his style 。

62. (D)　*isn't he* → **isn't it**　問的是 Everybody … party. 這整件事，故不能用 he，而要用 it 。

63. (C)　*another* → **the other**　兩者中的另外一個要用 the other 。

64. (B)　*nothing* → **anything**　根據句意，應用 anything 來表「隨時做他想做的事」。

65. (D)　*all them* → **all of them**　all 的後面不可緊接代名詞 。（詳見文法寶典 p.135 ）　* discharge〔dɪs'tʃɑrdʒ〕v. 開除

66. (A)　*who* → **whom**　whom 引導名詞子句，作 ask 的受詞，whom 在子句中，又作 inviting 的受詞 。

67. (B)　*than most* → **than that**　用 that 來代替前面提過的 the standard of living 。

68. (C)　*when* → **that**　It is（was）not until ～ that …「直到～才…」。

69. (A)　*Anybody never* → **Nobody ever**　在否定句中用 anybody 時，否定詞應出現在 anybody 前，如 There was nobody there.（＝There was not anybody there.）。

70. (D)　*them* → **those**　用 those 來代替前面提過的 the laws，以避免重複 。　* devise〔dɪ'vaɪz〕v. 計畫

Ⅱ. 71. others　72. another　73. those　74. it　75. itself　76. Such
77. myself　78. myself　79. one　80. others

Exercise 12

Ⅰ. 1. (B)　先行詞之前有 the only 修飾時，關係代名詞較常用 that 。（詳見文法寶典 p.153 ）

2. (C)　which 代替 He arrived … late. 整個子句。由子句前的逗點可知，這子句是補述用法的形容詞子句，所以不選(A) that 。

3. (D)　本題須關係代名詞引導形容詞子句，修飾 boys，而關代本身又作 with 的受詞，故選(D) whom 。

4. (A)　填關係代名詞作 seduced 的主詞，所以要用主格的 who 。
* seduce〔sɪ'djus〕v. 勾引

5.（ A ）　用 which 引導之形容詞子句，修飾 the one；(B)子句中缺少關係代名詞；(C)應把 which 之後的 it 去掉，以免主詞重複；(D)缺少動詞。

6.（ D ）　what 是複合關代，本身兼具先行詞和關代的作用，故前面不需要先行詞，which，that 則否。

7.（ B ）　than 接在 other 之後，表「除～之外」。

8.（ B ）　關代 as 代替 Most … him 整個句子，並引導補述用法的形容詞子句，補充說明Most … him；(C) that 不可用在補述用法的形容詞子句；(D) what 之前，不必有先行詞。

9.（ C ）　without question 修飾 believed，本題應用複合關代 whatever 來引導名詞子句，做 believed 的受詞；believe 是及物動詞，可直接接受詞，故(A)(B)中的 about 和 of 應去掉；(D)不合句意。

10.（ A ）　名詞子句中還缺少主詞，根據句意，應選主格的 whoever。

11.（ B ）　由子句前的逗點可知，這子句是補述用法的形容詞子句，根據句意，關代要用 which。

12.（ D ）　理由同第 6 題。

13.（ D ）　turn a deaf ear to「對～充耳不聞」。關係代名詞作介詞的受詞時，介詞可放在 which 或 whom 的前面或後面，但只能放在 that 的後面。（詳見文法寶典 p.154）

14.（ B ）　根據句意，應用 of which 來表所有格。

15.（ A ）　with fluency「流利地」，形容詞子句中應用 which 代替 fluency，作 with 的受詞。

16.（ B ）　for one's sake「為了某人的緣故」，形容詞子句中應用 whose 來取代 one's。

17.（ C ）　依句意，介詞應用 with，which 雖可作受詞，但只可代替「非人」，故應用 whom。

18.（ D ）　複合關代 whoever 引導名詞子句，作主詞；(A) Those who …作主詞；應用複數動詞；(B)(C)皆缺少關係代名詞。

19.（ B ）　根據句意，應用表所有格的複合關代 whosever 修飾 composition，並引導名詞子句，作 to 之受詞。

20.（ C ）　根據句意，應用表所有格的 whose，修飾 parents，並引導形容詞子句，修飾 boy。

21.（ A ）　what is ＋比較級「而且」，根據句意，應選(A) what is more 表好的方面。

22.（ B ） 依句意，應選(B) but（ ＝ that … not ）。它前面的主要子句一定有否
定的字，如 no，not 等，因而由前後的雙重否定，句意轉爲肯定。
（詳見文法寶典 p.160 ）

23.（ D ） 理由同上一題。

24.（ C ） than 後面省略 the war that（ ＝what ），as，than 後的 what 可省
略。

25.（ B ） 理由同第 22 題。

26.（ D ） 根據句意，子句應該用主動語態，因爲先行詞（ girls ）是複數形，所
以要用複數動詞。（詳見文法寶典 p.401 ）

27.（ A ） those who 「凡是～的人」。選(B)(C)，則 shall perish by it 缺少主
詞；(D) during 不能接子句爲受詞。
　＊ doctrine〔'dɑktrɪn〕n. 教條　　perish〔'pɛrɪʃ〕v. 毀滅

28.（ C ） be interested in 「對～感興趣」，子句中用關代 which 代替 the
subject，作爲 in 的受詞。

29.（ B ） 本題應用關係代名詞 whose 修飾 desires 和 impulses，並引導形容詞
子句，修飾 one 。　＊ impulse〔'ɪmpʌls〕n. 衝動

30.（ A ） the cure for … 「治療…的方法」，而不能用 sth.'s cure 。

31.（ D ） 由 better 可知應用 than，因作 than 的受詞，故關係代名詞用 whom；
(A) but 不合句意。

32.（ A ） 在限定子句中，受格的關係代名詞可以省略，本題中 whom 作 to 的受
詞，而被省略掉。

33.（ C ） 用 what 引導名詞子句作主詞，what 本身又作 need 的受詞；(A) what
本身即具有連接詞的性質，故不必加 that；(B) need 沒有進行式；(D)
缺少先行詞，不能用 which 。

34.（ D ） who 引導補述用法的形容詞子句，修飾 Chen Yi-an；(A)(B)皆無意義；
(C)缺少連接詞。

35.（ A ） 作 of 的受詞，故關代須用 whom；(B) who → **whom**；(C) all them →
and all of them；(D) which 只能代替「非人」。

36.（ C ） 先行詞 drug 是物，關代用 which，又由句意可知，應用現在完成式表
過去繼續到現在的動作或狀態；(D) what 本身可兼作先行詞，故 what
之前不須有先行詞。　＊ insulin〔'ɪnsəlɪn〕n. 胰島素

37.（ D ） 前面有 as 時，引導形容詞子句的關係代名詞用 as 。（詳見文法寶典
p.159 ）

38.（ A ） 前面有 such 時，引導形容詞子句的關代用 as 。（詳見文法寶典 p.159）

39.（ C ） 先行詞是句子時，引導形容詞子句的關代可用 as（或 which）。
（詳見文法寶典 p.160）　 * perceive〔pə′siv〕v. 察覺

40.（ B ） 關代 as 或 which 可代替一整個句子，但唯有 as 子句可放在句首。
* *play truant* 逃學

41.（ A ） what 本身可兼作先行詞，故 what 之前不須有先行詞，而 which 之前
一定得有先行詞，service 是不可數名詞，故用 little 修飾。

42.（ D ） 因前面有疑問代名詞 who，為避免 who *who* …的重複起見，所以用
that 代替第二個 who 。（詳見文法寶典 p.153）
* superstition〔,supə′stɪʃən〕n. 迷信

43.（ C ） 用 what 引導名詞子句作受詞補語。

44.（ B ） 由 town 可知，應用表地方的關係副詞 where，引導形容詞子句，修
飾 town 。

45.（ A ） 由 reason 可知，應用表原因的關係副詞 why，引導形容詞子句，修飾
reason 。

46.（ B ） 先行詞為 the day，故用表時間的關係副詞 when 。

47.（ D ） 先行詞為 Chicago，故用表地方的關係副詞 where 。

48.（ C ） 依句意應用表時間的連接詞 when 。

49.（ A ） 為簡潔起見，口語中常將關係副詞的先行詞省略（詳見文法寶典 p.244）。
本題原為 That's *the place* where the children sleep.

50.（ B ） 作 loves 的受詞，故用 whomever 。

51.（ A ） 依句意，要用關係副詞 how 來引導副詞子句；(B)(D)皆缺少先行詞；(C)
不合句意。

52.（ C ） 依句意，子句中應用關代 which 來代替 rich；(A) that 不可用在補述用
法的形容詞子句；(B) what 不可代替整個句子；(D) who 只能代替「人」。

53.（ D ） 根據句意，應用關係形容詞 which 引導補述用法的形容詞子句，which
本身又修飾 advice（「關係形容詞」，詳見文法寶典 p.166）。

54.（ A ） 用 whatever（＝ no matter what）引導副詞子句，表讓步；(B)
however 之後應有形容詞；(C)(D)皆不合句意。

55.（ C ） 由 clever 可知，複合關係副詞要用 however；(A)(B)(D)皆不可接形容
詞。

56. (B) 依句意，應用表時間的複合關係副詞 whenever（＝at any time when），故選(B)。

57. (D) 依句意，應用表地方的複合關係副詞 wherever（＝no matter where）。　* perseverance〔͵pɝsə'vɪrəns〕n. 毅力

58. (C) A is to B what C is to D「A 之於 B 猶 C 之於 D」。

59. (D) what with … and（*what with*）～「半因…半因～」。（詳見文法寶典 p.157）

60. (B) 只有關代 as 引導的補述用法的形容詞子句可放在句首，本題中 as 的先行詞是 he refused our request；(A) what＝(C) that which，不需要先行詞；(D) 關代 which 引導的子句，不能放句首。

61. (C) 用關係代名詞 whose 表示所有，修飾其後的名詞 smile 和 well-being。

62. (A) That is（*the reason*）why～「這就是為什麼～」。
　　　　* hushed-up *adj.* 隱瞞的　　scandal〔'skændl〕n. 醜聞
　　　　vulgarity〔vʌl'gærətɪ〕n. 粗鄙

63. (C) 理由同第 57 題。

64. (D) 由 vote for *sb.*「投票支持某人」可知，本題關代之前的介詞要用 for。
　　　　* representative〔͵rɛprɪ'zɛntətɪv〕n. 代表
　　　　voter〔'votɚ〕n. 選民

65. (B) 依句意，應用表地方的關係副詞 where。
　　　　* nourishment〔'nɝɪʃmənt〕n. 營養
　　　　fertility〔fɝ'tɪlətɪ〕n. 肥沃　　decay〔dɪ'ke〕v. 腐爛
　　　　sterile〔'stɛrəl〕n. 貧瘠的

Ⅱ. 66. (A) *whom → who*　　I am sure 是插入語，who 在子句中作主詞，故不可用受格 whom。

67. (B) *whomever → whoever*　　whoever 在子句中作主詞，故不能用受格，he thinks 是插入語。

68. (B) *who → whom*　　因作 believe 的受詞，故用 whom。
　　　　* marine biologist 海洋生物學家

69. (C) *has been → have been*　　which 用來代替 cities，故在子句中，應用複數動詞。　* bilingual〔baɪ'lɪŋgwəl〕*adj.* 兩種語言的
municipality〔͵mjunɪsə'pælətɪ〕n. 自治市

Ⅲ. 70. but　　71. whoever　　72. what　　73. as　　74. what *or* as　　75. which
76. but　　77. what　　78. what　　79. As

Exercise 13

Ⅰ. 1.（ A ） Democracy「民主政體」是抽象名詞，不必加冠詞。

2.（ C ） President（總統）之後有 of West Germany 修飾，有了限定範圍，故 President 前應加 the 。（詳見文法寶典 p.217）

3.（ D ） 公共建築、機關等名稱前，要加 the 。（詳見文法寶典 p.218）
  * residence〔′rɛzədəns〕 n. 住宅

4.（ C ） 在最高級形容詞前要加 the 。（詳見文法寶典 p.219）
  * mammal〔′mæml̩〕 n. 哺乳動物

5.（ A ） as 用於表讓步的副詞子句，相當於（al）though，其前的名詞不用冠詞，句型如下：（詳見文法寶典 p.529）
  名詞（不帶冠詞）＋ as ＋主詞＋動詞

6.（ B ） 語言名詞之後有 language 時，要有 the 。（詳見文法寶典 p.219）

7.（ A ） 兩個相對的名詞並用時，不用冠詞，由 was 可知主詞是單數，故選(A)。

8.（ C ） the 用在某些單數普通名詞前，可表示抽象觀念，本題中 the mother「母性」。（詳見文法寶典 p.49, 217）

9.（ D ） 本句為諺語：「一鳥在手勝於二鳥在林」，這裡的 a 相當於 one 。（詳見文文法寶 p.214）

10.（ A ） twice a week「一周兩次」。這裡的 a 相當於 each 或 every 。（詳見文法寶典 p.215）

11.（ B ） 本句為諺語：「同行是寃家」，這裡的 a 相當於 the same 。（詳見文法寶典 p.214）

12.（ A ） 根據句意，選(A)；(B)中的 the 應去掉；(C) *my picture* → *a picture of me*；(D)應改為 two more pictures 。

13.（ B ） * nationality〔,næʃən′ælətɪ〕 n. 國籍

14.（ C ） 表單位的名詞前要加 the , by the hour「按小時」。（詳見文法寶典 p.219）

15.（ C ） 海峽名稱前要加 the 。（詳見文法寶典 p.69）

16.（ D ） at sea「在航海途中」；(B) in the sea「在海中」。

17.（ C ） at half the price「以半價」。（half 的句型，詳見文法寶典 p.182）

18.（ D ） 在「 by ＋交通工具」的句型中，交通工具前不加 the 。（詳見文法寶典 p.219）

19.（ A ） enter college 進入〔就讀〕大學。

20.（ D ）　the＋形容詞＝人的單數名詞（詳見文法寶典 p.219）。本句為諺語：「唯有勇者才配得到佳人。」

21.（ A ）　the＋形容詞＝抽象名詞。

22.（ B ）　由句意可知，salt 有限定的範圍，所以前面應有 the。

23.（ C ）　the 可代替代名詞所有格，句型如下：
「動詞＋人＋介詞＋the＋人身的一部分」（詳見文法寶典 p.221），
catch *sb*. by the hand「捉住某人的手」。

24.（ B ）　pat *sb*. on the back「拍某人的背」。

25.（ C ）　look *sb*. in the eye「注視某人」。

26.（ D ）　have the＋抽象名詞＋to-V（＝be so＋形容詞＋as＋to-V）
「非常～地…」。（詳見文法寶典 p.70）

27.（ A ）　樂器名稱前要加 the。（詳見文法寶典 p.219）

28.（ A ）　supper，breakfast，lunch，dinner 前不加冠詞。（詳見文法寶典 p.222）

29.（ B ）　三餐名稱若有形容詞修飾時，要加冠詞。因無特別指明，用不定冠詞即可。

30.（ B ）　the＋序數＋名詞「第～的…」。

31.（ C ）　理由同上一題。

32.（ A ）　second 作「另一個」解時，前面應有不定冠詞 a。

33.（ D ）　the 用在某些單數名詞前表抽象的觀念，the church「聖職；教會的職務」。

34.（ C ）　the＋形容詞＝人的集合名詞，the deceased「死者」（單複數同形）。

35.（ A ）　運動名詞前不加 the。（詳見文法寶典 p.222）

36.（ A ）　what species of 後面的單數普通名詞不加冠詞。（詳見文法寶典 p.223）

37.（ B ）　在一件東西附屬於其他東西上而成為一件東西時，冠詞只用一個。
〔詳見文法寶典 p.225，（註2）〕

38.（ D ）　由 was 可知，主詞是單數名詞，應是 a black and white dog「一隻黑白相間的狗」，而不是 a black and a white dog「一隻黑狗和一隻白狗」。

39.（ C ）　double 的句型：double the＋名詞「～的兩倍」。（詳見文法寶典 p.182）

40.（ A ）　so 的句型：so＋形容詞＋a(n)＋名詞。（詳見文法寶典 p.216）

41.（ C ）　as 的句型和上一題 so 的一樣，請參照第 41 題。

42. (B) such 的句型：such a(n) ＋形容詞＋名詞。

43. (C) 河流名稱前要加 the（詳見文法寶典 p.63,218）；The Thames「泰晤士河」。

44. (A) tell the truth「說實話」。

45. (C) the ＋比較級＋of the two「兩者中比較～的」。〔詳見文法寶典 p.201.（註 1 ）〕

46. (A) 表示官職、身份、頭銜的名詞，作補語時，不用冠詞。（詳見文法寶典 p.221）

47. (C) the late「已故的」。

48. (C) Spring 之後有 of 1980 限制了範圍，所以前面要有 the。

49. (A) It is fun ＋ to-V「～很有趣」。fun 是抽象名詞，之前不需要冠詞。

50. (B) a large population「廣大的人口」。

51. (B) off duty「不值班」。

52. (D) 兩個相對的名詞並用時，不需冠詞，hand in hand「手拉著手」。
（詳見文法寶典 p.222）

53. (B) set up an alibi「證明案發時不在現場」。
* alibi〔'ælə,baɪ〕n. 不在場證明

54. (B) 報紙名稱前要加 the。（詳見文法寶典 p.64,218）
* subscriber〔səb'skraɪbɚ〕n. 訂戶

55. (B) knock 在此指「敲門聲」，是普通名詞，前面應加冠詞。
* **be absorbed in** 專心於

56. (C) 理由同第 14 題。　* slogan〔'slogən〕n. 標語；口號

57. (A) man to man「人與人之間相互比較」。

58. (C) 「動詞＋人＋介詞＋ the ＋人身的一部分」句型中的 the 不可用 his,
her …代替；take sb. by the arm「捉住某人的手臂」。
* picture gallery 畫廊　deposit〔dɪ'pazɪt〕v. 存放

59. (B) the middle 1700's「一七〇〇年代中期」。

II. 60. (B) *good swimmer → good a swimmer*　as 的句型：as ＋形容詞＋
a(n) ＋名詞。

61. (C) *of trade → of the trade*　most of the ＋名詞「大部分的～」。

62. (A) *kind of an → kind of*　kind of 後面的單數普通名詞不加冠詞。
* reluctant〔rɪ'lʌktənt〕adj. 難駕馭的；勉強的

63. (A) *an → a*　wealthy 是子音開頭的單字，冠詞應用 a。

64.（ A ）　*the church → church*　　after church「在做過禮拜後」。

Ⅲ. 65. a *or* the　　66. the　　67. an , a　　68. a　　69. x　　70. a *or* the

71. The , the　　72. the　　73. a　　74. a , the , a , the

Exercise 14

Ⅰ. 1.（ D ）　a living language「現行的語言」; alive 只作敘述用法 , 後面不可
接名詞（詳見文法寶典 p.191 ）。

2.（ C ）　something ＋形容詞。

3.（ D ）　be like ～「像～」;（A) alike 只作敘述用法 , 後面不接名詞;（B) be
similar *to* ～「與～類似」;（C)無此片語。
* *in many respects* 在許多方面

4.（ A ）　much ＋不可數名詞;（B) a little 在此不合句意;（C) many ,（D) few 之
後須接可數名詞。

5.（ D ）　a little「一些」＋不可數名詞;（C) little「很少」, 不合句意。

6.（ D ）　「the ＋形容詞」在此作複數普通名詞 , 表「～人們」。（詳見文法寶
典 p.192 ）

7.（ B ）　根據句意 , 應選(B) , too ～ to-V「太～而不能…」, little ＋不可
數名詞。

8.（ C ）　be welcome to-V「受歡迎～」。　　* *drop by* 順道拜訪

9.（ C ）　thousands of「成千的」; thousand（ *or* million ）前有數詞時 , 不
可加 s 。（詳見文法寶典 p.177 ）

10.（ A ）　a small salary「微薄的薪水」。

11.（ D ）　由 than 可知 , 應用比較級形容詞 fewer 修飾 children ;（C) less ＋不
可數名詞 , 在此不合。

12.（ B ）　a small number of「少數的」;（A) little ＋不可數名詞;（C) few ＋
複數可數名詞。

13.（ C ）　be unable to-V「無法～」;（A) impossible 是非人稱形容詞 , 不可
以人為主詞;（B) be incapable *of* ＋ V-ing「不能～」。（非人稱形容
詞的用法 , 詳見文法寶典 p.194 ）

14.（ C ）　remain ＋形容詞「保持～（狀態）」。

15.（ A ）　be worth ＋名詞「值～」; be worthy *of* ＋（動）名詞 *or* be worthy
to-V「值得～」;（C)應改為 worthy to be bought 。（ worth 和 worthy 的
句型 , 詳見文法寶典 p.443 ）

16.（B） enough＋名詞「足夠的～」；(A) plenty *of*「很多的」。

17.（C） $\left.\begin{array}{l}\text{most of the}\\\text{most}\end{array}\right\}$＋複數名詞「大多數的～」。

18.（D） any 用於否定句、疑問句或條件句；(C) some 多用於肯定句。

19.（B） no＋單數可數名詞（＝not a(n)＋單數可數名詞）；(D) none＝no ＋單數名詞。
* invertebrate〔ɪn'vɝtəbrɪt〕*adj.* 無脊椎動物
  spine〔spaɪn〕*n.* 脊骨

20.（A） alive（活著的）是限定形容詞，它的位置必須在它所修飾名詞的後面。（詳見文法寶典 p.188, 192）

21.（C） few＋複數名詞「很少～」；(A) scanty「（大小或數量）不足的」在此不合；(B) little＋不可數名詞；(D) a *little* number of man → a *small* number of men。

22.（B） some of＋複數可數名詞「～之中一些」；(A) A *fewer* → A *few*；(C) much，(D) a little of＋單數不可數名詞。

23.（A） quite＋a(n)＋形容詞＋名詞（＝a quite＋形容詞＋名詞）「相當～的…」。（詳見文法寶典 p.216）

24.（C） a large number of＋複數名詞「很多～」；(B) a large amount of ＋單數不可數名詞「大量的～」。

25.（D） of the same weight「重量相等」。（「of＋形容詞＋名詞」的句型，詳見文法寶典 p.546）

26.（C） lay 在此作形容詞，作「外行人的」解，是 expert 的相反詞。

27.（D） be glad（that）＋子句「很高興～」。

28.（A）「三杯黑咖啡」口語可說 three black coffees（詳見文法寶典 p.57）；(B) some 是不定數量形容詞，不可與數詞連用。
* platter〔'plætɚ〕*n.*（盛魚、肉用之）大淺盤
  shrimp〔ʃrɪmp〕*n.* 小蝦

29.（B） chapter five（＝the fifth chapter）「第五章」。

30.（D） be worth＋受詞「有～的價值」；(A) value 是名詞，作「價值」解；(B) cost 是動詞，作「花費（多少錢）」解，不可用於被動式；(C) be worthy 之後可接 of＋（動）名詞，或 to-V，「值得～」。

31.（A） It is＋非人稱形容詞（easy，necessary…）＋for＋*sb.*＋to-V「對（某人）而言～」。（詳見文法寶典 p.194）

32.(C)　理由同第31題。

33.(D)　It is certain that ＋子句「～是必然的」。

34.(A)　sympathetic 作「富同情心的」解；(C) pitiful 是「令人同情的」，
不合句意。

35.(B)　palm tree（棕櫚）是熱帶或亞熱帶的植物，故選(B) warm。

36.(A)　感官動詞 feel，taste 等以形容詞作補語。

37.(B)　理由同第36題。
　　＊ chicory〔'tʃɪkrɪ〕n. 菊苣（根可為咖啡的代用品）

38.(C)　find ＋受詞＋ p.p. 改為被動語態，則為主詞（原受詞）＋ be ＋
found ＋ p.p.；(A) to be abandoned，作補語時，在分詞前，to be
該省略。

39.(D)　be afraid 以 that 子句作受詞，故空格內需填動詞，選(D) seems。

40.(A)　動名詞的意義主詞，與句子的主詞不同時，須表示出來。I am sure
of its being true. ＝ I am sure（ that ）it is true. （詳見文法寶
典 p.426）；(B)動名詞 being 缺乏意義上的主詞。

41.(B)　quite a few「相當多」，含肯定的意味；(D)的意思與 Yes 不一致；
(A)(C)只能指不可數名詞。

42.(A)　a little late「遲一點」。a little 在此是表程度的副詞，修飾
late；(B) a few *late hours* → a few *hours late*；(C) *late* several
hours → *late by* several hours；(D)無此用法。

43.(C)　some 一般用於肯定句，但在疑問句中，若期望對方有肯定的回答，
則可用 some。（詳見文法寶典 p.130）

44.(B)　be respectful towards ～「對～表示尊敬」；(A)可尊敬的；(C)個別
的；(D)關於。

45.(C)　根據句意，應選(C) momentous「重要的」；(A)(D)瞬間的；(B)瞬間地。

46.(C)　unilateral 作「單方面的」解，因此應選(C) one-sided；(A)遍及全世
界的；(B)合作的；(D)懷惡意的。
　　＊ unilateral〔ˌjunɪ'lætərəl〕adj. 單方面的

47.(B)　根據句意，應選(B) eminent「傑出的」；(A)迫切的；(C)嫉妒的；(D)立
即的。　＊ untarnished〔ʌn'tɑrnɪʃt〕adj. 未玷汙的

48.(D) 根據句意，應選(D) mortal「會死的」；(A)道德的；(B)不道德的；(C)不朽的。

49.(A)「the＋形容詞」在此作複數普通名詞，表「～人們」，故動詞用複數。

50.(C) be close to「接近」；(A)(B)(D)皆無此種用法。

51.(B) 方位的表達法：「西南」south-west，「西北」north-west，「東南」south-east，「東北」north-east。

52.(D) keep good hours「早睡早起」。

53.(B) be equivalent to「等於」；(D)可利用的。
　　　　* equivalent〔ɪˋkwɪvələnt〕adj. 相等的

54.(C) something wrong with sth.(or sb.)「某物（或某人）有毛病」；(B) something the matter with＋sb.「某人有問題」。

55.(D) The early bird catches the worm.「（諺語）捷足先登。」。
　　　　* shrewd〔ʃrud〕adj. 精明的

56.(A) fall short of「未達到」；(C) fall behind「落後」。

57.(B) the last＋名詞「最不可能的～」（詳見文法寶典p.199）；(A)(C)不合句意；(D) hardly 是副詞，不能修飾名詞。

58.(C) every 和 each 都可指「每一個」，但 every 還可作「所有可能的」解，如：I have every confidence in him.「我完全信任他。」而 each 無此用法；(A) any 用於否定句；(D) all＋複數可數名詞。

59.(B) grave 在此作「嚴重的」解；(A)自私的；(C)守時的；(D)有能力的；皆不合句意。

60.(D) be preferable to～「比～好」（詳見文法寶典p.204）；(A)(B)(C)皆與than 連用。

61.(A) anything＋副詞＋形容詞，形容詞修飾 anything，副詞修飾形容詞。（詳見文法寶典p.187）

62.(C) time immemorial「太古」是慣用語。（詳見文法寶典p.189）

63.(B) 根據句意，應選(B) not a few「許多」；(A)(C)無此用法；(D) not a little＋單數不可數名詞。

64.(D) 理由同第9題。

65.(D) 根據句意，應選(D) prudent「謹慎的」；(A)大膽的；(B)強壯的；(C)害怕的。　* alert〔əˋlɜt〕adj. 留心的

Ⅱ. 66.（A）　*considerable* → **considerate**　　considerable 作「相當大的」解，不合句意，故應改爲 considerate「爲別人著想的」。

67.（D）　*a very little age* → **a very small age**　　at a very small age「年紀非常小時」。

68.（B）　*because of* → **due to**　　It is（was）because of ~ **that** … ，本題中缺少表結果的 that 子句，故應改成 due to 。
（參考英文正誤用法辭典 p.58）

69.（A）　*realizes* → **realize**　　few 或 a few 作主詞時，動詞要用複數形式。

70.（A）　*is* → **are**　　主詞 a number of things 是複數，故須用複數動詞。

Ⅲ. 71. wide　72. independent　73. free　74. many　75. good　76. Dutch　77. last

Exercise 15

Ⅰ. 1.（D）　much ＋比較級形容詞，very ＋原級形容詞。（修飾各級形容詞的副詞，詳見文法寶典 p.207）(A)比較級 younger 之前，不可加 more 。

2.（A）　take off（脫下）是由「動詞＋介副詞」所組成的動詞片語，當受詞是代名詞時，句型是「動詞＋代名詞＋介副詞」（詳見文法寶典 p.265）；(C) put off「延期」，不合句意。

3.（A）　downstairs 是副詞，前面不加介系詞或冠詞。

4.（B）　go home「回家」，home 作副詞，前面不加介系詞。

5.（D）　yet 用於否定句，作「還」解；(A) already 用於肯定句，作「已經」解；(B)(C)不合句意。

6.（A）　much less「更不用說」，用於否定句；(B) still more「更何況」，用於肯定句。

7.（C）　too ~ for ＋（動）名詞「對~而言太…」。
　　　＊ stern〔stɝn〕*adj*. 嚴苛的

8.（B）　頻率副詞＋一般動詞。（詳見文法寶典 p.265）

9.（C）　too ~ to …「太~而不能…」含否定的意味，而 any 常用於否定句中，故選(C)；(D)不合句意。

10.（D）　祈使句 Don't …的一般回答爲 No, I won't. 或 I'm sorry, but …
（詳見文法寶典 p.256）

11.（B）　回答問句時，Yes 表示肯定，no 表示否定，本題中，只有(B)的 Yes 和 a little 語氣一致；(A)(C)(D)都前後矛盾。

12.（ B ）　before 常與過去完成式連用，ago 則常與簡單過去式連用。
　　　　　（詳見文法寶典 p.247）

13.（ B ）　later「稍後」其前常伴有時間名詞；(A) late 應改爲 later；(C)
　　　　　latter 爲形容詞；(D) last 不放在時間名詞之後。

14.（ D ）　Do you mind…？的回答多爲 No, not at all. 或 Yes, I do.，但選
　　　　　(A) Yes, I do 則和 You can smoke here. 不合，故選(D)。

15.（ B ）　否定詞在句首時，句子中的主詞和（助）動詞須倒裝，其句型爲：否
　　　　　定詞＋助動詞（ or be 動詞）＋主詞。（詳見文法寶典 p.629）

16.（ B ）　根據句意應選(B)，How soon～？主要指的是時間的快慢；How fast
　　　　　～？則指動作上速度的快慢。

17.（ C ）　hardly 是副詞，作「幾乎不」解，通常放在 be 動詞之後，一般動詞
　　　　　之前；(A) *study* hard 和(D) studying *hardly* 都應改爲 *studying* hard
　　　　　「用功讀書」。

18.（ A ）　根據句意，finally 是用來修飾 decided，故選(A)；(B)(C) finally 可能
　　　　　用來修飾 decided，也可能用來修飾 take，句意混淆；(D)無此用法。

19.（ A ）　副詞＋enough to-V「～足以…」。（詳見文法寶典 p.417）

20.（ D ）　no～whatever「完全沒有～」，whatever 在此加強 no 的語氣。

21.（ A ）　用 on earth「究竟」加強疑問詞 what 的語氣；(B) *in world* → *in*
　　　　　the world「究竟」，放在疑問詞之後，也可加強語氣。

22.（ C ）　句中有助動詞時，already 的位置多在助動詞和動詞之間（詳見文法寶
　　　　　典 p.266）故用過去完成式。

23.（ B ）　still 表動作或狀態的持續，作「仍然」解；(A) yet 用於否定句，作
　　　　　「還」解，通常置於句尾；(C) already 多用於肯定句；(D) any more
　　　　　的位置須在否定字之後。

24.（ C ）　答句的主詞與動詞須與問句一致。

25.（ D ）　before long「不久」；(A)「不到很多天」不合句意；(B) some time
　　　　　「來日」是副詞片語，前面不接 before；(C) in *few* days → in *a*
　　　　　few days「再過幾天」。

26.（ A ）　near 本身即爲介系詞，可直接接名詞。（詳見文法寶典 p.194）(B) *close*
　　　　　→ *close to*；(C) nearly「幾乎」，是副詞，不合句意；(D) *next* →
　　　　　next to。

27.（ B ）　had better not ＋原形動詞「最好不要～」。

28.（ D ）　ago 和簡單過去式連用；ever since（＝ever since then）「從那時以後」，用於現在完成式。（詳見文法寶典 p.247）

29.（ C ）　much too late「（指時間）非常晚」。

30.（ B ）　連接兩個子句，須用連接詞，故選(B)，immediately 是由副詞轉變成的連接詞。（詳見文法寶典 p.496）

31.（ D ）　根據句意，選(D) respectively「分別地」；(A)不公平地；(B)相等地；(C)不同地，都不合。

32.（ A ）　連接兩個對等子句，須用對等連接詞，又(D) therefore「因此」，不合句意，故選(A) otherwise「否則」。（otherwise 的用法，詳見文法寶典 p.474）

33.（ C ）　far too～「太～」，far 可用來修飾 too 和比較級；(A) so much ＋名詞；(B) lots of ＋名詞；(D)（very）much 通常用來修飾過去分詞形的形容詞，尤其是表感情、心理狀態的情形。

34.（ B ）　for the most part「大體上」。

35.（ A ）　so ～ that ＋子句「如此～以致於」。（詳見文法寶典 p.516）

36.（ D ）　neither「也不」用於句首時，主詞與助動詞須倒裝；(A) I don't *too* 和(B) *either don't I* 應改為 I don't, *either*；(C) neither 本身已有否定含意，不須再和 not 連用。

37.（ B ）　for ＋時間「在～期間」，常與現在完成式連用。（詳見文法寶典 p.335）
　　　　　 ＊ doctoral〔ˈdɑktərəl〕*adj.* 博士的

38.（ A ）　so 置於句首時，主詞與 be 動詞須倒裝。（詳見文法寶典 p.643）

39.（ C ）　neither 用於句首時，主詞與助動詞須倒裝；neither 用於否定句，so 用於肯定句，故選(C)。

40.（ D ）　在對話中，常用 not 接在 hope，fear 等動詞後代替省略的否定子句（詳見文法寶典 p.129,640），I hope not.（＝I hope that your leg is not broken.）

41.（ A ）　「一～就…」的句型：（詳見文法寶典 p.497）
　　　　　 No sooner ＋ had ＋主詞＋ p.p. ＋ than ～
　　　　　 ＝ Hardly ＋ had ＋主詞＋ p.p. ＋ when ～
　　　　　 ＝ The moment（*that*）＋主詞＋過去式動詞，～
　　　　　 ＝ Directly（*when*）＋主詞＋過去式動詞，～

42.（ B ）　ever so ＝ very，ever 用來加強語氣。（詳見文法寶典 p.248）

43.（ A ）　shut ＋代名詞＋ off from ～「避開～」。

44.（ C ） not so much as「甚至不」。

45.（ D ） no more ～ than …「和…一樣不～」。（詳見文法寶典 p.202）

46.（ B ） how often 的問句須回答次數（ times ）（詳見文法寶典 p.241），又比較級前不加定冠詞，故選(B)。。

47.（ A ） 根據句意,應選(A) sometime「某個時候」,全句譯成:「那可憐的老人,病重到上個月某個時候去世。」;(B) sometimes「有時候」;(C) some times「幾次」;(D) some time「一些時間」。

48.（ A ） 用 a little 修飾比較級。(B)(C)(D)都不合。

49.（ C ） five o'clock *sharp*「五點正」。

50.（ D ） 「形容詞＋and」可當副詞用（詳見文法寶典 p.466）,選(D) nice and（＝very）。

51.（ B ） 根據句意,選(B) too（太）修飾 early;(A) so「這麼地」,不合句意;(C)(D)都不能修飾 early。

52.（ A ） hardly 的位置須放在助動詞和 be 動詞之間。

53.（ C ） seldom if ever「很少;簡直不」（詳見文法寶典 p.248）;(B) if any「即使有」。　* *be exposed to* ～ 受～影響

54.（ B ） 根據句意,應選(B)。

55.（ D ） scarcely ～ when …「一～就…」（詳見文法寶典 p.496）
　　　＝ hardly ～ when … ＝ no sooner ～ than …
　　　* patience〔'peʃəns〕*n*.〔主英〕一人獨玩的紙牌戲

Ⅱ.56.（ B ） *broad speaking* → *broadly speaking*「概括言之」。

57.（ D ） *does seldom* → *seldom does*　省略句中,頻率副詞須移至助動詞或 be 動詞前。（詳見文法寶典 p.266）

58.（ B ） *before* → *ago*　before 常與過去完成式連用,而 ago 則與簡單過去式連用。（詳見文法寶典 p.247）

59.（ B ） *can not* → *can*　hardly 是否定字,不須再加 not。

60.（ A ） *more better* → *better*　better 是比較級,不可再加 more。
　　　* key〔ki〕*n*.音調

Ⅲ. 61. There　62. only　63. much　64. too　65. too　66. almost
67. rather　68. up　69. otherwise

Exercise 16

Ⅰ. 1.（ A ）使用比較級時，必須把本身除外，常與 other（ 或 else ）連用。
（詳見文法寶典 p.208 ）

2.（ B ）比較同一人或物的兩種性質或狀態時，一律用 more ～ than … 「與其
說…不如說～」表示。（詳見文法寶典 p.201 ）

3.（ C ）根據句意，是表兩者間的相比，應用比較級 better，連接詞則須用選
擇連接詞 or，故選(C)。

4.（ A ）在比較的句型中，用 of the two 代替 than 時，比較級之前要加 the。
（詳見文法寶典 p.201 ）

5.（ A ）the ＋比較級～，the ＋比較級… 「越～，越…」。

6.（ B ）（ all ）the ＋比較級形容詞或副詞 「格外；越發」。

7.（ B ）be superior to ～ 「優於～」。（詳見文法寶典 p.203 ）

8.（ C ）know better than to-V 「不致於笨到～」。

9.（ C ）still less 「何況；更不用說」（用於否定句）。

10.（ B ）表反義的對等連接詞 yet 連接二個對稱句，more 的相反詞是 less。

11.（ C ）～ times as many ＋複數名詞＋ as … 「是…的～倍」。
（詳見文法寶典 p.182 ）

12.（ B ）not so ＋原級＋ as ～ 「不像～一樣…」。
＊ spectator〔ˈspɛktetɚ〕n. 觀眾

13.（ D ）the same ＋名詞＋ as ～ 「和～一樣…」。

14.（ C ）as many as 「多達」。

15.（ D ）not ～ so much as … 「與其說～倒不如說…」。

16.（ C ）用 of A and B（ or of the two ）來代替 than 時，比較級之前要加
the；the former ～，the latter … 「前者～，後者…」。

17.（ A ）prefer ＋（動）名詞＋ to ＋（動）名詞 「較喜歡～而不喜歡…」。

18.（ A ）as ～ as ～ can be 「極為～」。

19.（ C ）理由同第 5 題。like 作「喜歡」解，為及物動詞，其後一定得有受詞。

20.（ D ）理由同第 5 題，less 是 little 的比較級，而 lesser 很少使用，現在
的用法相當於 minor（次要的），如 lesser writer（二流作家）。
（詳見文法寶典 p.199 ）

21.（ C ）be inferior to ～ 「比～差」；要注意，同類的東西才能比較（詳見
文法寶典 p.208 ），mine ＝ my term paper。

22.（ B ） the latter half of ～ 「～的後半部」（指順序）；later 則指時間
上較晚。（詳見文法寶典 p.198）

23.（ A ） much 才能修飾比較級，very 則是修飾原級。根據句意，指時間上的
晚，選(A)。

24.（ A ） none the ＋比較級＋ for ～ 「一點也不因～而…」。
（詳見文法寶典 p.202）

25.（ B ） none the less 「仍然」。

26.（ A ） most 在此相當於 very，表絕對最高級。（詳見文法寶典 p.205, 262）

27.（ C ） 理由同第1題。

28.（ D ） 「最～」的句型：the ＋最高級＋of ＋人或物（複數）。
（詳見文法寶典 p.204）

29.（ D ） 比較級＋and ＋比較級 「越來越～」（詳見文法寶典 p.202）。根據句意，
選(D)。 ＊parking lot 停車場

30.（ A ） even 修飾比較級（詳見文法寶典 p.207）；(D) hardly 「幾乎不」，是副
詞。

31.（ C ） 三人以上的比較用最高級；(D) of all 與 compared to the others 同
義，不須重複。

32.（ B ） 絕對最高級前不加 the。（詳見文法寶典 p.205）

33.（ A ） much more 「更何況」，用於肯定句。

34.（ B ） not the least 「一點也沒有」。

35.（ C ） 由 I've ever seen 可知，應用優等比較的句型：
the ＋最高級＋單數名詞＋（that）… ever（詳見文法寶典 p.204）

36.（ D ） as ～ as possible ＝ as ～ as one can 「儘可能～」；(C)中的
possible 應去掉。

37.（ C ） no less than 「多達」（＝ as many as）。（詳見文法寶典 p.203）

38.（ D ） the ＋最高級＋單數名詞＋ in ＋場所（單數）。（詳見文法寶典 p.204）

39.（ A ） the last ＋名詞「最不～的」。（詳見文法寶典 p.199）

40.（ C ） more than 可修飾名詞、形容詞、動詞、副詞，表「非常；何止」；
本句譯成：「事情的結果讓他們十分滿意。」

41.（ B ） without（or not）so much as 「甚至不～」。

42.（ A ） to the best of ～ 「儘（某人之）所～」。
＊adequate〔'ædəkwɪt〕adj. 足夠的

43.（ D ）　sooner or later「遲早；總有一天」。(B)愈來愈少，(C)愈來愈多，
　　　　　　之後應接名詞。

44.（ C ）　the second（ or next ）best「次好的」。
　　　　　　* Philharmonic〔,fɪlhɑr'mɑnɪk〕n. 愛樂交響樂團

45.（（A ）理由同第 36 題。　　* feverishly〔'fivərɪʃlɪ〕adv. 狂熱地
　　　　　　folklore〔'fok,lor〕n. 民俗；民間傳說

46.（ B ）　not less ～ than …「也許比…更～」；(A) no more ～ than …「和
　　　　　　…一樣不～」；(C) not more ～ than …「不像…那樣～」。
　　　　　　（詳見文法寶典 p.202－203 ）

47.（ C ）　forty-two years later ＝ after forty-two years「四十二年之
　　　　　　後」。　* tulip〔'tjuləp〕n. 鬱金香

48.（ D ）　(A)… and perhaps *precious* than → and perhaps ***more precious***
　　　　　　than ；(B)… and perhaps *as more* precious than → … and perhaps
　　　　　　more precious than ；(C)不合句意。

49.（ B ）　根據句意，應選(B) no more ～ than …「和…一樣不～」。
　　　　　　* extinguish〔ɪk'stɪŋgwɪʃ〕v. 熄滅

Ⅱ. 50.（ C ）　*more prettier* → ***prettier***　　prettier 已是比較級，不需再加
　　　　　　more 。

51.（ B ）　*the worst* → ***the less***　　the ＋比較級～，the ＋比較級…
　　　　　　「越～，越…」。　* relative humidity 相對濕度

52.（ C ）　*the hardier* → ***the hardest***　　三者以上的比較用最高級。

53.（ B ）　*large* → ***the largest***　　對等連接詞 and 必須連接文法作用相同的
　　　　　　字，由 first 可知，large 應用最高級。
　　　　　　* ethnic〔'ɛθnɪk〕adj. 種族的；民族的
　　　　　　transcontinental〔,trænskɑntə'nɛntḷ〕adj. 橫貫大陸的

54.（ C ）　*more superior* → ***superior***　　（ be ）superior to ～「比～優秀」
　　　　　　即表比較，不必接 more 。

Ⅲ. 55. less　　56. any , other　　57. last　　58. better　　59. superior
60. as , as　　61. junior , by　　62. as , many　　63. less , than
64. never , more　　65. else　　66. second　　67. rather　　68. best
69. proud

Exercise 17

I. 1.(C) the French 指全體法國人，動詞要用複數。(詳見文法寶典 p.62)

2.(A) ten years 指「十年這一段時間」，意義為單數，動詞須用單數。
（詳見文法寶典 p.394 ）

3.(A) a pair of 指不可分離的一對東西（ 如 trousers ）時，為單數，動詞
應用單數。

4.(D) the number of ＋複數名詞「～的數目」，一般視為單數，動詞用
單數。(詳見文法寶典 p.396)
* casualty〔'kæʒʊəltɪ〕n. 意外死傷的人數

5.(B) A as well as B 作主詞時，動詞的數必須與A一致，又本題為過去
式，選(B)。(詳見文法寶典 p.400)

6.(C) bacon and eggs「薰肉和蛋」是一種食物，動詞用單數。

7.(A) A with B 作主詞時，動詞與A一致，選(A)。(詳見文法寶典 p.400)

8.(D) the United Nations「聯合國」，為單數，又根據句意可知須用主
動語態，選(D)。

9.(B) a list of ＋複數名詞「～的名單」，視為單數，動詞用單數。

10.(C) early to bed 和 early to rise 表同一觀念，動詞用單數。
（詳見文法寶典 p.398 ）

11.(B) more than one「不只一個」修飾主詞時，要用單數動詞。
（詳見文法寶典 p.396 ）

12.(D) audience（ 觀衆 ）指組成分子時，本身即複數形，用複數動詞。
（詳見文法寶典 p.53,394 ）

13.(A) 名詞子句作主詞時，動詞用單數。(詳見文法寶典 p.397)

14.(C) neither A nor B 作主詞時，動詞與靠近者一致，又 the Tigers 是
隊伍名，為單數，選(C)；(B) has gone「已經去」不合句意。
* pennant〔'pɛnənt〕n. 小旗

15.(B) a number of ＋複數名詞「許多～」，須用複數動詞。
（詳見文法寶典 p.396 ）

16.(D) mathematics「數學」是學科名稱，雖為複數形式，但意義為單數，
動詞用單數。(詳見文法寶典 p.393)

17.(C) 關係代名詞作子句主詞時，子句中的動詞，須與先行詞mosquitoes 一
致，選(C)。 * malaria〔mə'lɛrɪə〕n. 瘧疾

18.（ D ）　eighty dollars 指「一筆金錢」，意義爲單數，動詞用單數。
（詳見文法寶典 p.394）

19.（ A ）　every A and（ every ）B 作主詞時，動詞一律用單數。
（詳見文法寶典 p.399）

20.（ A ）　由句尾的 one of my favorite plays 可知，Romeo and Juliet 指的是莎士比亞著名的戲劇作品「羅密歐與茱麗葉」，動詞應用單數。

21.（ B ）　此句的核心主詞是 the use，爲單數，動詞要用單數。

22.（ C ）　此句的核心主詞是 advertisements，爲複數，動詞須用複數。(B) become 不可用於被動語態。

23.（ C ）　此句的核心主詞是 Mr. Jones「鍾斯先生」，動詞須用單數，又(A) has been proposed 是被動語態，不合句意，故選(C)。

24.（ D ）　由 than 可知，本題須用比較級，主詞 anything 是單數，選(D)。

25.（ D ）　本句主詞是 little change，爲單數，動詞用單數。
＊ intensive care unit 加護病房

26.（ B ）　核心主詞是 people，爲複數，故動詞用複數，又從 been interested 可知，本句爲完成式，選(B)。

27.（ C ）　對等連接詞 and 連接了 receive a good education，和 travel extensively 二個動詞片語，可知空格內必也是動詞片語，選(C)。

28.（ A ）　or 是對等連接詞，連接文法作用相同的片語，此句應選有不定詞片語的(A) to keep … reference 和 to sell his books 形成對稱。

29.（ B ）　理由同第 17 題。

30.（ D ）　主詞 each student 是單數，動詞用單數；(C) has been answered 爲被動語態，不合句意。

31.（ C ）　理由同第 10 題。

32.（ A ）　a watch and chain「一只掛錶」指一件東西，動詞用單數。

33.（ C ）　the editor and publisher「編輯兼出版者」指同一人，須用單數動詞（詳見文法寶典 p.398）；又 since 多與完成式連用，選(C)。

34.（ B ）　此句的核心主詞是 the fear，爲單數，動詞用單數。

35.（ D ）　此句的核心主詞是 conditions，爲複數，動詞用複數；(C) have been grown 爲被動語態，不合句意。　＊ refugee〔͵rɛfjʊˋdʒi〕n. 難民

36.（ A ）　此句的核心主詞是 No one，而 but nurses and doctors 是修飾語，所以用單數動詞。

37.（B） 名詞子句的動作發生在主要子句的動作（過去式）之前，要用過去完成式。

38.（C） 不定詞和動名詞都具有對稱性，又如：*To see* is *to believe*.「百聞不如一見。」（詳見文法寶典 p.432）

39.（B） 理由同第 38 題。

40.（D） and 是對等連接詞，連接兩個動詞片語，又根據句意得知，須用被動語態，選(D)。

41.（A） 主詞 six of the players 是複數，又根據句意，須用被動語態，選(A)。

42.（B） neither A nor B 作主詞時，動詞與靠近者（the teacher）一致，故知須用單數動詞，又根據句意，須用被動語態，選(B)。

43.（D） a person 的代名詞用 he，而非 you，選(D)。

44.（A） 在正常情形下，英文中句子的主詞應少更動，且須具有一致性，根據句意，本題主要是強調「**我們**（*we*）看見了塔」，故選(A)。

45.（B） 理由同第 38 題。

46.（C） 關係代名詞 who 是子句中的主詞，其先行詞是 many and many a man，須用單數動詞。（詳見文法寶典 p.395）

47.（A） the bulk of＋複數名詞「大多數～」，作主詞時，動詞用複數；the young 指「全體年輕人」，爲複數名詞。
　　　　 ＊ aspect〔ˋæspɛkt〕*n.* 方面

48.（B） not a few「許多」，爲複數，故動詞用複數，又根據句意可知，須用被動語態，故選(B)。

49.（B） 根據句意，可知 everything … to, everything … from, everything … despise，實際上是同位語關係，是一種加強語氣的用法，本題眞正主詞 everything 爲單數，動詞要用單數。

Ⅱ. 50.（A） *are* → *is*　　A with B 作主詞時，動詞與 A 一致。
　　　　 ＊ *press conference* 記者招待會

51.（C） *their* → *his*　　A like B 作主詞時，動詞、代名詞皆與 A 一致。

52.（C） *encouraging* → *to encourage*　　不定詞與動名詞具有對稱性，and 之前是不定詞片語，之後也必須接不定詞片語。

53.（B） *their name* → *his name*　　each A and B 作主詞時，動詞、代名詞皆用單數；request（要求）＋that＋主詞＋（*should*）＋原形動詞。
　　　　 ＊ registrar〔ˋrɛdʒɪˌstrɑr, ˌrɛdʒɪˋstrɑr〕*n.*（學校裡的）註冊主任

54.（ C ）　*has been* → *were*　　過去的事實，用簡單過去式，又主詞爲複數（factions），故用 were 。　＊faction〔'fækʃən〕*n*.黨派

55.（ D ）　*were* → *was*　　neither of＋複數名詞「兩者中沒有一個」，動詞用單數。（詳見文法寶典 p.395）
＊eligible〔'ɛlɪdʒəbḷ〕*adj*.合格的

56.（ A ）　*admit* → *admits*　　關係代名詞 who 的先行詞是 student，爲單數，所以子句的動詞須用單數。

57.（ B ）　*you* → *one or he*　　one 作主詞時，代名詞可用 one 或 he。

58.（ B ）　*have taken* → *has taken*　　either A or B 作主詞時，動詞與靠近者一致，one of his friends 的核心是 one，爲單數，動詞要用單數。

Exercise 18

Ｉ. 1.（ C ）　根據句意，應用 for「因爲」引導對等子句，表附加、推斷的理由。
（詳見文法寶典 p.477）

2.（ A ）　or 爲選擇連接詞，引導對等子句，在本題中，作「否則」解。

3.（ D ）　根據句意，應選(D) though「雖然」；(A)假如，(B)因爲，(C)所以，都不合。

4.（ C ）　which 用來詢問兩件事物中的「哪一件」，應直接回答所選之物，不可用 Yes 或 No 來回答；(D)*Milk is better* → *I like milk better*.

5.（ B ）　本題中 as 作「雖然」解，用於表讓步的副詞子句，句型爲：副詞＋as＋主詞＋動詞。（詳見文法寶典 p.529）

6.（ D ）　由兩子句不同的時代，可知兩個動作的發生有先後的順序，故選(D)；動作先發生的用過去完成式，後發生的用簡單過去式。

7.（ A ）　根據句意表條件，須選(A) supposing（＝if）「假如」。
（詳見文法寶典 p.457,522）

8.（ A ）　by the time（＝before）「在～之前」，引導表時間的副詞子句，大都指未來的時間（詳見文法寶典 p.495）；(B) till 本身即爲連接詞，可直接加子句。(C)即使，(D)雖然，皆不合句意。

9.（ C ）　Excuse me, but～「對不起，～」，這裡的 but 只是純粹的連接詞，沒有意義。

10.（ D ）　根據句意，應選(D) unless「除非」。　＊*apply to* 適用於

11.(B)　根據句意，應選(B)The moment「一～就」。（詳見文法寶典 p.496）

12.(C)　此句中，not 修飾的是 because 子句，而非動詞 despise，譯成「不能因為你有錢就瞧不起人。」(A)(B)皆不合句意。

13.(D)　so long as「只要」；(A)雖然，(B)除非，皆不合句意；(C) that 若是關代的話，在子句裡沒有代名的作用，且缺少先行詞；that 引導名詞子句，只能作句子的主詞受詞、補語或同位語，在本題中沒有它的位置。

14.(A)　now that「既然」引導表原因的副詞子句；(B) so that 不可置於句首；(C) unless「除非」不合句意；(D) when 用於現在式時，主要子句通常是未來式。

15.(A)　that 引導名詞子句，作全句的主詞；(B) which 和(D) what 亦可引導名詞子句，但也必須作子句中的主詞或受詞，在此不合；(C) so 不引導名詞子句。　＊ industrious〔ɪnˈdʌstrɪəs〕*adj.* 勤勉的

16.(B)　such ～ that「如此～以致於」。

17.(A)　lest 表否定目的，句型是：lest ＋主詞＋ should ＋ V「以免～」。（詳見文法寶典 p.514）

18.(D)　not ～ long before …「～不久，就…」。（詳見文法寶典 p.495）

19.(C)　nor 用於否定子句之後，句型是：～，nor ＋助動詞或 be 動詞＋主詞；(A) so 用於肯定子句之後。（詳見文法寶典 p.643）

20.(A)　在 not ～ long before 的句型中，可把 long 改為 far，來表示距離。〔詳見文法寶典 p.495（註3）〕

21.(C)　It is not until ～ that …「直到～才…」。（詳見文法寶典 p.115,492）

22.(B)　if 引導名詞子句，作 know 的受詞，相當於 whether（詳見文法寶典 p.485）；(A)(C)(D)皆不引導名詞子句。

23.(C)　It is ＋若干時間＋ *since* ＋主詞＋過去式動詞「自從～以來，已經…」。（詳見文法寶典 p.337,492）

24.(D)　while 引導的副詞子句，表時間，常用進行式（詳見文法寶典 p.490）；(A)直到，(C)除非，都不合句意；(B) during 之後不接子句。

25.(B)　只有 that 可引導名詞子句，作 report 的同位語。

26.(A)　Do you mind if ＋子句？「如果～你介意嗎？」

27.(B)　根據句意，應用 as 來連接兩個逐漸演變的狀態。（詳見文法寶典 p.490）

28.(D)　No ～ but …（沒有～不…）是雙重否定，句中常有 so 出現，此句相當於 No man is so old *that* he can *not* learn.（詳見文法寶典 p.519）

29. (B)　由句尾的 or not 可知，應用 whether 來引導名詞子句，作動詞 know 的受詞。（詳見文法寶典 p.484）

30. (C)　Some ～, *while* others …「有些人～，而有些人…」，while 在此 為表反義的對等連接詞（詳見文法寶典 p.471）;(A)(B)(D)都不合句意。

31. (D)　no sooner ～ than …「一～就…」。（詳見文法寶典 p.496）

32. (B)　根據句意，應選表條件的連接詞 once「一旦」。（詳見文法寶典 p.523）

33. (A)　late 只能放在動詞後，修飾動詞。

34. (C)　此句是 it 加強語氣的用法，句型為: it is (*or* was) ＋所要加強的 部分＋ that ＋其餘部分。（詳見文法寶典 p.115）
　　　　＊ disperse〔dɪˋspɝs〕v. 四散

35. (D)　在 " The reason ＋子句＋ is … " 之後，通常接 that 子句，但口語中 有時也用 The reason is because …，此種用法較不正式，不選為正 確答案（詳見文法寶典 p.509）;(B) since 不引導名詞子句;(C) what 亦可 引導名詞子句，但必作子句中的主詞或受詞，故不合。

36. (A)　for fear (that) ＋子句「以免～」，表否定目的（詳見文法寶典 p.514）;(B) so as to-V「以便～」和(D) so that ＋子句「以便～」 都不合句意。

37. (B)　not ～ but …「不是～而是…」。（詳見文法寶典 p.474）

38. (D)　由句中兩個子句可知，必須有連接詞，故選(D);(C) because of ＋名 詞「因為～」，不合句意。
　　　　＊ magnetize〔ˋmægnəˏtaɪz〕v. 使磁化

39. (B)　in case (that) ＋子句「以防～」（詳見文法寶典 p.514）;(A) in time「及時」，是副詞，不能引導子句;(C) 除非，(D) 即使，不合 句意。

40. (C)　because ＋子句，because of ＋名詞（片語）。（詳見文法寶典 p.509）

41. (C)　nevertheless 是表反義的連接詞，作「然而」解，其前常用分號。 （詳見文法寶典 p.472）

42. (A)　so ～ that ＋子句「如此～以致於…」。

43. (D)　(just) as ～, so …「…就像～那樣」，so 後的子句可倒裝。 （詳見文法寶典 p.502）

44. (C)　根據句意可知，應選(C);(B) despite 是介系詞，須接名詞（片語）; (A) 除非，(D) 因為，不合句意。
　　　　＊ sprain〔spren〕v. 扭傷

45. (A) so far as ～ is concerned「至於～」。

46. (C) 根據句意可知，應選(C) on condition that ＋子句「只要～；假如～」。

47. (B) as if ＋主詞＋過去式或were「好像～」，是與現在事實相反的假設法。（詳見文法寶典 p.371 ）

48. (D) 主詞＋doubt whether＋子句「某人懷疑是否～」，由whether引導名詞子句，作動詞 doubt 的受詞。

49. (D) 根據句意，及第二個子句的倒裝，可知空格內應填否定字，選(D)。

50. (A) 本題中 as 作「雖然」解，用於表讓步的副詞子句，句型為：形容詞＋as ＋主詞＋動詞。（詳見文法寶典 p.529 ）
    * deceitful〔dɪˈsitfəl〕 adj. 欺詐的

51. (B) 理由同第 17 題。

52. (C) 理由同第 43 題。

Ⅱ. 53. (D) *as well as → and*　　　A as well as B 的重點放在A，不合此句句意（在台灣學會中文是當然的，故重點應置於法文），故應改為一般的 and 。

54. (A) *both → x*　　　both 與 and 連用。as well as 則單獨使用。
    * anthropology〔͵ænθrəˈpɑlədʒɪ〕 n. 人類學

55. (A) *that → whether*　　　根據句意，應改為 whether 。

56. (A) *Neither Emily has mentioned → Emily has mentioned neither*
    neither ～ nor …是對等連接詞，必須連接文法作用相同的單字、片語或子句，根據句意可知須連接 time 和 place，故把 neither 放到 time 之前。

57. (A) *so → such*　　　「 such＋a(n)＋形容詞＋名詞」相當於「 so＋形容詞＋a(n)＋名詞」，但如果名詞是複數時，只能用「 such＋形容詞＋複數名詞」這句型。（詳見文法寶典 p.517 ）

Ⅲ. 58. because　　59. that　　60. while　　61. and　　62. Whether　　63. but
64. if　　65. before　　66. till *or* until　　67. nor　　68. As　　69. as　　70. but
71. before *or* when　　72. but

Exercise 19

Ⅰ. 1. (C) at ＋時間的一定點。（詳見文法寶典 p.555 ）

2. (B) on ＋日期。（詳見文法寶典 p.591 ）

3. (D) next Friday（＝on Friday next）「下星期五」。
（詳見文法寶典 p.199）

4. (A) by ＋時間，作「最遲在～之前」解，相當於 not later than 。
（詳見文法寶典 p.566）

5. (D) since 作介詞時，受詞須爲指示特定時間，而不是一段時間，並常與現在完成式連用。（詳見文法寶典 p.493）

6. (D) behind schedule「誤時」；(A)準時，(B)守時的，(C)按時，都不合句意。

7. (B) for ＋一段時間，表「經過的時間」，常與現在完成式連用。
（詳見文法寶典 p.335, 571）

8. (C) 根據句意，應選(C) during「在～期間」。

9. (A) at the beginning of ～「在～初」；(B)(D)→ *in* the middle of；
(C)→ *at* the end of 。

10. (B) after a little while「過不久」；(A)→ *in a little while*「不一會兒」。

11. (B) in addition to ～「除～之外」；(A) in order to-V「爲了～」，
(C) in respect to「關於」，(D) in search of「尋求」，都不合句意。

12. (C) on ＋特定日子的上下午。（詳見文法寶典 p.591）

13. (A) *sb*. ＋ be 動詞＋ starved to death「某人被餓死」。

14. (C) 原料＋ be made into ＋成品；(A)成品＋ be made of ＋材料，用於成品仍保有材料原來的性質形狀；(B)成品＋ be made from ＋材料，用於成品不保留材料原來的性質形狀。（詳見文法寶典 p.575）

15. (C) in the cause of ～「爲了（主義、目標）」，本題譯成「李先生爲民主犧牲生命。」。（ in 在此作「爲了～」解，詳見文法寶典 p.581）
＊ *lay down one's life* 捐軀

16. (D) to 在本題中表方向，作「朝～；向～」解，相當於 in the direction of 或 towards 。（詳見文法寶典 p.600）

17. (B) with ＋受詞＋ p.p. 或 V-ing（作受詞補語），表示「某一動作的附帶狀態」。（詳見文法寶典 p.462, 608）

18. (A) from under the earth「從地底下」。

19. (C) under these circumstances「在這些情況下」。

20. (A) on duty「上班；值班」。

21. (C)　among 表示三人以上的分配；(A) between 表示二者之間的分配，在此
不合。

22. (A)　within a stone's throw「在一石之擲的距離內」。

23. (D)　根據句意，應選(D) by「藉著」。（詳見文法寶典 p.567）

24. (C)　to one's surprise and relief「使某人驚訝和放心的是」。
（詳見文法寶典 p.600）

25. (B)　smell of ～「有～的氣味」。

26. (D)　take ～ for … 「把～當作…」。

27. (C)　result in「導致」；(B) result from「起因於」。

28. (A)　have every reason for ＋（動）名詞「有充分的理由～」。

29. (D)　be 動詞＋older than I by three years「大我三歲」，by 在此表
相差的程度（詳見文法寶典 p.566）；older than me 是非正式用法，不
選為正確答案。

30. (B)　dance to the music「配合著音樂跳舞」，to 在此作「配合」解。
（詳見文法寶典 p.601）

31. (B)　根據句意，選(B) in spite of ＋名詞（片語）「儘管～」；(A) although
之後應接子句。

32. (C)　get hurt in a car accident「在車禍中受傷」。

33. (A)　根據句意，應選(A) look for「尋找」，句中的 in the dictionary 是
副詞片語，修飾 look；(B) look on「觀察；面向」，(C), (D) look to
（ to 為介系詞）「照顧；依賴」，都不合句意。

34. (B)　deprive sb. of ～「剝奪某人的～」。（詳見文法寶典 p.585）

35. (D)　thank sb. for sth.「感謝某人某事」，for 表原因。
（詳見文法寶典 p.572）

36. (A)　die of ＋疾病「死於～」；(B) die by 表「死亡的手段或方式」。
（詳見文法寶典 p.584）

37. (C)　by ＋數量單位，作「以～計」解。（詳見文法寶典 p.566）

38. (A)　have ～ to do with … 「和…有（某種關係）」。

39. (B)　be free of「免除」。

40. (D)　（be）named ～ after … 「以…（的名字）命名為～」。

41. (A)　be similar to ～「和～類似」。

42. (C)　remind sb. of sth.「提醒某人某事」。（詳見文法寶典 p.279）

43. (B)　resort to ＋（代）名詞「訴諸（某種手段）」。

44. (D) read between the lines「領會言外之意」。

45. (A) to the minute「準時；一分不差」。

46. (B) 根據句意；應選(B) from 表「來源；出處」。(詳見文法寶典 p.575)

47. (C) on the grounds of「因為」。

48. (D) distinguish between ~ and …「辨別~和…；區別~和…」。
   * barley〔ˈbɑrlɪ〕 *n*. 大麥

49. (B) in the direction of ~「朝~方向」。(詳見文法寶典 p.579)

50. (A) look forward to V-ing「期待~」。

51. (C) on all fours「爬行」。

52. (B) concentrate ~ on …「集中~於…」。

53. (D) congratulate + *sb*. + on ~「向某人祝賀~」。

54. (A) thanks to「幸虧」。

55. (B) idea 之後通常接 of + V-ing，選(B)。(詳見文法寶典 p.433)

56. (C) on the faculty of our school「我們學校的一位教職員」，on 表示「為~的一分子」。(詳見文法寶典 p.593)
   * faculty〔ˈfækl̩tɪ〕 *n*. 一學校中的全體教員

57. (D) lend *sb*. a hand with *sth*.「幫助某人做某事」。

58. (B) It goes without saying that + 子句「不用說~；當然是~」。

59. (B) live on ~「靠~過活」。

60. (D) never ~ without + V-ing「沒有~不…；每~必定…」。
   (詳見文法寶典 p.440)
   * shabby〔ˈʃæbɪ〕 *adj*. 破舊的　　fortnight〔ˈfɔrtnaɪt〕 *n*. 兩禮拜

61. (C) 根據句意，應選(C) without，no ~ without + V-ing 是雙重否定，句型同上題。

62. (A) 根據句意，選(A) be true of「適用於」；(C) be true to「忠於」。
   * binocular〔baɪˈnɑkjələ〕 *adj*. 雙眼並用的

63. (D) difference between ~ and …「~和…的差別」。

II. 64. (A) *Despite of* → *Despite*　　despite 本身即為介系詞，不必再加 of。
   〔詳見文法寶典 p.532，(注意)〕

65. (C) *bored of* → *bored with* or *bored by*　　become bored with (or by) ~「厭倦~」。
   * quotient〔ˈkwoʃənt〕 *n*. 商數
   intelligence quotient「智商（略作 I Q ）」

66. (D) *on* → *in*　　get in「搭乘（小車，如 taxi，car 等）」
67. (C) *of* → *to* or *for*　　without regard to（ or for ）「不顧～」。

Ⅲ. 68. on or upon　　69. to　　70. to　　71. of　　72. under　　73. To or By
74. over　　75. above　　76. beneath　　77. from　　78. through　　79. with
80. with　　81. to　　82. of　　83. of　　84. at　　85. for　　86. with　　87. in
88. at　　89. for　　90. of

Exercise 20

Ⅰ. 1. (A)　副詞 down 置於句首，主詞與動詞必須倒裝。（詳見文法寶典 p.631 ）
　　　 * *in torrents* 傾盆大雨

2. (C)　here 放在句首時，如果主詞是名詞，則主詞和動詞須倒裝。
　　　〔詳見文法寶典 p.643，（註2 ）〕

3. (B)　否定詞放在句首時，助動詞（ 或 be 動詞 ）須放在主詞前，形成倒裝
　　　（ 詳見文法寶典 p.629 ）；hardly ～ before（ or when ）「一～就」
　　　（ 詳見文法寶典 p.496 ）。

4. (D)　little「幾乎沒有」，本身具有否定意味，放在句首時，助動詞（ 或
　　　be 動詞 ）須放在主詞前，形成倒裝。

5. (D)　under no circumstances「絕不」放在句首時，倒裝理由同第 3 題。

6. (A)　否定詞在句首，所以助動詞 have 要放在主詞 the enemy 前，形成倒
　　　裝。

7. (C)　副詞 then 放在句首時，主詞和動詞須倒裝（ 詳見文法寶典 p.631 ），此句
　　　相當於 A beautiful sight was then seen.

8. (B)　Here you are.「你要的東西在這兒。」（ 詳見文法寶典 p.250 ）

9. (D)　本句的主詞是 How many people，不須再用助動詞來造疑問句，這句
　　　型就和疑問代名詞（ who，what 等 ）等主詞時的句型一樣。（ 請參考文
　　　法寶典 p.146 ）

10. (C)　「 only ＋副詞片語 」放在句首時，助動詞（ 或 be 動詞 ）須放在主詞
　　　前，形成倒裝。（ 詳見文法寶典 p.631 ）

11. (C)　本題是考與過去事實相反的假設法中，條件子句的倒裝：Had you
　　　come earlier ＝ If you had come earlier。（ 詳見文法寶典 p.365 ）

12. (B)　such 在此作主詞 his diligence 的補語，置於句首時，主詞與動詞須
　　　倒裝（ 詳見文法寶典 p.516 ）；(A) so 是副詞，在此句型中，不能作補語用。

13.（ A ）　本句爲 it 加強語氣的用法，句型是：It is（ or was ）＋所加強的部分＋ that ＋其餘部分，改爲疑問句時，如果所加強的部分是人時，則變成 Who ＋ is（ or was ）it ＋ that ＋其餘部分？（詳見文法寶典 p.115）
　　　　　＊ concerto〔kən'tʃɛrto〕n. 協奏曲

14.（ D ）　I'm afraid *not*. ＝ I'm afraid *that she is not coming tomorrow*. 在對話中，常以 not 代替否定子句。（詳見文法寶典 p.129）

15.（ B ）　until（或 till ）所引導之子句的主詞，和主要子句的主詞相同時，until（或 till ）子句中的主詞和 be 動詞可省略〔詳見文法寶典 p.491，（註 3 ）〕；Don't speak until（ *you are* ）spoken to.「別人問到你時再開口。」

16.（ D ）　用 although 引導表讓步的副詞子句，修飾主要子句的動詞 set 。

17.（ D ）　根據句意，應選(D) if at all「即使有的話」，作插入語（詳見文法寶典 p.137）；(A) if ever「即使有」，常與 seldom 連用（詳見文法寶典 p.248）；(B) if any「即使有的話」，常與 little 連用；(C)不合句意。

18.（ C ）　根據句意，應選(C) if not all「若非全部的話」。

19.（ A ）　although（ *he was* ）born in Canada 是插入的副詞子句，修飾 Peter ；although 所引導的副詞子句，句義明確時，可省略主詞和 be 動詞（詳見文法寶典 p.645）；選(B)，缺少連接詞，選(C)，缺少連接詞和主詞，選(D)，應去掉 he 。

20.（ B ）　You can not have your cake and eat it, too. 本句爲諺語，意爲「魚與熊掌不可兼得。」（請參考「英文諺語詳解」p.195，第781項）。

21.（ C ）　not ～ but …「不是～而是…」。（詳見文法寶典 p.474）

22.（ D ）　more often than not「時常；大半」（＝ as often as not ），是副詞片語，倒裝放在句首，表強調。　＊ *in person* 本人；親自

23.（ D ）　neither「也不」置於句首時，主詞與助動詞須倒裝，而 neither 本身已有否定含意，不須與 not 連用（詳見文法寶典 p.463）；(A)→ I don't, *either*.

24.（ B ）　由 How kind 和句尾的驚嘆號（ ! ）可知，此句爲感嘆句，句型爲「How ＋形容詞（或副詞）＋主詞＋動詞!」（詳見文法寶典 p.4）

25.（ A ）　敍述句的動詞是肯定，附加問句的動詞要用否定；本敍述句的動詞爲 had to，附加問句的主詞前要用 did，故選(A)。（詳見文法寶典 p.6）

26.（ D ）　含有 hardly 的句子，是否定句，所以附加問句的主詞前只能用 do，does 或 did，故選(D)。（詳見文法寶典 p.7）

27.(C) 複句的附加問句以主要思想的子句爲準，故選(C)。（詳見文法寶典 p.7）

28.(B) 由 Let's 引出的祈使句，肯定的要用 shall we。（詳見文法寶典 p.6）

29.(A) 肯定祈使句之後，表「邀請、勸誘」時，附加問句用 won't you。
（詳見文法寶典 p.6）

30.(C) 「 only ＋副詞子句」放在句首時，助動詞（或 be 動詞）須放在主詞前，形成倒裝。

31.(B) 「 not until ＋子句」放在句首時，助動詞（或 be 動詞）須放在主詞前，形成倒裝。（詳見文法寶典 p.492，629－630）

32.(A) 補語放於句首，主詞與動詞須倒裝。（詳見文法寶典 p.636）

Ⅱ.33.(B) *nothing* → ***anything***　　nothing 與 nobody 形成雙重否定，不合句意，應改爲 anything。

34.(B) *they lost* → ***did they lose***　　否定詞 Not only 置於句首，助動詞（或 be 動詞）必須放在主詞前面，形成倒裝。（詳見文法寶典 p.629－630）

- 文法系統化，淺顯易懂。
- 題型富變化，活用文法。
- 反覆式練習，加強記憶。
- 大而清晰的字體，做了還想再做。

LEARNING PUBLISHING CO., LTD.